BRIGHTLING

Sovereigns of Bright and Shadow Book Two

I0522780

C. E. Page

The characters and events in this book are fictional and any resemblance to actual persons, living or dead, is purely coincidental.

First Published 2021 in Australia by Enchanted Castle Press

Copyright © Cassandra Erin Page 2021

The moral right of the author has been asserted.

All rights reserved. No part of this book may be reproduced or transmitted by any person or entity (including Google, Amazon or similar organisations), in any form or by any means, electronic or mechanical, including photocopying, recording, scanning or by any information storage and retrieval system, without prior permission in writing from the publisher.

ISBN: 978-0-9925548-6-6

A catalogue record for this work is available from the National Library of Australia

Cover by: Joolz & Jarling – Julie Nicholls & Uwe Jarling
Map by: Fictive Designs
Formatting by: Enchanted Castle Press
Edited by: Creating Ink – Anna Bishop

Author website: www.cepageauthor.com

V4 061221

BRIGHTLING

SOVEREIGNS OF BRIGHT & SHADOW

BOOK TWO

C. E. PAGE

ENCHANTED CASTLE
— PRESS —

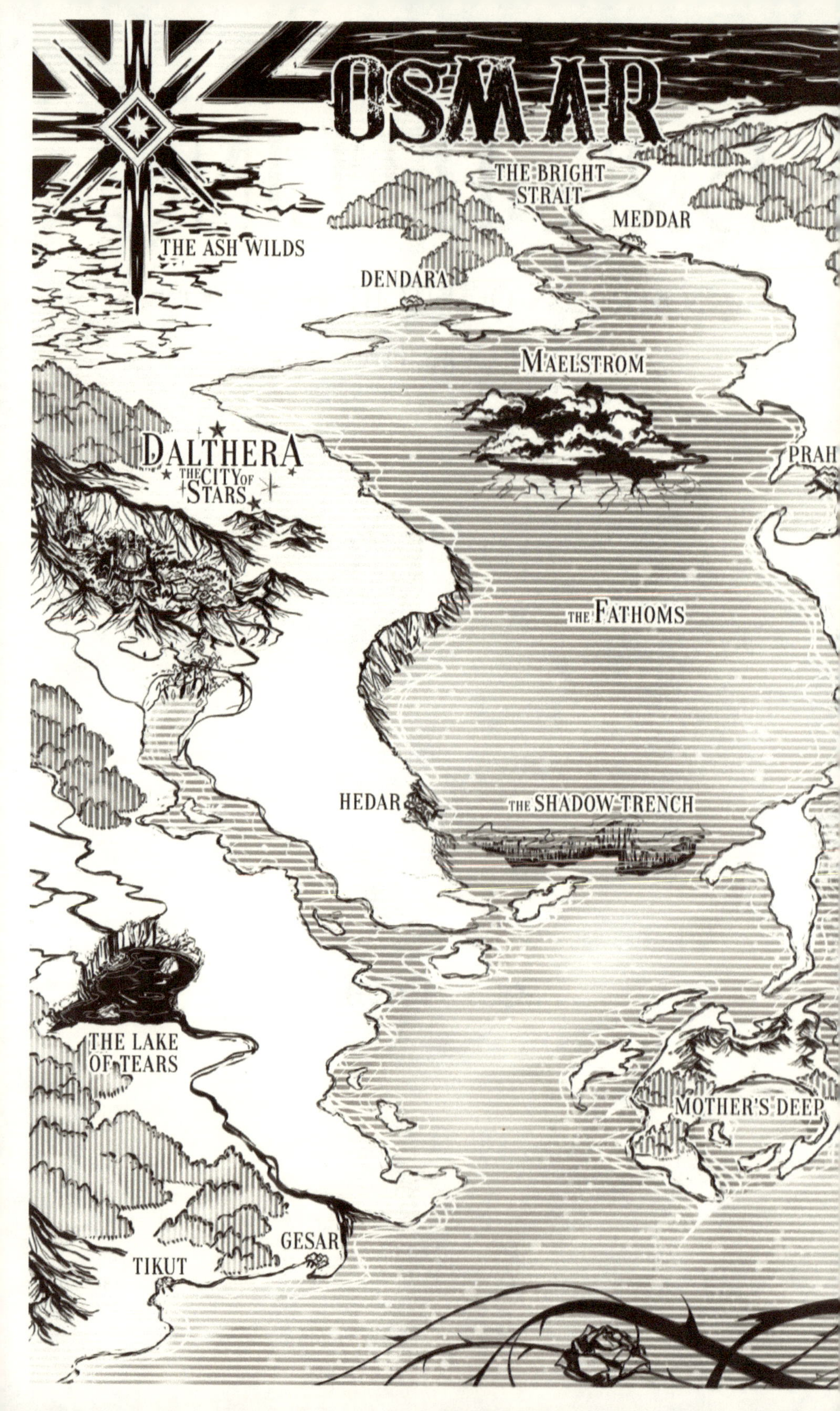

OSMAR
THE ASH WILDS
THE BRIGHT STRAIT
MEDDAR
DENDARA
MAELSTROM
PRAH
DALTHERA
THE CITY OF STARS
THE FATHOMS
HEDAR
THE SHADOW TRENCH
THE LAKE OF TEARS
MOTHER'S DEEP
TIKUT
GESAR

HARTSWOOD
DEL HAROL
LITTLE BROOK
MERSTON
WARREN'S GROTTO
DUNHOLD
FORT BRAEMAR
THE FENLANDS
HILLSIDE
KILTON
SWINTON
LONE OAK
FENGATE
LOCH BASTIEN
THE CROSSROADS
NEW BRENNA
KALHANNA
BELDAREN

To Noel and Margaret McKenzie,
thank you for supporting this dream of mine and always asking:
"How is the book going?"

CHAPTER ONE

MARGOT

Days passed like cold honey—slow, almost stagnant. Margot threw herself into refining the treatment for corruption. But as the weeks trickled by, it was getting harder to keep herself distracted from the dread that crept in itching fingers across the back of her mind. Dread that was fed by her nagging thoughts: there was no cure, and the woman she considered her sister and another of her closest friends had leapt needlessly to their deaths. Working softened the cruel voice that told her it was all for naught. So, she worked. And she waited, hoping for a sign that her worries would prove unfounded.

High Mage Niall had provided a collection of rooms in the east wing of the college for her to use as a laboratory and clinic. She presumed it was because he was tired of sharing his study with several people at a time. Like his daughter, Nea, Niall preferred his own space and could go days devoid of human contact without it impacting him negatively. But not Margot. The worst part of her internment in King Evard's *care* had been the isolation.

Maybe that was the only solace she could take from losing Nea a second time. That Nea wasn't alone—Garret was with her.

With a sigh, she returned the jar of dried Mother's balm to the shelf. Her efforts to refine the treatment had greatly dwindled her supply, and though Niall had taken measures to propagate more of the rare plants, it would be some time before they had the quantities needed to effectively treat all the cases of corruption that were appearing.

She pressed her hands against her lower back and stretched. It was high time she took a break. After hanging her apron on the hook by the door, she headed towards the room of reflection to check on the portal.

Light played across the surface of the water, reflecting shimmering patterns over the archway set into the wall at the far end of the pool and making the stones look alive. But it was nothing more than a stubborn wall of rock and faded magic that refused to offer even the tiniest clue about the fate of her friends.

With a huff, she rubbed her hands over her face. If she thought it would make a difference, she would plead with the Bright Mother to give her a sign. But the older she got, the less she believed Nonna's stories about the Mother coming to the aid of her faithful. She'd seen too much suffering, felt the bitter sting of grief too many times.

The fresh sweetness of orange oil filled the air a second before a warm hand slid into her own. She met Molly's cornflower-blue eyes and gave her fingers a small squeeze before lifting her free hand to trace the edge of Molly's jaw and draw her in for a quick kiss.

As Molly pulled away, she gestured to the portal. "You know sitting here staring at that thing isn't healthy?"

"What if they need help when they come back and no one is here for them?"

"It's been six weeks. We have no way of knowing ..." The pause spoke the words Margot dreaded, but Molly continued quickly, "*when* they will return. And as soon as anything comes through that portal, Niall's wards will let us know. You should take his advice and put your mind to something practical."

"I know, Mol." Margot chewed the side of her thumb. "I've been trying. But this reminds me of those first few weeks after Kalhanna. I only just found her again and now ... both of them could be ..." A lump caught in her throat and she blinked. "Mother damn it."

Molly looped her arms around Margot and pulled her in for a hug. "They are both resourceful and honestly not all *that* easy to kill. Plenty of people have tried and scored themselves early graves in the process. So, I am sure they're not going to let some trans-dimensional realm get the better of them."

Margot leant back and studied Molly.

"What?"

"That's probably the nicest thing I've ever heard you say about Nea."

"Oh, did I forget to mention that I still don't trust her motives and think she knows far more about what is going on than she says she does?" Molly chuckled and gave her a light jab in the ribs. "Seriously though, whatever I think about Nea, she seems to care about Garret. And I have come to realise that regardless of her other ... questionable traits, she does tend to go out of her way to protect those she loves."

"You're getting soft in your old age, and I think you secretly like Nea," Margot said with a grin.

Molly rolled her eyes. "I admire her tenacity. And Garret trusts her, so she can't be all bad. After all, he isn't easily swayed by pretty appearances or silver words, unlike Declan." A sad smile touched her features. "Declan would have *loved* Nea."

Margot's gaze dropped to her fingers. The strange sensation that was the presence of Declan's spirit had been a near constant beside Nea. And though she had only ever experienced Nea's side of their interactions, she got the impression they had formed a close friendship. "I think you're right; they would have gotten on quite well."

She glanced at the portal again then brushed her hands on her knees and got to her feet. "Hungry?"

"Always." Molly grinned and took the hand Margot offered her. "Aveline promised me some of her famous spiced apple cake for helping her distract Niall earlier, and it is high time I collect on that payment."

"Why did she want to distract Niall?"

"Your guess is as good as mine. Though Niall is not the only one who could use a *distraction*."

Margot yelped as Molly's finger prodded her ribs again. "What was that for?" She pulled her attention away from the portal once more.

"You can't go two minutes without staring at that bloody thing. Come on. Let's go eat."

Margot gave the arch a final glance as Molly led her away.

Molly's effort to cheer her up had briefly reinforced the hope that Nea and Garret would be alright, but already the thick fingers that had enclosed her heart the moment the portal had faded were settling back into place.

✖

Margot placed the beaker carefully on the bench as a knock sounded against the door frame. She wiped her hands on her apron and turned to face Leith, who gave her a tired smile.

The events of the last few months had aged him, though if she was honest, not in a bad way. He'd always been carefree and charming, having little time to worry about consequences. Whilst he still possessed his easy demeanour, it had matured under the weight of the darkness the world faced.

"I am not interrupting anything I hope?" he said as he stepped into the room.

"Just the creeping melancholy of hopelessness and existential dread."

One of his eyebrows flicked up. "Are you alright?"

"I'm *fine*. We have no actual cure for corruption, two of my dearest friends disappeared through a portal to Mother knows where, and it is very likely they are both dead—"

"It's only been two months."

She dropped her gaze and swallowed. "I don't like not *knowing*, and this—" She gestured to the mess of half-completed experiments around her. "I'm starting to understand why Samson went mad."

He opened his mouth, but she cut him off.

"What if there is no cure and this treatment is the best we're going to get? But it's not just that ..." She chewed her thumbnail. "Samson had been suffering the effects of corruption for a long time when he came to the conclusion it could only be cured by finding its root in the Between. And both Nea and Garret were infected before they went through portal. What if he was wrong? What if the corruption wanted him to go into the Between for another reason? What if—"

"Hey now." Leith strode forward and wrapped his arms around her shoulders, pulling her against his chest in an embrace that smelled of sweet jasmine tea and Osmarian spice. He drew back, his hands still on her shoulders as his grey eyes searched hers. "It's not like you to give up hope, Margot."

"I—no. I'm not. It's just so hard, and I don't think I can keep doing this ... I'm not Declan or Nea."

"No, but you are a *healer*. One of the best, and you have people who need you. You might not have a cure, but you have a treatment that can ease the suffering of the afflicted and buy them time while we wait for Nea and Garret to return."

She rubbed her hands over her face. "And if they don't return?"

He frowned and cast his gaze to the floor before giving her a shaky smile. "We'll cross that bridge when we get to it. Now I didn't come in here just to give you a pep talk. I wanted your opinion on something."

"And that is?"

"I want to steal Amelia from Father."

He what? She coughed, then swallowed to clear her throat. "That is not what I was expecting. It's not possible to remove Amelia from the south wing. Even if it was—and the fort wasn't under your father's control—it would be very ill advised. She's a monster who can't be killed and can infect others with corruption. Why would you want to embark on what is surely a suicide mission?"

"Niall can remove the binding, and we can bring her here and contain her. It would be safer to have her away from Father, don't you think?"

"I agree that it would be safer if Evard didn't have access to her, but it would be too dangerous to attempt. And how do we control her once the binding is removed?"

"Bind-shackles—"

"Were ineffective. Niall exhausted every avenue he could think of before binding her to the south wing." She leant against the bench.

Leith folded his arms.

"I understand. The waiting ... all the unanswered questions, they're killing me too, but we can't make rash decisions out of frustration." She chewed her thumbnail. "What if we sent someone to Braemar undercover?"

"Like a spy?" He rubbed his chin.

"Exactly. They could relay information about Evard's activities there and that may allay some of your concerns."

"It's not a bad idea, but who would we send?"

"Me," Harvey said with a grin as he stepped through the door. "I volunteer."

"Evard's men know that you deserted to join Garret. If you show up at the fort and they reveal you, Evard won't hesitate to kill you," Margot said.

Harvey waved her concern away. "Sure, if I joined as soldier, but people often see only what they are told to. If, say, I had darker hair, a disfiguring scar, a new name and occupation ..."

"A disfiguring scar? If you're talking about magically changing your appearance, the wardens in Evard's service will see straight through it," Margot said, flicking a glance at Leith imploring him to back her up.

Leith, however, was rubbing his chin and studying Harvey with a calculating smile.

"Okay, so maybe *not* a disfiguring scar ... but I need to do something. I am tearing my hair out from boredom." He turned his attention to Leith. "We can figure out the logistics, but you want intel, and I am offering myself up."

"It's not the worst idea—"

"You've got to be kidding me!" Margot threw her hands in the air. "Spying on Evard is a good idea, but if you send Harvey to the fort, you will be signing his death sentence. There has to be someone else."

"I won't risk anyone else," Harvey said.

"That's what Garret said right before he leapt through a portal, most likely to his death."

Harvey let out a laugh. "Sure, it was Garret's *altruism* that made him go dashing off through the portal."

"The feat required a warden. Of course Garret would sacrifice himself rather than send anyone else to what could be their death," Margot said.

Harvey chuckled. "Exactly. But chivalry aside, I imagine he'd follow *Nea* anywhere. And who could blame him? If I had a woman like that, I'd do anything to—" He glanced sideways at Leith. "Ah, that is ..."

Leith folded his arms and frowned at the floor.

Harvey made a good point; one that Margot could exploit to get this foolish idea out of his head. "And what would *Janey* think about you gambling your life on whether or not Evard's men will recognise you?"

He had the decency to look chastened. "Janey? Why would what Janey thinks have any bearing on it? And regardless, I'm sure she'd understand how important gathering information about Evard's plans is."

"I know you're getting bored with waiting for your father to make his next move, but you need to think this through," Margot said as she turned to Leith again. "Garret would never send anyone in without a sound plan."

"Which is why we need to call a meeting. Harvey, go and inform Niall and the others to meet us in the second-floor training room," Leith said.

"Right away." Harvey snapped his fingers then turned on his heel and hurried out the door.

Leith studied Margot for a moment. "You don't approve."

She let out a sigh. "It's not that I don't approve. Harvey can be a little too enthusiastic at times, but he has a good head on his shoulders; it's one of the reasons Garret likes him. But I still don't think you should send him to Braemar. No matter how we disguise him, there are people who will see straight through it. It's just too dangerous."

Leith rubbed his fingers over his chin. "Maybe that is why it will work. No one would expect us to be foolish enough to send in someone recognisable, so they might overlook him." Her rebuff must have shown on her face because he quickly added. "Or not ... Maybe the others can come up with a better plan."

Margot rubbed her hand over her eyes and took a sip of her tea, grimacing at the cold liquid. Leith, Emil, Molly, and Harvey were standing around a table a short distance away, arguing. The surface between them was covered in a collection of maps and notes.

Beside Margot, Janey made a noise and shifted in her seat. Catching Margot's eye, she shrugged and rolled her eyes as she gestured to the arguing group and signed. "*This is ridiculous.*"

Margot nodded. "I think they all need a time out."

Janey grinned and brushed her chestnut hair behind her ear. The jagged scar that covered her throat caught the light as the sound of someone slamming their hands on the table drew her attention back to the others.

"This argument has been circling for the last two hours. It's giving us nothing but heated tempers and headaches," Niall said. He was leaning against the wall across from Margot, a smooth disk of pinkish metal in his fingers. "Maybe we should all take a breather and reassess the options." He danced the coin across his knuckles before he caught it.

"We don't have the luxury of time here—" Leith fell quiet as the coercing fingers of Niall's keen stirred across the back of Margot's neck.

"Time is one thing we do currently have, my boy." His violet gaze pinned Leith. "Evard has not made any significant moves since Fort Braemar, and whilst we have seen an increase in reported cases of corruption, we have no real evidence that he is planning anything."

"But we can't be certain. Just because we can't see evidence of a plan, doesn't mean he doesn't have one."

Niall's knuckles paled as he squeezed the metal disc and his mouth twisted bitterly. "I have an *explicit* understanding of the way your father's mind works."

It was clear that Niall had single-handedly raised his daughter. There were so many traits they shared—the inability to sit still, the mercurial moods; even the way they both chewed their lips when thinking.

"Sending someone to Braemar to gather information is a *good* idea, but you can't go running off with your pants around your ankles."

"You should have told Nea and Garret that before they went jumping through portals," Emil quipped.

"I did. But Nea has always been like a hurricane trapped in skin when she gets an idea in her head." He smiled warmly then chuckled. "I imagine Garret is wishing he let her go alone right about now."

Emil let out a bark of laughter in response.

"So, what should we do? Who should we send to Braemar?" Molly asked. "If Harvey is out, so are the rest of us, especially as magical disguises are not an option."

Niall fidgeted with the coin, rolling it across his knuckles as he worried his lower lip. "Of course!" He caught the disk with a flourish and pushed off the wall. "I'll be right back."

"That's where Nea gets it from then." Harvey chuckled.

When Niall returned, he was carrying two pieces of braided leather with smooth ovals of metal at their centres. They looked like the warded bands he'd given Nea and Garret to hide them from the finder. "I was experimenting with these a few years ago before I started working on the portable wards. Hold out your wrist." He directed the last at Harvey. When Harvey lifted his arm, Niall tied one of the bands around it. "Now this is extremely experimental magic. If you feel any dizziness, tingling in your extremities, tongue swelling, or loss of vision, I need to know."

"You didn't think to tell me that before you tied it around my wrist?" Harvey asked as he studied the band.

Niall shrugged. "I've never tested it on a non-mage before. Anything?"

Harvey shook his head. "I feel normal."

"Good. Now to program it."

The subtle brush of Niall's keen ghosted across Margot's neck again, and the oval of metal in the band glowed pink for a moment.

"Hmm ..."

"What was supposed to happen?" Margot asked.

"So that tingling you mentioned—" Harvey's words were cut off as he doubled over gripping his stomach.

Margot leapt to her feet, followed quickly by Janey. They both hurried over, but Niall lifted his hand to stop them. "No need to panic."

"Mother's tits, you could have warned me about the—" Harvey let out a moan and dropped to the floor where he started convulsing.

Margot rushed forward and placed her hands on Harvey's shoulders. Her keen swelled warmly at her core and she let it out. A strange sticky magic covered him from head to toe, but there was nothing else that was causing the convulsion. She took hold of his chin to steady his shaking face as she rolled back his eyelid to check his pupils. The iris contracted and changed from steel blue to hazel. She released his face and jumped backwards. "What in the realms?"

His blond hair darkened to a deep brown, lengthening until the ends brushed his shoulders. Then he sat up as though nothing had happened. His face was narrower, his features sharper. If Margot hadn't seen the transformation, she wasn't sure she would believe it was Harvey.

"What?" he asked, glancing from one face to the next until his gaze settled on Margot.

"You might want to look in a mirror." Her attention switched to Niall. "Why did you bring two?"

"In case the first one didn't work and we needed to find another candidate. I did mention the magic was experimental, but it seems to have worked splendidly."

Janey turned to Niall and signed. "*Is it permanent?*"

"It shouldn't be. When he removes the band, he should, in theory at least, return to his usual self."

Janey nodded and gave Harvey a small smile.

Leith clapped his hands together. "Well, that solves that problem. Since you have two of them, maybe we should send someone else with Harvey as a safety precaution."

"What, so we can spend another hour arguing about who to send?" Emil asked.

"I'll do it." Molly stepped forward.

"What? No," Margot said a little too quickly. "I mean ..."

"It's alright. I'll be careful." She gave Margot's hands a squeeze then held her wrist out to Niall. "Hit me with it."

"But ..." Margot bit down on her objection.

"You're absolutely sure about this?" Niall asked.

Molly gave a firm nod. "Yes."

"Alright ..." He tied the band around her wrist before charging it with his magic.

"Shit." Molly dropped to her knees with a cough, her fingers gripping the floor as she started panting.

"It kind of feels like you ate something rotten and your skin is being flayed off," Harvey said as he watched Molly writhe about with mild interest. "Did I convulse like that?"

Janey gave him a light slap on the arm then placed a hand on Margot's shoulder.

Finally, Molly sat up. Her pretty cornflower eyes were now a similar shade of hazel to Harvey's, and her creamy blonde hair the same deep brown. Her features had also sharpened considerably. Her nose, which had been slightly off centre due to being broken when she was younger, was now perfectly straight, her delightfully plump lips thinner. She and Harvey appeared similar enough that they could easily pass as siblings.

"Mother's tits!" Harvey exclaimed. "Am I *that* different?"

Janey nodded.

"I thought it might be a good idea to make you look like family. That will give you a decent backstory and reason to be seen in each other's company. So you won't arouse too much suspicion." Niall looked rather impressed with himself.

"Is it bad?" Molly asked as she inspected the now brunette end of her braid.

"It's *different* ... but I don't hate it," Margot said and pressed a kiss to Molly's lips before frowning. "Are you sure about this, Mol? I can't go with you. What if something happens? I'd never—"

"I promise I'll be careful."

"What about wardens or other mages—wouldn't they feel the magic?" Margot asked Niall. She couldn't sense magic radiating off either Harvey or Molly, but she wanted to be sure.

"I can't feel anything unusual about them," Emil offered.

"If you touched the band, you'd feel the magic, but it is self-contained like the portable wards. You would really have to be looking for it to feel it. The enchantment should hold up against suppression as well." Niall held a hand out to Emil.

A numb bubble of suppression lowered over Molly and Harvey, but their new appearances didn't waver.

Emil let out a whistle. "Declan would have been having a field day with this."

"It's settled then. Let's sort out your backstory and get you both on your way," Leith said.

Margot shared a worried glance with Janey.

Every fibre of her being was telling her this was still a bad idea, but now she couldn't tell if it was her instincts or her concern for Molly that was the driving force.

CHAPTER TWO

NEA

Nea opened her eyes and took in the dark puddles littering the floor. After a few blinks, it became clear they were discarded clothes. Heat flooded her back as a firm body pressed against it, and a heavy arm looped around her waist, pinning her to a well-muscled chest.

She wanted to close her eyes and sink into the comforting warmth of the bed, but something was bothering her. Like the dream she had been having had left scars across her mind. With a deep breath, she centred herself and summoned a mage light. The pale lilac orb bobbed above the bed as she sat, slowly shifting the arm around her waist. Its owner stirred and grumbled sleepily, then opened his grey eyes and gave her a lazy smile.

"Leith?" Tension pulled across her forehead and she pressed her fingertips to it.

He chuckled. "You were expecting someone else?"

She shook her head, more to try and clear her thoughts than to answer him. "Sorry. I just had the strangest dream ... I think it was a dream ... I'm a little disorientated."

"You know the cure for a bad dream?" He sat and ran his finger along the bare curve of her shoulder.

She rolled her eyes. "That was a terrible line."

"It made you smile though." He grinned and brushed his lips against hers. "And I do so love your smile." One hand supporting her weight, he guided her onto the pillow as he dropped a trail of kisses along her jaw and down the side of her neck.

"Leith, I don't think now is a—oh."

His hand dipped between them, tickling the sensitive skin below her navel and tracing a path farther south.

"Leith!" She pushed her palms against his chest, and he relinquished his hold on her, allowing her to sit.

A look of confusion brushed his features.

"Doesn't this feel strange to you?"

He glanced around the room and shook his head. "It feels no different to normal, though you're not usually this highly strung ... If you're still worried about Father ..." He traced his index finger in delicate circles along the curve of her shoulder again.

She pulled the sheet up to cover her chest and frowned. There was a need to be worried about Evard, wasn't there? Something was missing. A niggling sensation stirred at the very back of her mind like a blossoming headache.

"Nea!"

She blinked. "Sorry. I was lost in thought."

He gave her an affectionate smile. "Of course you were. You can't help yourself. But you know there's something we could be doing right now that would drive all those niggling thoughts away." As he spoke, he edged closer.

A look of mock exasperation settled on her features, then she let out a yelp of laughter as he pounced and pulled her onto the bed. They rolled in a tangle of flesh and sheets until Leith was pinned beneath her.

"Now this view ..." His voice was a lust-filled whisper as he snaked his hand behind her neck and guided her lips to his.

The kiss started gently but quickly became feverish in a way that left her lips feeling hot and tender. One of Leith's hands cupped the base of her skull, fingers twisting into the roots of her hair, while the other possessively gripped the flesh of her side. She felt a smile shift across his mouth as he flexed and flipped them over so Nea was beneath him again. His lips left hers to press a scorching path across her chest and between her breasts—

A knock at the door elicited an irritated groan from Leith that tickled the skin of her stomach. "Someone better be dead—"

"Leith," she chided him as she slipped from his clutches and threw on the first item of clothing she could find before crossing the room.

The messenger on the other side of the door blushed and cleared his throat as he became fascinated with the trim around the threshold. "My lady, the king requires your presence for the trial."

Trial? She bit her lip and tried to focus, but her thoughts had become squirrely things that slipped through her fingers and darted away. "Tell him I am on my way," she responded automatically and closed the door.

"Everything alright?"

Her attention snapped to Leith where he was propped on the bed, the planes of his chest highlighted by the dim glow from her mage light. "Yes. Your father requires my presence."

"It is time for the trial already?"

She ran a hand through her hair. "Apparently." Whose trial she wasn't sure, and she was about to ask when he cut her off.

"I didn't think it would be so soon, but we shouldn't keep Father waiting." He got up and found his pants then grinned at her. "I'll be needing that back now."

In her haste to answer the door, she'd pulled Leith's shirt on. "I suppose you do need it." With a smile, she slipped it off and tossed it to him before she turned to find her own clothes.

When they walked into Evard's throne room, it was too bright and too warm. Light shone off the grey stone walls and heavy green drapery. The fire in the massive hearth was an ominous orange glow that every so often spewed sparks with a loud crackle and pop.

Evard sat on his mahogany throne, his chin resting on his tented fingers as he surveyed the group of people before him. Tight pressure crawled up the back of Nea's skull. The prisoners were all mages. Leith stepped forward and took up the smaller throne beside his father, his gaze becoming hooded and his mouth a grim line.

"My darling Nea." Evard stood and opened his arms to her. "Come and let's get this distressing business done with so we may celebrate the dawning of the new era."

She bit down on her lip and dug her nails into her palms. This was all wrong. There was something about Evard's demeanour, a softness to his features that had never been there before. Or had it? She pressed her fingers to the middle of her forehead.

"Are the headaches still troubling you, my dear?"

When had Evard gotten so close? As his long fingers reached for her, she rocked back a step. "I'm fine." Something was thrashing in the back of her mind, tiny fists pounding against the bars of an impregnable cage. "I mean, no offense, my lord." Licking her lip, she glanced at the bound mages. "Shall we?" She lifted a hand to draw his attention to them.

Evard's posture shifted as he faced the prisoners. The warm compassion was replaced with cold indifference, and he strode forward to pull a man to his feet.

Icy dread squeezed around Nea's heart. *Tobias?* She studied the other mages. Though they had their backs to her, she knew them all too. They were from Kalhanna. Her gaze then found the dark-haired warden leaning casually against the wall, running the blade of a small knife against an oily whetstone. His smile was warm, but his eyes held a deep cruelty. *Willem.*

No, this wasn't how it had happened. She looked at Tobias again and found only hatred in his features.

Evard was talking, but the words couldn't penetrate the rush of blood that surged through her skull. Thick fingers squeezed her throat and gritty ash coated her tongue. The air she gulped over dry lips refused to fill her lungs. *Is this how fish feel when they are dragged from the water?* The cold floor slammed against her.

"She's too strong," said a frustrated female voice Nea didn't recognise.

"What did you expect? She belongs to *Him.*" Another voice. This one male and almost soothing.

Something inaudible followed by a familiar sound—a pestle grinding herbs against a mortar. She tried to open her eyes, but they remained firmly shut.

"You're trying too hard to overwrite the memory. That period of her life was too traumatic. She'll never accept it as anything else. If you want to keep her subdued, you'll need to use another."

"I know what I am doing," the woman snapped.

The clearing around Nea was silent. Still. Like that moment before an earth-shaking boom of thunder when the entire world seemed to hold its breath. Waiting.

A whimper behind her broke the stillness, and she turned to find a boy, no older than three or four, sitting in the middle of the field. His dark auburn hair tangled with leaves and bark. He was picking debris from the scrapes on his palms, tears cutting a path through the grime on his cheeks. Nea swallowed and stepped towards him.

His head snapped up. He had grey eyes so like Leith's, they knocked the breath from her. Those eyes widened in fear and he let out a sob as he scuttled backwards.

"Sorry. I didn't mean to frighten you," she said, but his gaze went straight through her.

"There you are!" a voice said behind Nea seconds before a girl with the same deep red hair as the boy went running through her body.

Nea patted herself down and then waved her hand through the form of the girl, who was now crouched over the boy.

"You don't exist here because this isn't your memory." Nea's attention was drawn to the youth leaning against the trunk of the tree nearby. He rolled a dark red apple around in his hands, inspecting it. When he looked up and shook his auburn hair out of his eyes, they were the same steady grey as the boy's. One was ringed by the mottled shadow of a healing bruise. He was probably fifteen at her best guess, broad and tall, but he had a touch of lankiness that he hadn't quite grown into.

"This is a memory? Whose memory and why am I here? *How* am I here?" She trawled through her mind for the answers, and the thing caged there slammed against the bars of its prison, but they remained steadfast. Pain surged across the back of her skull and settled in her temples.

"I don't know *how* you're here. You shouldn't be." He took a bite of the apple, the movement highlighting the scar that intersected his top lip, and his keen-sense brushed her.

Warden. But there was something different about the feel of his keen, like it held deep-rooted secrets.

He chewed thoughtfully. "You're not a normal necromancer, are you?"

"And you're not a *normal* warden," she threw back.

A warm grin broke the corner of his mouth as he took another bite of the apple.

Nea turned back to the children. The girl was trying to coax the boy to her, but he kept shying away.

"Come on, Garret, please? Mama will only punish you harder if you don't come home now," she pleaded.

The boy, Garret, shook his head and pointed over the girl's shoulder before miming something with his hands.

The girl made a frustrated noise and leapt to her feet. "Use your words!"

Garret flinched.

"I'm sorry." She crouched again and spoke softly. "I know you're not dumb. That's not why you don't speak. I have heard you talking to the wrens by the stream."

The older boy made a noise and Nea glanced his way.

"Please, Garret, come home with me," the girl implored.

Garret shook his head again and said one word. "Dead."

"Dead? What's dead?" The girl's face paled and her mouth drew into a hard line. "What did you do?"

Garret's eyes grew wide, and he shook his head harder while tapping the centre of his chest.

"There they are." A group of adults broke through the trees. An older woman, who had the same hazel eyes as the young girl, rushed to the children and started fussing.

The other two Nea knew. The first was a woman with a long iron-grey braid, and the second a younger man with deep brown hair that brushed his shoulders. Both had the same dark violet eyes. The man, Nea's father, had a strange pack strapped to his back.

"Where's Mama?" the girl asked, and the woman with the hazel eyes rocked back on her heels, drawing a deep breath.

"She's ... Bridie, your mother ..."

"She's dead," Nonna said, not unkindly, but in that matter-of-fact way Nea had hated when she was younger.

"Mother!" Niall said. "You can't break the news to a child like that."

"Dead?" The girl squeaked, then something flashed in her eyes and she rounded on the boy again. "What did you do to her! She was right about you! You ... you ... WRETCH!"

"Bridie, that's enough! Garret didn't do anything," the hazel-eyed woman reprimanded. "Garret, wait. Don't run."

The boy had gained his feet and ran full pelt between Nea and the teenager. Nonna started after him, but Niall grabbed her arm.

"No, you fix this mess." He indicated Bridie, who had collapsed against the woman Nea now assumed was her grandmother. "I'll find the boy." He started after Garret.

Nea followed her father, and with a sigh, the youth tossed the core of the apple away and wandered along beside her. "Curious? Did the boy do something to his mother, other than simply be born that is? You've got an interesting experience with mothers as well, don't you? At least yours didn't poison herself because she couldn't cope."

Nea ignored his questions; she had no idea why she was witnessing this boy's memory, but now that her father and grandmother were involved, she was intrigued.

They followed her father to a small stream. Garret sat on a large flat rock at the water's edge, his face buried in his knees. Niall cleared his throat, and the boy leapt to his feet, slipping on the rock and teetering towards the water.

"It's alright." Niall launched forward and grabbed the boy's shirt before he fell into the stream. "Now ..."

Garret struggled against Niall's grip.

"That's enough of that. I'm not going to hurt you. I know you didn't do anything wrong." The smooth fingers of her father's keen stirred the air.

If he wanted to, he could force the boy to be compliant, but that wasn't her father's way. Slowly, Garret stopped struggling and drew a shuddering breath.

"I'm going to let you go. Please don't run." He released the boy, then took a step back and unbuckled his pack before deftly shifting it around to his front and peering inside. The pack wiggled and then made a small sound, and Garret, who had been warily studying Niall, crept forward.

"Out you come then." Niall lifted a baby from the pack. She blinked and twisted around, her wide violet eyes taking it all in. Her head was covered in a thick patch of stormy curls. Garret took another careful step towards Niall, drawing the attention of the infant.

"That's you then," the teenager said to Nea.

"It's alright. You can come say hello," Niall said softly as he sat and placed the child on his knee. She couldn't have been more than seven or eight months old.

Garret edged closer.

"I'm Niall. Your grandmother probably told you I was coming to see you. And this is Nea."

The infant reached her hands out towards Garret and made a bunch of cooing sounds.

"Nea," Garret said as he took another step forward and held his finger out. His keen-sense stirred as she took hold of the offered finger. "She's *different*."

Niall smiled. "She is. And I see you can talk. They told me you couldn't."

"I ... don't want to," he mumbled, not taking his eyes off the baby.

"And why don't you want to talk?"

Garret shrugged.

"I can't help you unless you want me to, but I can take away the bad things or make them not so bad."

Garret's eyes met Niall's for the first time. Something desperate shimmered in their grey depths. "You can fix me?"

"You're not broken."

Garret shook his head. "Mama said I'm going to be a monster like him. I don't want to be a monster."

"Like who?"

"I don't know. Just *him*."

"You're being quiet," Nea said to the teenager beside her.

"I'm just letting you absorb the information presented. That's what you do, isn't it? Take everything in and then use it to your advantage later."

"You speak as though you know me."

"Given where you are, is that really a surprise?"

No, but it was more than that. "I don't know you. Should I? Obviously we met once *long* ago, but I don't recall ever meeting you again." Pain sliced across her mind as the thing there gripped the bars of its cage. They bent but didn't break.

"Abigail has taken Bridie back to the house." The hazel-eyed woman had joined Niall and Garret. "I think it would a good idea for you to alter her memory of today. Garret's too."

Niall nodded. "Garret and I were just discussing that."

"He spoke to you?"

"He speaks quite well actually."

She sniffed as she watched Garret showing infant Nea a spotted blue feather. "These ones eat insects. These ones"—he held out another feather: olive-green with a sheen like oil on water—"eat the berries."

"I taught him that," the woman said. "We'd sit here and watch the birds, and I taught him about them. He never seemed to respond though."

"He has a very sharp mind. And as his mutism is obviously selective, it is most likely a response to the treatment his mother gave him. She couldn't separate the boy from his father, and he has suffered unnecessarily for that." Niall's tone became bitter.

Garret's grandmother nodded. "And the other matter?"

Niall chewed his lip and flicked a sad glance from Garret to Nea before delicately brushing his fingers through Nea's curls. "Mother and I discussed it with Warren, and we have come to the conclusion that it is for the best. If Evard were to discover the truth ..."

The woman's brow lifted. "*Warren* agrees we should lock it away?"

Nea's father made a sound that could have been a laugh or a sigh. "No. Warren believes we are making a dreadful mistake. However, the alternative ..."

"I understand ... It won't harm him, will it? He's already been through so much."

The baby tilted her head and reached for the older woman. With a small smile, Niall handed her over. "There are risks, of course, but I shall do my best to ensure they are both safe."

"Grandmama, look!" Garret had a butterfly sitting on the palm of his hand. The wings were tattered and unmoving. As he held it out, a cool coil of keen stirred the air. The wings fluttered as the butterfly righted itself then took flight.

The woman's gaze snapped to the baby and then to Niall. "Did she?"

He shook his head. "It would seem that the need for haste has become imperative."

"I wish you could see your face right now," the youth said, snatching Nea's attention from the scene.

"He's a warden. How did he reanimate the butterfly? And what are his grandmother and my father talking about locking away?"

"You'll get the answers when you are meant to. And, honestly, I don't make a point of understanding it all. That's what you do. You figure it out, then you fill me in. We'll make a pretty good team eventually."

Something tugged behind Nea's navel and bile bit at her throat. The landscape around her flicked.

"Don't worry. We'll meet again. Our paths were always meant to converge." With that, the teenager disappeared as the world fell out from beneath her.

She hit the ground running. The image of the person she had been talking to slipped through her fingers and shattered across that part of her mind she couldn't access.

Wet loam shifted under her feet as trees flashed past. Behind her, someone let out a squeal of laughter. She glanced back. A group of girls, their heads adorned with crowns of flowers, were darting through the trees. Ahead of her was another a group. Snatches of their conversation reached her.

"He went this way."

"I can't believe it was really the prince."

"Don't get your hopes up. You saw the way he was looking at the necromancer."

Then they were gone, and Nea found herself in a quiet clearing. She leant against a tree and lifted the crown of flowers from her hair, gently thumbing the bright blooms. The sound of someone clearing their throat came from above her, and she looked up. Leith was perched in the branches, his feet dangling lazily beneath him. He gave her a wide smile and dropped to the ground next to her.

"Well, fancy meeting you here." His fingers found a loose coil of her hair as he slid them along her jaw and cupped the back of her neck.

She swallowed and gripped the crown tighter; the scent of wild flowers filled the air as the space between their bodies became unbearably hot.

Heat burned her face. A campfire. Someone who wasn't Leith but had the same steady grey eyes ... A name on the tip of her tongue—

The rough skin of Leith's thumbs rubbed against her cheeks, and her breath snagged in her throat as his lips brushed lightly against hers in an almost-kiss that chased her churning thoughts away and turned her knees to water.

"I wouldn't trade you for a thousand willing maidens." His voice was husky, and she could almost taste the honied mead on his breath.

She was dying to get lost in him. Her fingers traded their grip on the crown for the sides of his shirt, crushing the fine fabric and anchoring their chests together. Leith made a noise low in his throat—something between a groan and growl—as his lips claimed hers. His hands dropped to her waist, and he pinned her to the tree with a force that could have stolen her breath had he not already claimed it. She arched her body against his, hungry to feel every inch of him.

As soul-devouring as the kiss was, the prisoner stirred in the back of her mind. The cage rattled. She was forgetting something. The hunger she felt for Leith was tinged with sorrow. No, not sorrow. Regret and fear ... and something she couldn't quite place—

With a gasp, she pulled away from him and drew a series of sharp breaths to feed her starved lungs. "This isn't right."

"It feels perfect to me." He toyed with the loose lock of her hair.

It wasn't right. It wasn't real. It wasn't ... "You're not Leith."

An indignant look was quickly replaced with a warm smile and too-sweet tone of voice. "Of course I am."

"No, you're not. This isn't real. It's ..." The thing at the back of her mind gripped the bars of its cage—strong enough to bend them but not quite enough to break free. "It's ..." Pain blossomed across her brow and she pressed her fingers against it. "I have to get out of here." She pushed away from him.

"Nea, wait. You're not thinking straight." He made a grab for her, but she danced away.

"You're losing her again." A male voice echoed through the forest, and she spun around, searching for its source as the trees started to shimmer and fade.

"Shut up!" a woman's voice ordered.

The world flickered at a nauseating speed. Leith's face was replaced by a woman with bright pink hair, but before Nea could get a good look at her features, she was gone again.

Strong hands closed on Nea's shoulders and she twisted, trying to get away.

"What's he doing? No!" the woman's voice yelled. "Stop him."

"Stop fighting it, Shadow Girl." The voice in Nea's ear was gravelly, foreign, and yet—strangely soothing.

She drew a slow breath and the world stopped flickering. The trees came back, but Leith was gone. Heavy hands still restained her but the grip was gentle enough that if she wanted to break free, she could.

"That's it. Deep breaths now. The witch has lost her hold on you."

Nea focused on her breathing. Each inward rush of cool air was a balm that soothed away the hot-cold prickles that crawled up her spine; every exhale slowed her racing heart.

After several moments, she shook off the hands holding her and turned.

He was a towering man with intricate black tattoos that covered the rust-coloured skin of his bare chest. His long black hair was secured in a neat braid that rested over his shoulder. A smile touched the corners of his dark eyes and cracked his full lips as he rested the heel of his palm on the hilt of one of the hand axes sheathed at his belt.

"Who are you?" She rubbed her forehead and took a step back. "And where am I?"

"Rourke, and you're currently in a trap."

"A trap?"

"Do you remember how you got here?"

She frowned. Whenever she tried to access her memories, they slid away from her. But she got the impression of ... a portal and a man with grey eyes who wasn't Leith. Pain stabbed at her temples and she rubbed them in small circles. The thing at the back of her mind slammed against the bars of its cage.

Rourke nodded. "It will come back when we free you. Come on. We need to go hunting." He indicated she follow.

"Hunting what?" She wasn't sure whether she could trust him or that she should. Her keen-sense didn't pick up anything malicious about him, quite the opposite actually, but she wasn't sure she trusted her own judgement at the moment.

"The thing that stole your essence."

"The one you called a witch?"

He let out a low chuckle. "No. She'll keep. We're hunting a devourer."

A devourer? Where had she heard that term before?

She closed her eyes as Nonna's voice said, "... *beings of thought and memory. They are predatory in nature, though they don't usually seek to leave the Between. Rather, they attempt to trap their prey and slowly absorb its life force.*"

A headache threatened at her temples again, and she gripped her head, rubbing her fingers through the roots of her hair.

Rourke gave her a pat on the shoulder. "Best to leave your memories alone for now, Shadow Girl. They'll come back after we defeat the devourer."

Nea nodded. "Alright. Let's go hunting."

CHAPTER THREE

GARRET

Garret frowned at the ceiling. Every night it was the same. He woke before dawn with his niece, Nora, curled against his side and the tacky residue of forgetfulness at the back of his mind. He knew this wasn't real. This place he was in that was trying so hard to be his home, but he also couldn't remember why he was here. It had something to do with the violet-eyed woman who haunted his dreams he was sure. Though he couldn't remember her name, and the dreams kept most of her features hidden in shadow; but nothing could hide her eyes. They stared straight through him and seared the very fabric of his soul.

When the realisation that he was trapped in this façade of normality had initially hit him, he had fought it. However, after the fourth or fifth time of waking up in his bed with a splitting headache, he learned it was easier to just accept it. Still, it didn't sit right with him. There was an insistent pull in the back of his mind telling him he couldn't linger here, that there was something vital he was supposed to be doing.

He rubbed his hands over his face before getting up, careful not to disturb the sleeping girl beside him. She mumbled and burrowed deeper into the blanket as he tucked it around her then grabbed his boots and headed into the kitchen.

The fire had burned to a patch of glowing coals that he stirred before placing on another log and going outside into the cool pre-dawn. Bright stars studded the indigo sky around the thin crescent of the moon.

One of the indicators that this place wasn't real was the moon. Though the days went by, it remained unchanged—a silver sickle that taunted him. He drew a bucket of water from the well and frowned at his distorted reflection before splashing his face. The cold water did little to drive the images of the violet-eyed woman from his mind. Like the moon, she was goading him, insisting he was forgetting something important, but not offering up any clues as to what it might be. He would have liked to ask Declan for his opinion, but he was back at Loch Bastien ... No, that thought didn't seem right. Whenever his mind shifted to Declan, a weight closed around his chest and the sense that he was forgetting something increased tenfold.

Running a damp hand through his hair he scanned the moonlit farm. A brown cow was standing in the door to the barn chewing its cud, but otherwise nothing stirred. Taking another bucket from the well, he headed back inside to make some tea and porridge. There was no way he was getting to sleep again tonight, so he might as well continue the charade of normality.

The smell of porridge brought Bridie from her room. She stretched and hid her yawn behind her hand. "Are you sure you don't want to see the town healer about this insomnia? Perhaps there is a tea that he can suggest; one to help you sleep." As she spoke, she walked over and checked the pot hanging by the rekindled fire before taking a seat at the table.

"I'm fine, Bridie. Just restless. I should really be getting back to Loch Bastien."

Her mouth twitched and her eyes narrowed, but the look was quickly replaced with a forced smile. "You can't go back before Nora's birthday. She'll be heartbroken."

He shrugged as he measured out a spoonful of dried apple and spices into a cup. "I've been away long enough as it is."

A frown flickered at the corner of her mouth again.

Garret gritted his back teeth as a prickle of pain started at his temples. "I'm sure Nora will understand."

"This is the first birthday without her father."

"I can't replace Kieran!" His tone was harsher than he intended. With a sigh, he said more softly, "I have a life and I need to get back to it." He added honey to the tea mix before pouring the freshly boiled water over it.

Bridie folded her arms and sniffed as he placed her tea in front of her. "You really have no problem abandoning us in our time of need?"

He bit the inside of his cheek and busied himself by adding a handful of dried fruit to oats bubbling in the pot and giving it a stir.

"Silence was the stern reply," she said as he placed a steaming bowl in front of her.

"What do you want from me?" He was tired of this game. She wasn't like this every morning; only the days he was entertaining ideas of escaping this false reality. The ache had shifted from his temples to behind his eyes.

A triumphant curve touched the corner of her mouth as she dipped her spoon into her breakfast. "I just want what any sister wants for her brother."

Bullshit. He sat across from her and they ate in silence.

Nora and Pierce emerged, and their mother busied herself getting them breakfast.

After he finished his meal, Garret threw himself into farm work. Doing something with his hands helped clear his mind. It also kept him away from the thing that was pretending to be Bridie. He fixed the broken hinge on the barn door, helped Pierce move the stubborn cow out to the south field, and took Nora for a walk along the stream where she found a spotted stone for her rock collection.

That evening, they were all in the kitchen. His grandmother was sitting in her chair by the fire, her hands busy carving a small rabbit out of piece of apple wood. Nora and Pierce were playing a game of knuckles at her feet, and Bridie sat by the table, a pile of mending beside her.

Garret poured hot water over the leaves in the cup in front of him. The scent of chamomile and peppermint brought the violet-eyed woman to surface of his mind. Only this time she wasn't featureless. When he closed his eyes, he could clearly make out her pale skin and her slightly fuller lower lip rolling between her teeth as she raked a hand through her storm-grey curls. Her name was on the tip of his tongue—

"Who's that cup for?" Bridie asked, stealing the image of the woman away.

He glanced at the steaming cup sitting by her elbow, then at the one next to his grandmother and his own. "I guess I wasn't thinking." He went to place the cup next to his, but at the last moment lifted it to inhale the fresh scent again before taking a sip.

Images burned across his mind. Memories? He took another sip of the tea and tried to focus on the image of the woman as she flashed by again. He saw her shackled in a dim jail cell, her posture defeated but her eyes bright with dignity. Then she was sitting across a campfire, her brow furrowed and her hands moving as she spoke in hushed tones. The image changed again to the repository below Loch Bastien, her hand pressed against the massive palm of the sentry golem—

"Uncle Garret?" Nora's voice cut through the memories, and he stared at her fingers curled in the side of his shirt. "Uncle Garret, I asked if you're going to stay for my birthday. Mama said you needed to get back to the college, but you can stay, can't you? It's only a few more days."

"A few more days ..." He didn't have a few more days. He wasn't even supposed to be here. The throbbing inside his skull was dulling the edges of his vision. He focused on the greenish liquid in the cup and willed himself not to collapse. The kitchen was too hot—he needed to get out. The cup fell from his fingers and clattered against the bench, spilling its contents across the scarred wood.

"Are you alright, Garret? Maybe you need to sit down," Bridie said as her fingers settled on his shoulder.

When had she gotten so close? He shook her fingers away and took a step back.

"Uncle Garret?" Nora's eyes were wide, almost too wide to be human.

He licked his lip. "I'm fine. I just need some air." As he said it, there was a knock against the door. He moved to it and tugged it open to reveal Declan wearing his usual lopsided grin.

"You won't believe the lengths I've gone through to find you, old boy."

Bridie let out a small, frustrated growl, but Garret ignored her as pain burrowed through his skull again. Declan lifeless on the back of a cart, his throat slit—

"You're supposed to be dead."

"We can discuss that later. Right now, I need to get you out of here so we can find Nea."

Nea. The name brought the violet-eyed woman to the front of his mind, and the weight of the memories made his knees weaken. Behind him, Bridie snarled.

"That's our cue to leave." Declan grabbed the front of Garret's shirt and dragged him through the door.

Outside, the world was breaking apart. Great cracks had formed in the earth, and trees floated in the air, their roots creating an impregnable cage around the farm. Dark shapes crawled through the suspended roots, skittering things that made sounds like a hoard of insects.

"That's new," Declan said as he drew Garret to a stop in the middle of the farmyard.

"He belongs to me, deathwalker. You will not take him." Bridie's voice was distorted in a way that grated down Garret's spine and made his insides squirm.

Garret turned to face her. Her body was changing—arms and legs becoming long and disjointed, hair shifting from rich auburn waves to limp coils of muddy-green. Like her limbs, her midsection started to lengthen and distort, her ribcage expanding and her stomach concaving as her skin pulled tight, highlighting her bones. Her mouth opened in a red slash to show rows of pointed yellow teeth.

Fetid breath rushed over Garret and Declan as Bridie fell forward onto all fours, her teeth gnashing towards them.

"Well, shit," Declan said as lightning crackled over his knuckles.

Garret studied the flickers of magic. Why couldn't he *feel* them? He swallowed and tried to focus on his keen-sense, but there was nothing there. Icy fingers gripped his heart. He'd never been without his keen-sense. It was as essential to his body as breathing.

The thing that had been Bridie let out a wail and charged. Garret dove out of the way, and Declan unleashed his magic. Blue lightning flashed, and the scent of burning flesh and hair filled the air. Garret reached for his sword, but his hand found only empty air where the hilt should have been. Spotting an axe by the wood pile, he rushed over and snatched it up. He faced the creature, twisting out of the way as its talons sliced towards his stomach.

A crackle sounded, and the creature screamed as it was shrouded in a cage of lightning. When the lightning dissipated, the thing dropped to all fours again and started making a high-pitched yipping sound. Garret swung the axe. The blade met little resistance as it connected with the creature's neck. Its head flew through the air and landed near Declan's feet as the body melted into a puddle of black ooze.

A hiss behind Garret drew his attention. Two more of the creatures were prowling towards him, maws dripping as they ran impossibly red tongues along jagged yellow teeth. He backed away to stand beside Declan.

"If we die here, Nea is going to resurrect us and kick our arses. You know that, right?" Declan said as he eyed the advancing monsters.

"Then I suggest we try not to die." Garret tightened his grip on the axe and shifted his weight.

The creatures charged, and Garret dropped low as one reached him. Its talons whooshed through the air as Garret rolled under its belly and thrust both his feet upwards. His heels connected with the monster's ribs and it was flipped onto its back. Garret gained his feet and circled the creature. He lifted the axe and brought it down. The blade thudded harmlessly into the dirt as he was lifted from his feet.

Yellow teeth snapped a hair's breadth from Garret's face as he dangled above the ground. He slammed his fist into the monster's nose, and it let out a roar that smelt of fetid mud and frostbitten flesh. Garret swung himself forward and grabbed either side of the creature's face, pressing his thumbs into its dark eyes.

It wailed and released him. He rolled as he hit the ground. After grabbing the handle of the axe, he swung it as he twisted to his feet. The blade caught the belly of the creature and black ooze poured over it, scorching the wood and pockmarking the metal. Garret let go of the handle and leapt back as the creature staggered forward, its talons making another grab for him. It hissed and fell onto all fours, then with a last guttural moan dissolved into a heap.

Declan landed next to Garret panting as the smell of burning refuse filled the air, and the creature he had been fighting collapsed before melting as the others had.

"Still in one piece?" he asked Garret.

"Mostly. Any idea what those things were?"

"None absolutely." He gave a wide, slightly askew grin. "But I can tell you I am going to drive Nea crazy with questions when we find her."

"If we find her." Garret gestured to the roots still imprisoning the farm. "Do you know how to get out of this place?"

Declan studied the cage. "No. But I am sure we can figure it out. I got in easily enough." He walked over and placed his hand on one of the roots. There was a flash, and he was thrown onto his back, his hair standing on end.

"Maybe you should try," he said as Garret pulled him to his feet.

Garret eyed the cluster of roots and focused on his keen-sense but found only numbness. Rubbing the scar above his lip, he tried suppressing the source around the tangle, but his keen refused to stir. He gave Declan a look. "Something is very wrong."

A wrinkle formed between Declan's brows as he studied Garret. "What do you mean?"

"My keen is gone. I can't feel your magic, and I can't use my suppression."

Avid curiosity chased Declan's frown away. "Really? I wonder if that's something to do with this cage we are in, or perhaps being physically in the Between affects wardens differently to mages. Do you think it's similar to the effect of bind-shackles on a mage? Not that you manipulate the source the way a mage would, but maybe because the air is so saturated with it here—"

"Now is not the time for you go chasing theories!" Garret ran his hands over his face. After months of thinking Declan was dead, to have him here in the flesh was beyond strange. So many emotions were warring in his mind. He was grateful that Declan appeared alive and well in this realm but was too overwhelmed by everything else that was happening to give it any more thought. He leant his palms against the twisted roots in front of him.

The moment his skin touched the dirt-shrouded wood, it groaned and rolled back, showing a twisting tunnel bathed in a soft, green-hued light. Someone stood at the end of the tunnel. She was too tall to be Nea. Her starlight-coloured hair caught the green light, and then she was gone.

"That looks promising," Declan said, peering into the passage.

The roots groaned again and started to constrict. There was no time to consider what to do. Garret gave Declan a shove into the opening of the tunnel, and they both broke into a run, the roots raining dirt on them as they shuddered shut, blocking off the tunnel behind.

As they ran, chased by the collapsing roots, the light grew brighter and the shuddering of the tunnel more violent until they were spewed out into the soft grass of a wide field. The knee-deep green blades that stretched above them were studded with flowers every colour imaginable. The flowers seemed to be whispering among themselves, bobbing this way and that even though there was no breeze. They twisted their pollen-dusted centres towards Declan and Garret as they sat up.

In the distance, large iridescent orbs floated a few feet above the flower-studded grassland. Colours shifted over them in alluring patterns, almost like mage light. But these orbs were more like giant soap bubbles with twisting dark shapes contained within.

As Garret studied the spheres, they appeared to draw closer.

"My best guess is that Nea is somewhere in one of those. They seem to lead to memories, but we need to find the right one. Has your keen returned?" Declan asked.

Garret shook his head. His keen-sense was still agonisingly mute. "How did you find me?"

"You were in one of those sphere things, but it felt different to the others. We could—"

"Ahem!" a small voice said behind them.

They both turned, and Declan let out a laugh. The voice belonged to a young girl wearing a blue dress that was covered in more ruffles and bows than Garret imagined her adult counterpart would ever be caught dead in. Her hands were firmly on her hips. The look on her face was one he was familiar with—her mouth a tight line and exasperation in her deep violet eyes. She shifted her weight, and the storm-grey ends of her high ponytail danced against her shoulders.

"Nea?" Declan asked.

She tilted her head. "Well, I'm not Emil."

Declan laughed. "You never know. Things here are *tricky*, after all."

Nea bit down on her lip. "And what exactly are you doing here? It's dangerous."

"We're trying to find you actually."

"No, you're not. You're trying to find *her*. The me I will become one day. We're not the same. Too much has happened to us." She glanced at her skirt and her nose wrinkled. "Though she'd still hate this dress."

"So, if you're not our Nea, who are you and what are you doing here?" Declan asked.

Nea tilted her head as though listing to something. "I'm a memory. You are in a memory field you know? That's why it's so dangerous. It's easy to get lost in the pleasant moments, and then the devourers will get you. They don't get fresh food very often." She chewed her lip again. "The witch has promised you to them so that she can keep Nea. She needs her to complete the deal with the one who calls himself the Master of Shadows."

"The Master of Shadows. Is that the same as the Shadow Man?" Garret asked.

She scrunched her nose up. "Yes and no. I guess that is what you call him in your world, but here the distinction between the two mantles is *complicated*. Regardless, I don't like him. He's too nice."

"Too *nice*?" Declan asked.

"People are only *that* nice when they want something."

"That's an astute assumption from someone your age." Declan chuckled.

She folded her arms over her chest. "I'm ageless here. Though this version of me just turned seven. Hence the dress. Soph—*Mother* was visiting Del Harol, and Father thought if I looked like a normal girl, she might change her mind about me. But I won't change my mind about her. I ..." She clamped a hand over her mouth as though she had said too much.

Seven—the same age as Nora. Garret hoped she and the rest of his family were alright. They had made it to Hartswood, but there had been no time to check in on them before going through the portal.

"Anyway, we shouldn't stay here much longer. If you want to find the way out, you'll need to find your version of me. She keeps moving around though. The sage has sent her apprentice to help her. They are hunting the queen."

"They're hunting a queen?" Declan asked.

Nea rolled her eyes. "Not *a* queen, *the* queen. The biggest and meanest of the devourers in this nest. The witch is using the queen to keep you all trapped here ... so the devourers have food"—she pointed to them both—"and the witch can give Nea to the Master of Shadows. Weren't you listening at all?"

Garret traced his finger along his top lip to hide his smirk. "Alright. Do you know where we can find our Nea?"

She tilted her head again and chewed her lip, then she pointed to a mass of bubbles. "She's that way. You'll find her in the memory with the wolf."

"The memory with the wolf?" Garret turned back to the girl, but she was gone.

CHAPTER FOUR

HARVEY

Harvey prodded his cheeks as he examined his reflection. It was taking longer than he thought it would to get used to his new features. He cracked his neck then splashed water on his face before running his fingers through his hair.

"Bryce and Tessa, brother and sister, looking for work," Molly said from her perch on the bed. She'd been repeating it several times a day since they had left Del Harol.

"Surely you've memorised it already, *Tess.*" He grinned at her reflection.

"It needs to be seamless. If they suspect anything off about our story ..."

"We'll be fine. Who are our parents?" He turned to face her and pulled his shirt on.

"Ian and Chloe. They owned a small farmstead just outside Varth, but we lost them both two winters past in the epidemic that swept through the village and surrounding areas."

"Any other siblings?"

"Only one, Hannah, taken by the same fever that took our parents."

"See? You're all over it." He picked up his pack from next to her on the bed. "It's time we got ourselves to the fort."

Though they could have reached Fort Braemar the night before, they had decided to stay in the village below it. Molly had wanted to pen a letter to Margot and practice her backstory another dozen times. Harvey, on the other hand, had spent his evening with the locals, gathering information about the goings on at the fort since Evard had taken control of it.

The townsfolk had been tight-lipped, and there was a tension that hadn't been present before. A discontent that seethed beneath the surface. It was worth informing Leith.

Molly was silent as they wandered along the road that led from the village to the keep. Occasionally she would toy with the leather band around her wrist and let out a huff. Harvey had learned early on to leave her be when she was in this mood, but she'd need to snap out of it before they reached the fort.

It wasn't the first time he wondered why she had offered to come along. Since they had rescued Margot from Evard, Molly had barely let her out of her sight. It seemed strange that she would agree to something that created so much distance between them. Trouble in paradise? Their overtly passionate goodbye would suggest otherwise. Perhaps, like him, Molly was just bored with sitting around waiting for Evard to do something. That was most likely the case. He'd known Molly since they were teenagers playing at being soldiers and dreaming of one day becoming high-ranking members of the king's guard. She didn't do well with just waiting and watching the world play out around her.

"Sickle for your thoughts?" Molly said.

"Oh, so you're done contemplating your navel, and you're ready to talk to me again," he said with a grin.

She gave him a light shove with her shoulder.

He stopped and ran his hand through his hair. "It's not too late for you to turn back if you regret coming along. I can do this alone you know?"

"You? Do something as delicate as this alone? Come on, Harv. You know subtlety has never been one of your strengths."

"I can be ridiculously subtle when the mood takes me. It just doesn't happen all that often, that's all ... But I'm serious, Mol. If you want to go home to Margot, now is the time. Once we reach the fort, there's no turning back until—"

"I *know*. Margot will be fine without me for a while, and Del Harol is the safest place for anyone at the moment." Her gaze dropped to her feet before snapping up again, a smile lifting the corners of her mouth. "Truth be told, I feel guilty because I'm excited to be doing something other than sitting on my backside watching the mages theorise about Evard's motives. Mother preserve me, it seems to be all they do."

Harvey laughed. "Glad I am not the only one. If I heard Niall say, 'Perhaps we're looking at this from the wrong angle' or 'have you considered ...' one more time, I think I would have asked you to put me out of my misery."

Molly's grin widened. "That's all it is though. Once we step into the fort, I promise I will be completely focused."

"Okay." He started walking again.

A guard stood forward to block their path as they reached the gate. "State your business."

Harvey cleared his throat. "I am Bryce, and this is my sister, Tessa. We were told the fort was in need of new staff, and ..." He fell silent as a man wearing the dark leathers of a warden stepped out from the shadows. He had sharp features and a beak-like nose. John.

John's eyes narrowed as he studied them and rubbed the stump where his sword hand had been. Harvey swallowed. John would be using his keen-sense and he hoped Niall was right about the enchanted band.

After a few more agonising heartbeats, John nodded to the guard and disappeared. Molly let out a nervous chuckle that drew the attention of the guard. She cleared her throat. "I bet that guy is great at parties." She grinned a little too wide, but the guard snorted a short laugh.

"Come on. I'll take you to the head of staff." He nodded to the other soldier on duty, who turned his to face the road.

The bulk of debris from the battle in which Evard had claimed the fort had been cleared away, but the courtyard still showed scars from the fight. A wooden palisade had been erected in the blasted-out section of the outer wall, and the side of the stables that had collapsed had not been rebuilt.

When they reached the foot of the stairs that led into the fort itself, a woman with her greying hair peeking out from under a green kerchief came down to meet them. She paused and wiped her hands on her apron. "Who do you have there, Micha?" She eyed them like a farmer assessing his stock.

"Bryce and Tessa. They've come looking for work." He gave them a nod and then headed back towards his post.

The woman walked a slow circle around them. "What sort of work are you chasing?"

"Anything you have. Tess is a good cook, but she won't turn her nose up at harder duties, and I was training to be a master of the horse before the plague, but I'll take on anything you throw at me. We have recommendations." Harvey fished a small stack of letters from his pack and held them out.

The woman's nostrils flared, and she took a step back. "Plague?"

"Two years ago, in Varth, it took the rest of our family. We've been accepting any job that has come along since."

She nodded and took the letters. "It was a terrible year for sickness that one. You're from Varth then? Farmers?"

"Our parents were," Molly said.

The woman chewed the inside of her cheek. "I'm Sarah. I oversee the house staff and could certainly use another pair of hands. You should report to my husband, Reg, in the stables." She indicated

Harvey. "He will likely have work for you if you're not afraid of manual labour." Turning her attention to Molly, she gave her a short nod before beckoning her to follow.

"I'll see you later, Tess," Harvey said brightly as he headed off to find Reg.

Workhands were in short supply, and Reg had put Harvey to work straight away. Within the week, they had the frame for the stable rebuild standing, and as Harvey wiped the sweat from his brow, Reg clapped him on the back. "I could've used you a month ago." He grinned as he pressed a pinch of smoke bush into his pipe and lit it.

As the acrid scent of the smoke filled the air, Harvey coughed and scrunched his nose up. He'd never liked smoke bush. It settled in his lungs, stole his breath, and reminded him too much of the man who'd replaced his father.

Reg snorted and gave him another clap on the back before scowling at something on the other side of the courtyard. Harvey followed his line of sight to John, who was frowning in their direction. The warden had seemed overly suspicious of Harvey. Molly had told him he was just being paranoid. John had been ignoring her, so it couldn't be that he could feel the enchantment. Or at least that's the conclusion Molly came to.

"Damn mage-sniffer needs to mind his own business," Reg muttered around a draw from his pipe.

"You don't like the wardens?" Harvey tried to keep his tone light.

"Some of 'em are decent folk. The old commander, Garret, he was a good sort. Gave me quite a shock when they said the king wanted him tried for treason." He nodded and tilted his pipe towards John. "That one though? He's an adder in the haystack." He studied Harvey for a few puffs. "He seems a bit obsessed with you. Yer not a mage in hiding?"

"Me a mage?" Harvey let out a laugh. "I wish. Do you think I would be building walls by hand if I could just snap my fingers and get them up?"

Reg's laugh turned into a hacking cough, and he spat. "I s'pose not. Just be careful around that one. He's *mean*."

"I'll keep out of his way."

"Good. I don't fancy losing such a useful set of hands."

Molly came over to them and smiled brightly at Reg as she handed him a small package. "Sarah thought you might be hungry."

"Where's mine, Tess?"

"Sarah said you can get it in the kitchen after you fix a shelf for her."

Reg had been unwrapping his roll and gave Harvey a nudge towards the kitchen. "Off you trot. It's not a good idea to keep Sarah waiting."

When Harvey entered the kitchen, the first person he noticed was Maurice. He bit down on his tongue and gave the cook a curt nod. Maurice didn't bother to get up from his seat in the corner. He lifted his flask by way of greeting and then took a swig.

"You here to fix the shelf? It's in there." He indicated the larder.

"Thanks," Harvey said as politely as he could manage. The sooner he got this shelf fixed, the better.

He ducked into the larder and found the offending shelf easily enough. He cleared a space and set to work.

"Did Tessa fetch Bryce?" Sarah's voice carried clearly through the kitchen.

"He's in there," Maurice muttered.

Sarah poked her head in the door of the storeroom. "Do you need an extra set of hands? Maurice is out here."

"It's fine, Sarah. I can manage on my own."

"Good, good." She disappeared again. "Get off your arse, Maurice. We've had word from the capital. Commander Leon will be arriving by first frost with a small contingent of mages and wardens. That gives us a couple of weeks to ensure we are prepared for the increase in numbers."

Harvey set the shelf back in place and tested it. With a nod, he stepped into the kitchen, wiping his hands on a rag. "As good as new, Sarah. Anything else you need?" He gave her a wide smile.

"Not at the moment, Bryce. Why don't you help yourself to some lunch before you head back out to Reg?"

"Thanks." He grabbed himself a roll and some cheese. "Expecting a few extra bodies soon, are we? Anything I can do to help?"

"Not at this stage, love. You just focus on getting that stable rebuilt." Sarah smiled warmly, but Maurice's eyes narrowed.

"Is Captain Trenton due to return before the new commander or after?" Maurice asked.

"Trenton should be back in the next day or two. He's the captain on the king's guard stationed here," she added for Harvey's benefit. "Quite a lovely man once you get through that gruff exterior."

Harvey knew Trenton. He'd trained with him and then served under him for a while before being recruited by Garret. Trenton had little time for bootlickers like Leon, so things were about to get very interesting. He took a bite of his roll and waved to Sarah. "Thanks for the lunch. If you need anything else, just give us a yell." She waved him away, and he ducked out the back door of the kitchen into the courtyard where he nearly collided with John.

"Watch it, *stable boy.*"

"Sorry," he muttered and kept his head down as he hurried away.

He'd need to check in with Molly as soon as he got a chance. Maybe she had heard something he hadn't. Either way, they had to get a letter to Leith to let him know about the developments. If Evard was sending a group of wardens and mages to the fort, what did that mean?

CHAPTER FIVE

NEA

Nea leant her head against the trunk of the tree and closed her eyes. She and Rourke had been dipping in and out of memories for what felt like days, but they had yet to find their elusive quarry. Pain still blossomed when Nea tried to connect the dots between the older and more recent memories. It seemed anything that had happened over the last several years, at least, had been locked away in that prison at the back of her mind.

Every time she questioned Rourke about her missing memories, he told her to leave it be. That what had been taken from her would return once they found the devourer queen and freed Nea from her influence. He *had* divulged that when she'd used the portal at Del Harol, it acted like a beacon, announcing her presence to the more powerful denizens of the Between. Hence her current predicament and Rourke's assumed role as her guardian.

She opened an eye at the sound of him crouching in front of her. He held out a cup of tea. The steam rising from it in a gentle coil was laced with a sweet aroma that made her scrunch her nose up. Still, she opened her other eye and took it. She'd had several cups of the too-sweet tea, and as Rourke had promised, it had kept her from being tricked by the memories and falling back into the trap he had rescued her from.

Rourke settled himself across from her and stirred the flames of their small fire. The thing at the edge of her mind gripped the bars of its cage, and a flash of recognition stabbed the centre of Nea's chest. It was not a moment with Rourke she was remembering, but someone else. Someone tall with dark, auburn hair highlighted a deep, burnished copper by the firelight. She closed her eyes and inhaled the sweet scent of the tea. Grey eyes stared back at her, a wrinkle of concern between them as his fingers worked a small blade against a lump of wood. Creamy curled shavings fluttered to the ground as he tilted the carving, inspecting it. Something tugged deep within her stomach and she opened her mouth to speak, but the image scattered like ripples across the surface of water.

"The witch is losing her hold." Rourke's voice rumbled, and she glanced towards him. "This is good. It means we are getting close." He placed his cup aside and stretched. "You should sleep. You'll need your energy for the devourer."

"What will happen when we find it?" She cradled her cup in her hands.

"We will kill it, and you will get back the memories the witch stole. Then you can complete the task you came here for."

"Do you know what that task is?"

Rourke fixed her with an appraising stare. "The knowledge would do you very little good at this point in time. Especially as you will forget it by morning."

"Alright, what *will* you tell me? Did I come here with someone else or on my own?"

He folded his arms. "You did not come alone, but I fear that your companions have met a gruesome fate. The witch sacrificed them to the devourers in order to lay her trap for you."

She tried to conjure up the image from before. It had been a man, but now his features slipped through her mind like oil on water. "Companions? Did they have names?" Names had power. Perhaps the sound of theirs would break through the last of the spell that was keeping her memories trapped. Though Rourke seemed adamant she would only be free once the devourer queen had been dealt with.

Rourke studied her and let out a breath before answering. "You think that by hearing the names it will release you from the enchantment. It's clever, Shadow Girl, but it won't work."

"Humour me?"

He gave a low rumbling chuckle. "You'll just give yourself a headache, and as I said, you'll need your strength for the devourer. Drink the rest of your tea."

She scrunched her nose up at the remaining liquid in her cup but downed it without another word. Hopefully, come morning, they would finally locate the devourer, and Nea could get the answers that kept eluding her.

Strong hands cupped the back of her neck as a rough thumb traced her lower lip. She tilted her head back, the scent of clove clouding her senses. A pulling sensation stirred behind her navel ...

"May I ..." The words vibrated against her skin.

This wasn't real. The moment she opened her eyes, the dream would scatter like thistledown on the wind. But this place felt safe — safer than she could ever remember feeling.

Something warm dripped onto her stomach and the metallic scent of blood replaced the clove. Her eyes flew open. The man above her wore a mask of pink-gold robrillium, his auburn hair caked with blood and ash. One of his hands was pressed to a wide gash in his side from which black-streaked blood was weeping. The other held a dark-bladed knife, the tip pressed against the skin the between her breasts. He twisted the blade and her blood welled around it. Ash coated her tongue, and the sky turned dark.

"Why?" The word slid between her lips as she lifted her fingers to unmask the man.

His mouth curved wickedly before opening to speak—
"Shadow Girl!"

She bolted upright, her forehead colliding with someone else's as she probed her chest.

"Easy now. You were dreaming." Rourke rubbed his head as he sat back on his heels.

Nea swallowed. The taste of blood and ash stained her tongue, and the centre of her chest burned as though the blade was still twisting into it. She glanced around; predawn light tinted everything a strange washed-out shade of grey. "Well, I'm awake now. We should find that devourer." She got to her feet and helped Rourke gather their things. The sooner they found this devourer the better.

It didn't take them long. Rourke led her to a large floating sphere that contained a bucket of blackberries and a bunch of wild flowers. He nodded, and Nea lifted her hand to press her palm against the bubble. It burst under the pressure, then she tilted forward and was falling.

She landed in a small meadow. The laughter of children playing reached her, and she sat up. Nearby, a girl and a boy were having a mock sword fight with a pair of straight sticks. The girl's storm-grey curls were a wild tangle around her flushed face, leaves and other bits of debris sticking to them. The boy had long dark hair, which shone in the sunlight as he danced around the girl, feigning an attack to the right. Just beyond the sparring pair was another girl with soft golden ringlets, who was picking wild flowers.

"If Nea breaks your fingers again, Emil, I am not going to mend them," she said as she settled in the grass with her flowers and started weaving them into garlands.

"She's not going to get close enough to break my fingers again." Emil laughed as he dodged a strike from Nea. "Ouch!"

Nea's stick slid down the length of Emil's and collided with his knuckles. He shook his hand and took a step backwards as Margot gave him a smug look.

Adult Nea glanced sideways at Rourke. "Why didn't I go into her body like I did every other time?"

"I am not certain, but be on your guard."

"Can the children see us?"

He shook his head. "You couldn't see me until I wanted you to. It is the same for them."

Nea slowly circled the playing children before turning her attention to the bushes that surrounded the meadow. She could remember this as clearly as if it had been yesterday. In a moment, her younger self was going to hit Emil on the knuckles again—

"Ouch! Nea, stop doing that!"

"I can't help it if your defence is sloppy," Nea whispered as the younger version of herself said the very same words to Emil, a triumphant gleam in her bright eyes.

A foreign laugh sounded, and Nea's gaze snapped to the two figures who were just emerging from the trees to the right of her. The laugh belonged to a tall, finely built man with a mop of jet hair that looked windswept despite the complete lack of breeze. Beside him was a broader man with dark auburn hair.

She pressed her hand to the centre of her chest. The sight of the second man had stirred up the dregs of her dream and along with them the searing kiss of the blade against her skin. The man's attention snapped to her, his deep grey eyes narrowing slightly before relief washed over his features.

"Nea!" He strode towards her, but the dark-haired man raced past him and all but collided with her as he lifted her off her feet and into a hug.

"Stars above, you can't believe how good it is to see you!" He placed her delicately on her feet again as the other man reached them.

Nea looked from one to the other then back at Rourke.

"You are our Nea?" the grey-eyed man asked her.

"I don't know ..." Pain tightened behind her temples. "I'm sorry, but I don't know you."

The dark-haired man studied her. There was something familiar about his forest-green eyes. "Come on, Nea. It's me, Declan. I haunted you for the better part of two months."

She shook her head.

"She won't remember until we kill the devourer," Rourke said.

"Then let's find it." Grey-eyes held his hand out. "I'm Garret."

"Rourke." He shook the offered hand.

"Declan," the dark-haired man said automatically. He was busy studying Nea with an intensity that made her shift her shoulders.

"Declan and Garret," she said carefully, testing the names. The thing at the back of her mind pounded against the bars of its cage. She *should* know them.

"Exactly," Declan said.

She held her hand out. "May I ..." The words brought the dream rushing back, and she repressed a shudder. Garret held his hand out as well, and Nea laid her palm against his. Her keen flared in a cold spike, sending a shower of lilac sparks into the air.

She'd never seen anything like it, and clearly neither had Declan because he exclaimed, "Mother's tits, what was that?"

The sparks of magic settled on Garret and Nea's still clasped hands as pain seared up the back of her skull. A cascade of memories tumbled across her mind: a little boy in a clearing, a nonchalant youth leaning against the trunk of a tree, steady hands working a blade over a lump of wood, teasing out a shape, a—"Fox!"

They all looked at her as she exclaimed.

"You carved me a fox." She reached for her satchel, but it wasn't there. Cold dread gripped her chest. "Rourke, where's my satchel?"

"The witch probably has it, Shadow Girl."

Her heart thundered behind her ears, but she looked back at Garret. She *knew* him like a fragment of her soul was laced with his. Even if the memories were locked deep, her keen recognised him. "Garret ..." She tested his name again and pain sliced through her head. She gripped it and doubled over. *Our paths were meant to converge.* More memories. Garret standing with her in the reflection pool at Del Harol, chasing a silver-haired girl around a forest clearing as they both laughed—"I remember you."

"Oh, of course you remember *Garret.*" Declan threw his hands in the air in mock exasperation. "Never—"

A scream silenced Declan, and they all turned. The children were running for a tall tree. Emil reached it first and swung into the branches. He lowered a hand and dragged Nea up after him, but Margot's skirts had become tangled in the blackberry brambles beneath the tree.

Adult Nea's eyes snapped to the wolf that was prowling towards the struggling Margot.

"Jump, Margot," young Nea yelled as she reached down, trying to grab Margot's hand, Emil's fist bunched in the back of her shirt to hold her steady.

"I can't. My skirt is caught." Margot sobbed and tried to scramble up the trunk as the wolf advanced.

"Margot!" young Nea screamed as the wolf charged.

A blur dropped out of the tree and collided with the side of the wolf, knocking it off balance as its jaws snapped an inch from were Margot had been. Young Nea sat up in the grass and then scuttled backwards as the wolf advanced on her. It lunged and she screamed, throwing her hands up. The source twanged like a bowstring snapping under too much strain, and the wolf's snarl was cut short in a pained yelp.

The meadow grew deathly silent. Young Nea lowered her hands to stare at the body of the wolf, its teeth in the grass by her toes.

Adult Nea had started forward, but she stopped in her tracks as a man came racing into the field. His violet gaze settled on young Nea and the dead wolf. He rushed over, scooping her into a hug, his hand cupping the back of her head.

"Are you alright?" he asked against her hair.

"He was going to eat Margot." Young Nea's wide violet eyes peeked over her father's shoulder at the wolf, and she let out a shudder before burrowing deeper again.

"What did you do?" It wasn't her father who spoke, but an older woman with the same storm-grey hair as Nea. When Nea didn't respond, she took a step closer. "*Nea.*"

"Mother, now is not the time—" Nea's father started, but Nonna cut him off.

"You can't keep coddling her, Niall. See that?" She thrust a finger at the body of the wolf. "That proves what I was telling you. Now, take Emil and Margot home." She fixed her gaze back on Nea. "What did you do to that wolf?"

Niall released Nea and moved to Margot and Emil. "Come on."

"Nea didn't mean to do anything wrong, Nonna." Margot rushed to Nea's side.

"Go with Niall, Margot." Nonna's voice was like ice and her eyes did not move from young Nea where she stood, her fingers twisting tightly in the fabric of her shirt.

Nonna waited until the others were out of sight and crouched to inspect the body of the wolf before rising again and looking down at Nea. "You must *never* do this again."

"I don't know how I did it. The wolf was going to eat Margot and I didn't want it to. I wanted it gone. That's all. I promise I didn't want it to *die.*" Young Nea's voice broke on the last word, and she fell against Nonna's legs sobbing.

"Shush now. That's enough of that." Nonna crouched to Nea's height and cupped her cheeks, her thumbs dashing the tears away. "You need to be strong; you've been dealt a hard hand in this life, but the Mother does not give us that which we cannot endure."

Young Nea sniffed and rubbed at the remaining tears. "I ... I'm fine."

"Good girl. Now come on. We need to get you to Warren. You must learn how to control yourself, so this doesn't happen again."

"But you said I was *never* to do it again."

"That's right. You need to learn how to control it so that it doesn't get the better of you in the future and we can avoid further *accidents*." Nonna's gaze flicked to the body of the wolf. "Come on now." She held out her hand.

"You are certain the devourer is here?" Adult Nea turned to Rourke. "This memory hasn't been tampered with."

His mouth pulled into a grim line. "It's here alright, Shadow Girl. We just need to flush it out. Perhaps now is a good moment to make our presence known." He tilted his head towards the place Nonna and young Nea were still standing.

Nea swallowed and glanced at Declan and Garret before stepping out into the meadow. She met a slight resistance but pushed forward, and the memory around her shimmered.

Nonna's attention snapped to her and she pulled young Nea behind her, out of sight. "Catch up to your father."

Young Nea's brow knit. "But Nonna—"

"Go now!" Nonna pushed her the way Niall had gone with Margot and Emil, not taking her eyes off adult Nea. "You're not supposed to be here."

"I want what was taken from me and then I'll leave."

A strange smile pulled across Nonna's mouth and she let out a bitter laugh. "My children and I are hungry, and we were promised a feast." She jutted her chin towards Declan and Garret. "If you agree to pay the same price as the witch then I will return what was taken."

Nea shook her head. "I'm not honouring that deal. You will give me back my memories or I will take them. I am done playing games." She let her magic build, the comforting cool of it coiling behind her navel.

"I thought you might say that. Very well." Nonna's body tripled in size and she fell forward onto her hands as her arms became long and disjointed, her fingers blade-sharp claws that dug into the soft earth. Her size increased again, and twisting horns sprouted from her skull as her mouth widened to a red gash studded with wicked, ice-white teeth.

Declan and Garret stepped up on one side of Nea and Rourke the other. Static magic charged the air and Nea glanced sideways. Arcs of lightning danced around Declan's fingers. He gave her a wink.

The monster that had been Nonna was now prowling from side to side. It was almost the size of a small house, and though roughly human in shape, it prowled on all fours. Its tongue lolled out and dripped black-streaked saliva that sizzled as it met the delicate blades of grass.

Nea swallowed and shifted her weight from one foot to the other.

"Easy, Shadow Girl. Wait for the right moment," Rourke said calmly, his hand tightening on the hilt of his axe.

The air was coiled vice-tight, and still the creature prowled, watching them, as though waiting for the cue to lunge. Nea almost couldn't bare it any longer. Her magic quivered in icy spikes, craving freedom. It was a beast that was not meant to be restrained, especially here where the source soaked the entire fabric of the world.

"I can't—" Nea whispered.

The devourer let out a blood-curdling wail and sprang forward. Nea was wrenched out of the way as it landed right in the place she had been standing. The skin under Garret's fingers shone purple, highlighting the silver spiderweb marks that marred her wrist. She'd asked Rourke about them, but he'd been elusive, telling her it didn't matter until after they got her memories back.

Garret pulled her behind him and hefted Rourke's spare axe in his free hand as the creature lunged for them again.

Nea let her magic out. The place her skin still touched Garret's burned bright, and her magic surged stronger than it ever had. A primal force that charged into the creature and caused it to hiss and writhe as the magic searched for the edges of its soul. Everything had a soul, a life force, but this thing was an empty void. Finding no target, the magic recoiled, hitting Nea in the chest. Garret lost his grip on her wrist as she was knocked clean off her feet.

"Are you alright?" He helped her up.

Pain shot through her side and she let out a groan. "I'm fine."

"We could use a hand over here," Declan yelled as his magic crackled through the air. "Like, now!" He skidded backwards as the hind foot of the creature kicked out and caught his middle.

Rourke was dancing around in front of the devourer, moving faster and lighter than someone of his size should have been able to.

"This one is different to the ones Declan and I fought before. Any ideas how to kill it?" Garret asked as he sliced the axe into the grasping hand of the creature, lopping off one long claw-like finger.

Nea started to shake her head, then a story Nonna had once told her filtered up through her thoughts and the thing in the back of her mind squeezed the bars of its cage. "We need to tear it's heart out."

"It's heart?"

"Yes. It's a construct of thought and memory. It has to have a heart-stone like a sentry golem. Something that holds it toge—" A yelp of pain cut off her words as Garret pulled her out of the way and Declan went flying past them.

Garret gave her a look of concern. "I'm sorry. How bad is—"

"It's fine." She bit down on her lip and drew a few shallow breaths. "Just a bruised rib or two. Nothing I can't endure."

He looked from her to the creature then back again. "How do we reach the heart?"

"We need to flip it onto it's back so I can get to the chest cavity."

The meaty thwack of an axe thudding into flesh sounded, followed by a grunt.

"I don't know if you've both noticed the giant abomination trying to kill us!" Declan said as his keen charged the air again.

"Get it onto it's back?" Garret asked.

"That would be the easiest way."

"Alright." He tightened the grip on the axe and then joined Declan and Rourke.

Hand pressed to her side, Nea moved out in front of the creature. "Hey! Over here!" She picked up one of the discarded sticks the children had been using as swords and rushed at the creature, drawing its attention.

As it whirled to face Nea, Garret lunged and it let out a hiss, snapping its leg high out of reach. The leg hovered in the air, the foot hanging by a flap of skin and ragged flesh as black blood splattered onto the grass. The creature hopped about and snapped at Garret, its teeth tearing the sleeve of his shirt.

Rourke dashed forward and ploughed his axe into the arm of the creature. It reared back and over-balanced before toppling sideways. Nea leapt onto it as it fell. She let her magic charge the air around her fingers as she drove her hand into the centre of its chest. The skin gave a slight resistance then split, sending a spray of black ooze and purple magic around her wrist as her arm disappeared into the icy muck that was the devourer.

The creature writhed beneath her as she groped around in the fetid sludge that formed its body. Her fingers brushed the rough edge of something hot and she drove them deeper, grasping for the solid lump.

Magic zinged up her arm as her hand tightened around the rough stone and yanked it free of the creature's chest with the wet sucking sound of thick mud. The stone shone a sickly green against her palm, and she closed her fingers over it again, flooding it with her magic. It vibrated then crumbled to ash.

The thing in the back of her mind bent the bars of its cell, then they gave way and a torrent of thoughts and feelings rushed through her body. She fell forward, panting as pain bloomed in her side and sliced her mind to ribbons.

Someone yelled. The ground lurched and the sky above shattered, then she was falling.

CHAPTER SIX

GARRET

Slabs of colour rushed past Garret as he fell through the inky darkness. He had lost sight of Declan and Rourke the moment the world had shattered, but Nea's limp form was plummeting just ahead of him. She collided with the broken shards of the memory with a shower of pale purple sparks. He couldn't feel her keen, but he knew it would be an icy breath-stealing cold, not the usual comforting cool. A chunk of meadow came close, and he used it as a springboard, willing himself to fall faster and catch up to Nea before they hit the speck of light that was widening beneath them with each passing second.

He caught her, shielding her against his chest as the light surrounded them and the world flipped.

The scent of forest and sounds of birdsong reached him, and he opened his eyes. Branches of a lush green canopy stretched above him; the earth beneath his back was cool and slightly damp. Nea shifted, and he released his grip on her. She sat slowly and gulped deep breaths as though she'd barely escaped drowning. The small wince she gave with each inhale was concerning, but the thought was stolen as her violet gaze found his. The forest around them seemed to hold its breath as she studied his face. She lifted her hand slowly and touched her fingertips to the curve of his jaw. Her brow wrinkled and she rubbed it as she shut her eyes.

When she opened them again, they widened, and her breath hitched in her throat. "Garret?" she whispered so softly he barely caught it.

He knew what she was experiencing. The memory that had held him had seemed so real, and when he had finally broken free, he had questioned everything around him. His grip tightened involuntarily on her hips. Even now, he wasn't certain she wasn't going to fade through his fingers like smoke dispersing on the breeze.

"You're actually here. This is not some twisted figment ..." Her weight shifted in his lap as she turned to take in the forest around them. "I'm free and ..."

Her gaze snapped back to his and he thought he saw the glimmer of tears along her lashes before she threw her arms around his neck and buried her face against his chest.

"You're *real*. I thought I'd never—" She coughed and winced.

"Are you alright?" He lifted his hand to smooth her hair but lowered it at the last second.

She straightened again. "I'm fine. I think that recoil of magic bruised my ribs. Are *you* alright?"

He propped himself up beneath her and followed the line of her gaze to his arm, which was red with blood. "I didn't even realise I got hit." Now that he saw the blood though he could feel the throbbing pain beneath his sleeve.

Nea took hold of the injured arm and rolled back the sleeve to show a long, curved gash. Her fingers were cool and where they met his skin, little shimmers of violet glowed. He frowned. He'd thought dealing with the devourer would fix his keen, but everything was still numb and silent.

Nea tilted her head and worried her lower lip between her teeth. It was a look he had become familiar with over the weeks they had spent together. Usually it meant she was processing an idea, but it could also mean she was about to act on an impulse and do something unpredictable and most likely dangerous.

"Nea?"

Her attention moved from his arm to his face. "Did you see that? It happened before when we touched in the memory. I thought it was just something to do with the magic of the trap, but ..." She deliberately touched his arm, sending a flicker of sparks across both of their skin. "I've never seen or *felt* anything like that before. It's almost like part of my keen is trapped under your skin and trying to get back to me ... Is that what it feels like for you?"

Garret bit back a sigh. Strange, unexplainable magic usually made his skin crawl, but he'd give anything to feel it now. The thought that his keen-sense might never return sent a twist of dread through his stomach.

"Garret? What's wrong?" Concern shone in the depths of Nea's eyes as a loop of her hair fell forward to obscure them.

He closed his fist to fight the urge to brush it behind her ear. "I can't *feel* anything. My keen-sense is completely numb."

She tucked the curl away. "You have no keen-sense? Can you still suppress magic?" The curiosity that touched her features was tinged with worry.

Garret shook his head.

Her brow furrowed. "I ... how? Is it like bind-shackles? I've never heard of a warden—"

"Well now, this is cosy." Declan's voice was an indulgent purr, and Garret didn't need to turn to know he was wearing a wolfish grin.

Nea blinked and her gaze dropped to her hands, which were splayed across Garret's chest. Her cheeks darkened and she leapt to her feet with a wince. "Before you start being insufferable, it's not what it looks like. I was just experimenting with something."

Declan let out a bark of laughter and propped his shoulder against a tree as Garret rose. "Experimenting? You can *experiment* with me anytime, my lovely."

Nea rolled her eyes and let out an exasperated sigh, which was broken by a hiss of pain.

"Are you sure those ribs are only bruised? If they are broken—" Garret started, but Nea cut him off with a raised hand.

"They're fine." She settled her gaze on Declan. "Have you seen Rourke?"

Declan shook his head. "No, I lost sight of everyone after you killed that devourer." A mischievous gleam came to his eyes as he gestured to the place Garret and Nea had been sitting. "So, if the pair of you weren't working through that pent-up tension you've got going on, what *were* you doing?"

"This." She reached out and touched Garret's arm, causing the magic to shimmer and spark again. "See that? *Feel* that?" Her eyes lit up as Declan tilted his head.

"That's remarkable." He studied Garret. "Can you feel it?" When Garret shook his head, Declan asked. "Did you tell Nea about your lack of keen?"

Garret nodded and opened his mouth to respond, but Nea cut him off.

"Wait a minute. You're corporeal here." She took a step forward and gave Declan's chest a small shove before wincing again. "And Garret can see you."

"So it would seem. Tell me, is it just Garret that your magic reacts to?"

Nea chewed her lip. "I don't know."

Declan held his hand out palm up, and Nea touched the centre of it with her finger. Nothing happened.

"Curious." Declan looked between them. "Do you think it's something to do with coming through the portal? Do you think your magic may have gotten a bit scrambled? That might explain Garret's missing keen."

Nea shook her head. "It's not completely impossible, I suppose, but it is doubtful. Portal accidents generally involved missing limbs or death, not *scrambled* magic. And honestly, though it is possible for mages to share their magic with each other, the effects are never long term. And this seems to be something else entirely. Perhaps—"

Garret cleared his throat and they both turned to him. "As fascinating as watching you both try to figure this out is, do you think now is the right time?"

Nea and Declan shared the tendency to become obsessively focused when presented with a puzzle. Given the chance, they would spend the rest of the day talking in circles until one of them had an epiphany.

"Garret's right. We should try to work out where we are. The sooner we do that, the sooner we can start trying to find the root of corruption and get ourselves home. Who knows how much time has passed while we were trapped in that memory field," Nea said, pressing her hand to her side.

"Should we wait for Rourke?" Declan asked.

Nea shook her head. "He'll find us. I am sure."

"Which way?" Garret asked.

Nea closed her eyes, and Declan watched her with a tilt of his head until she lifted her hand and pointed. "That way."

She started walking in the direction she had indicated, and Declan fell into step beside her, already running through theories of why Nea's magic kept reacting to Garret.

Garret followed them, scanning the trees for any sign of Rourke or danger.

The dappled light coming through the canopy had started to darken when they reached a small clearing. It didn't look like a bad place to camp, but the forest was foreign to Garret so there was no knowing exactly what they would encounter come nightfall.

"I don't think we should stop," Nea said, drawing his attention. She was scratching the inside of her wrist. The corruption marks had dulled to a soft silver that shone with a strange iridescence in the half-light.

"Is that bothering you?" Garret asked.

She studied the mark and shook her head. "No, it's silent. What about yours?"

"Likewise." The mark on his side appeared much like Nea's now did—a web of silver—the nagging sensations and voice in his head blissfully still. His suppression had been able to keep it under control, but he couldn't have fought it forever. Exhaustion would have soon claimed him. He didn't know how Nea had endured it for so long.

"I would think that being here where the source flows so freely would have the opposite effect," Declan said. "Do you think that distillation of mage bane and Mother's balm really was the cure and this travelling to the Between was a fool's errand?"

"No. I don't know why the corruption is dormant here, but it isn't the distillation. That did help at the time, but it ..." She chewed her lip. "... satiated? No ... soothed would be the better word. It pacified the corruption in some way, but it wasn't silenced. Now if the mark wasn't there, I wouldn't know I had it at all."

"Curious." Declan tapped his finger against his chin and his eyes glazed over. "The corruption is silenced, Garret's keen seems to have disappeared, and then there's that strange thing your magic keeps doing ... This place is great!"

Nea blinked at Declan. "Great? Have you forgotten about the memory field and the devourers already? Or have you noticed that while we've been standing here discussing this, the trees have been shifting? This place is unpredictable, and the majority of the things that dwell here are not benign."

Garret examined the trees. They had, in fact, been shifting, drawing closer and erasing the game trail he and the others had been following. A sound broke through the silent trunks—a curse?

Nea obviously heard it too because her attention immediately snapped in the direction it had come from. "I don't think we are alone."

"Rourke?" Declan asked.

Nea shook her head. "Whoever it is, their keen is different to Rourke's and there's more than one." She edged towards the sound, and Garret caught her wrist.

"I'll go."

Something shimmered in her violet gaze and the corner of her mouth tucked in like she was biting the inside of her cheek, but she stepped back to stand with Declan.

Garret moved forward carefully, and the trees shifted to reveal a tiny clearing.

"... if she finds out about Rourke." A woman sat on a large boulder, her back to him. Her azure blue hair was so long the ends of it danced against the stone near her hips.

"She won't find out though. Unless you decide to tell her, that is." The man in front of her had feathery antennae nestled in his goldenrod hair. He polished a monocle as he spoke.

"Of course I won't tell her. But, Wade, we have to be careful—you especially. Frell already suspects—"

A twig behind Garret snapped, and he swore under his breath as he backed farther into the trees.

"Well?" Declan whispered behind him.

Garret fought the urge to roll his eyes. Of course the pair of them couldn't stay put. He pressed his finger to his lips and indicated the clearing.

Nea had her head tilted in the way that she did when her keen encountered something she found intriguing. Before Garret could stop her, she stepped around Declan and himself and out of the trees.

Wade was gone, but the woman was still there. She stiffened and twisted to face them. Like Wade, she had long feathery antennae.

But they weren't as strange as her crystalline eyes that seemed to reflect the light in a myriad of colours before settling on a soft burnished gold.

"By the Bright," she intoned as she slid from the stone and took a step towards Nea. She lifted a hand and Garret tensed, but she lowered it again. "Oh no, no, no." Her tongue traced her lips. "You're not supposed to be here." A shiver ran over her form. "Sorry, I am being terribly rude. It has been … one of those days. I'm Zephyr." She smiled brightly and held her hand out.

Nea took the offered hand and gave it a shake. "Nea. I'm sorry to bother you, but we're a little lost." She half-turned to indicate Garret and Declan and winced before gripping her side.

"Oh, you're hurt." Zephyr rushed forward, her hands lifted. "I can mend flesh better than anyone." Azure magic flickered across her fingertips.

"You're a healer?" Nea's brow furrowed. "You don't *feel* like one."

Zephyr waved as if to shoo Nea's confusion away. "I am Nundle; we are many things. May I?" She indicated Nea's side.

Nea gave her a nod, and Zephyr traced her fingertips over the injury. Nea gritted her teeth and let out a groan before Zephyr stepped back and settled her gaze on Garret.

"I can mend that arm too." She stepped towards him then stopped, her attention switching to Declan. Her head gave a bird-like tilt and she blinked before smiling at Garret again and placing her fingers on his arm. "My, you are a strange bunch, aren't you?" She inspected the scar left in the wake of her magic and gave a small nod. "Well, that's all sorted now. We probably should be getting back to the troupe before it gets too dark. It is not advisable to sleep in the woods."

"The troupe?" Garret asked.

Zephyr nodded. "The Nundle. We are wanderers and entertainers, and Frell's magic keeps us safe in these wilder parts of the world. I am sure she will not mind extending that protection to a few extra souls."

Garret glanced at Nea. She was chewing her lip and studying the other woman like she were a particularly vexing puzzle.

As though feeling his eyes on her, her gaze shifted to him and she gave a tired smile before saying to Zephyr, "If the troupe won't mind, I certainly would rather not camp out here."

Zephyr gave a small clap and looped her arm through Nea's, startling her. She didn't seem to notice as she led Nea away through the trees. Declan shook his head with a smile as he watched the two women for a few moments before giving Garret a pat on the shoulder and following them.

They broke from the trees into another large clearing. Painted wagons were set up around the outer edge and beside them giant black and blue striped caterpillars were curled, seemingly resting. As they entered the edge of the camp, a petite woman with long feathery antennae like Zephyr's came striding over. She had vivid pink hair and her crystalline eyes switched to a pale sea-green as she studied their small group.

"Well, hello." She leant on the silver shepherd's crook she was carrying. "Lost in the wood, were you?"

"You don't mind, Frell—" Zephyr grew silent as the other woman lifted her hand.

"Of course not. It wouldn't do to have her wandering the woods after nightfall." Her eyes were locked on Nea as she spoke, and Garret fought the urge to step between them. There was something about her stare that set his hair on end.

"Wonderful. This is Nea, and that is—I'm sorry. I was so caught up before I didn't get your names."

"Declan and Garret," Declan said, indicating himself and then Garret.

"Nea," Frell repeated. "That's a very pretty name. Zephyr, if you wouldn't mind taking Nea to see Wade, I will have Urden make the tea. You two may follow me." She directed the last at Declan and Garret.

Frell led them to the central fire where a man with grass-green hair was tending a bubbling pot.

"We have guests, it would seem," Frell said as the man looked up. "Declan and Garret, this is Urden. He will make you a tea that will dissolve any unsavoury attachments you may have picked up in the woods. My magic will keep most undesirables out of the camp, but beings in this realm can be very tricky things." Without another word, she sauntered away and fell into conversation with a young woman with flame-orange hair.

"Here." Urden held out two cups.

"Thank you," Garret said, automatically accepting the offered tea.

He examined the pinkish liquid. A heady floral aroma was rising from it that made him scrunch his nose before taking a tentative sip. *Too sweet.* He resisted the urge to spit the liquid back into the cup and swallowed it with a grimace. Nea would hate it.

Declan chuckled. "Interesting brew, isn't it?" he said as Garret flicked a look in his direction.

Urden gave a small laugh. "It does get better, or maybe you just get used to it. Are you hungry? Stew is almost ready, or we have a selection of fruits." He held out a plate of assorted fruits and pastries.

Garret was famished, but the shining fruit on the plate held no appeal. Not with the lingering taste of the tea and the way his head was swimming. "Not right now, thank you."

"Of course. Please make yourselves comfortable. I'll see if I can catch Wade in a little while to get you a change of clothes. You look like you've been wandering in the woods for a week."

Once Urden left, Garret turned back to Declan. "You don't find this strange? Their open hospitality? The way Frell was staring at Nea? It almost reminds me of Evard."

Declan made a noise. "I'm sure she's nothing like Evard. And Nea is comfortable enough to stay. That should speak volumes."

He wasn't wrong. Garret wouldn't say Nea had accepted the troupe with open arms, but she wasn't being overly standoffish either. Perhaps there wasn't anything to worry about. With a sigh, he studied the liquid in his cup again before taking another sip. The second mouthful was no better than the first.

CHAPTER SEVEN

NEA

Zephyr led Nea across the camp to an ornately painted wagon with deep-purple stairs and a rack of patchwork clothes out the front.

"Wade!" Zephyr yelled up the stairs, announcing their presence.

"No need to yell, Zeph." A man popped his head out the door. He had goldenrod hair and a monocle over one of his brightly faceted eyes. "Oh my. The hare has entered the fox burrow." His voice was soft, and Nea nearly didn't catch the words. He leant closer and lifted the monocle to study her, his eyes changing from that multitoned hue to a very pale lilac–grey. "It's about time you got here." He inhaled deeply and stepped down to offer Nea his hand. "Darius Wadellyn the third, tailor of the Nundle troupe. It is a pleasure to make your acquaintance, Nea of Hartswood, Daughter of Shadow."

She wasn't exactly sure how to take this man or the fact that he seemed to know who she was when she had yet to introduce herself. "Ah ... a pleasure to meet you also, Darius."

"Please, none of that formal nonsense. Everyone around here just calls me Wade." A serious look flickered across his features as his attention shifted to something over her shoulder.

Nea turned. Frell was watching them from the other side of the camp. Her stoic expression shifted to a warm smile when she caught Nea's eye.

"Now what can I do for you, hmm?" Wade asked, drawing Nea's gaze back to him. "A gown of the finest silk to make all the men stare and all the other ladies weep with jealousy?" His voice had the practiced air of a salesman as he pulled a smock from the rack. A shimmer of magic stirred the air in a playful flurry, and the strange patchwork fabric shifted shape and colour. The plain smock was now a seductive gown of deep vermillion silk with flame-coloured salamanders embroidered on it. The salamanders seemed to move across the fabric, coiling through drifts of shining gold beads.

"No that's—"

"Something much simpler, yes? You're not the type for extravagance." He rolled the last word over his tongue and thrust the gown at Zephyr. "Let me see. Ah, yes, this. This will do nicely."

He pulled another gown from the rack. This one shifted into a soft blue fabric that pooled delicately over his arm. Emerald and silver dragonflies flittered around the neckline and through the tall bulrushes embroidered over the skirt.

"Do you have something that isn't a gown?"

With a frown, he thrust the second dress at Zephyr. "Practicality, is it?" He disappeared into the wagon and returned with a bundle of clothes, which he tipped into Nea's arms before placing a pair of dark leather boots on top. "Try these on." He gave her a push towards the dressing screen nearby. "Quickly now. In case I need to make alterations."

She emerged a short while later in a pair of form-hugging pants that disappeared into the knee-high boots that were as soft as butter with laces right up the front. Her top half was clad in a linen shirt with elbow-length sleeves under a royal-purple waistcoat. The coat had a flared skirt-like tail that fluttered against the back of her thighs. The garment hadn't avoided the elaborate embroidery: sleek brown stoats and bright wrens played among the tangling hedgerow embroidered right around the hemline. "I am not sure this is right either."

"It's perfect!" Wade clapped his hands together.

Nea tried to tug the sleeve over the grey corruption marks. "I'd rather these sleeves were longer."

Wade tisked. "Whatever for, my dear? Those marks are a badge of honour."

"Corruption? A badge of honour?"

"They are scars that show you fought, and you won."

"But I didn't win."

Wade pursed his lips. "No? Well, it is only a matter of time. Now what are we going to do about your hair?"

"My hair?"

"Yes." He clicked his fingers at Zephyr, who was lounging on the stairs, her bright eyes watching Declan with unfettered interest.

"He's so shiny," she muttered dreamily.

"Zephyr! Stop making doe eyes at the human and fix this." He gestured to Nea's hair as Zephyr snapped to attention.

"It's fine. I like it simple. But if you have a comb or a brush, I can at least get the tangles out."

Wade let out a sigh and handed Nea a wide comb. The ivory teeth were set into a dark wood handle covered in carved roses. Once upon a time, the blooms had been painted a soft pink and the leaves a dark green, but most of the colour had been worn away. The sight of the comb brought a lump to Nea's throat and she nearly dropped it. "Where did you get this?"

"That old thing has been in the family for generations. It used to be part of a set, along with a brush and a matching mirror," Wade replied.

Nea studied the comb a few heartbeats longer then started on the tangles in her hair. Once it was snarl-free, she braided it, and Zephyr held out a length of purple ribbon to secure it.

"Much better. Now ..." Wade patted the lid of a small wooden box, his confident, all-business demeanour shifting as a frown tilted the corner of his mouth.

Zephyr reached for the box, but as her fingers met the wood, she snapped them back as though stung. "*Wade?*"

Nea's gaze flicked from one to the other. Magic fluttered in the air between them. Zephyr frowned and settled her hands on her hips as one of Wade's eyebrows rose. Then his mouth twisted angrily and his grip on the box tightened.

Nea cleared her throat, drawing their attention back to her. "If you're done now, I should return to my friends." She started to move away.

"Wait," Wade said sharply. "Just one last thing." He opened the box to reveal a rose-shaped pendant on a long chain. The silver metal caught the light with a violet sheen. "Many things in this realm would seek to harm, but this will offer some protection."

"If Frell finds out ..." Zephyr started, then cast a glance about.

"I know what I am doing, Zephyr. Besides, it doesn't belong to Frell. It belongs to Nea."

Nea shook her head. "I've never seen that before in my life."

"Of course you haven't. There was no way to get it to your realm after—never mind. It's a gift. Please take it. However, Zephyr is right. Don't let Frell see it."

"I don't want to cause any trouble." Nea rocked back a step. There was something very odd about the troupe, and she didn't want to get caught up in whatever power struggle was bubbling beneath the surface.

Wade sighed and tucked the box away. "Very well. I won't force the matter further, but it is here if you want it. Now off you go and enjoy the evening." He shooed Nea and Zephyr away.

Zephyr hummed under her breath as they wandered through the camp. She led Nea not back to Declan and Garret, who had only moments before been sitting by the central fire, but towards one of the larger wagons. The man sitting on the butter-yellow steps stood as they approached.

"This is Urden. Urden, this is Nea." Zephyr pointed from one to the other.

"A pleasure," Nea said.

"Likewise, Daughter of Shadow. Frell asked me to see about some sleeping arrangements for you and your companions. You are welcome to share our wagon." He thrust his thumb at the door behind him. "The others will find a bunk with either Wade or Amber and Zeph. I'd offer you sleeping rolls to bed down by the fire if that suited you better, but I think it's going to be a wet night."

"The shining one can bunk with us," Zephyr said a little too quickly and blushed. "I mean, if that suits?"

"Shining?" Nea asked.

Zephyr regarded her through her long navy lashes. "Yes, his keen is like light refracted through glass. It's so pretty."

Nea's gaze searched the campsite again for a sign of either Declan or Garret. She found Declan over by Wade's wagon. He had exchanged his usual attire—the simple shirt and brown pants he had died in—for a pair of dark pants and an emerald-green jacket, the sleeves of which he was adjusting as he glanced her way and gave her a small wave.

Zephyr made a noise and Nea glanced at her. "Is he—are you—you're not ... you know?"

"Not what?" It dawned on Nea what Zephyr was getting at and she collapsed against the side of the wagon with a laugh. "Declan? Oh, Bright Mother no."

"Good to know." Zephyr's grin was suddenly feline as she stretched.

Urden rolled his eyes but his smile was warm. "Here," he offered Nea a cup of tea.

She blinked at the cup. The swirling steam rising from it was heady and floral and turned her stomach to water. "I'm fine, thank you."

"It's a precautionary treatment. There are things that dwell in the forest that might have attached themselves to you. The tea will dissolve any such attachments," he said with the coercive tone that Margot used when she wanted her patient to take a bitter medicine.

Nea took the cup and touched her lip to the edge of it before taking a tentative sip. It was vile: sweet and floral with a bitter kick at the end that could have saved it, except it was too sharp to be palatable. Worse than Penny's favourite Osmarian jasmine tea.

"That is something else." She ran her tongue along her lip to chase away the numbness left by the tea and gave a small shudder.

"The first sip is always the worst," Zephyr said. "I find it best to try and throw it back in one go."

Nea closed her eyes and swallowed the remaining liquid with a grimace. "Ugh. Well at least it's done with now."

Zephyr laughed. "Come on. Let's get you something to eat."

She grinned, and Nea couldn't help grinning back. There was just something unexplainable about the troupe that melted her uneasiness and stirred up memories of the person she had been before Kalhanna. The thought didn't hurt as much as it should have, as though the horror had been soothed and the anger dulled. It might have concerned her if the warm heaviness of contentment hadn't just settled in her stomach.

Nea stretched and opened her eyes as she slowly sat and took in the room. She was lying on a bed covered in a mountain of lush pillows embroidered with sprays of bright wild flowers and small grey rabbits. The room itself was small, and every available bit of wall contained an overflowing shelf stuffed with all manner of container, book, and contraption. The yellow door opened, throwing a slant of buttery light across the floor.

"I thought you might like a little breakfast, my dear." Frell's pink hair and long antennae appeared in the doorway before the woman herself. She moved to the bedside and held up a silver tray containing a cup of tea and a considerable number of pastries and fruits.

Nea's stomach turned as she stared at the extravagant breakfast. She would have preferred something simple. "Thank you, Frell," she said as she took the cup of tea and a dark red apple from the tray. Inhaling the sweet steam from the cup, she scrunched her nose and sighed.

Frell placed the tray aside before perching herself on the edge of the bed and settling an expectant gaze on Nea. "Do you not like the tea?"

Nea studied the pinkish liquid in the cup. "It's different to what I would normally drink." She glanced at the door. "You didn't have to bring me breakfast, Frell. I could have eaten with my friends." She would have preferred it. The Nundle were accommodating almost to the point that it made Nea's skin crawl.

"It was nothing." Frell folded her hands in her lap. "And in truth, I wanted a moment *alone* with you."

Nea had been about to take a bite of her apple, but she lowered it. Usually when people said that, they wanted something.

"I thought it would be best to avoid your stoic friend. It has not escaped my notice that he does not trust me."

"Trust has to be earned," Nea said before taking a bite of the apple. It was all the things an apple should be: sweet and tart and crisp. "Especially with Garret—it would not have escaped his notice that you think I am some kind of legend come to life. And he will not change his mind about you until he has a good understanding of your motives." She took a sip of the tea and instantly regretted it. It wasn't quite as vile as it had been yesterday, but it was still too sweet and too floral for her liking.

"I don't just *think* you are. I can feel it in my bones. You are a child of the Shadow blood. You would only be here if you had come to break the walls separating our world from yours so the Master of Shadows could once again be free." Something indescribable flickered in Frell's gaze.

"Then you are wrong. I am not here to release the Shadow Man. I am here to find the root of the corrupting disease that plagues mages in my realm."

Frell's mouth twisted. "The corruption exists because the balance has been broken for too long. If you were to release the Master from his prison, the balance could fix itself and the corruption would cease to plague your people."

Nea placed the tea aside. "I doubt that it would be that simple."

"You can doubt it all you want, but it is the truth." She eyed Nea's discarded cup with a frown.

"Why do you want the Shadow Man free? I can't imagine that would be a good thing for your people ... or anyone for that matter if the legends are anything to go by." Nea finished the apple and placed the core on the edge of the tray.

The other woman drew a deep breath. "*History* is always skewed in the favour of the victor."

"That doesn't *always* mean that the loser was undeserving of their fate. Life is not black and white. It is all shades." Nea folded her arms. "I appreciate the breakfast and the hospitality, but if you expect me to repay you by doing something that could completely destroy my world—"

"I would never ask you do anything of the sort." Frell's incredulous look was ruined by a twitch at the corner of her mouth. "I just want you to be open to *all* the avenues that may lead you to your goal." She got off the bed and moved to the door. "I'll leave you to enjoy the rest of your breakfast. We'll be breaking camp soon ... Don't forget your tea."

When the door closed again, Nea picked up the teacup. She gave it a tentative sip then grimaced. Didn't peppermint exist in this realm? Placing the cup aside, she slid from the bed and pulled her pants on. As she buttoned the waistcoat, she examined the food on the tray. Margot would have appreciated the flaky pastries with their fruit-filled centres, but she had always had a sweeter tooth than Nea. Her stomach rumbled, and she selected a bread roll then left the wagon.

The camp was a bustle of activity. The Nundle rushed about, packing crates and securing the strange caterpillar-like beasts into their harnesses. Across the extinguished fire, Garret was helping Wade heft some boxes and the rack of clothes into his wagon. Nea wandered over to them.

"Morning, Nea," Wade said brightly as he bounded down the purple stairs. "Would you like to ride with me today or has Frell already offered?"

Nea would rather avoid Frell right now. The conversation had been innocent enough, but she didn't have a desire to revisit it any time soon. "Frell hasn't mentioned it. If you have room, I'd be happy to join you."

"There's more than enough room. You can ride in the back or up front with me. The choice is yours."

Garret joined them. "Morning." He nodded to Nea.

"Good morning, Garret. Did you sleep well?" Nea asked.

He rubbed the back of his neck. "Well enough. I was worried all this was just a dream and I might have woken up back at the farmstead."

"Well, if we are dreaming, then I don't think I ever want to wake up," Declan said as he joined them. "Did you ask Frell about that thing with your keen? She seems like the type who might know," he asked Nea.

She shook her head. "No, it didn't come up." She was not sure she wanted to mention it to Frell.

"There's something wrong with your keen?" Wade asked.

"I wouldn't say wrong. It's ... go on," Declan said to Nea.

"Really, it's nothing. Probably just something to do with travelling through the portal," Nea said.

Declan rolled his eyes then grabbed hold of Nea's wrist. He pressed her fingers to the bare skin of Garret's forearm. A shimmer of purple magic twisted over their skin and a magnetic pull throbbed behind her navel. Wade adjusted his monocle as Nea snatched her hand back.

"Declan," Garret reprimanded. "Do we need to have the discussion about boundaries again?"

Wade was studying Nea and Garret with interest. That sensation that Nea now realised was Nundle magic stirred the air around him. "It is almost like an oathing."

"An *oathing*?" Declan asked, his dark brows rising.

Wade chuckled. "Yes. It's old magic even by our standards. It—"

"It's not an oathing." The back of Nea's neck was suddenly hot, and Declan's mouth twisted into that wolfish grin.

"Why, Nea, you've gone a delightful shade of pink. Any reason the idea of an oathing would cause that?"

She let out a huff. "Stop being facetious. You know as well as I that forming an oathing is an extremely complicated process and not something that can simply happen by accident."

"Indeed. Not to mention the bound parties must both be—"

"Wade, Frell needs you for a moment." Zephyr came bouncing over, cutting Wade's response short.

As Wade wandered off to complete the summons, Zephyr looped her hand around the crook of Declan's elbow, drawing his attention to her. "You're still planning on riding with Amber and I today, aren't you?"

"Of course." Declan gave her a soft smile, which turned into a smirk as he glanced sideways at Nea. "Tell me, Zeph, do you know what an oathing is?"

Zephyr's eyes went wide. "Magic that isn't to be practiced or spoken of."

Nea opened her mouth, but Garret cut her off. "Then we won't discuss it further." He gave Declan a pointed look.

"Alright. I'll leave it alone, but I need *something* to keep my mind busy."

"Why don't you focus on Garret's missing keen then? Because that is the more pressing issue," Nea said.

Declan brightened at the suggestion. "Perfect."

He let Zephyr lead him away as Wade returned looking red-cheeked and ruffled. "Right. Well, there's no use standing around. Are you riding inside or with me?" he asked Nea.

"I might ride inside if that's alright?"

"Certainly. Garret?"

"I'll sit up front with you."

Wade nodded and ushered Nea up the stairs. His wagon was like Frell's in that it was certainly bigger on the inside than it appeared from out. His bed didn't have as many pillows as Frell's, but the ones that were there were covered in embroidery of hedgehogs and stoats frolicking in swathes of autumn leaves. The shelves were much neater than Frell's also, some of them containing baskets of ribbons and bolts of exotic-looking fabrics.

After showing her how to latch the door from the inside, he started down the steps but then turned to face her again. "Best not mention the complication with your keen and Garret's to Frell. Even if you're not oath-bound, it's not a good idea for her know about it." He whistled as he skipped the last step and rapped on the boards beside the door.

The stairs quivered then rattled and clacked as they rolled themselves up, tucking in neatly against the side of the wagon. Nea secured the bottom half of the door and then the top as she had been shown, then she settled herself into Wade's large armchair.

Whatever was going on with her keen and Garret's, she was sure it wasn't an oathing. That required a complex ritual to form the bond, and such pacts were generally sealed by an exchange of blood. No, it had to be something different like their keens getting mixed up when they went through the portal. She wasn't ready to explore the implications of it being anything else.

CHAPTER EIGHT

MARGOT

"I need to be out there!" Margot threw her hands in the air and paced away from Leith.

"There is nothing more you can do for them than is already being done," Leith said gently.

Margot knew that, but it didn't make her feel any better. She should be on the front lines helping people. Instead she was stuck in this laboratory working day and night to make sure they had enough of the corruption treatment to aid the cases that kept cropping up.

"I know you want to help, Margot, but you're already doing everything you can. No one else has your ability with medicine."

Tobias had, but he'd died with the others at Kalhanna. So many good healers lost and Nea changed forever all because of Evard's spite. She shook her head and leant against her work bench. "There is nothing else I can do with the ointment now. The other healers here can reproduce it easily enough. I need to get out of this college. I want to see for myself what is happening out there."

Leith folded his arms.

"I won't go near the capital."

"No, you'll go to Hartswood." Niall walked through the door, followed by Penny.

The mind mage was one of Nea's oldest friends and had been present in the aftermath of Kalhanna, where she'd let Nea transplant a fragmented soul under her skin. Margot had studied the golden mark on Penny's palm, but aside from it having a soft thrumming keen that differed to Penny's own, it seemed to be a natural part of the mage and not a foreign impurity.

As the other woman settled into an empty chair, she gave Margot a small smile and swept her sleek, chestnut hair over her shoulder.

"Why Hartswood?" Margot asked, flicking her attention back to Niall.

"You need to stretch your legs, and I need to get this to Mother." He held out a small wooden box. The pinkish-gold chains wrapped around it rattled against each other.

"That's the box Nea retrieved from Loch Bastien, isn't it?"

Niall nodded. "Yes, I believe it belongs to Warren."

"Have you opened it?"

"Of course not. It belongs to *Warren*."

"Who's Warren?" Leith asked.

"Nea's grandfather. He's a little ... eccentric," Penny said as she mimed a spiral in the air beside her temple.

"*Right*. And why does it need to get to Hartswood?" Leith turned to Niall.

"I am not exactly sure, but Mother wanted it retrieved from the Loch Bastien repository, so it's probably important ... Or it's random junk ... It's always hard to tell with Mother."

"Fine. I'll take it to Hartswood, but from there I am heading to Loch Bastien to check on things," Margot said holding her hand out for the box.

Niall passed it to her. The wood was old and cracked but magic sung along the chains. Magic that was tight and constrictive, as though it was the only thing holding the object together. There was something else. A whisper that tickled her fingertips and drifted sleepily up her arm—a call to action, but for what she couldn't decipher.

"Take Penny and Emil with you if you insist on going on to Loch Bastien after Hartswood," Leith said.

"I can manage on my own."

"It was an order, Margot. I won't deny that the extra intel from Loch Bastien would be welcome, given that we only have rumours to go off at this stage. But I don't want you going alone. It's too risky." He ran a hand through his hair.

"Okay." She gave Penny a half-smile. "Go pack your bags, Pen. I'll find Emil and let him know." Her grip on the box tightened as she made for the door. The magic clinging to it throbbed in a steady rhythm, matching the beat of her heart. Somewhere deep at her centre, a voice whispered in words too soft to understand, gentle and warm, like sliding into a lover's embrace after a long time apart.

When they entered the garden at Hartswood, a woman Margot didn't recognise was bent over a plot of tomatoes. Her deep auburn hair caught the late summer sunlight in hues of dark gold and copper. She straightened and stretched before turning her attention to the three of them. There was something familiar about the woman's features that Margot couldn't quite place. Maybe it was the shape of her mouth or her eyes, which were a lovely shade of soft hazel that hinted closer to green than brown.

"Hello. Abigail mentioned we were expecting company. I'm Bridie." She brushed her hand on her apron and held it out.

"Margot. And this is Penny, and Emil." Margot gave the offered hand a shake. "I'm sorry, but I feel like I should know you. Have we met before?"

Bridie chuckled. "No, we haven't, but I believe you know my brother."

"Your brother?"

The smile that pulled across Bridie's lips was unmistakeable.

"Oh, you're Garret's sister. He did say you were coming to Hartswood."

"Abigail and Grandmother can be found in the back garden. I'll go fix some tea." She started towards the house.

"I'll come with you. I should let my father know I'm here," Emil said, jogging to catch up with her.

Margot led Penny around the side of the house. A group of children were running about laughing. Margot recognised the youngest, Henry, with his storm-grey curls, and Kenna with her cloud of ash-grey ringlets. The blond boy and the young girl with a sheet of silver hair she didn't recognise. They must have been Bridie's children. Bran was sitting at the base of the large oak reading and gave Margot a wave as she walked past. She was surprised at how much he had grown since she had seen him last. He must have been fifteen or sixteen now.

Nonna's laughter reached her, and she continued forward to find her sitting with another woman who had the same hazel eyes and jawline as Bridie, her grey hair braided and arranged in a neat bun. She looked up as Margot and Penny approached.

"Well, hello. Who do we have here?"

Nonna turned and gave Margot a smile. "This is Margot. You might remember her. She's Darla's youngest."

The woman nodded. "I can see Darla in her."

"And Penelope. I don't know if you ever met Killian and Verity?"

"Can't say I have."

"Exceptionally skilled bloodline. Penelope was Niall's protégé." Was that a touch of pride in Nonna's voice?

"*Exceptionally skilled bloodline*? I am not a horse, Abigail," Penny quipped. "It is a pleasure to meet you ..."

"Camille." The woman offered and held her hand out.

As Penny lifted her hand to shake Camille's, Nonna grabbed it and flipped her palm up. The sunlight caught the whorl of gold that marked her skin, and Nonna let out a hiss through her teeth. "Where did you get this?"

Camille glanced at Margot, who shrugged.

"Nea put it there," Penny said plainly.

"Shadow's teeth, what was that girl thinking!" Nonna exclaimed. "She's got too much of that old bastard running through her veins."

"Which old bastard, Abigail dear?" Camille chuckled and took a sip from her cup.

Nonna made a sound that was half-laugh half-snort and traced the swirl on Penny's skin.

"Do you know what it is then?" Penny asked, tugging her hand back.

"Of course I know. Do you?"

"It's a soul," Penny replied, rubbing the centre of her palm.

"It's not just any soul—it's a brightling."

"A brightling?" Margot asked.

"Sometimes referred to as a brightborn. They are extremely rare, rarer even than deathborn. Unlike deathborn, which can occur only in the three arcane bloodlines, a brightling might pop up in any bloodline, including those that have never had magic. But there are specific events that need to occur for the emergence of a brightling."

Bridie arrived with a tray of tea things.

"Sit and I'll tell you a story," Nonna said to Margot as Bridie placed the tray down and headed back towards the house.

"Nonna, please can't you just tell us plainly?" Margot didn't want a story. She wanted straight answers.

"Once, long ago, when the world was still young ..." Nonna started, and Margot gave a reserved sigh as she sat herself on the grass beside Penny, who held out a cup of tea.

"... a young woman lived in a cottage in the centre of a beautiful meadow. One day, a young man was riding through the forest that bordered her meadow and he heard her singing. He slowed his horse and crept through the trees to spy on the woman as she tended the plants in her garden.

Every day for a full cycle of the moon the man returned to the edge of the forest and watched the woman work. One day, however, growing unsatisfied with just watching, he approached her. She told him to leave, that he wasn't welcome in her garden. He told her he had watched her work from afar, enchanted by her singing, and that he had fallen in love with her. Again, she told him to leave, that he wasn't welcome, to go and never return.

Angered by her rejection, the man struck her and told her that she would belong to him and no other. He fell upon her and raped her right there among the flowers of her garden.

A month passed and then another, and it became clear that the man's seed had set a child in her womb. She went to her garden and gathered pennyroyal and brightsbane—the herbs she knew would purge the infant from her. After letting the herbs brew from dawn to dusk, she drank the tea and fell instantly into a fitful slumber. As she slept, the Bright Mother came to her and touched the child, protecting it from its mother's wrath.

At midsummer, the woman awoke in the throes of labour, and the child was born by the time the sun was high in the sky. A little girl, so sweet natured she made her mother weep from guilt. The girl was special beyond measure. Though she herself possessed no keen, she could absorb the magic from those around her. She could twist it and turn it against its owner or wield it as though it were her own."

"Wait. She could absorb the magic from others and wield it? What does that mean?" Margot asked.

Nonna gave her a pointed look. "Exactly what it sounds like. The child could channel the magic of others and use it without having any keen of her own."

Margot chewed the side of her thumb. Garret had channelled Nea's keen; they had assumed it was to do with the corruption. That was the only logical explanation, of course, but what if it wasn't just Nea's magic he could channel? No, he was as shocked as Margot and Nea had been at the time. If he could absorb and channel anyone's magic, then surely he would have known or someone would have noticed before now.

"Do you have another question?" Nonna asked, cutting through her churning thoughts.

Margot shook her head to clear it. "Specific events need to be met for the emergence of a brightling. They need to be the result of a failed abortion. What else?"

"It was once said that they were only born when the world was on the verge of a great cataclysm. But generally, there has to be an element of divine intervention in their gestation. Whether that is a failed attempt at abortion or something else. And they are always born at midsummer."

"Always born at midsummer? But hundreds of children the world over could be born at midsummer."

"Hence the point about divine intervention. A brightling isn't a seemingly random accident like a deathborn. They are *chosen*."

"When was the last known brightling born?"

Camille and Nonna shared a look. "The last recorded emergence of a brightling was about three hundred years ago."

"When Port Brenna sank?"

Nonna nodded.

"Last *recorded*," Penny said, placing her cup down and folding her hands delicately in her lap. "What are you not telling us?" Her magic stirred in gentle fingers across the back of Margot's skull.

Nonna's eyes narrowed. "I suggest you don't go prying in my mind, girl, unless you're ready to encounter truths that would send the bravest soldier running for his mother." She smoothed her hand over her lap. "The truth will out when it is time, and you're not here for fairy stories about enchanted children. Did you bring the box?"

"You can't just do that! You're the one who brought up the brightling. What does having it inside Penny mean?"

"It means that Evard can't use it to tear down the barrier between worlds."

"I thought that is what he needed a deathborn for."

"Nea is the only deathborn in several centuries who has the right kind of keen to rend holes in the barrier. Evard knows this. He also knows that Nea would never willingly destroy the barrier, but if he has a brightling, he can just absorb her keen and do it anyway."

"But can't any deathborn necromancer destroy the barrier."

Nonna shook her head. "Nea isn't *just* a deathborn. She's *something* we have never encountered before. We never told her, thinking it was best to just let her believe she was a regular deathborn, and I fear now that was a dire mistake."

Camille patted Nonna's knee. "We did what we thought was best with the information we had at the time. Just like *they* are doing now." She indicated Margot and Penny, but Margot got the sense that she was talking about more than just them.

"What do you mean Nea is something else?" Penny asked.

"Nea was born at the height of midwinter when the barrier between worlds was at its thinnest. And she was *dead.* I have witnessed the birth of deathborn in the past. They certainly appear dead to the untrained eye, but there is something about them, a thin thread of source undetectable to those who don't know what they are looking for. Nea didn't have that. She was a complete void, a *deera solvec* in the old tongue. Daughter of Shadow. I don't even know if the soul that resides inside Nea is truly human or something else, something older perhaps."

"And you didn't think Nea should know? That she's not ... that she might not be ... Oh, I see why you might have kept it from her." Margot frowned.

Penny shook her head. "Nea *is* human. At least in essence, regardless of where her soul came from."

One of Nonna's brows lifted. "I am inclined to agree with you."

"Is a brightling human then? Or are they like Nea?" Margot asked.

"That is a good question. Scholars would argue they are something other than human, but they would argue the same for mages in general. At one stage there was a schism in the council of sages as to whether mages and keen-less should be classified as different species. Utter nonsense, of course. If we consider Nea to be human despite the uncertain origins of her life force, then we can safely assume brightling are human also." Nonna drew a long breath. "But again, you didn't come here to discuss metaphysics." She held her hand out.

Margot retrieved the box and placed it in Nonna's open palm. "Do you know what's inside?"

Nonna tilted her head as she examined the chains around the box. "I believe it is an anchor—a piece of old magic. The type that was once used to create the spirit-glasses and portals. This particular piece of magic, however, is the kind used to bind a soul."

"Like Amelia is bound to the south wing of Braemar?"

"Not exactly. Niall used rune magic for that, similar to that used to create a sentry golem."

"Does that mean any mage could do what he did to Amelia?"

"No," Camille answered. "Niall has spent the better part of his life studying the old magics. What he did requires a sound understanding of the mechanics of runic magic and a great deal of skill backed up by raw power."

"But Nea didn't use rune magic to do this," Penny indicated the mark on her palm.

"Because she didn't need to," Margot said. "Nea can manipulate *any* soul to the point where she can rip them from their bodies ..." Realisation hit her. "She's a walking anchor! Could she banish Amelia?" She directed the question at Nonna.

A proud smile curved across Nonna's lips. "More than likely." She rolled the box around, studying it from every angle. "You need to take this to Warren. I would have asked Nea to, but she's currently beyond our reach."

"Why take it to Warren?"

Nonna handed the box back to Margot. "Because he is the only one who can destroy it. If it falls into Evard's hands, there will be no stopping him."

The magic clinging to the box vibrated against Margot's skin. It didn't want to be destroyed. She shook her head to scatter the whispers as she slid the anchor into her pack. "How do we find him?"

"I know the way. I've been there with Nea," Penny replied. "Just how much do you know about Evard's plans?" she asked Nonna.

"More than you and less than Nea. If that fool of a girl had confided in me instead of running off and trying to handle things herself ..." She drew a heavy breath. "No matter. The important thing now is that we control what we can control."

Margot finished her tea with a nod and then stood. She had wanted to head to Loch Bastien, but it now appeared she was going into the Fenlands. The anchor's magic still quivered at her fingertips. Maybe it didn't need to be destroyed. Maybe they could hide it or maybe ... maybe they could use it.

"Are you coming, Margot?" Penny's voice cut through the whispers.

"I'm coming." She chewed the side of her thumb as she followed Penny towards the house. Maybe there was something in the library that could tell her more about magical anchors. The whispering voice that seemed connected to the box didn't feel malicious. It wanted to help, and Margot needed to make sure that destroying it wasn't a huge mistake.

CHAPTER NINE

HARVEY

Harvey rubbed his lower back as he stretched before accepting the water skin Reg offered him. He took a mouthful and handed it back. Several weeks had passed since he and Molly arrived at the fort, and the rebuild on the stables was nearly complete.

"Good work. Just that last section to thatch and we're done," Reg said as he lit his pipe.

Harvey waved the cloud of smoke away from his face. "Are we moving onto the wall next?" He flicked his hand in the direction of the broken outer wall.

"Nah, we still don't have the stone for that. Trenton wants an outer palisade built. I've no idea what for. And then there's the new commander on his way. I am sure he'll have his own ideas about what needs to be done." Reg chewed the end of his pipe and grunted a laugh. "A keen-less in charge of the order—never thought I would see the day."

"Maybe after what happened to the last few commanders of the capital garrison, there aren't any wardens who actually want the job. A more superstitious person might say it's cursed."

Reg let out another laugh, which turned into a hacking cough. "More likely the king is a hard man to please."

"Yeah, just ask the mages at Kalhanna." *Shit, I shouldn't have said that.* He gave Reg a sideways glance. The other man was chewing the end of his pipe, staring into the distance.

"Aye," he said softly with a nod after a few moments. "'Twas nasty business that. Necessary though, if you believe the king's rhetoric. Best not talked about anyway." His attention shifted to the maid who was crossing the courtyard.

"Sarah would like all staff to report to the kitchens," she said as she reached them.

"Come on then." Reg snuffed his pipe and tapped the ash out, pressing it into the dirt with the toe of his boot.

When they stepped into the servants' entry of the fort, the entire house staff were gathered in the hallway with Sarah barking orders at them. The crowd slowly cleared, and Harvey and Reg approached Sarah.

"What's going on, love?" Reg asked.

"We've just had word that Princess Catriona is coming with Leon. This fort is in no fit state to be housing a princess!" She fisted her hands in her apron. "Sending someone like *her* to this backwards part of the world. What is Evard thinking?"

"Anything we can do to help?"

"Yes. Bryce, get yourself upstairs and help Tess. There are a few things that need fixing and a crate in the blue room that needs to be taken to the library. Then see if she and the others need help with the guest rooms. Who knows what other nobles will turn up once word gets out that Catriona is in residence?" She shooed him away as she turned to Reg.

Harvey headed upstairs and found Molly standing in the doorway to the room she and Margot used to share.

"Tess," he said quietly as he touched her elbow.

"All our things are gone," she said softly. "I knew they would be, but the first time I saw it ... I came up here when we first arrived. The only thing I found was this." She opened her hand. Sitting in her palm was a mouse carved from wood.

"Garret?"

She nodded. "We need to leave before Catriona gets here. She's a mind mage. If she—"

"Tessa, are you there? I need help with—Oh, hello, Bryce." A maid came along the hall towards them.

Molly slid the mouse into her pocket. "This room is done," she said brightly, flicking her hair over her shoulder.

"Great. Can you help me with the master suite? Then it is just the blue room at the other end of the hall. Actually, there is a crate in there on the desk that needs to be taken down to the library; would you mind, Bryce?"

"That's one of the things Sarah sent me up for, and apparently there are a few things that need fixing."

The maid nodded. "The shutter in the green room is jammed, and the hinges on the door into the end room need attention." She pointed over her shoulder.

"I'll fix those first then."

Last time Harvey had been in Declan's room it had been utter chaos. But now there was no sign that Declan had ever inhabited the space, save for the crate on the desk overflowing with books and other personal effects. Harvey picked up the book on top and flipped through it, not really paying attention to the writing on the pages.

Declan's death had hit Garret harder than he had let on. It wasn't a surprise really. The pair had been brothers in all but blood. Harvey had thought Nea was the catalyst that had upended everything, but she was only one part of it. He didn't regret throwing his life with the guard away to follow Garret into an unknown future that could very likely end with all their deaths. No, given the chance, he'd make the same choice every time. He placed the book back on the top of the pile and picked up the crate and left.

As he was crossing the hall that led to the south wing, a noise stirred in the darkness. Amelia appeared, and the markings on the floor flared with light. She might have been an attractive girl once; the lines of her face showed some promise. But her cheeks were too gaunt, the gleam in her pale eyes edged with madness. Her dark hair shifted, revealing a small purple birthmark at the corner of her collarbone as she tilted her head, a slow smile spreading across her lips.

"This one wears a face that is not his own," she whispered, leaning as far forward as the marks on the floor would allow.

Harvey ignored her and started to move away.

"Don't you want to play with me?"

He turned to face her. "No."

A pout replaced the smile. "I will happily trade secrets for companionship. That's why you're here, isn't it? You want secrets."

"I'm not interested in making any kind of deal with you."

"No? Then why are you still here? I can tell you about the fate of your friend *Garret*." She purred Garret's name, her teeth sinking into her lower lip. "Or I can tell you how to free me. That's what the handsome princeling wants, isn't it? To liberate me from this prison."

"Only to place you straight into another."

"I wouldn't mind if he was my jailor." She leant against the wall and traced her fingers along the neck of her nightgown.

"Right, well, I'll leave you to your fantasies." He started to leave.

"You'll return. I can feel it. You're curious. Of course you are. Because, like me, you're not who you pretend to be, and that provides a sense of kinship. Even if you don't want to acknowledge it, you can feel it in your core."

Don't turn around, Harvey. Just walk away. He couldn't help himself. Shifting his grip on the crate, he faced her again.

A triumphant smile slid across her lips, but it curled quickly into a snarl.

"What are doing here, *stable boy*?" John's voice had an edge of ice, as usual he was flanked by Arthur.

"Still shadowing your master like an obedient dog, Arthur?" Amelia's voice was light. "He'd not show you the same loyalty."

Harvey tightened his grip on the crate and moved to step around John, but the warden lifted his arm to block the hallway.

"Not so fast. I asked you what you were doing here. Surely you've been warned about this area of the house and its ... *resident*." His lip curled, matching Amelia's as he shot a glance at her.

"I've been warned. I was just on my way to library from the upper guest rooms." Harvey hefted the crate. "Now if you don't mind, this thing is heavier than it looks." It wasn't, but he needed an excuse to get away.

"It would be a terrible shame for you to stumble too far down this hallway. Do you know what she could do to you if you crossed those marks on the floor?" John stepped forward, forcing Harvey to take a step back.

"Leave him alone, John," Arthur said quietly.

"Not now, Arthur," John barked and took another step into Harvey's personal space. He pressed his hand against the front of the crate and gave it a shove.

Harvey stumbled backwards and met a wall of heat. John frowned and gave him another shove. The air grew hotter, and the rune marks shone so bright, Harvey had to squint to see.

Amelia's indulgent laugh sounded. "Oh, did you forget that there are only a handful of people who can enter my cage?"

"They told me anyone could cross the rune marks except you," John growled.

"I'd have corrupted the entire house and been out of this prison long ago if that were case."

"But Nea and Garret—"

"Are not bootlicking bottom-dwellers like you."

John's mouth pulled into a tight line and his fist clenched.

"Touched a nerve, did I?" She gave an indulgent little chuckle that seemed out of place with her usual demeanour.

"They're all terrified of you, but one of these days I'll wipe that smile off your face, abomination."

"I look forward to the day you try. It's been a long time since I got to corrupt a warden, but they are my favourite toys. How quickly all that righteousness crumbles when you give them a little taste of power." She licked her lip.

John gave Harvey another shove into the barrier and let out a snarl.

"John." Arthur put a hand on his shoulder. "Come on."

"That's it, Arthur. Take your master away before he embarrasses himself," Amelia cooed.

John shook Arthur's touch off and took a step back, rubbing his palm over the stump where his hand had been. "I'll figure out exactly what you are, *stable boy,* and when I do—"

"That's enough, John." Another voice joined them as a man with hair the same shade of brown as his eyes entered the hallway. He folded his arms over his chest and glared at John.

Harvey stiffened and fought the urge to salute. Old habits were hard to break, apparently.

"This is none of your business, Trenton," John growled.

"Well, I'm making it my business." He settled his gaze on Harvey. "Bryce, isn't it? You are one of the lads helping Reg with the rebuild."

Lads? Trenton wasn't that much older than Harvey was. "Yes, sir," he replied, chancing a glance at Amelia, but she had disappeared.

"Back to work then. I've just passed on my plans for the second palisade."

"I'm not finished—"

"Yes, you are." Trenton cut John's objection short.

John's lips pressed into a hard line. "You might be top dog around here now, Trenton, but that will change the minute Leon arrives. Personally, I can't wait to see you taken down a peg or two."

"Leon lost any authority he had in the guard when the king appointed him commander of your order."

Harvey took that moment as his chance to escape. He hurried from the hallway, John's glare boring into the back of his shoulders until he turned the corner.

With a roll of his wrist, Harvey inspected the practice sword in his hand and tested its weight before casting a glance around. The golden light of afternoon was quickly making way for dusk, and no one else seemed to be about. This was risky, but his mind was full of thoughts stirred up by the events of the day and sweating them out felt like the best solution. He still hadn't had a proper talk with Molly about what to do with the knowledge that Catriona was coming. Should they cut their losses now? Catriona might not be able to feel the enchantment, but she could easily pluck the information from their minds.

He gave the sword an experimental twirl and took up position facing the dummy. It wasn't just Catriona. It was the altercation with John. Could John feel the enchantment? He suspected Harvey was not what he seemed.

A tremor rolled through his fingers and along his arms as the blade met the side of the dummy. He shifted his weight, moving backwards with fluid steps before advancing again.

Each thud against the dummy sent vibrations through him that shifted the thoughts around his mind, reorganising and quieting them.

Sweat stuck his shirt to his back as he landed one last strike at the point where the dummy's oval-shaped head met the broad edge of its shoulder. Panting, he gave the sword a final twirl and moved to the edge of the field.

As Harvey approached the equipment lock-up, a shape stepped into his path. It wasn't full dark quite yet, but there had been enough pooling shadows to hide Trenton from him.

"I didn't think you were *just* a labourer." His tone was even. "You've had formal guard training."

Harvey rubbed the back of his neck. "Yeah."

Trenton folded his arms. "Why didn't you apply for a position on the guard?"

"That part of my life is behind me ... sir." He added the last with a downcast glance.

"Soldiers who have *left that part of their life behind them* don't tend to reach for a sword to sweat out their problems." The corner of Trenton's mouth twitched. "Would you like to try out for the guard?"

Yes. But no. It would be much harder to be *Bryce* if he was on the guard. The guard was Harvey's life, not Bryce's. He let out a long breath. "No. I tried that once, but I am not suitable."

"What I just witnessed would prove otherwise."

"My temper is a liability," Harvey said a little too quickly.

"You're hot-headed? Most young soldiers are. I fail to see how that has any bearing on suitability." Trenton had always been a bit like a dog with a bone when he found something he wanted.

"Look, Tr—sir, I mean no disrespect. I'm honoured that you would consider me a suitable fit, but I've tried the whole soldier thing and truth is I'm not good at blindly following orders. I picked a fight with the wrong captain and ended up thrown out on my arse." It wasn't an outright lie. Harvey didn't follow orders that grated against his moral code—that's how he ended up working with Garret.

"You're saying you're insubordinate? True, that's not a good quality in a soldier, but it also means you're a critical thinker, which can be useful." Trenton scratched his jawline. "You remind me of a soldier I trained with. He could be a bit of a hothead, but he wasn't to be underestimated."

Harvey nodded. "Did something happen to him?"

"He deserted."

"Deserted? Do you know why?"

Trenton made a sound somewhere between a laugh and a huff. "Because he's a bloody fool." He leant against the wall of the equipment shed and studied his hands. "I suspect he learned something of what is going on and he made a choice. It's one we're all going to have to make in the coming days." He sounded like Garret. Maybe that was what happened to you when you were the one in charge; you instantly aged ten years and became a gruff old philosopher.

"What do you mean we've all got to make a choice?" Harvey tried to keep his tone light.

Trenton studied him then pushed off the wall and clapped him on the shoulder. "Look, what you've told me about your past doesn't make for a good reference, but I think I could use you. I won't press the matter further, but give it some thought and let me know."

Harvey studied Trenton's back as he walked away. He had hoped running a few sword drills would clear his mind, but it had only served to provide him with a new series of concerns.

CHAPTER TEN

GARRET

After several hours rolling through the forest, the troupe pulled into a small village. Children came running from all directions as several of the Nundle climbed down and started handing out small bags of brightly coloured sweets. Frell called for the wagons to stop as they reached a clearing on the other side of the town.

Wade jumped from the driver's seat and turned to Garret. "We'll only be here long enough to trade for some supplies, but if you wanted to stretch your legs, you have time," he said as he moved to the side of the wagon and rapped on the boards next to the door.

The purple stairs rattled as they rolled out, and the door opened to reveal Nea. She buttoned the front of her waistcoat as she descended the stairs to join them. Her normally braided hair was free and tumbling down her back in thick, curling waves. All the black dye had finally faded, and it had returned to its natural stormy grey. She met Garret's eye and gave him a small smile.

"I just mentioned to Garret that he might like a chance to stretch his legs. We're going to trade for supplies then move on, but you'll have an hour or two respite before we're ready to go," Wade said.

Nea placed her hands against the small of her back and stretched. "That doesn't sound like a bad idea."

Wade nodded. "I recommend heading along that street and taking a left at the end—lovely little spot. And farther along there's a tavern that serves the best spiced mead this side of the Night Estate." He dug in his pocket and produced a handful of hexagon-shaped coins. "Here." He passed the coins to Nea. "Now off you go. We won't leave without you." He ushered them away as Urden and Frell came over.

Frell's expression was neutral as she watched Garret and Nea pass.

"Should we see what Declan is up to?" Nea asked as she examined the coins. They had a rose stamped on one side and an eight-pointed star on the other; the Nundle referred to them as hexies.

Garret cast a gaze over the line of wagons and spotted Declan with Zephyr and a small bunch of village children. Declan had crouched to the height of the children, his hands swirling the air in front of him as an orb of water formed above his fingers. The children all gasped in delight as the ball shimmered silver-blue before breaking apart into a school of those fancy long-finned fish Osmarians liked to keep. "I think he's quite happy where he is."

As Nea followed his gaze, she let out a rare chuckle. "He does look in his element. Also, it might be nice to avoid an hour or two of innuendos and sideways smirks."

Garret rubbed the scar above his lip. "Indeed."

They headed along the street Wade had mentioned. It followed the path of a small stream, and every so often branched off over a small wooden bridge. The road they were on came to a small pond with an island in the middle of it. The island was covered in ducks and geese and as Wade had promised, just beyond the pond, over a little, red-painted bridge, was a tavern. And sitting at one of the tables out the front was Rourke.

Nea appeared to spot him at the same moment Garret did. She lifted her hand to wave then started over the bridge.

Rourke nodded in greeting when they reached him and indicated they take two of the empty seats at his table.

As they sat, a girl came over and smiled brightly. "I'm Daisy. Would you like to hear today's specials?"

"Two meads and one of those fancy plates with the cheese that Aster has been doing lately," Rourke answered for them.

"No problem." Daisy hurried off.

"You're travelling with the troupe?" Rourke asked.

Nea nodded. "We found them after the memory shattered. Zephyr said it would be safer than travelling the wilds alone."

Rourke scratched along his jaw. "She's right. How are you finding them?"

"They are very *accommodating*," Nea said.

Garret made a noise in his throat, and Rourke's attention snapped to him. "Accommodating is certainly one word for it," he offered in response.

Rourke let out a deep chuckle. "They're mostly a good-natured group of people."

"Where have you been?" Nea asked.

Daisy returned with a tray. She placed their drinks on the table, followed by a large plate covered in different cheeses, slices of fruit, and wedges of a strange crisp bread.

"I haven't been far away. I had some business that needed attending to. But I've been keeping an eye on you. Frell and I don't get along. She doesn't like my kind or really anyone who has a differing opinion to hers," Rourke said once Daisy was gone again. "But the troupe is the safest place for *you* at the moment. Not to mention the fastest way to get to your destination."

Garret reached for one of the slices of apple at the same time Nea did. Their fingers brushed and that strange purple magic shimmered over their skin. Rourke tensed, his gaze moving to Nea.

"Do you know what that is? It keeps happening," Garret asked as he took a different slice of apple from the plate.

Rourke studied them both, and the hairs on Garret's arms stood on end. Nea shifted. Was Rourke using some kind of magic? Having no keen-sense wasn't getting any easier. After a few moments, Rourke gave a decisive nod.

"So, you know what's going on?" Nea asked.

"Not exactly. Something has happened in your past—an event when a piece of your keen has become woven together with Garret's. It is—"

"Wait. You felt my keen?" Garret sat forward.

"Of course. It's not like anything from this realm, but I know what you are. And your kind, much like mine, were originally created for a specific purpose."

"But Garret's keen is gone," Nea said.

Rourke shook his head. "It's not gone. It just works differently in this realm to yours. Here." Rourke held his hand out for Nea, and she laid her palm against his. "Close your eyes and focus."

Nea did as instructed, and then Garret *felt* her—subtle and cool at the very edges of his senses. Fresh air to drowning lungs. Nea released Rourke's hand and the sensation of her keen stopped. But he had felt it for those few precious heartbeats. His keen wasn't broken, it was something else ... Dormant?

"Why is it like that?" Nea asked.

Rourke scratched the underside of his chin. "Honestly, I don't know. I haven't had any experience with ward mages, but I do have a contact I can ask."

"Ward *mages*?" Nea's brow wrinkled, and she bit her lip.

"You don't consider them mages?"

Nea started to shake her head. "Most don't. Warden keen works so differently to mage keen that in general people consider them to be opposites. It makes sense though that they are actually just another variant of mage." She studied Garret. "Now is probably not the time to be exploring semantics though. Do you know how to extract the piece of my keen that has been trapped with Garret's?"

"The keens are woven together like a cloth now. I don't know that your keen could be extracted entirely, but surely you've noticed that Garret isn't the only one harbouring a foreign keen?"

"What do you mean?" She sat forward.

"For a piece of your keen to take root in Garret, a piece of his had to be sacrificed, and the fracturing of your keen created an opening."

"There's a piece of my keen tied up with Nea's?"

Rourke nodded, and Garret rubbed his hands over his face.

"What was done cannot be reversed, but it can be stabilised. Do you know when this might have occurred?"

Nea stared into her cup then her head snapped up. "When you channelled my magic. That must have been when it happened."

"Wouldn't we have noticed that at the time. Or ..." There had been plenty of moments when they had touched before going through the portal, but it wasn't until they arrived in the Between that Nea's magic had started reacting to him.

"Magic works differently in your realm," Rourke said simply. "Though I am fairly certain ward mages are not supposed to be able to *channel* magic."

"Could corruption have affected it at all?" Nea asked

"Perhaps."

"When Garret channelled my magic, he was trying to isolate it from the corruption."

Rourke nodded. "That actually makes a bit of sense. What happened when you tried to separate the two?" He turned his rust-coloured gaze to Garret.

"They were tangled together. I followed the thread of Nea's keen to its source and then a hedge of roses appeared, and I ended up in the Between. Not physically. It was completely different to travelling through the portal."

"A hedge of roses?" Rourke looked at Nea.

"The barrier between our world and this one," she replied. "What will happen if we don't stabilise the woven keens?"

"It is hard to say as there is really no precedent. At worst, I would say that your keens will keep weaving together until they reach some kind of balance. But that will have an irreversible effect on your magic both in this world and your own."

"How do you stabilise it?" Garret asked.

Rourke flicked a look between them. "I am not sure you'll like it. It will tie the pair of you together irrevocably, at least in a magical sense."

"Are you talking about an oathing? That is what Wade thought this was." Nea sat back and cradled her cup as she chewed her lower lip.

"An oathing *might* work ... but if so, it would only be a temporary fix. No, I was talking about something much more permanent. A death ward."

The colour drained from Nea's face, and she straightened so fast her mead splashed into her lap. Daisy appeared at her side and held out a cream-coloured rag. Nea took it and blotted at the spilled liquid.

"What is a *death ward*?" Garret asked when the girl had disappeared again.

Nea smoothed her palm over the surface of the table, watching the movement of her hand rather than meeting his eye. "*Old* magic. A more permanent form of an oathbond. Extremely dangerous, they often went wrong with catastrophic results. Rourke, I don't think it's wise."

Rourke shrugged. "It might not be wise, but do you take your chance with the unstable sharing of keen? We could try a standard oathing first or there might be another way, but I'll need more time ... just—"

"There you both are." Wade bustled up the stairs to the tavern. "Hello, Rourke," he said before his attention switched to Garret and Nea again. "We'd better be getting along. Frell is ready to move out."

Nea offered the coins Wade had given her to Rourke, but he waved them away. "I'll look into it further."

She nodded then joined Wade.

"Garret." Rourke touched Garret's elbow, holding him back as Nea and Wade started walking. "Frell cannot know about the woven keens, nor can she know that you channelled Nea's magic."

Garret studied Nea's back as she wandered away, chatting with Wade. "You told Nea she was safest with the troupe."

"She is for now. Frell's magic protects the caravans as they wander through the wilder parts of the world, and she knows just how rare someone like Nea is. But be on your guard. The lines between friend and foe are very fickle creatures in this world, and even good people can be misled by their own intentions." He released his grip then started into the tavern, pausing to say over his shoulder, "Zephyr and Wade know how to find me if you need me."

When Rourke disappeared inside, Garret moved off after Nea and Wade. He'd have to ask Nea more about this death ward, but given her reaction, perhaps it was better he asked Declan if he knew anything about it first.

Late afternoon saw them set up camp in another forest clearing. Garret approached Declan, who was helping Urden with the central fire.

"Just in time, Garret," Declan said brightly as he stood wiping his hands on his pants. "You can help me gather some wood."

He followed Declan into the trees and when he could no longer hear the sounds of the camp, Declan turned to him with a wide, lopsided grin firmly in place. "So, where did you and Nea disappear to earlier?"

"Why don't you ask her?" Garret picked up a large branch.

"I already did." Declan frowned.

"And what did she tell you?"

"She dodged the subject by asking me if I figured out why your keen has disappeared. Then Frell called her away for something ... probably a cup of tea. That woman is obsessed with tea. Have you noticed?"

He had noticed, and he didn't know how Nea and Declan could stomach the strange tea she constantly offered. "Have you heard of a death ward?"

Declan's eyebrows just about disappeared into his hair. "I've read about them. They are not exactly the kind of magic *you* would approve of. They are extremely dangerous and something that I would never mess around with ... and that's saying something, really. I mean, I managed to get my soul jammed between worlds by playing with long-dead magic." He tapped his chin. "Why are you asking about them?"

Garret focused on the forest around them before turning back to Declan. "We ran into Rourke in the village, and he said that Nea's keen has become woven with mine and that unless we stabilise it, there is no telling what it could do. He believes a death ward may be the only way to stabilise it."

"Your keens have become woven together?" Declan shredded a leaf and watched the pieces fall to the forest floor. "When? How? Can't they be unwoven? How did Nea respond to the idea of a death ward?"

Garret ran a hand over his face. "Nea seemed to think it had happened when I accidentally channelled her magic and—"

"That sounds impossible but also makes a ridiculous amount of sense. I wonder if it's a warden thing or a *Nea* thing. If it's a warden thing then that has huge implications ... If wardens can channel the keen of any mage ..."

"It might actually be related to corruption. And Rourke believes it is permanent and can't be simply *unwoven*. As for Nea's response to the idea of a death ward ... She didn't take it well."

Declan ran a hand through his hair. "Didn't take it well? What does that mean?"

Garret toyed with his scar. "The idea seemed to frighten her."

"That doesn't bode well at all."

"No, it doesn't. Why are they dangerous enough to make even someone like Nea pause?"

Declan leant against a tree and folded his arms. "You realise I only have a few a cryptic accounts from a handful of long-dead scholars to go from?"

"That's never stopped you before." Garret grinned, and Declan let out a low chuckle.

"Essentially, a death ward would work by tying the souls of two individuals together. They were irreversible and they only worked in cases where the parties involved trusted each other completely. You'd be giving a literal part of your soul over to Nea, and she you. Not even death could part you." He tapped his chin. "Which is probably one of the things that Nea found confronting. As a necromancer *and* a deathborn she already has a *complicated* relationship with death."

"And a death ward is different to an oathing?"

"In essence they are different versions of the same thing. However, the bond created by an oathing is constrained to the parameters of a special agreement or pact. They are time sensitive and, even in long-term cases, are broken by death. There was a period of history where many mages chose oathings instead of formal marriages." His grin was wolfish as he said the last part.

Garret shook his head; he knew better than to bite when Declan played this game.

They each gathered an armload of branches then returned to the camp. Nea was sitting by the central fire talking to Urden. She took a sip from the cup of tea she was nursing and scrunched her nose up. Garret wasn't sure why she persevered with it, though it seemed to be the only tea the Nundle knew how to brew. He dropped his load of wood by the fire then headed over to Wade's wagon.

Wade was perched on the top step pulling a needle and thread through a piece of fabric. A golden mage light danced around him, illuminating the unfinished embroidery. He was humming a tune but stopped and looked up as Garret arrived. "What can I do for you, Garret?" His attention turned back to his work, his fingers moving almost too fast to follow as a leaping hare took shape.

"You wouldn't have any tea-making supplies, would you?"

"Of course." He thrust his thumb over his shoulder and shuffled sideways so Garret could pass. "Though I'm sure Frell will make you a cup if you ask."

"I'm after a few specific herbs, ones I am not sure Frell knows exist."

Wade stared at him for a few moments then let out a laugh. "I'm sure you'll find what you're looking for. Everything is labelled."

Sure enough, Garret located several jars containing the herbs he was seeking. He measured out a few scoops into a pot and then went outside again to find some water.

A short while later, he joined Nea by the fire and held out the cup of tea. One of her grey brows flicked up as she took it from him, but when she inhaled the scent, she smiled widely and placed the half-full cup of Frell's tea aside.

Feeling eyes on him, Garret glanced over his shoulder. Frell was watching him, her mouth a thin line.

"I was beginning to think peppermint didn't exist in this realm. You remembered the recipe," Nea said.

Garret nodded and settled on the grass beside her. He held his cup up. She touched hers lightly against his and then took another sip.

They sat in silence for a while. Occasionally Declan's laughter would reach them. He was playing a game of liar's dice with Zephyr and several of the other members of the troupe. Not far from the gaming group, Frell and Urden sat talking quietly with Wade. Every so often one of them would glance Nea's way, and after a while Wade got up with frown and left to join the dice game. He whispered something to Zephyr, who glanced at Garret.

"Declan seems to be in his element," Nea said, drawing Garret's attention to her.

"It's good to see." He sighed and studied the liquid in his cup. "It's not something I ever thought I would witness again."

"I imagine not." Something flickered in the depths of her gaze. "Garret, I ... I don't know if he'll return to our world with us. He has no physical form to return to. The fact that he is corporeal even here in the Between is a pure miracle as far as I can tell. The magic he used ... I've never seen it's like before, so I can't predict what will happen."

"It's alright. He's already told me as much." He leant back on his hands; his fingers were so close to hers, the air between them felt bowstring tight.

Nea shifted and swallowed. "Truth be told, I am not sure what is going to happen to any of us when we find the root of the corruption. I don't know if we can go back or if we'll be stuck here."

"Do you have any ideas of where to start looking for the corruption?"

"No. Frell seems adamant that corruption exists because the *balance* is broken. She told me that the only way to fix it was to set the Shadow Man free."

"The spirit who pretended to be Declan when I channelled your keen?"

"The same." She drew her knees to her chest and rested her chin on them. "That would be disastrous for our world, and it would be playing right into Evard's hands."

"Evard wants to free the Shadow Man?"

"Not exactly." She bit her lip. "Ultimately he wants to cheat death. But it goes deeper than that. He wants power ... He wants ... *godhood.* To unseat the Shadow Man and usurp his powers. It won't work the way he thinks it will, but he is beyond seeing reason, has been since before ..." She drew a deep breath and was silent for so long, Garret wasn't sure she was going to speak again until she said softly, "Something is *wrong* here."

"What do you mean."

"It's ..." She studied him. "My memories are still broken. Back in our world, I can't think of Kalhanna without them threatening to drown me. But here it's ... everything is ... *numb* ... I don't like it."

Now that she mentioned it, she had been different here. Not as raw ... and he hadn't noticed her withdrawing to that place that made her breath hitch and her eyes go vacant. He suspected that in those moments she was reliving what had happened at Kalhanna, but he had the decency not to ask her. If she wanted to talk about it, she would.

"It's getting late," she said as she played with the end of her braid and stood. "Thank you for the tea."

"Goodnight, Nea," he whispered as she left. She was right. There was something definitely wrong here. The heaviness that had settled in his stomach the day Declan broke him out of the memory trap shifted in a way that brought a bitter flavour to the back of his tongue. He finished the last of his tea, but it did nothing to chase the taste away.

CHAPTER ELEVEN

NEA

The next day went much like the day before. They broke camp in the morning and travelled until mid-afternoon. However, the forest around the clearing they stopped in was different. The air here stirred ticklish fingers through the hairs on the back of Nea's neck, and strange shadows darted through the trees.

She stretched as she studied the dark tree line. Something out there was calling to her, raising a distinct pull behind her navel and stirring whispers at the back of her mind. It wasn't the corruption. That still seemed to be dormant.

"Something to warm your weary bones?"

Nea leapt sideways as Frell approached, holding out a cup of tea.

"Sorry, I didn't mean to startle you."

"I was just ..." Nea cast another glance out at the trees.

"Best to ignore it. Here, this will help." Frell pushed the cup into Nea's hands.

The sweet floral scent didn't seem so off-putting today. She took a sip and found that whilst it still wasn't a pleasant tea, she was growing accustomed to it.

A small smile curved the corners of Frell's mouth. "Have you had a chance to think about my proposal in regard to the Master of Shadows?"

The fleeting numbness that accompanied the tea gave Nea a moment's pause before she answered. "Yes, and my stance on the matter has ..." She shook her head as a fog settled on her thoughts. "... not changed."

"You're sure about that?"

"Yes. It is too dangerous. There has to be another way to deal with the corruption."

"I told you the balance needs to be fixed or any solution you find to your plague will only be a temporary one."

Nea took a large mouthful of the tea, more to buy herself time to respond than because she was enjoying it ... She glanced into the cup. When had she finished it?

"Just consider what I've told you." Frell smiled as she took the empty cup from Nea and walked away.

Nea looked back at the dark trees. What had just happened? She rubbed a hand through her hair. Her thoughts were scattered, and there was a niggle at the back of her mind. Almost like a warning.

"There you are."

She turned as Declan approached.

"I'm starting to think you've been avoiding me."

"You're the one who has been *busy*."

He grinned. "I was dead you know; I think I am entitled to a little *indulgence*."

She opened her mouth to respond but thought better of it.

"All joking aside, do you have a moment to talk?"

"You did spend several months haunting me—what's one more moment?"

He gave her a look of hurt that dissolved into a smile. "I left myself wide open for that one. Garret told me about your meeting with Rourke."

"He did?" She folded her arms.

"The woven keens, the *death ward*. That's—"

"Out of the question for now."

The eagerness on his face fell.

"We have no way of knowing what will happen or if it is actually necessary. I haven't noticed any further differences in the response of my keen to Garret's."

One of his dark brows lifted. "So, you've been testing it then?"

"No. But I think I would notice if my magic was changing."

"Do you think there might be complications with forming a ward because you're a deathborn?"

She frowned. "Not complications as such, but as far as I know, no one has ever tried to form one with a deathborn. So, there is no telling what might happen. Speculation aside, it wouldn't be fair to Garret."

A slow smile smoothed across his features as he studied her. "Did you get Garret's opinion on that?"

"I don't need to. There is too much that could go wrong, and even if it did work ... it is no light matter, tying your soul to someone. He'd never be able to escape it—to escape me."

Declan folded himself onto the ground and patted the grass beside him. "It seems that he's not going to be able to escape you anyway with the whole mixed-up keens thing, and I don't think he minds all that much, to be honest."

She sat and ran her fingers through the grass. Whenever the Nundle set up camp, the clearing they chose always shifted to accommodate them. Growing in size and shape, the grass changed to a lush spongy green. "I'm not interested in playing this game, Declan."

"That's good, because for once I am not playing." His forest-green eyes darkened as he said it. "Forget about what a death ward would mean for you and Garret on a personal level for a moment." His tongue traced the seam of his lips. "Though the sooner the pair of you—"

"Declan!"

"Sorry. Old habits." He lifted his hands in surrender. "Before I died, long before actually, when my father was first infected and I started studying corruption in the effort to find a cure ..." He let out a huff and shook his head. "... I happened across a myth that I thought had no credit until you gave me the revelation about corruption being a soul disease."

"Are you talking about the story of how the Shadow Man became trapped in the Between?"

"Yes. Not really the story itself but the disjointed musing of the scholar who studied it. She seemed to think that there was some truth to the story, and that by imprisoning the Shadow Man and damaging the Bright Mother in process, the mages of the time had severely weakened themselves. She used the breakdown of the portal network among other things as evidence of this." He shredded blades of grass as he spoke. "She also touched lightly on deathborn, stating they were our salvation. The keys to the prison we had created for ourselves. I thought she was raving mad of course. But then you came along, and all those pieces started to click into place. Corruption is a soul disease related to the Shadow Man, deathborn are actually real and not some time distorted myth ..."

"And how is all this related to death wards?" Nea lay on the grass and studied the sunset-tinted clouds.

"To fix the corruption, you need to be able to control it, and only the Shadow Man can do that. But if the Shadow Man is released, then we can all kiss our arses goodbye. Unless someone, a deathborn, was able to usurp his place."

She sat up. "That is utter lunacy."

"Is it though?"

"It's what Evard is planning. At least the part about taking the place of the Shadow Man."

His jaw dropped. "Okay, so it's not the sanest of plans, but think about it. If you were to usurp the Shadow Man's powers and—"

"I would completely lose myself in the process."

"Except if a piece of your soul was safe. You could take the Shadow Man's power, fix the corruption, foil Evard's plans, and reunite the pieces of the Bright Mother. Then she could strip you of the godhood, put the Shadow Man back where he belongs, and return you to the land of the living." He leapt to his feet and started pacing.

"You make it sound simple, but it's not. There is too much that could go wrong. Not to mention to trap the Shadow Man originally, the Bright Mother had to be broken to make his prison."

"But what if she didn't have to be?"

Nea collapsed on the grass again. "You're not going to let this go, are you?"

"Not until a better hypothesis presents itself. All I am saying is be open to the idea of it."

Be open to the idea of it. Frell kept asking her to do the same thing. Numbness and the taste of bitter floral tea coated the back of her tongue.

"Nea?" Declan crouched over her.

"Sorry?"

"You seemed to zone out for a moment there. Are you alright?" he asked, his brow furrowing.

"I'm fine."

His eyes narrowed, and the corner of his mouth tightened. "I know that's a lie. What's the matter?"

She sat slowly and glanced back at the camp. "I think Frell's trying to manipulate me."

He offered her a hand up. "You're sure? Have you mentioned it to Garret?" His voice had taken on a heavy tone.

She shook her head as he pulled her to her feet. "No. I'm just … something doesn't feel right, and I don't want to mention it to Garret until I am absolutely sure that is what is happening."

He nodded. "I doubt he'd take it well. He's already suspicious of the troupe." The serious look on his face changed as he caught sight of something over Nea's shoulder. "Zephyr, my lovely, what we can we do for you?"

"Dinner is ready." She smiled brightly and slipped her fingers around the crook of Declan's elbow. "Come on before you both miss out."

Nea trailed behind them, her thoughts churning. Magic that was not her own had settled in her veins, heavy and numbing. Was it Garret's keen or was it something else entirely? Was she right about Frell or being paranoid because ever since she had arrived in the Between, she hadn't felt like herself? As though some integral part of her psyche had been taken from her.

She absently took a plate of food from Urden and settled on the grass next to Garret. His grey gaze studied her, and she shifted her shoulders.

"Is something wrong?" he asked quietly.

Nea looked across to where Frell was sitting, her pink hair reflecting the orange light from the fire. The other woman smiled as her crystalline gaze settled on Nea. "I'm fine, just a little tired." Nea turned her attention back to Garret.

He traced the scar above his lip but didn't say anything.

The man behind Nea hummed a soft lullaby as he worked soothing fingers through her hair, followed by the long strokes of a hairbrush. He placed the brush on the table beside her and separated her hair into sections before starting to braid it. Nea picked the hairbrush up. It was heavy in her small hands, the wooden handle darkened in patches with age. The roses carved into it so worn down in places, the pink and green paint had long rubbed away. She ran her thumb against the bristles. "Why does Sophia hate me?"

The man's hands paused. "She doesn't hate you. It's complicated, and you probably won't understand—"

"Until I am older. I am tired of being told that, Father." She pulled

away and twisted to face him. "I never did anything to her, and she acts as though she'd rather I didn't exist. Why do you bother parading me before her? She's never going to change her mind about me." She slammed the hairbrush on the table and clenched her fists.

"Nea," he reprimanded softly.

"It's not fair. She's allowed to be nasty and hate me, but I must always be on my best behaviour. I don't want her to like me. I don't need her. I HATE HER!" The source shuddered as she screamed the last words. A crack formed on the face of the hand mirror that matched the hairbrush.

"Nea!" The weight of her father's keen pressed on her, forcing her boiling emotions down to a simmer. "You must control yourself."

Nea picked up the mirror. Her reflection's hair appeared pink for a fleeting moment. "I'm sorry, Father," she whispered as she placed it down again. "I just ..."

"Come here." Niall held his arms out, and she rushed into them. He settled her in his lap as he took up a seat on the bed. "If you don't want to see Sophia again, I won't make you." He smoothed his hand over her hair as she pressed her face into his chest.

"I don't want to. I don't need her." She hiccupped. "Not when I have you." She gave him a watery smile, and he pressed a kiss to her forehead.

"I'll always be here. Now let's finish your hair. It's well past your bedtime."

A scream tore through the night, startling Nea from sleep. She sat up and the blanket that had been on her shifted. No, not a blanket. A dark jacket that smelled of clove. Another scream sounded and she leapt to her feet, clutching the jacket to her chest. What was she doing outside by the fire? Had she fallen asleep here? Frell was sitting across from Nea, her pink hair appearing orange as she stirred the coals and sent a flurry of sparks into the air.

"You can go back to sleep." Her crystalline eyes reflected the embers.

"But the screams ..."

"Overdramatic ghouls who are tired of being ignored, but ignore them we shall."

Nea shivered as a scream echoed again.

"Here, the tea will help you sleep." Frell poured a cup of tea from the pot by the fire.

Nea didn't want tea. Hot-cold needles were dancing a path across the back of her skull. Something was very wrong. She glanced around, not seeing evidence of Garret or Declan anywhere. "Where are my friends?"

"They are fine. Declan is with Zephyr." She held out the teacup pointedly as another scream came from the trees.

"Where's Garret?" Nea's heart was battering painfully against her ribs.

"Here, this will help." Frell stood and approached with the cup.

"I don't *want* tea. Where's Garret?" A tremor had crept into Nea's hands, the source around her quivering in response, and she gripped the jacket tighter.

Frell's mouth pulled into a thin line and she glanced at the forest. "He didn't listen. He refused to take the tea."

"I have to find him." Nea started towards the tree line.

"I cannot allow that. You are too important to lose to the wood." Frell grabbed hold of Nea's arm, and a quiver of magic touched her mind. "I must insist you take the tea and go back to sleep."

Nea pushed against the compulsion. "No. I am going after Garret, and I suggest you stop trying to compel me unless you wish to feel the bite of *my* keen." She shook herself free of Frell's grasp and darted into the forest.

CHAPTER TWELVE

GARRET

Nea often spoke in her sleep and that must have been what had woken him now. She was probably having that nightmare where she called out; more memories from Kalhanna no doubt. She'd likely be mortified if she knew how often her nightmares had woken him over the weeks they had spent travelling together from the capital to Loch Bastien. He studied her sleeping form nearby. She always looked like a doll carved from marble in her sleep, and now was no different—her brow smooth and relaxed, her long, dark lashes resting against her pale cheeks. She murmured softly then rolled over and shivered. Garret slid his jacket off and laid it over her.

He sighed and rubbed his hands over his face as someone cleared their throat.

Frell was sitting by the still-burning fire, a pot of tea beside her. "You and Nea chose an interesting place to sleep. Though I can't really blame you. It is a beautiful night."

Garret glanced back at Nea. Something had been troubling her and she hadn't wanted to stay in Frell's wagon, so Wade had supplied a pair of sleeping rolls.

"Would you like a cup of tea?" Frell asked, lifting the pot.

"No, thank you."

"You don't like tea? I can get you something stronger."

"I'm fine."

Frell shrugged and stirred the coals. "Suit yourself." She poured a cup.

A scream tore through the night, and Garret whirled to face the direction it had come from. It had sounded like a young girl, and immediately he thought of Nora.

"I would ignore that if I were you," Frell said calmly.

"But—"

"It is nothing that concerns you." The corner of her mouth twitched as she held the cup out. "Here, have a cup of tea. It will help you go back to sleep."

Another scream. This one more desperate than the first. Garret's shoulders tensed.

"Help me! Please." The scream came with words now, fragile and pleading and so very like Nora. Garret started towards the voice, but Frell appeared in front of him, holding out the teacup. There was something in her eyes that churned his stomach.

"If you go into the wood, you will not return. What would Nea think if you threw your life away for some girl." Frell's voice was sweet but it did nothing to hide the barbs beneath the words.

He glanced at Nea's sleeping form. She was usually a light sleeper. Why hadn't the screams woken her? Or anyone else in the camp for that matter? They were so loud they rattled down his spine and set his teeth on edge. "She'd understand."

Frell's eyes narrowed, but the corner of her mouth twisted up. "That hero complex will be the death of you."

Another scream, this one blood curdling. He stepped around Frell and charged into the forest.

Sound echoed off the wide trunks all around him, and he spun on the spot trying to pinpoint where it was coming from.

"Help me!" To the right.

"Please." To the left.

A scream sounded directly in front of him, and he went running towards it. He broke through the trees into a moonlit clearing. At the centre sat a woman with dark red hair and a glowing white nightgown. She looked up when he approached, and the scent of warm apples stirred a flickering memory in the back of his mind. Red curls, warm apples, a bitter taste on the back of his tongue.

"Garret?" she asked, her voice rasping as though she had been the one screaming. "It is you, isn't it? Oh, how you've grown."

He froze, pinned in place by an invisible force.

The woman walked towards him and lifted her hands to cup his face. "You're so handsome."

He tried to pull away as her burning-cold fingertips brushed lightly over the scar that split his top lip, but he couldn't move, couldn't speak.

"I was worried you would grow to look like your father, and I couldn't bear the thought of seeing him every time I looked at you. You do have his eyes."

A branch broke behind Garret, and he tried to turn but the woman held his face firmly. "Wait, don't you remember me? Of course you don't. You were so small."

Garret wanted to shake his head. This couldn't be his mother. She was long dead. She hadn't cared enough about Garret or Bridie to save herself after their father died.

"That's not true. I loved you both so much."

Not enough to keep living. As the thought crossed his mind, her hazel eyes locked onto something over his shoulder.

"No! He's mine." There was venom in her voice.

Garret tried to turn again, but she held him firm.

"You will not take him from me again! You made so many sweet promises, but there was only cold darkness and despair."

"I did nothing to you," Nea said.

"Lies. You took them all, turned them against me."

"You have me confused with someone else I am afraid."

"No, you did this. You did! You stole them."

"*You* chose to love a dead man more than the children who needed you." There was a distinct coldness to Nea's tone. It was one Garret hadn't heard before.

Lilac magic danced over his mother's skin and her eyes grew wide. She released him to grip her own head as she dropped to the ground screaming.

Able to move again, Garret hurried to Nea's side.

His mother straightened and smoothed a hand over her hair as she panted. "You'll not steal him when I have only just found him again. Garret, please, I love you as only a mother can. I made a mistake before, but I have had time to reflect. I'm so sorry I left you."

He looked out of the corner of his eye at Nea. Her mouth was a thin line.

"Then tell him the truth. Admit the real reason you *left*."

"She's trying to poison you against me. Don't you know what she is? Her kind are rotten to the core. Abominations of the natural order."

A tremor ran through Nea at the word *abominations*.

"I trust Nea more than most and certainly more than some spectre in the woods."

"But I'm your *mother*. I know now it was wrong to let Frederick's death control me. If I had my time over, I would choose differently."

"No, you wouldn't. I've seen your kind more times than I would like to, and it always ends the same. It was weak and selfish," Nea said.

"It was not weakness! Evard took *everything* from me! How could I love *his* bastard knowing there was every chance he would grow to be as heartless as his father," she shrieked. "If the pennyroyal and brightsbane had worked, I—"

"You tried to purge the pregnancy." Nea's eyes widened, and she swallowed.

Garret's mother paled as she switched her attention from Nea to him. "I made a mistake; you have to believe me. I was so relieved when it didn't work. She's trying to turn you against me. Her kind only know how to spit venom and lies."

"Evard is my father?" Garret looked from his mother to Nea. "You knew?"

She bit down on her lip and nodded. "I suspected. Almost from the first moment we met."

"How did you know? Who else knows? Does Declan? Margot?"

"I never mentioned it to Declan or Margot. It wasn't my place to say anything, and whilst I was fairly sure, I couldn't be certain."

"Garret, please?" His mother's voice had taken on a pleading tone that burrowed with barbed fingers into the back of his skull. "She doesn't understand a mother's love. How could she when her own mother rejected her rather than raise an abomination."

Nea flinched as though stung.

"That's why she abandoned her own child." His mother's hazel gaze flicked to Nea. "He was such a sweet little thing, wasn't he? With those stormy curls and steel eyes. His father's eyes. You couldn't stand it, could you? Seeing that resemblance after he had betrayed you and left you to face Kalhanna alone."

"Henry's resemblance to Leith had nothing to do with it. It was what Evard would do to him if he found out. I did what I had to, to keep him safe." Nea's voice took on that cold tone again. "It's interesting you brought up Sophia, considering you also chose to reject a child who needed you, to treat him like an abomination because of the circumstances of his birth. But regardless of what I think of my own mother, I would rather have her than you. Because whatever Sophia might be, she is not a coward."

Garret's mother let out a shriek and charged at Nea. Violet magic flashed through the air and the earth beneath their feet shook. His mother staggered to the side but regained her footing. With an agile leap, she landed on Nea, knocking her to the ground. Garret raced forward and grabbed her by the back of her nightgown, pulling her off Nea and tossing her aside. She fanned her fingers and vines sprouted from the ground. They lashed towards him, but he threw his hand up on instinct, reaching for his suppression. Cold washed through his stomach and his mother gave a startled gurgle. Garret could feel the air around her like a shroud laying over a body. He had somehow grabbed onto that shroud and couldn't untangle his keen from it. He tugged, and his mother screamed. A cool hand touched his arm, then the steady thrum of Nea's keen rolled down his spine. It smoothed over the shroud, deftly untangling it from Garret's keen. Then it cracked like a whip and Garret's mother disappeared in a cloud of violet ash.

Nea's breath was coming in sharp gasps and she sagged beside him, catching herself before she hit the ground. She drew a slower breath as she fell onto her backside in the grass.

"Are you alright?" Garret asked as he crouched beside her.

"I will be," she replied meekly.

"I did it again, didn't I? I channelled your magic?"

She shook her head. "No, that was your keen or maybe the part of mine that is trapped inside you, but that was all you. It took everything I had to stop you from killing yourself along with her."

"How? My keen is dormant here."

"I don't know, but Rourke did say it wasn't dormant. It just works differently in this realm."

Garret swallowed as he studied that dark trees around them. "Evard ..." He shook his head. There was no way he could finish that sentence.

"Knowing it now doesn't change anything. It has always been the truth, even though you weren't aware of it. You might have been a different person if you had always known, but you didn't. So, you're still ... you." She straightened and winced, her fingers moving to press against her collarbone.

"You're hurt."

"It's fine." She inspected the blood shining on her fingertips in the moonlight. "Just a scratch."

He settled on the grass beside her. "How did you know so much about her past? Is it because she was a spirit and you're a necromancer?"

"A little. Necromancers get *impressions* from spirits. Like the residue of emotions or thoughts, but I knew about your mother's past because when I was trapped in the memory field, I entered one of your memories by mistake. It was the day your mother died. That would have been enough except ..." She chewed her lip. "Do you remember ever meeting my father before we emerged from the portal at Del Harol?"

"As far as I know, that was the first time I had met him, despite my grandmother apparently being rather close with yours. Why?"

"Because both Nonna and my father were in that memory, and so was I."

"But you couldn't have been older than one, maybe two. My mother died the autumn before I turned five."

"I wasn't quite a year old. My birthday is—"

"Midwinter."

She gave him a strange look.

"Margot mentioned it." He rubbed the back of his neck. "The first year she was at Loch Bastien, she convinced the cook to let her into the kitchen to bake some Osmarian celebration bread. She said it was tradition and even if you weren't there, she wanted to honour it." He bit back a grin. "And every year since then, she's insisted on celebrating. At least Molly handles the bread now. Margot might be good at making tonics and salves, but she cannot bake to save her life."

Nea let out a genuine laugh. "No, she definitely cannot." She leant on her hands, her fingers brushing his. Violet light shimmered between them.

"I can understand a necromancer like Abigail being there for my mother's death, but why your father?"

"I don't think either of them were there for your mother. I think Camille sent for my father because she was worried about you. The child I encountered in that memory ... a four-year-old, who should be laughing and learning about the world, was so beaten down by his own mother that he refused to talk. He thought there was something wrong with him, that he needed to be *fixed*." Bitterness edged her voice.

"I don't remember it ever being like that."

"I suspect my father had something to do with that. He doesn't like to tamper with the minds of others that way unless he sees it as a necessity. I know you don't remember, but I'm sorry you had to go through it."

"I'm not. As you said, knowing the truth now doesn't change anything."

She studied the pile of glimmering ash that had been the spirit and drew a breath before letting it out again in a soft huff. "I need to tell you something else ... When I was in that memory ... ah ..." She rubbed a hand through her hair, pulling some of it free from the braid in the process.

"It must be serious if you're short of words."

That prompted a small laugh. "It's ... *hard*. I am not certain if it was an accurate part of the memory or a fabrication. Regardless, for a while now I've been developing this theory. And I didn't want to say anything until I was sure because I know how you feel about strange and unexplainable magical phenomena." She twisted her hands together.

He placed a hand on hers to stop her wringing fingers, setting a shimmer of sparks over their skin. "I promise not to—what does Declan say? '*Freak out and retreat inward*'."

She regarded him through her lashes and lowered her hands to her lap again. "Alright. In the memory you ... reanimated-a-butterfly." She said the words so fast he didn't catch them.

"I did what?"

"Reanimated a butterfly. Your grandmother thought it was me but, whilst I know I am not like other necromancers, I was definitely too young for that kind of mastery of keen, and my father confirmed that it wasn't me."

"Impossible."

"Improbable, not impossible. We already know you can channel my keen with the ease of someone actually born with it."

He stood and paced away from her. "What are you trying to say? I was born a necromancer? I'm a *warden,* and until you and the corruption came along, there was no indication of that not being the case." Clenching his fists, he let out a breath and turned to face her again; he had, after all, just promised he would remain calm and listen to what she had to say.

"You weren't born a necromancer; of that I am certain. But I don't think you were born *just* a warden either." She got to her feet and took a step towards him. "Do you know what pennyroyal and brightsbane do?"

"I've spent enough time around Margot to know that pennyroyal is used to end an unwanted pregnancy."

"Yes, but it's not always effective. When you add brightsbane, however ..." She shook her head. "... I've never heard of pregnancy outside of Nonna's stories surviving such a tonic, and it can take the mother almost as readily as it takes the child."

He got a brief glance of the sincerity and concern swimming in her eyes before her gaze fell to her feet.

"Garret," she said delicately and closed her eyes before giving a self-resigned nod and opening them again. "... I think you're a brightling, and I think—I know that not only my father and Nonna knew, but Camille did too. What's more, they knew and they chose to lock that part of your keen away. I don't know why. Maybe they thought by doing so they could avoid what is coming to pass."

The way she said *brightling*, the twist of her mouth and the weight of the word, it reminded him of the moment she had revealed that she was deathborn. Like it held the same severity.

He drew a long, slow breath, trying to still the pounding behind his ears. "And a brightling is?"

"A person who can manipulate and channel the keen of others without having a keen of their own. I've never heard of one being born a warden. In fact, generally they are born keen-less, but I know Evard was doing experiments on bloodlines trying to create a new *breed* of mage. One that would negate his need to wait for someone like me to come along. The timing is right, and the fact that Evard is your father—" She sucked in a hard breath and pressed her hand to chest. "I want to be wrong. I want it to be a string of coincidences and nothing more, but too much lines up. Did Evard ever give an indication that he knew who you were?"

"No. He never treated me any differently to anyone else under his command."

That wasn't a whole truth, and Nea clearly knew it too because one corner of her mouth pulled tight and her right brow inched upwards. "Perhaps he didn't know, or he knows *who* you are and not *what* you are. That would make more sense. After all, he never gave me any indication you existed, and that is the sort of thing he couldn't help but gloat about."

"If you're right and I am a brightling, what does that mean?"

"I honestly don't know. And I could be wrong. Unless you were born at midsummer because that would be too big of a coincidence to—" The humour in her tone faded at the look on his face. "You *were* born at midsummer?"

"A whole month early, according to my grandmother."

She rubbed her fingers along her brow. "We need to see if you can channel the keen of someone other than me, but I think it can wait until we are back home in our realm. It would not be a good idea for Frell to find out the truth. Anyway, we should probably be getting back to the camp."

Head churning with more questions, he fell into an easy step beside her. Occasionally their hands brushed, each touch sending a shimmer of magic dancing over their skin. Unless they figured out a way to stop that from happening, it was going to be hard to hide their woven keens from Frell for much longer.

The darkness around them was taking on that grey quality of night, giving way to day as they walked in the direction of camp. Or at least where they thought camp was. Sound travelled strangely in the wood, and though they headed towards the sounds of the troupe having breakfast, Garret wasn't certain they were going in the right direction until the trees thinned and they stepped out into the circle of wagons.

When Declan spotted them, a wide smile replaced the concern he had been wearing. "Snuck off for a midnight tryst in the forest, did you?"

Nea let out an exasperated groan and stormed past him to the fire where Urden was making a pot of tea.

"If by tryst you mean a battle of wills with an angry ghost, then sure," Garret said.

Zephyr came bounding over and threw her arms around Declan's neck. "See, I told you it was nothing to worry about."

"That you did." He extracted himself from her grip and lightly kissed her temple. "Would you mind giving us a moment?"

She pouted but skipped away towards Nea.

Declan watched her go and then looked back at Garret. "Sounds like you had an interesting night."

"That's an understatement. You found nothing out of the ordinary last night? Didn't hear anything strange?"

Nea had told Garret the screams had woken her and that Frell had tried to force her to drink the tea as well, but she'd refused just as Garret had done. He was thankful for that. He wasn't sure what would have happened in that forest if Nea hadn't arrived when she did.

"Nothing. I had the best sleep of my life; I didn't even realise you and Nea were gone until I came outside this morning and found this." He handed Garret his jacket.

Garret shrugged the jacket on. He couldn't imagine not being able to hear those screams; they had vibrated through his very soul.

"Are you alright, old boy?" Declan gave his shoulder a shake.

Garret shook his head to shift the daze that had settled on him. "Last night was ..." He drew a breath. It had been eye-opening in more ways than one, and he wasn't sure he was ready to discuss it yet and certainly not here at the camp where Frell could easily overhear. "Have you noticed the strange fixation Frell seems to have on Nea?"

"I'm not blind. Even before Nea mentioned it yesterday."

"What did Nea say?"

"She thought Frell was trying to manipulate her."

Garret swore under his breath. "She said nothing to me. If I had known—"

"Nea wasn't sure that *was* the case, and she didn't want to tell you because she was worried it would colour your already suspicious opinion of the troupe. But if Nea's fears are true, then the implications are not good." He ran a hand through his hair. "I tried to get some information out of Zephyr last night, but she was tight-lipped. It is clear she knows something, but I don't know if she's holding back because she wants to or because she has no choice."

"The pair of you seem to be getting quite *close*. Are you sure that's wise given what Nea told you about Frell?" Garret toyed with the scar above his lip.

Declan gave him a sly look. "Just because you're too polite to throw Nea against the closest wall and work out some tension, doesn't mean *I* can't enjoy myself."

"*Declan.*" Garret folded his arms over his chest.

Declan lifted his hands in surrender. "I think for the most part the intentions of the troupe are benign, and Zephyr is a bit of an outcast given she has magic very similar to Frell's. I am not sure how it works, but from what I can gather the leader of the troupe is chosen based on a certain type of keen. Zephyr is forced to hide her keen and there are times she speaks of Frell with a distinct bitterness." He glanced across to where Nea and Zephyr were chatting. "Which is why I believe there is some compulsion keeping her from speaking and not an actual desire for secrecy."

Garret opened his mouth to respond, but Declan cleared his throat and tilted his head towards the flame-haired girl who was coming over with two cups of tea.

"Would you like some tea?"

"No thank you," Declan said.

She turned her gaze on Garret and held out one of the cups. Garret glanced across to where Nea was politely refusing a cup from Frell. He looked back at the girl in front of him. "I'm fine. Thank you."

She frowned but wandered off.

"It's not like you to turn down a cup of tea," Garret said.

Declan chuckled. "Maybe you're finally rubbing off on me, but I found it odd that Frell kept insisting we drink that strange floral tea. At first it was understandable. It was touted as a curative for any nastiness we may have encountered in the forest, but I noticed the more I drank the more it dulled my thoughts."

Dulled his thoughts ... Nea had mentioned her emotions felt numb. But when Garret drank the tea, it didn't seem to affect him. It just tasted vile, and though he'd been told that it would get better it never did. Maybe it was because he was a warden. He was about to ask Declan but Frell came over.

"I am glad to see no real harm befell you in the wood."

"No physical harm at least." He clenched his back teeth together.

"I did you warn you to ignore it, but you had to go running off and be the *hero*. I would have left you to your fate, but Nea had other ideas. She seems to be rather attached to you, which could prove problematic."

"Problematic?" He shared a look with Declan.

"Yes, make no mistake, her importance in what is coming to pass far outweighs yours. Last night proved that she will deliberately put herself in harm's way to protect you, and I can't have that. I will—"

Declan cleared his throat. "I am sure Garret will be more careful in the future, Frell. We wouldn't want to disrespect your *hospitality*."

Her eyes narrowed but she nodded and then walked away.

Declan blew out a breath. "Well, old boy, you've certainly managed to kick the hornets' nest this time."

CHAPTER THIRTEEN

MARGOT

Margot hadn't found the answers she was seeking in the Hartswood library. However, she did find a letter tucked into the back of one Nea's old journals. The note wasn't written in Nea's hand, which was a delicate mix of loops and curves that slanted ever so slightly to right. This hand was tighter, producing neat but thin letters that scrawled across the page like the spindly legs of a spider.

Dearest Nea,

I thought your opinion of me may have been sullied irreparably after our disagreement over the morality of Rembrandt's theories of soul transplantation. I am pleasantly surprised to see that this is not the case. Though I fear I cannot help you regarding the stability of the barrier. I personally have not encountered any thinning here in Osmar, which would suggest that the efforts of your associate are restricted to Beldaren at this stage. However, I cannot understand something like the barrier being restricted to geographical borders. Perhaps the weakening is like a plague that extends exponentially from an epicentre. I shall keep an eye on it in case that is what we are facing.

It does wound me that you do not trust me with your associate's identity, given the troubling nature of their research. I had thought we might be beyond our little game of cat and mouse. Do I sense a reawakening of those passionate debates in the future? I am game if you are. All ripostes aside, if this associate succeeds in tearing the barrier and letting loose the denizens of the Between, then the damage to our world would be irreparable as I am sure you understand. I hope your involvement in the matter is merely theoretical. I would be loath to lose you to some foolhardy experiment involving the very fabric of eternity.

I shall look for this Book of Souls in the Arcanarium at my earliest convenience, though Arcanius Greffon still has not forgiven me for that incident in the phylactery vault. Perhaps you would have better luck with him given that he was all too eager to overlook your involvement in the matter. Come to think of it, you still owe me for that. I shall be more than happy to collect next time you deign to grace The City of Stars.

Ever your faithful debate partner,

Mateus

Nea had once mentioned a necromancer by the name of Mateus. From memory, he was an apprentice at the Arcanarium in Osmar at the same time Nea was there studying. But Nea had obviously cared enough about his opinion to reach out for his aid before Kalhanna. Why had she trusted him when she had retreated from so many others she cared about? She hadn't revealed Evard's identity to him though, so perhaps she was simply after his academic opinion as the letter seemed to imply. It still pressed on the wound Nea's disappearance had left. Had she spent those three years galivanting around Osmar? No, that was just Margot's jealousy talking.

The years Nea had originally spent studying in Osmar were during the time Margot was finishing her own studies at Kalhanna and finding her feet as apprentice to Evard's court physician. She regretted that she hadn't had the time to be off having wild adventures with Nea. If she had, then maybe things would be different. Maybe Evard would never have encountered Nea, and his grand plan would still be a fairy tale well beyond his reach.

But no. Nea had met Leith whilst she was in Osmar, and Evard had been looking for an arcane advisor. A role that was almost purpose built for Nea. It was a whole mess of linked coincidences that made Margot question her stance on destiny. She didn't want to believe that someone or something was out there pulling strings and moving parts to get all the players in the places they needed to be. That certain events couldn't be avoided no matter how hard you tried or what choices you made. If that was the case, then what was the point of everything? Why allow autonomous choice at all?

With a huff, she folded the letter and tucked it neatly in the back of the journal. She hadn't found the journal in the library; it had been wedged into the hidey-hole in Nea's old closet. Garret's niece, Nora, now inhabited the room. She'd watched with avid curiosity from her perch on the bed while Margot thumbed and prodded the decorative trim looking for the secret switch that opened the compartment. Once she'd got it open, she found a collection of old letters, two journals, and other various items that Margot assumed held sentimental value given she couldn't feel any residual magic clinging to them. She'd taken the journals and returned the rest to the hole.

"You've been awfully quiet," Penny said, drawing Margot's attention to where she sat on the other side of their small fire.

"Just trying to get my head around being the puppet of some divine force with no real autonomy."

"And here I thought Nea was the philosophical one," Emil said as he pulled the lit end of the stick he was holding out of the fire and waved it to douse the flames, leaving a glowing coal at the tip.

"We always have autonomy, Margot ... Well, unless someone is tampering with our minds and using us as a literal puppet, but I can assure you that is not the case currently." Penny gave her a wry grin. "You've read that letter several times now. Who is it from?"

"Mateus."

Penny's dark brows lifted. "I wasn't aware that you knew Mateus."

"I don't. It's a letter he wrote to Nea."

Penny chuckled. "Is it a naughty letter? Do you need my help explaining some of the *positions*? I can use Emil to demonstrate."

Emil stuck the end of the stick back into the fire and cleared his throat. "I am sure that won't be necessary."

"It's not *that* kind of letter. She asked for his opinion on the barrier and for his help securing a certain book. Why would you think it was a naughty letter? Nea's not really the type."

"True. But Mateus ..." She drew a long breath and grinned. "... is an exquisite example of human beauty. Not only that, but he is also the youngest in a line of Osmarian necromancers who can trace their origins back to before the Bright War. You must know that necromancers are very picky about their bloodlines. It only stands to reason that he and Nea would have made a good match. Why do you think she was sent to Osmar for study in the first place?"

"Nonna wouldn't do that to Nea."

Penny shrugged. "Who knows what schemes Abigail has churning in that rabbit warren of a mind. Care to share why a simple letter has you questioning the meaning of *destiny* and your place in it?"

"It's not just the letter. It's everything leading up until now. I need Nea here to explain it all. She knows more than she is letting on. This is enough to tell us that." She held up one of the journals. The other was sealed by some kind of enchantment, and she hadn't been able to open it let alone read its contents.

"But good luck getting her to tell you. Nea can be just as bad as Nonna and Niall at keeping secrets," Emil said. "If she was more open about everything, then we wouldn't be in this mess in the first place."

"Nea kept it secret because she didn't want to pull everyone she loved down with her," Penny said. "She was committing high treason right under all our noses, and only let Francesca and Tobias in because she needed to access the repository at Kalhanna. By then,

Evard's plans were too far in motion to stop. That was also right around the time she told Leith the truth about his father, and we all know how he took that."

"Of course he took his father's side. Nea had no ironclad evidence against Evard."

Penny's mouth twisted into a smirk. "Say that again, Emil."

"Of course he took his father's side?"

"I think she means the part about Nea having no real evidence against Evard," Margot said softly. "And every time she tried to hint at it, no one took her seriously. Evard was charismatic and clever. None of us noticed the danger until it was too late. I think even Nea thought she could redeem him before the purge."

They fell into silence after that. The fire between them occasionally sent little showers of embers into the air with a crackle and pop. Eventually Emil moved to his sleeping roll and Penny to hers a short time after, leaving Margot alone with her thoughts. She pulled the box from her bag and rolled it in her hands, letting the pink-gold chains catch the light of the fire. She desperately wished it would tell her its secrets, but since they had left Hartswood, it had been stubbornly silent.

The fastest way to reach Warren was to enter the fenlands at Fengate. The only alternative was to secure a boat somewhere along the coast and enter the Fenlands from the south, but that could add at least another week to their journey.

As they reached the outskirts of Fengate, however, Margot started to wonder if they had made the right choice. The farmsteads along the main road were all silent, several nothing more than blackened ruins. The few people they passed refused to make eye contact or dropped what they were doing and hurried away out of sight.

The state of the town proper made Margot's heart sink. It was a shallow reflection of its former self. Charred husks of buildings stood like sentinels among their boarded-up brethren. Notices had been nailed to the sides of those buildings that still stood. The signs wore angry red letters condemning mages living outside the colleges and imploring their keen-less neighbours to turn them in. Margot swallowed. Had this been Evard's intention from the very beginning? To force a schism between keen-less and mages and destroy the world while they were all distracted?

She glanced sideways at Penny, who nodded grimly towards the only structure that didn't look abandoned: The Rowdy Badger. Thin light spilled out onto the darkening street from the grimy windows, but the usual cacophony of laughter and song that drifted from the establishment was silent. A stark contrast to the last time Margot had been here with Garret.

"Are you sure it's wise for us to go in there?" she asked.

"We don't have much choice. It will be dark soon, and I don't fancy navigating the fenlands at night," Penny replied.

"We'll be careful. Worst case we can always head back to the farmland and stay at one of those abandoned homesteads," Emil said.

Margot chewed her thumbnail. "Maybe we should just do that."

"And miss out on a chance at information? There's a reason Garret frequented places like this, and it wasn't because he enjoyed the *atmosphere*." Emil handed the reins of his horse to the stable boy, who had emerged from the back of the tavern. "Don't bed her down yet. We might not be staying," he said as he slipped the boy a few coins.

Margot and Penny handed the reins of their horses over also and followed Emil into the tavern.

Inside was warm and bright and not completely devoid of life. Groups of people sat around the scarred tables talking quietly or gambling. It certainly had none of the usual raucous charm, but there was an undercurrent of mirth that was not present outside. As the door swung shut behind Margot, Penny, and Emil, several heads turned to stare warily in their direction. Margot lifted her hand and cleared her throat, but Penny grabbed her fingers and led her with purpose towards the bar, ignoring the looks from the locals and seemingly oblivious to the three men who had stood and touched the hilts of their swords.

When they reached the bar, Penny dropped a few coins on the counter and leant against it as she waved to the barkeeper. Emil slid in next to Margot, his back against the bar as he kept his eyes on the men with swords.

"Hey," Penny called down counter. "What's a girl got to do to get a drink—" A meaty hand slammed onto the wood beside Penny, and her attention snapped to it. She turned slowly until she was facing its owner and flicked her hair over her shoulder. "Can I help you?"

"You and your little friend need to leave." He sniffed in Margot's direction. "We don't want your *kind* here."

Margot felt the heavy fingers of suppression roll down her spine. *Warden.* She didn't recognise him.

"Easy now. We're not looking for trouble," Emil said carefully as he stepped around Margot to place himself next to Penny. "We just need a warm meal and a room for the night, then we'll be on our way."

"They can't stay here." The warden pointed a thick finger at Penny and Margot in turn. "I'm sure you saw the signs on your way in."

"You're a warden," Emil said as he scratched the underside of his chin. "So, you know by now that my friend here is a healer." He titled his head towards Margot. "And by my count there are at least four people in this room who are in need of her services ... but you're still going to chase her away?"

"They can't stay here!" the warden said again and touched his sword.

"No need for that." Emil scooped up Penny's coins and handed them to her. "Come on. It's obvious the king has brainwashed these good people."

"He didn't brainwash 'em; he slaughtered 'em. Any who were found to be harbouring a mage," one of the other men said.

A telling smile twitched across the corners of Emil's mouth and he nodded as he turned towards the man who had spoken. "Yeah, he slaughtered them. He did the same to Dunhold. He's been doing it since he purged Kalhanna, but no one has had the stones to stand up and say *enough*. So, he'll keep doing it until all of Beldaren is completely under his heel, and you'll only have yourselves to blame." He guided Margot and Penny towards the door.

"Hold up, Emil." Another warden, this one with short blond hair and a star-shaped scar on the back of his hand, blocked the door. "Gerald is an opinionated fool who doesn't speak for everyone in this room."

"Let them go, Dale. They're not welcome here," Gerald growled.

"Fuck off back to your corner to brood, Gerald," Dale said before turning his attention to Emil again. "I heard you disappeared into the mountains with Garret. What are you doing in Fengate?"

A sharp intake of breath drew Margot's attention to Gerald, who stopped and spun to face them. "Conspirators of the traitor are to be taken into custody," he growled, his hand moving to the hilt of his sword again.

Dale rubbed a hand over his face. "Excuse me a moment." He stepped around the three of them and vaulted over a table, his boot landing squarely in the centre of Gerald's chest.

The tension in the room snapped like a string under too much pressure. Gerald's friends rushed forward to pull Dale off him. Emil cracked his knuckles and joined the fray, throwing a punch into the jaw of one of the men holding Dale that made Margot's teeth ache in sympathy.

Margot and Penny pressed themselves into a corner as several other patrons scrambled to join the fight. Tables were overturned and chairs went flying.

"Bright Mother be damned," Penny said as she leapt onto the bar. "Alright, you lot, that's enough!" Her keen, normally smooth and seductive, slammed down as a crushing compulsion.

Everyone stopped immediately and stared at her.

"Right. If you are quite done exchanging blows, perhaps we can clean up this mess and get back to our evening in as civilised a manner as you backwater yokels are capable of."

Margot wasn't sure insulting them all was a good idea, but as Penny spoke, she slowly decreased the weight of her keen and no one seemed to protest the remark. They sheepishly went about righting the room. Even the wardens joined in, none of whom had tried to suppress her, but she had snapped the compulsion down so quickly. Maybe they hadn't had time to react.

As Penny climbed off the bar, Margot noted that the mark on her palm was glowing softly. She closed her fingers over it and turned a wide smile to the barkeeper. "Now how about we try this again. My friends and I would like a meal and a room." She slid her coins back onto the bar and added a few more to the pile. "I am sure this should be sufficient to compensate you for the inconvenience of housing fugitives ... Oh and ..." Her keen stirred again, this time in sensual fingers that smoothed along Margot's spine.

The barkeep leant forward as Penny beckoned him with a curl of her finger. She whispered something in his ear, her magic giving one last flare before settling again.

Emil joined them just as the barkeeper was setting several mugs of dark ale in front of Penny. He touched his fingers to the split in his lip and winced. "Did you have to rattle everyone's skulls so savagely, Pen?"

She took a gulp of her drink and shrugged. "It worked, didn't it?"

"Sure, but I think I'm going to have a headache for days."

"You'll live." Dale clapped Emil on the shoulder as he joined them. "Nice work. You just reminded me why I need to be wary of mind mages. Shame they don't always come in such a pretty package."

Penny's smile was sly as she took another sip from her mug. "I take it you disposed of the trash?" She tilted her head towards the vacant table Gerald and his friends had been occupying.

Dale frowned. "Gerald has always been a bit of a thug, but he's mostly harmless. The breakdown of the order is hitting him harder than he's letting on."

"Breakdown?" Margot asked.

He nodded. "It's been happening since the purge. A shift here, a change in rank there. Garret was doing his best to keep things together in the capital and the rest of us were happy to follow his lead, but then he up and deserted and the king has labelled him a traitor. Doesn't make sense to me; Garret's not the type to desert without a fucking good reason."

"No, he's not." Margot nodded. "Thank you for stepping in. We didn't have to stay."

"You're welcome," he grunted.

"I'm Margot, and this is Penny. You seem to know Emil already."

"Dale," he said, picking up the cup the barkeeper set down for him and tilting it in a small salute before drinking deeply.

"Should we expect more trouble?" Emil asked, beckoning them to follow him to Gerald's vacated table.

Dale shook his head. "I doubt it. The patrols stopped coming through a month back. Though if you're worried about Gerald, you needn't be. He'll scamper off and lick his wounds then be just as ornery tomorrow." He settled into a seat and gave Margot a pointed look. "Emil was right. There's a few people who could use the services of a healer."

She glanced around the room and noted serval patrons watching her. "Right. If you'll excuse me."

Margot spent the rest of the evening tending to the sick and injured. Most had patched themselves up with crude remedies that did just as much bad as they did good. The town healer had been dragged off when Evard had first attacked. No one seemed to know what Evard was looking for, but occasionally someone would flick a look in Penny's direction. What was more distressing was the talk of a pit of bodies behind the capital—bodies that refused to stay dead.

CHAPTER FOURTEEN

HARVEY

Harvey landed a solid strike, causing his opponent to stagger backwards and rub the centre of his chest.

"Come on. You can do better than that," Harvey said, shifting his weight onto his back foot and lifting his hand to beckon the soldier forward again.

"Alright, let's call it there," Trenton's voice sounded over the grunts and thuds of the sparring men. "Bryce, a word." He waved Harvey over as the others started to disband.

"I know that was sloppy. I—"

"Sloppy? You've got more skill than some soldiers who've been training for decades." He held out a waterskin.

Harvey took a long drink before tipping some onto his hand and splashing his face.

"I'm pleased that you have decided to give the guard a chance. However, you're going to have to choose whether you keep working with Reg or join the guard completely. I gave you a week to figure it out, but now I need your answer."

Harvey frowned and scratched the scruff under his chin. The guard felt like home—the steady routine, the aches in places he didn't know could ache. But he also liked working with Reg. Still, with Leon due in the next day or two, a position on the guard would give him more opportunities to gather information. "Alright." He held his hand out. "I'll officially join the guard."

Trenton shook his hand firmly. "Pleased to have you. You can move your things to the barracks as soon as you're ready. Now, if you'll excuse me." He gave Harvey a final nod then left.

"Hello, Bryce. I've a got a message for you."

Harvey turned to the girl with a messenger bird tucked in the crook of her arm.

She gave him a bright smile and held out a letter. "It's from your uncle in Little Brook."

"Thanks."

With a curt nod, she skipped away again.

Harvey slid his finger under the seal and unfolded the parchment. Two small discs of pinkish metal fell onto his open palm. At first it appeared to be just as the girl had said—a message from his uncle in Little Brook—but as Harvey's eyes drifted over the words, they shifted, the letters seeming to rearrange themselves until they said:

Harvey,

You must avoid contact with Catriona at all costs. If that is not possible, these charms should offer some protection. You and Molly are to keep one on you at all times. They will block her ability to access your mind. But be careful.

Sincerely,

Niall

P.S: I've enchanted the parchment so only you can read this, but please ensure you burn it. If a warden were to get hold of it, your cover would be blown.

"Right." He refolded the letter and slipped it into his pocket along with the metal discs, and then went off to find Molly.

She was in the garden with one of the other maids. Her attention snapped to him as he approached. She'd always been annoyingly alert. He gave her a small wave. "Hi, Tess, do you have a minute to talk? I've decided to take Trenton up on his offer to join the guard."

Molly sat back on her heels and rubbed her fingers on the bottom of her apron. "Are you sure that's wise?"

The maid beside Molly stood, lifting her basket of produce. "I'll meet you inside, Tess." She gave Harvey a nod as she moved away.

"It feels right, Tess, and it's a second chance at what I always wanted," he said. Then when he was sure the maid was gone, he added softly, "With Leon arriving soon, it will put me in a good place to get closer to him."

"You need to be careful. But you didn't just come to tell me you joined the guard. You have had word from Del Harol, haven't you?"

He nodded and pulled one of the pink metal discs out of his pocket. "You need to keep this on you at all times. Stitch it into the lining of your clothes if necessary. It will protect your mind from Catriona."

Molly slid the coin away out of sight. "Do you really want to rely on something like this? Maybe we should just cut our losses now."

"I want to know why Leon and Catriona are coming here. I didn't tell you, but I spoke with Amelia—"

"She's insane and manipulative, Harv. You can't believe a single word out of her mouth."

"I know. But ..." His argument died on his lips. Molly was right. He'd been warned about Amelia's nature ... and yet, there was something that told him maybe she was just as much a victim of circumstance as the rest of them. "Look, Mol, if you want to leave you can. We can come up with some story about you needing to go help *Uncle Nevil* or something, but I want to know what Evard plans to do with Amelia. I think we *need* to know." He kept his voice to a whisper.

"I'm not going to leave you here alone, but you need to promise me that we'll go at the first sign of real trouble."

He drew a long breath as she studied his face, waiting for his answer. "Alright. I promise."

All the staff had been gathered in the main courtyard of the fort to await the arrival of Leon and Catriona. Harvey straightened the collar of his new guard uniform and then dipped his hand into his pocket to press against the charmed coin Niall had sent him. He hoped it worked.

Trenton gave a signal, and as one the retinue snapped to attention.

Leon rode through the gate first; he had traded his old bay gelding for a gleaming sand-coloured warhorse. Harvey noted the warden crest which covered the front of Leon's shining breastplate. The wardens weren't generally the sort for pomp and ceremony. Even the commanders tended to stick to dark leather armour with little embellishment or insignia. Harvey bit back his chuckle at the thought of what Garret would make of Leon's spectacle.

Behind Leon, came Catriona, her sapphire silk skirt fanned out over the horse's rump. She leant sideways and said something to the man riding beside her. Harvey didn't recognise him. He looked to be in his late thirties, tall and thin with dark shadows under his eyes, but his hair was a sleek sheet of silver. *Necromancer.*

The group stopped at the foot of the stairs that led into the fort and Leon dismounted. He cleared his throat and looked pointedly at the two young stable hands. One leapt forward and took the reins of the horse and led it away. Leon helped Catriona down, his hands lingering on her waist as he whispered something in her ear that brought a wicked smile to the corner of her red-painted lips.

When the other horses had been taken away, Leon, Catriona, and the necromancer took up position at the top of the stairs, and Harvey chanced a look in Molly's direction. She swallowed and gave him a small smile.

"What a delightful welcome." Leon's voice rang out. "You may be wondering why the king has chosen to send three of his most prized advisors to this misbegotten place at the foot of the mountains."

If Leon was trying for Evard's commanding charisma, he was falling short and just sounding like the pretentious prick he was.

"Many of you were present for the battle in which we liberated this fort from the … *filth* that had called it home."

Harvey bit the inside of his cheek.

"I wish to commend those of you who fought on that fateful day. Without you, we would not be as close as we are to crushing the dregs of the foolish resistance. Your king wants a bright future for all his people, and this fort is to become the first beacon of that future." With a flourish, he turned on his heel and marched through the doors. Catriona and the necromancer followed him without a word.

"Well, that was something," Harvey muttered as Trenton dismissed them.

"I'll say. His failure to catch one little mage doesn't seem to have dampened his inflated self-importance," Micha, the guard to his left, said with a short chuckle.

"He was hunting a mage?" Harvey knew Leon had been hunting Nea, but Bryce didn't. "I didn't know he was a warden."

"Because he's not," another guard by the name of Callie said. "But the king has still given him command of warden garrison in the capitol."

"And how do the wardens feel about that?"

Callie shrugged. "I imagine they aren't too impressed with the idea, but what can they do? The order has signed themselves over to the king, and he has declared Leon commander … So it shall be." A wicked smirk rolled across her mouth. "Still, I wouldn't mind seeing him taken down a peg or two, and I'd sure like to be there when he finally corners that mage. I saw what she did to Harold."

"What sort of mage is she?"

"They reckon she's a necromancer, but if she is, she's not a normal one," Micha piped up. "I doubt Leon will have much luck finding her anyway. It took nearly three years to hunt her down, and then rumour has it that Warden Commander Garret found her by accident. Just stumbled upon her in the middle of the road, and then she—"

"Then she used her feminine charms on him and she's the reason he turned traitor." Callie batted her eyelashes and laughed. "You know better than to listen to crazy rumours, Micha."

Harvey grinned. There might be a *little* bit of truth to that rumour, but Nea certainly wasn't the sole reason for Garret's desertion. He'd already been on that road long before Nea came along.

"Why else would he betray the king?" Micha asked. "I met him once, you know? He was an honourable man. There wouldn't be much that would cause him to desert."

Callie planted her hands on her hips. "So, you're saying that somewhere out there is a woman who is just waiting to corrupt you and force you to forget your honour and your oath to king and country?"

"Now come on, Callie. That's not what I said, and I didn't say I believed the rumours. Just it seemed odd that someone like the commander would suddenly throw everything away like that ... Maybe there was magic involved. I've heard of mages who can read your thoughts and plant ideas in your head."

"Yeah, but she's a necromancer. They can't do that," Callie said.

Harvey scratched his chin. "So, if Leon is supposed to be hunting this mage, why is he here now?"

Micah licked his lip. "Who knows, but supposedly Hartswood is not far from here."

"Hartswood?" Harvey asked.

"Yeah, it's the grey-hairs' sanctuary. Necromancers are weird even for mages. They don't congregate in those fancy colleges, and their sanctuaries are always hidden by magic—only able to be found by those who have been *invited*." Micha's tone became hushed, like he was telling a tale at a fireside.

Callie rolled her eyes. "You and your stories, Micha. Of course necromancers like to keep to themselves. Could you imagine all the people who would turn up on their doorstep wanting to speak to their dead loved ones? Healers get that too—people banging down their door for this treatment or that. If they'd taken the same precaution as necromancers, maybe Kalhanna would still be standing."

The mention of Kalhanna brought a heaviness over the group. Callie kicked a stone by the toe of her boot and swallowed.

"We'd best get back to it," Micha said. "Don't want to get caught slacking off with Leon around."

No, they did not. Leon had always been an arse, but something over the last year had changed him. It had happened slowly at first, but since Nea's emergence, he had become bloodthirsty and cruel— an almost perfect copy of Evard.

CHAPTER FIFTEEN

GARRET

They finally reached a larger city several days after the incident with the ghost in the forest. They hadn't had a chance to discuss what had happened further, and with each passing day, Nea seemed to be growing more distant, like she was reverting to the person she had been when he encountered her on that road outside Little Brook. Except it was more than that. Declan had mentioned she had been unfocused and when pressed, she had insisted that she was fine; that she was just tired due to the headaches she had been having, but there was no need to fuss over her.

Garret glanced sideways at Wade. He'd like to ask him about it, but a small part of him wasn't sure how much he could trust any of the Nundle. The sooner they parted ways, the better.

The wagons rolled through the town gates, and children came running out as they had at every other village they had passed through. Above the heads of the children, Garret caught sight of Rourke. He nodded once to Garret then disappeared into the shadows.

The troupe finally stopped in the large field on the other side of town, and the Nundle got to work setting up the camp.

"I implore you to reconsider, Frell." Wade's voice stopped Garret as he was carrying a crate past the back of Frell's wagon.

"You know why it must be done," Frell said coolly.

"No, I know why you *think* it must be done, and I never agreed to this. You could have just asked her for her help instead of taking away her free will."

"She's a tool created for a specific purpose. She has no real free will, and you know that," Frell spat.

"You cling to that theory because it suits your need. She's a *person,* Frell, not a tool for you to abuse because you signed a contract in your own blood eons before she was born." Something thumped against the side of the wagon. Wade's fist?

"You don't have to agree with me, Darius, but let me make myself abundantly clear. If you or that little upstart Zephyr stand in my way, I will banish you both beyond the Sorrow Wood. Is that understood?"

"Yes, Frell." The door of the wagon creaked open, and Garret backed away out of sight.

Wade came down the stairs and glanced left then right before walking with purpose across the field to his own wagon. Garret placed the crate down and then strode after him. He waited for Wade to go inside then knocked on the door.

A curse sounded and the door was wrenched open. "I'm not in the"—Wade's golden eyebrows lifted as he spotted Garret—"mood."

"What are Frell's plans with Nea?"

Wade licked his lips and started to close the door. "I'm busy, Garret. Can you come back later?"

"No." Garret held the door open. "I really can't."

"Bright confound it. Get inside before you draw too much attention to yourself." Wade stepped back and then latched the door behind Garret after he'd entered the wagon.

Garret settled in Wade's chair as Wade propped himself on the end of the bed and folded his arms.

"I want the truth. What does Frell plan on doing with Nea?"

"She wants Nea to release the Master of Shadows."

"Nea would never agree to that."

"Frell thinks she can force Nea to do her bidding." He drew a breath. "But she's had to resort to drastic measures because Nea is too strong for her to control."

Garret clenched his fists. "What sort of drastic measures?"

"Frell has used an enchantment on her, one that will slowly take away everything that makes her *Nea* and leave a blank slate in its wake."

"A blank slate?" It occurred to Garret that he hadn't seen Nea since they arrived in town several hours ago. "Where is Nea now?"

Wade twisted his hands. "Frell took her."

Garret leapt to his feet, hitting his head against the ceiling. "Took her where?" he growled.

"I don't know, but Zephyr—"

He didn't wait for Wade to finish. He wrenched the door open and dashed down the stairs.

When he opened the door of Zephyr's wagon, he was confronted with the sight of Declan naked amongst the mountain of pillows on the bed with Zephyr draped over him. She shifted, and the sheet of her hair slipped away to reveal more of her bare skin. Garret cleared his throat and averted his eyes.

Zephyr chuckled. "Come to join us, have you?"

"No, I'm looking for Nea."

"Nea? I haven't seen her." Guilt quivered on the edges of Zephyr voice. Her feet hit the floor, the boards creaking under them. Garret chanced a look at her and found she had wrapped a blanket around her chest to cover her form.

"Wade told me you might know where Frell has taken her," he said.

"Frell took Nea?" Declan jumped up and pulled his pants on.

They both levelled their gazes on Zephyr, and she let out a rough breath. "She needed to get Nea away from the pair of you. The enchantment wouldn't stick while you were there reminding Nea of who she was and why she was here." She dropped onto the edge of the bed. "She won't hurt Nea. She *needs* her. I'm sorry. I didn't want any part of it, but Frell ..."

"Threatened you," Garret said.

Declan moved over and placed a hand on Zephyr's shoulder.

"I'm sorry. I thought it would be easy, but then I got to know Nea and ... Actually, it doesn't matter how I feel about Nea. It's not right to do that to a person."

"Do you know where Nea is now?" Garret asked.

"No, but I know where you can start looking. There is a warehouse in town that the troupe use. She may have stashed Nea there." She twisted her hair around her fingers. "When you do find Nea, I suggest you don't bring her back here. There's a tavern in town called The Ogre's Footprint. It's one of the last places Frell would go, but Rourke will probably be there. I know he's been shadowing the troupe."

"How do I get to this warehouse?"

They followed Zephyr's directions to the warehouse. Two Nundle were lounging against the wall out front. Garret placed a hand against Declan's chest and forced him into the shadows.

"What now?" Declan asked.

"We need a distraction."

Declan rubbed his fingers over his chin then grinned. "One distraction coming up." He stepped brazenly out of cover and strode towards the guards. "Good afternoon, gents."

"You're not supposed to be here," one of them said, stepping forward.

"I guess I got turned around. New city and all that." He lifted his hands and wind howled down the alley behind Garret. It ripped towards the front of the warehouse, hitting the two men square in the chest and throwing them against the wall with a bone-jolting crack. Neither of them stirred.

Garret joined Declan as they stepped over the unconscious bodies and into the warehouse.

"Nea?" Declan called. "Are you in here?"

"If Frell—" Garret stopped dead. An arm was hanging over the edge of a blanket-covered table to the side of the room. The pale silver marks that marred the skin seemed to shine in the dim light. He hurried over and threw the blanket back. Nea's dark lashes were resting against her cheeks, her chest barely rising and falling.

"Nea!" Declan joined him beside the table and placed his fingers against her pulse. "She's still alive." He took hold of her shoulder and gave it a gentle shake. "Now is not the time for a nap, my lovely."

Garret had seen this before. When he'd first met Nea and asked her to investigate Declan's room, she had fallen into a sleep they could not wake her from, one that almost convinced him she was dead. "I don't think that's going to work."

"We have to do something. If Frell finds us here ..." Declan gave Nea another shake. "Come on."

"Let's get her somewhere safe. Last time she fell into a sleep like this, it took hours for her to wake." Garret nudged Declan out of the way and scooped Nea up. "We'll take her to that tavern Zephyr mentioned." He shifted her weight so she was easier to carry then headed for the door.

"Garret, what if Frell succeeded? What if she doesn't wake up?"

She had to. They needed her—he needed her.

The second they entered The Ogre's Footprint, Garret saw Rourke. He was sitting on his own at a table in the back corner. The other patrons were giving him a wide berth. He waved Garret and Declan over, took one look at Nea's unconscious form, and led them to a private room in the back.

"Lay her down there."

He indicated the bed, and Garret complied.

"What happened?"

"Frell did something to her," Declan said, wringing his hands together.

"Wade said Frell needed to make her a blank slate so she could use her to free the Master of Shadows." Garret paced to the window.

Rourke sucked a breath through his teeth. "Then there's no time to waste." He dragged a chair over to the bed. "Sit."

"Sit?" Garret asked.

"If you want to save her, you're going to have to do exactly as I say."

Garret sat as instructed, and Rourke took hold of Nea's hand. He laced her cold fingers with Garret's then placed his own hand on top. "Frell has trapped her in a prison in her own mind. You'll have to find her and break her free. I just hope we're not too late."

"Wait—" Garret didn't get a chance to finish what he was saying before the colour drained from the world and he landed on his back in a grassy field. An apple tree stretched above him and perched in its branches, watching him, was a young girl. She was around Nora's age; her feet were bare, and her storm-grey hair was a wild mess under a crown of yellow flowers. She smiled widely and then leapt from the tree, landing next to him as nimbly as a cat.

"You're not supposed to be here, are you?" Her violet eyes glittered as she tilted her head to regard him.

"That all depends." He watched her as she circled him.

"Who are you? Are you a knight here to save the princess? She is perfectly capable of saving herself, you know?"

"Normally I would agree with you, but this time she needs help."

She stopped in front of him again, her eyes narrowing. "You didn't answer my question."

He almost laughed then. From the look and her tone, there was no doubt this girl had grown up to be the Nea he knew. "I am here to break the enchantment that has Nea trapped. My ... the grown up Nea."

She pressed her lip between her teeth. "You haven't revealed your name; how can I decide if you're a friend if you don't tell me your name?"

In the stories Aveline had told him and Declan when they were younger, names held power in certain realms and giving them freely was often a mistake. "You haven't told me your name either."

"But that's not fair. You know my name already—you came here to find me."

"How do I know you're really Nea though? You might have been sent to trick me."

A warm smile he'd only seen a handful of times on adult Nea's face curved the corners of the girl's mouth. "That would be a grand story. The hero tricked by the very being he came to save. I'm not here to mislead you though." She tilted her head again. "You don't have to tell me your name. I already know it because you will be important to me when I am her."

The words gave him pause. Nea was certainly becoming important to him, but was this version of her implying that his Nea felt the same way?

A slow smile curved across the girl's lips again as she studied him, most likely waiting for him to piece everything together as her adult counterpart would.

He shook his head. There would be time to wonder about what it meant later. Right now he needed to find Nea. "So, are you going to tell me how to find her?"

"I'm going to show you. The witch was very clever; she tried to change the memories to convince your Nea to work with her, but Nea is far smarter than that. The witch's honied words and altered dreams were no more effective than the bully king's brutality." She walked towards a door in the trunk of the apple tree that hadn't been there before. "When she realised that Nea wouldn't submit, she took all the important memories and locked them away. But she went too far." She placed her hand on the doorknob.

"What do you mean she went too far?"

"In her haste to gain control, she grew careless and took away ... *everything*. That's why your Nea is dying."

Garret swallowed. "Nea is dying?"

"You can still save her, but I don't know if you are willing to pay the price. And besides, she can't be saved until the witch's spell is broken." She twisted the knob and the door opened to reveal a misty path.

Garret followed her across the threshold and found himself in a bedroom. Two young girls were lying on the bed. A pair of mage lights danced above them, one soft green and the other lilac.

"... and then as the knight lay dying, the sky above him opened and the rain began to fall." One of the girls lifted her hands and made the action of rain falling. "And a woman came to his side. She was robed in the golden light that follows a storm, her hair silver spun from starlight. She took the knight into her arms and asked him his one regret—"

"He regretted that he let his sister choose the bedtime story again." The second girl sat up, her blonde curls reflecting the mage light. "Nea, this story is awful. It doesn't have a happy ending."

"A story doesn't have to have a happy ending to be good. But how do you know this version doesn't end happily?" Nea sat and folded her arms.

Margot pursed her lips. "Because it's the story of the first warden, and everyone knows that it doesn't end well for him. The Bright Mother heals him, makes him swear to serve her, and then after all of that doesn't even resurrect his one true love. The only person it ends well for is the Bright Mother."

Nea let out a laugh. "Oh, Margot ... Fine, you choose the story, but I'll tell it."

"I want the story of Nethara and Feralyn."

Nea made a face. "But—"

"You said I could choose."

"Fine." Nea flopped back on the bed and Margot joined her. "Once long ago, when the Bright Mother still roamed the realm of men, there lived a hunter named Nethara ..."

A door opened in the wall across from Garret, and the young Nea beside him slipped her hand into his. "We should move on. Unless you want to stay and hear the story?"

Garret shook his head. "Why are we here?"

"This was the first memory the witch tried to warp. She wanted to take away Nea's love for Margot, but though they aren't connected by blood, they are truly sisters. And love, though capable of great destruction itself, is a terribly hard thing to destroy." She led Garret through the door, and they emerged into the room of reflection at Del Harol.

The Nea here was older again, probably around eleven or twelve. She was standing in the pool at the foot of the portal archway, her hands and one cheek pressed against the stones as though she was listening for something.

"Nea, for the thousandth time, leave the portal alone. It's dead," High Mage Niall's voice said from behind Garret.

"No, it's not, Father. I know dead things, and the portal is not dead. It's just ... sleeping."

A smile quirked the corner of Garret's mouth.

"This time the witch tried to twist Nea's innate curiosity. But by its very nature curiosity is a slippery thing, and Nea's more so than most," the Nea beside Garret said.

"Just leave it alone please and come here," Niall said.

Nea pushed off the portal and splashed across the pool to her father.

"Here, Warren left this with Nonna last time he visited. He said you might find it *enlightening*." He handed her a scuffed journal, one that Garret recognised.

"Whose journal is it?" Nea asked.

"A necromancer by the name of Samson."

Nea thumbed through the book. "Did Warren say why I would find it enlightening?"

"No. But you know what Warren is like."

Another door opened and Garret started heading towards it.

"Wait. We're getting closer, but the next few memories could prove difficult to witness. The witch changed tactics and tried to use the darker moments from your Nea's past," the Nea beside him said. "You may see things that your Nea would rather you didn't"

"I have no choice but to move forward."

"I know. But I wanted to warn you regardless. Your Nea will understand why you had to, but that doesn't mean it won't hurt," she said softly before tugging him toward the door.

They entered another bedroom. This one was decadent. The bed had green silk curtains, and lying on it, her bare back to them, was Nea. She sat, the ends of her hair dancing above the purple birthmark on her hip. Garret had seen that birthmark before on the other deathborn they had encountered, but he'd never seen Nea's. He averted his gaze and swallowed as she slid from the bed.

The young Nea beside him chuckled. "She's not modest. She won't care if you have a little look."

"What's bothering you?" a familiar voice said from the bed, and Garret's attention snapped to Leith as he sat.

Nea had pulled her clothes on and was resting against the desk, watching Leith.

"If it's Father, I told him—"

"It doesn't matter what you tell him. He's become ... unhinged. I can't believe that you don't see it." She ran a hand through her hair.

"He's been a bit *intense* of late sure. But, Nea, you can't expect me to believe that he is actually capable of—"

"Francesca—"

"Is using you to push her own agenda. Can't you see that? She has planted these ridiculous ideas about Father in your head so you'll take her side. I know my father."

One corner of Nea's mouth tightened. "I really don't think you do, and if you think that I would let someone else manipulate me then you really don't know me either." She started for the door.

"Nea, wait." Leith grabbed her wrist as she reached for the handle. "I'm sorry. There's just so much going on, and Father wants me to go to Osmar to meet Catriona, but I don't want that. I want—"

"You should go."

The colour drained from Leith's face. "What?"

"It is clear that no matter what I say you will choose to believe your father rather than myself. But regardless, you should go to Osmar." She shook her hand free of Leith's.

"But ..." Leith looked at his fingers.

Nea's features softened as she watched him. "Leith ..." She touched his cheek and pressed a soft kiss to his lips. "We both knew from the start that this was—"

"But I love you."

She flinched as though the words had struck her.

"And you love me."

Her hands found the door handle behind her and she shook her head. "I'm sorry, but I don't know that I do." After wrenching the door open, she raced out into the hallway.

Garret followed her and found himself in a study lit by the glow of the fire crackling in the hearth and one floating lilac mage light. Nea was at the desk, a book in front of her and her mouth a grim line. The door opened and she glanced up. She swallowed and stood. Garret turned to see who had entered the room: Evard.

"How goes the study, my dear? Any breakthroughs I should know about?"

Nea stood and tucked the book under her arm.

"You did find something, didn't you?"

Her fingers tightened ever so slightly on the tome. "Nothing of consequence."

"You have always been an appalling liar." He moved forward and held his hand out. "Give me the book."

Nea's gaze darted to the door before returning to Evard.

"You're not a fool. You know you won't make it to that door." Steel hid beneath the calm, velvety tone of his voice. "Give. Me. The. BOOK!"

Nea flinched. "You want the book?" She started to hold it out towards him then drew a deep breath and hurled it into the hearth.

Evard let out a roar and charged for the fire. He snatched the tome from the flames and threw it on the floor, stamping it out with his foot. Nea made a dash for the door, but Evard grabbed the back of her shirt and slammed her against the wall. Garret clenched his fist and started forward, but a small hand on his arm stopped him.

"We're in Nea's memory remember? You can't prevent what is about to happen," the young Nea said.

Evard's hands tightened around Nea's neck and she gripped them, her feet kicking against the wall as she struggled.

"If you weren't an integral piece of my plan, I would kill you now for your insolence. But I do not have the time to wait for another of your kind to be born, so you listen to me."

Nea fought harder, bringing her knee up and forcing it into Evard's stomach. He dropped her and she darted for the door, but Evard recovered and reached it first, slamming it shut. *Why isn't she using her magic to fight back?* The thought had barely sounded when lilac shimmers filled the air.

"You're not a killer and even if you were, I have protection remember?" He pulled a pink metal pendant from under his shirt.

Leith had one just like it. He said it protected him from Catriona's mind magic.

"Now stop this foolishness and listen to me. You will tell me how to breech the Between and then you will play your part like a good little girl or I will turn everything and everyone you care about to ash. Do I make myself clear?"

Nea backed up to the desk.

"Answer me!" Evard roared.

"Yes, you have made yourself clear."

"Good. Now enough games that you know you can't win." He moved closer.

"Oh, I can assure you I am done playing." Nea lunged, a penknife clutched in her hand. She landed on Evard, knocking him onto his back as the knife dug a rough path down the left side of his face.

Dropping the knife, she dove for the door, her blood-covered hands slipping on the handle. She wrenched it open and charged out into the hallway. Garret raced after her as she barrelled along the winding corridors to another room. Slamming the door open, she slid inside and raced around, her breath coming in frantic pants and sobs as she threw various items into her satchel.

After closing the satchel, she opened the door again to reveal Leith, who had his hand lifted as though he had been about to knock.

"Surprise! The meeting finished early. I thought we could—Nea, are you alright?" His attention dropped to the blood still on her hands.

She shook her head. "I have to leave. I have to get to Kalhanna before ..." She covered her mouth with the back of her wrist and blew out a breath.

Leith took hold of her shoulders. "What happened?"

"Your father ..." A deep sob escaped her, and she shook herself free of his grasp. "I have to go. I'm sorry." She darted around him.

"Nea, wait." He turned to chase after her just as Evard and several of his guard came around the corner.

Evard had a bloody rag pressed over one side of his face. "Seize her! She is not to leave this castle."

"Did you do that to Father?" Leith asked, but Nea spun on her heel and raced away.

Garret followed her again, but as they passed through a door, he found himself in the courtyard at Kalhanna. Nea was sitting on the ground, the mutilated body of a woman in her lap as she hummed a lullaby and tears cut paths through the grime on her cheeks. Lilac magic danced over the woman in Nea's arms, and then she let out a final breath. A sound that was half-scream half-sob tore from Nea's throat, and she lifted her gaze to several soldiers who were picking their way through the carnage.

Her breath heaved into her chest and she stood as the men approached.

"King's in luck. The necromancer is still alive."

Nea's fists clenched, and the men all halted and shared a look. The air around Nea had grown dark and churning with flickers of lilac and deep violet flashing through it.

"Come—" The man who started to speak let out a wet gurgle as blood ran from his mouth, cutting off his words.

"She didn't want to kill them," the girl beside Garret said softly. "But the magic in her blood had overtaken her, and she couldn't control it."

The other two soldiers lifted their swords.

"Stand down," one said, though his voice was shaking.

"This is what the witch wants. For Nea to become the monster she has always feared she could become. But Nea is too kind and brave to become a true monster. She'd destroy herself before something like this happened again," the girl said as the other Nea clenched her fists and both soldiers fell to the ground screaming.

"Why did we have to go through all those memories?"

"Because I had to figure out if you could really save her." She held her hand out, and in her palm was a key made of a dark metal. "I can't follow you through that door. But you don't need me anymore anyway." She pointed to the threshold that had appeared in front of them. It was completely entwined in the thorn-studded branches of a briar of roses. The blooms scattered amongst the dark green leaves were a soft pink. "Well, go on. She's waiting for you."

Garret lifted the key, and the branches peeled back to reveal an ornate lock made from the same dark metal in the middle of the door. He slid the key into the lock and the door opened.

The room on the other side was bare save for a large cage in its centre in which Nea sat. She leapt to her feet and grabbed the bars. "Garret? Is it really you?"

"It's me." He moved to the cage and touched her fingers.

She gripped his hand. "I knew you'd figure it out."

"How do I get you out of there?" The cage appeared to have no door.

"You don't."

He turned as Frell entered the room.

"I knew you would prove trouble. Now you will leave this place and return Nea to the warehouse, and I will let you live."

"She isn't really here," Nea said behind him. "I think to break this cage you need to figure out what she took from me."

"What she took from you?" He looked back at Nea. "She couldn't take anything. She tried but failed each time. She ..." He thought back to something Nea had said several days ago about her emotions being numb. Frell couldn't take Nea's kindness or her curiosity or tenacity, but there was something she could—something that was intrinsic to the Nea he knew. "She took your pain and your anger and your guilt. All the things that you use to keep yourself prisoner."

A smile pulled across Nea's mouth. "Well done," she said as the bars of the cage collapsed into piles of dark dust and she fell to her hands and knees.

"Look what you've done!" Frell yelled and started forward, but Garret stepped into her path. "Get out of my way. She's useless to me if she dies."

"This is your—"

"Garret ..."

The softness of Nea's tone cut through him and he knelt beside her. "How do I fix this?"

She shook her head. "You can't." Her fingers brushed the edge of his jaw. "You need to find Rourke and get him to send you home. Tell Margot I'm sorry—" Her eyes fluttered shut.

"No ..." The world faded, and he found himself beside Nea's bed, her hand still sandwiched between his and Rourke's. "Nea! No, no, no. We still need you." He felt her pulse. It was a weak thump ... thump ... thump. "Help her," he implored Declan and Rourke.

"I'm not a healer, Garret. You know that." Declan pressed his hand over his mouth.

Rourke shook his head. "There is only one way that I know of, but you have to be willing to pay the price that it will cost the pair of you." He indicated both Nea and Garret.

"Do it."

"I can't, but I can take you to someone who can."

"She won't survive the journey." The skin beneath his fingers was turning to ice as a soft blue chased the pink from her lips.

"I can anchor her life force to one of ours. It will stabilise her in this state. We have to move quickly though." He flicked a glance between Declan and Garret.

Garret nodded. "What do you need me to do?"

"Give me your right wrist." He drew a knife and made an incision in Nea's left arm. Her blood seeped, sluggish and dark, from the cut.

Garret held out his wrist, and Rourke drew the knife across it. Blood welled instantly and Rourke pressed the wound to the matching one on Nea.

Ice flooded Garret's veins, and for the first time since they'd arrived in the Between, he could feel his suppression rising. Nea's keen was a distant throb growing fainter with each heartbeat. A twisting magic caught hold of the icy flicker of Nea's dying keen and wild heat replaced the ice, bringing with it his keen-sense and the familiar numbness of suppression.

Rourke released him. "We'd best dress those wounds. I can't knit flesh back together." There was a breathless quality to Rourke's voice and sweat ran in a thin line from his right temple. He brushed it away with the back of his hand. "Soul magic has never come easily to me."

"Shadow's teeth." They all turned to the door where Zephyr was standing, her golden eyes wide and her hair tussled, a thin graze of pink marking her right cheek.

"Move it, girl. We don't have the time to be lingering in doorways." Wade's voice sounded behind her.

Zephyr stumbled forward as Wade pushed around her. He stopped short as his eyes fell on Nea's seemingly lifeless form. Garret understood the horror on his face. She looked so much like a corpse that if not for the reassuring thrum of her keen twisting under his skin, he'd believe she was dead. Wade's lilac-grey gaze landed on Garret and travelled down his arm to the thin slice and the blood that was dripping over his palm.

"I bought us time to get her to Moira," Rourke said.

Zephyr blinked and moved forward. "Show me," she said softly as she indicated Garret's arm.

He lifted it, and she hovered her fingers above the wound. Warmth pooled in his stomach and thin tendrils of azure magic coiled across his skin. He bit his lip as the sides of the cut pulled together into a neat white line.

She released him then healed Nea's cut before turning to Rourke. "We need to move now. Frell is on the warpath, and it won't be long before she finds us here."

CHAPTER SIXTEEN

MARGOT

Dale decided to join them as they left Fengate. He said it felt like doing the right thing despite the odds, and his knowledge of the Fenlands had proved invaluable. Though the road had been raised above the water to allow easier travel to both the east and south, the north way had fallen into disrepair. The marsh had reclaimed sections of the road in the form of deceptive pools that looked no more than knee-deep but could swallow a man to his chest. And there were sticky stretches of mud that clung to their horses' legs and threatened to pull them down.

Despite the treacherous footing, the landscape was beautiful. Lilies and other water plants with flowers of various shapes and sizes dotted the deep pools amongst the tall marsh grasses. The blooms were painted in hues of mauve, soft yellow, and pink, but Margot's favourite were the small feathery white ones that looked like stars of frost floating in the swallows.

The wet sucking sounds their horses' hooves made as they picked a path down the disused road joined the cacophony of noise that filled the air around them. The flit-buzz of insects and the deep ba-roak of frogs was shattered by the occasional lilt of birdsong or splash of something unseen moving through the shallows.

As beguiling as the fenlands were, they held dark secrets and a horrific past. Centuries ago, the waters had run red with the blood of the fallen as a great battle raged. The details had been mostly lost to time, but local legend was that on certain nights you could hear the sounds of warriors still locked in battle and apparitions would lead unwary travellers into the marsh and drown them. It was most likely over-imagination and superstition that led to the stories, but there was no mistaking the cool shifting prickles that ran up her spine or the tingle that charged her hair and made the short curls stand on end. The barrier between worlds was thin here. Perhaps there was a grain of truth hidden under the exaggerated ghost stories. Regardless, she wouldn't like to be travelling the Fenlands at night.

By the time the sun was high, they had entered a section of marsh where the road was flanked by twisted trees. Margot's horse's ears flicked and it and tossed its head. Something heavy dropped from the closest tree into the marsh water with a loud splash, and the horse shied, nearly throwing her from the saddle.

"Shhh. It's alright." She rubbed the animal's neck as she scanned the murky water. Large ripples ringed out from the base of the tree, but nothing else stirred.

"I don't like this," Penny said as her horse's nostrils flared.

Ahead of them, both Dale and Emil were also having trouble with their mounts. Dale's danced about and bumped into Emil's, which lowered its ears and took a snap at the neck of the other.

Penny let out a yell as her horse reared back. Something pale came hurtling out of the water, and a line of red opened along the horse's stomach. It teetered sideways as another creature charged towards it, and Penny was unseated.

Emil dove after Penny as her head disappeared beneath the water, a grey arm looped around her neck.

The screaming horse was dragged down also and then everything went still as red bloomed across the surface of the water. Bile rose in the back of Margot's throat as she stared at the place Penny and Emil had disappeared then looked to Dale.

Seconds ticked by. There was a splash and Emil's head broke the surface. He dragged Penny up and boosted her onto the back of his horse, then vaulted up behind her. "Go!" he yelled.

Margot planted her heels into the sides of her horse, and it surged forward. She glanced at the red water where Penny's horse had disappeared and shuddered.

They didn't break pace until they reached higher ground and what looked like the ruins of a small town. A moulding signpost bore the name Holbrook. Margot had seen that name before, but where? A plague ... a plague so contagious and devastating that entire towns were set ablaze or abandoned or both.

"We need to keep going. I've been through here once with Nea, but she said whatever you do, do not stop until you reach the hollow oak," Penny said weakly.

"I should check—"

"*Nea* said don't stop." Penny cut her off.

"Alright." As Margot said it, pale shapes appeared in the water at the edges of the road—gaunt, grey bodies with sharp teeth and lank clumps of hair clinging to their balding heads. They might have been human once, but whatever they were now they were *wrong*. Cold magic crept down Margot's spine, thick and suffocating like deep mud.

Dale and Emil didn't wait. They urged their horses forward, along what had once been the main street of the town. A guttural howl rose as the creatures splashed after them. The end of the road disappeared through a massive archway made in the centre of an ancient oak. Emil and Dale charged through it ahead of Margot. When she reached the void in the tree, the air became treacle thick. It pulled at her hair and dragged across her skin. Then she was on the other side, the pressure of the ward dissipating instantly.

Behind her, the grey creatures threw themselves against the invisible barrier, snarling and gnashing their teeth.

"Why can't they cross?" she asked.

"The barrier probably only affects dead things," Emil said as he watched the creatures with disgust.

"Nea said as much," Penny panted. "They are some kind of reani—" Her words were silenced as she slumped forward so fast Emil nearly lost his grip on her. A steady trickle of blood ran from the torn flesh of her arm and across the shoulder of Emil's mount.

Margot slid from her saddle and rushed over. She pressed her fingertips against the inside of Penny's wrist. A faint pulse beat just under the skin. Green smoke slid over the sides of the wound as Margot drew the source to her. Slowly, she focused on bringing the edges of the tear together. They resisted at first as though something were fighting back against Margot's keen, but then she gave a heavy push and Penny's skin melded into a jagged scar. "We need to get her somewhere safe so I can have a proper look at her. Are you alright, Emil?"

He nodded.

"Perhaps someone else should take her to spare your horse."

"He'll be fine," Emil said as he gave the horse's shoulder a thump. "Do you know if we're any closer to Warren?"

"It's not far now. When we reach the rock that looks like a rabbit, we'll be there," Penny mumbled as she rested her head against Emil's shoulder, her eyes still closed.

"A *rock that looks like a rabbit*. Alright, Margot, it might be best if you take point and Emil rides in the middle with Penny. I'll keep an eye on our rear," Dale said.

Margot nodded and guided her horse to the front of the group.

They rode for several more hours, the marsh slowly giving way to a dense forest. The road had diminished into a game trail, and their horses had to pick their way carefully through the undergrowth, avoiding the raised roots and tangling vines.

Finally, the trees thinned out and the path widened again. It was still not wide enough for two abreast, but the grabbing branches had retreated providing a cleared way through. Just head of Margot was a large grey boulder. If she tilted her head, it looked kind of like a giant rabbit hunched in the grass.

"It really does look like a rabbit," Dale said from behind her. "But now what? There's nothing here except a sheer cliff face. Do we keep following the road?"

"There's a door," Penny said, her voice still sounding drained. "Margot, you'll need to feed it your magic."

"Feed what?" Margot twisted in her saddle to face Penny.

"The *bunny-rock*," Penny replied with a shadow of her normal smile.

Margot dismounted and moved to the boulder. She placed her hand delicately on the curved top and let her keen out in a warm rush. The stone shone green momentarily as it absorbed the magic, then a loud grating sound filled the air and the wall behind the rock rolled back on itself to reveal an archway leading into the cliff face.

"Just be careful. Warren isn't fond of visitors, so I'm not sure what to expect," Penny said as Margot remounted her horse and guided it through the opening.

The other side of the archway expanded out into a great cavernous grotto. Lush ferns and bushes laden with berries were lit by sunlight streaming from above. The bank of the small stream that wound its way through the space was littered with red-leaved Mother's balm and small clumps of tassel moss. A familiar click-whoosh sounded, and Margot flinched as a crossbow bolt thudded into the tree beside her.

"I suggest you lot clear out. The next one won't miss," a voice from above said.

Margot shielded her eyes. An old man was sitting on a rock ledge across from them. He had a crossbow levelled on the centre of her chest.

"Wait, we're friends. We just want some answers and then we'll be out of your hair," Margot said, lifting her hands.

"All my friends are long dead, girly. Turn yourselves around and off you go."

"Okay, so we're not your friends, but we're friends of Nea," Margot said.

Warren lowered the crossbow a fraction. "Friends of Nea you say? Alright, I'll give you one answer." He disappeared from sight and then moments later stepped out of the bushes beside them. "Right then, what do you want?"

"Mother's grief you move fast for an old man," Dale said.

A smile quirked the corner of Warren's mouth, but it faded when his gaze landed on Emil and Penny. "What happened to her?"

"We were attacked in the swamp. She's lost a fair bit of blood."

Warren's blue eyes narrowed. "What attacked you? A wraith?"

"A whole group of them if you mean those undead things outside of the ruins," Emil responded.

Warren clicked his tongue and shook his head. "Not good. Not good at all. Bring her inside."

"I thought you wanted us to leave," Dale said.

"I'd prefer it that way, but I can't leave her in that state. Terrible way to die that is. Get her down off that beast and follow me. She doesn't have much time." He snapped his fingers and started towards a little shack set onto another outcrop over the stream.

Emil helped Penny slide from the horse then moved to pick her up.

"My legs are not broken thank you, Emil." She tilted her chin and took a step forward but stumbled. With a reserved sigh, she turned back to Emil. "I don't want to be carried, but I won't turn down assistance."

Emil chuckled and looped an arm around her waist then slowly guided her after Warren.

"Come on, healer. You'll be needed," Warren called over his shoulder.

Margot handed the reins of her horse to Dale and then hurried after Emil and Penny.

"Put her on the bed and then off with you." Warren directed Emil as he started sorting through the jars on his shelves.

Emil did as he was told, and then gave Margot a small smile as he ducked out the door.

"What do you want me to do?" Margot asked.

Warren sniffed the contents of the jar he was holding then frowned. "Nothing right now. I need to draw the death out first then you can patch her up again. Would have been easier if you hadn't healed her before, but we'll make do ... Aha, there you are!" He placed a jar full of a strange red powder onto the table. "Alright. Now you'll need to reopen that wound."

"Reopen her wound?"

"Yes."

"That's not how healing magic works."

Warren gave her a look that was distinctly unimpressed. "It's exactly how healing magic works, girly. Doesn't matter if you're mending or breaking—you're manipulating living flesh."

"It's not as simple as that and regardless, the cre—"

"Pfft!" Warren rolled his eyes. "Bloody college mages and your creeds and self-imposed limitations," he muttered as he dug in a drawer. "You can't stand there and tell me you've never used your keen to harm in self-perseveration." He pulled a tarnished knife out of the drawer and started towards Penny.

"Wait!" Margot said.

He turned, and one of his snowy brows lifted.

"I'll do it." She moved over to Penny's side and took hold of her arm. "Sorry, Penny, but this is going to hurt."

"I can handle it. I'm more concerned about what he means by drawing the death out to be honest." Penny gave a weak chuckle.

Margot brushed her fingers over the scar on Penny's wrist and focused on undoing the magic from earlier. At first, she met a tight resistance, then Penny let out a moan as beads of blood welled in the centre of the scar. Penny's moan became a scream as the scar burst open, blood flowing freely again.

"Good, good. Move out of the way," Warren said, and the second Margot moved, he smeared a red poultice over the freshly opened wound.

The cold kiss of necromancy slivered up Margot's spine as Warren's magic rose and a purple shimmer twisted over the poultice before absorbing into it. Penny's flesh hissed and the golden whirl on the centre of her palm began to glow. Swirling gold patterns like the fluffy heads of storm clouds painted themselves across Penny's hand and along her forearm. The poultice dried the instant the golden marks touched it, and then it flaked and lifted off in a red cloud that floated in the air for several heartbeats before collapsing onto the bed beside Penny.

Penny lifted her arm and studied the marks and the smooth, completely healed skin. Warren made a noise and grabbed hold of her wrist.

"Where did you get this?" He prodded the golden whirl in the centre of her palm. "Of course ... *Nea*. Mother confound it what was that girl thinking? She should know better." His attention snapped to Penny's face. "Do you know what it is?"

"Only what Abigail told me."

"And?"

"A brightling soul."

Warren grunted. "And do you know why Nea put it in you?"

"She wanted to keep it away from Evard."

"Right. You." He snapped his fingers at Margot. "You said that you came here for answers. Why didn't Nea give them to you?"

"She ... she can't. She's out of our reach at the moment."

"Out of your reach? Please don't tell me that fool of girl used the portal at Del Harol."

Margot closed her mouth tightly.

"Mother's grief what was she thinking?" He rubbed his hands through his hair and his sleeve fell back revealing a purple flower-shaped birthmark on the inside of his wrist. "Where's the box?"

Margot pulled the box from her bag. Its magic clung to her skin as she passed it to Warren. He traced the chains with his fingertip and gave a nod.

"Are you going to destroy it?" Margot's mouth was suddenly dry.

"It can't be destroyed. It needs to be put back where it belongs, but for that we need Nea or someone like her."

"Aren't you like her?"

He shook his head. "There's no one this side of the barrier who's *like* her."

"But you're a deathborn, aren't you? I saw your mark, and there are others too. Nea is not the—"

"Of course I'm a sodden deathborn, but Nea's not."

"What do you mean she's not? She has a mark just like yours on her hip, and she seems to think that is what she is."

"She doesn't know the truth herself. A decision was made to keep it from her because none of us truly understood it. She should have been a deathborn—all the indicators were there—but she was like nothing any of us had encountered before."

His fingers tightened on the box, and its magic flared in a hot flash down Margot's spine.

"I told the others keeping the truth from her was a mistake. One I fear we are paying for now. But there is no sense dwelling on what could have been. Right now, we need to do what we can to stop Evard getting all the pieces he needs together."

Something stirred the hairs on the back of Margot's neck. "How do we do that? Nonna seemed to think you could destroy it. But you said yourself it can't be."

"No, but it can be placed beyond Evard's reach in the same way that the brightling soul was."

"You mean you can put it inside someone? Isn't Nea the only one who can do that?" Penny asked.

"When we're dealing with souls, yes, but this isn't a soul. It's a tool, and that's a different thing all together." His gaze settled on Margot. "We just need a willing volunteer."

Yes. This was what the magic inside the box wanted—it wanted to be free again to serve its intended purpose.

"I'm not sure that's a good idea," Penny said. "Can't we just hide it somewhere?"

"It's the surest way to keep it from him. Unless you want to take it into the howling chamber in the catacombs beneath the Bright Temple, but there's no guarantee Evard won't find it there."

Margot had been in those catacombs. Did he mean that strange archway with the oppressive magic and whispering voices? "I've been there, I think." She chewed her thumbnail. "When we were escaping from Evard, a priestess helped Sonia and I get into the catacombs. There was an archway that was shrouded in this strange magic, and beneath it we could hear the dead the talking."

"That's the howling chamber. You didn't go in, did you?"

Margot shook her head. "No, we were told not to enter any of the side passages until we reached a particular tomb. One that contained the bodies of several deathborn."

"A bunch of fools. Their folly is where Evard got his mad plan to begin with." Warren scowled.

"You know about them? They had something to do with corruption."

"They are the origin of it! Their machinations created it. If they had had an anchor, they probably would have succeeded in tearing down the barrier, and none of us would be here now."

"Wait. They were trying to tear down the barrier, but Samson was trying to find a cure for corruption to save Evette."

"She wouldn't have needed saving if she had just left well enough alone. Samson should have known better and burned the sodding book when he found it."

"What book?"

"The Book of Souls."

A rock landed in the pit of Margot's stomach. The letter from Mateus had mentioned the *Book of Souls,* and it seemed that Nea had been searching for it, but why? Did she know what it contained? Did the Arcanarium have a copy? Had Mateus found it and sent it to Nea as promised? "What did the book contain?"

"I don't know exactly; I've never read it myself given that it was lost centuries ago, but I know that Evette wasn't corrupted until after she read it and started experimenting with things she shouldn't. Samson was clear enough about that."

"You said Samson found it."

"Yeah, or it found him."

"And it has been lost? Nea was searching for it." Margot pulled Mateus's letter from her bag and handed it to Warren.

He skimmed the parchment before landing his gaze on Margot again. "Do you know if she found it?"

Margot shook her head. "Why would she be looking for it?"

"Maybe she wanted to stop Evard from getting it," Penny offered. "If she realised what it was."

"Perhaps. However, Evard was already scheming before Nea was even born. I suspect he has had the book all along. And Nea would have known that, so why ask Mateus to look for it in the Arcanarium?" Warren said.

"Unless it's a clue," Margot said. Nea knew that Margot was aware of her hidey-hole in the bottom of the wardrobe. Most of the letters in there had been bundled together, except this one. It had been tucked neatly in the back of one of the journals. The journal Margot could read contained musings on her research for Evard, but

nothing that rang any alarm bells. The other journal, however ...
She pulled the two journals out of her bag. Sure enough, the second
journal's covers remained unmovable as though they were glued
together, and no matter what she did she couldn't open it.

"Nea suspected Evard was up to something when she took on the
position as arcane advisor, but she simply thought he was trying to
find a way for keen-less to be able to use magic. This journal tells
us as much. It is not until the later entries that you get a sense that
things were worse than she originally thought." She handed the first
journal to Warren. "But I can't even open this one. Nea's keen is all
over it, but whatever is in these pages, she doesn't want anyone to
know." She passed it to Warren.

He ran his finger down the spine and the chill of his keen coiled
around Margot's chest. "I doubt any of us are going to be able to
read these pages any time soon. She's put an enchantment on it
that is connected to her life force. It won't lift unless Nea herself
choses to remove it or she dies. Why do you think the request for
the *Book of Souls* was a clue?"

"Nea left these where she knew I would find them. I don't think
she expected to survive Kalhanna, so if that enchantment is
supposed to lift when she dies, then she thought that by the time I
found them I would be able to read the second journal. The request
for the *Book of Souls* could be pointing us to the Arcanarium or it
could be pointing us to Mateus himself ... Or, as you've suggested,
it could be that Evard already had the book and she knew that, and
it was her way of telling us what we were facing."

"That's an awful lot of what-ifs, Margot," Penny said.

"It is, but unless this journal suddenly decides to give up all its
secrets, maybe getting in touch with Mateus might be our best
course of action." As she said it, the magic clinging to the journal
gave a heart-stopping shudder. It glowed bright lilac for a moment
then the covers flopped open on Warren's palm.

Icy fingers closed around Margot's throat as a dead weight landed in her stomach. She drew a ragged breath and turned to Penny only to find her own dread mirrored in the wideness of the other woman's eyes and the way her hand was pressed over her mouth.

What had happened to Nea?

CHAPTER SEVENTEEN

HARVEY

Harvey leant against the back wall of the barracks and tilted his face towards the star-spangled sky. He drew another deep breath of cool air to chase the suffocating feeling from his chest. It had been some time since a nightmare had left him gasping in a sweat-soaked tangle of sheets.

Rubbing a hand through his hair, he glanced at the fort. There was a light in one of the downstairs windows. It didn't make sense; he was sure that window was in the south wing, and Amelia seemed to prefer the dark. Come to think of it, he'd never seen a light in that section of the fort before.

Using the shadows, he crept towards the window and then hazarded a glance inside. The necromancer, who had been introduced as Kieran, was pacing the rune-marked barrier. Leon stood behind him, his arms folded and his mouth set in a frown. Amelia was nowhere in sight, which was unusual as she always appeared when someone came too close to the *bars* of her cage.

"I don't know enough about rune marks to undo the work that was done here," Kieran said. "Perhaps if we put her in another body, we could move her across the barrier."

"And how do we do that? *Nea* was the only one able to cross the barrier." The way Leon said Nea's name lifted the hairs on the back of Harvey's neck.

"That *is* interesting." Kieran moved his hand towards the barrier. The rune marks lit up and he tilted his head as though listening to something. "Perhaps if the person crossing the barrier was already dead? But then I am not certain that magic can cross the barrier either … No, there must be an anchor point somewhere. We simply need to find it."

Something moved behind Leon then Catriona came into view. She slid her hand over Leon's shoulder and fanned her fingers across his chest as she turned her attention to Kieran. "Perhaps the pair of you should slip back to bed, let Amelia and I have a little talk, woman to woman."

The coin in Harvey's pocket grew warm. Was she using her magic on them?

"There is no need for the compulsion," Kieran said. "Until I figure out the anchor, there is nothing more for me here." He stepped around her and moved out of sight.

Catriona smiled and pressed her lips along Leon's jaw. He tilted his head away and took a step back.

Harvey didn't hear what Catriona said next as a hand slid over his mouth and he was hauled away by the back of his shirt.

He twisted free and spun to face his attacker. Trenton stood there with a finger pressed to his lips. He tilted his head to indicate Harvey follow him and then walked towards the sparring field.

"What are you doing skulking about in the middle of the night?" Trenton asked as they stopped in the shadows by the outer wall.

Harvey bit the inside of his cheek. He liked Trenton, but he wasn't sure he could trust him. "I couldn't sleep, so I decided to take a walk."

"It didn't look like you were *taking a walk*." Trenton folded his arms. "What did you learn?"

Harvey blinked at him. "I'm sorry?"

"You heard me. What is Leon up to in the south wing?"

"I don't—"

"I know you were spying on him." Trenton rubbed a hand over his face, and for a moment he appeared *tired*. The type of tired Garret had been in the months before he had finally rebelled against Evard. Like he had reached the limit of hiding behind a façade, of keeping the two halves of his life in careful balance. "And I know you're not exactly who you say you are."

Harvey swallowed. "I—"

"I don't care about that. What I care about is what Leon is up to."

"I'm not sure yet, but I think he is looking for a way to extract Amelia from the south wing."

Trenton paced a few steps away and then back again. "Who do you work for?"

"I'm sorry?"

"Who sent you here? Did they know Leon was coming? Is it Warden Commander Garret?"

Harvey shook his head. "Who do *you* work for?"

"Mother's breath you remind me of Harvey at times," Trenton muttered. "The official story is that I work for the king like everyone else stationed here."

"And unofficially?"

Trenton folded his arms and let out a sigh. "Unofficially? I was never Evard's man. My allegiance has always been to Leith, but the bloody fool ran off before half of us knew what was happening."

"Why are you telling me this? I could just reveal it to Leon, and you'd be charged for treason."

Trenton let out a breath as he studied Harvey. "You could, but I don't think you will. You know that soldier I've told you about before?"

Harvey licked his lip and wrapped his fingers around the charmed band at his wrist. "Yeah?"

"You're a lot more like him than I thought. You can't spend years in the close confinement of a barracks and not get to know the people there with you. Really know them. I'd say you *were* Harvey, except that's impossible. No one can change their features that much." He shook his head. "But that similarity tells me you're not likely to turn me in. That and the fact that I know there's no Uncle Nevil in Little Brook who you've been sending letters to." He pulled out a folded piece of parchment. "I intercepted this yesterday morning. Funny thing is ..." He unfolded the letter, and it was completely blank.

"Seems someone might have been playing a trick on you." Harvey tried to keep his voice even.

"Maybe." He held the parchment out to Harvey. "Or maybe it's enchanted so it can only be read by the one it's intended for. I could see easily enough if I took it to the wardens. But I don't know that I trust them much these days."

"You're loyal to Leith?"

Trenton gave a nod.

Even if Trenton was lying, which wasn't likely as Trenton had never been fond of liars, Harvey couldn't escape the fact that he had been caught red-handed. He could take the letter now or Trenton would hand it over to John. Either way, his cover was blown. However, if Trenton *was* loyal to Leith, Harvey would likely find himself another ally here at the fort. If not, then he'd be dead before the sun rose.

He swallowed and took the letter; the moment his fingers brushed the paper, words coiled across it in Niall's neat scrawl. With a resigned huff, he flipped the letter around so Trenton could see the damning evidence for himself.

Trenton's breath hissed through his teeth. "How is this possible?" His gaze flicked from the parchment to Harvey's face.

"It's an enchantment. It really is *me* under this skin." Harvey turned the letter back around and folded it.

"You expect me to just take your word for that?"

Harvey rubbed the back of his neck. "No. But I know you don't like liars."

"That's common enough knowledge."

"True, but I know that when you were five you lied for your oldest brother, so he could go and see that girl he was sweet on. And when your father found out, he beat you half to death for lying. It wasn't the beating. It was the fact that your father was a rotten drunk and lied to himself about it every day. That's why you don't like liars, and why you can't stand the smell of drink."

Trenton crossed his arms.

"And I know that because you told me after I confided in you about my stepfather and how he used to get one too many in him and beat us. Me and my mother, anyway. He never laid so much as a finger on Lorie." He pressed his lips together and swallowed the bitterness that had coated his tongue. "That was the day that I got Lorie's letter telling me he'd—"

"I remember." Trenton placed a hand on his shoulder. "Mother's breath, Harvey. You could have come to me sooner."

"I didn't know where your loyalties lay."

"I can understand that. The way John's been acting around you, I half-expected you to be a renegade mage or something ... Can he feel the enchantment? Is that why?"

"I don't think so. I think he is just suspicious. He stopped us on our first day coming through the gate, and if he picked up on it then he said nothing. He's been mostly ignoring M—Tess. He seems to be fixated on me for some reason."

"I am guessing Tessa is under a similar enchantment."

Harvey nodded. "She is, but don't ask me to reveal her identity because I won't. You can trust her though."

"What are you doing here? How much *can* you tell me?"

"We were just gathering information. Leith wanted to know what Evard was up to here, particularly in regard to Amelia."

"I suspect he wants to move her. Leon is tight-lipped about his plans, but I caught him and Kieran discussing it, arguing really. Kieran wanted to go to Hartswood and find a vessel, said it would be easier than trying to extract her."

Harvey frowned. "A vessel?"

"Your guess is as good as mine, but Kieran seemed to think they would find one at Hartswood. Leon wouldn't have it though. He's waiting for something. He told Catriona that his finder directed him here."

That rang a bell. "He was using a finder to track Garret and Nea." The wards at Del Harol had shielded them while they were there though. He didn't know how it worked, but it obviously had.

"Nea? The one who killed Harold?"

"The same."

The tip of Trenton's tongue ran along his lips. "Was she here?"

Harvey shook his head. "But Garret was, during the siege. I think because the finder couldn't locate Nea, Leon switched his focus to Garret. He probably hoped to find evidence of them both here. But why not kill two birds and extract Amelia while he's looking for clues?" He scratched the edge of his jaw. "I need to find out more about this vessel though."

"I'll help where I can, but you need to be careful. John is already suspicious of you, and Leon has always been an arse. Now he's an arse on a power trip. If he suspects—"

"I know," he snapped. "Sorry. I appreciate the concern, Trenton, but honestly, it is just good to know someone else is on my side."

Trenton nodded. "I imagine it is. I'm not the only one. I won't reveal your identity to the others, but they'll be here when you need them." He clapped Harvey on the back. "Well, there's not much night left. Best be heading back to the barracks and catching what little sleep you can."

"I don't imagine I'm going to get any." He gave Trenton a smile and then started off towards the barracks. He'd need to snatch a moment to read Niall's letter and then tell Molly that Trenton knew the truth. It felt good to have Trenton on his side, but it also set prickling uncertainty at the base of his spine. The more people who knew, the higher the danger of being found out.

Morning was starting to grey the sky as Harvey ran through sword drills against his invisible opponent. He had returned to the barracks after his chat with Trenton, but his mind had been too busy to allow sleep. After tossing and turning for a little over an hour, he had decided it was better to be out doing something than lying in the dark with his turbulent thoughts. Drills and sparring were the two things that could clear his head and bring him back to his centre; that and talking to Janey. Her silent presence was surprisingly comforting. Most people just saw a mute with a horrific scar and they either felt pity or revulsion. But Janey was always cheerful. She'd been dealt one of the harshest hands in this life, but she took it in her stride with a smile and boundless inner strength. *The Mother does not give us more than we can endure.* That was the line the temple sisters always gave, but why must one person endure more than another? And what about people like his mother who had *endured* until it killed them.

His blade embedded in the side of the practice dummy sending a reverberation up his arm that threatened to rattle his teeth. He wrenched it free and wiped the back of his hand over his brow.

"Get it together," he muttered to himself. He turned his attention to the thin line of orange that was just cresting the horizon, painting the sky in splashes of deep orange, apricot, and gold. Drawing a deep breath, he gave the sword a decisive flick and twisted away from the dummy.

The blade sang as it slashed through the air and his muscles fell into the time-honed rhythm. Slowly, his thoughts cleared as he focused on the whoosh of metal, the satisfying ache that was slowly building in his muscles, and the sweat that was rising on his brow and slickening his grip.

With a yell, he spun and set his blade in a rapid arc, his muscles contracting at the last moment and pulling it up short a hair from the neck of the dummy.

Someone clapped to his left, and he flicked a look at them: John. What did he want?

"I knew there was more to you than it seemed. Trenton can play it off as natural talent all he wants, but only soldiers who have trained for years, if not decades, can move like that." He looked down at the stub where his hand had been. "I was like you—raw talent honed into a weapon. My sword was not an accessory to my body, it was part of it. Very few soldiers ever truly achieve that, and it was stolen from me."

Harvey licked his lip. "That must have been hard to come to terms with."

"I don't need your pity," John snarled. "Your technique is strange for a regular soldier. Your lot are trained differently to wardens, but you carry yourself like you have spent a great deal of time training with not only members of the guard, but the order as well. In fact, I would go as far to say your style is reminiscent of one warden in particular."

"I can assure you I've never trained with the order."

"No?" John took a step towards him. "What are you then?"

"I'm sorry?"

"You're not a mage. I know that much, but your curiosity about Amelia and your unusual way of comporting yourself tell me you are hiding something."

Harvey swallowed. "I think you're half-mad. There's nothing special about me. I'm not a mage, and I am certainly not a warden or whatever it is you might think I am."

"John, there you are." Arthur came running. "Leon needs you."

"He can wait!" John rounded on Arthur. "Tell him I'm busy."

Arthur opened his mouth then glanced at his feet. His nose scrunched and his eyes blazed as they snapped back to John. "Tell him yourself." The words coming from his own lips seemed to surprise him.

"Excuse me?"

"You heard me. I am done being your errand boy, John. You are becoming a bully just like Willem."

"I am your superior," John growled. "How dare you talk to me—"

"No you're not, John. You just think you're better than me and that gives you a right to order me around, but I am sick of it."

Harvey hid his smirk behind his hand; it was about time.

John started to say something, but Arthur cut him off. "I'm not finished. Maybe Garret was right … Maybe … No. It's not a maybe. Garret *was* right. There's rot in the order. It started before Kalhanna when people like Willem got a little power and started making deals with Evard. And it's just been growing and growing. And it might be too late to save it now, but I'm going to try." He turned on his heels and stalked away.

"Where are you going, traitor?" John started after him.

Arthur stopped. A quiver ran through his body and he swung around, throwing a punch that sent John staggering. "I am not a traitor. I swore an *oath* to the Bright herself. We all did, or have you forgotten that?" He drew a huff of breath and walked away.

"Evard will hang you or worse if you desert, Arthur."

Arthur just kept walking.

Harvey let out a low whistle. "Never thought I'd see that." He wished Garret had been there to see it also.

"How dare you?" John stepped towards him.

"Lay one finger on my recruit, John, and I'll take the other hand," Trenton said, drawing John's attention to where he stood flanked by Callie and Micha.

John muttered under his breath and then thrust a finger in Harvey's direction. "I'll get the truth."

"Better run along to Leon." Harvey waved him away.

John gave Trenton a glare as he barged past Callie, knocking her with his shoulder.

"You alright, Bryce?" Callie asked.

"Yeah, I think he's more than a little unhinged but mostly talk. You missed seeing Arthur finally stand up to him though." He chuckled.

"We caught the last of it. Good on him I say, but he wants to watch his back now," Micha said.

"I don't think he plans on sticking around," Trenton said. "Not after he openly admitted to agreeing with Garret."

"Give me a minute." Harvey handed his sword to Callie then went running after Arthur.

He found him just outside the warden barracks, a pack on his shoulder.

"Where are you going?" he asked.

Arthur's attention snapped to him. "I don't know. I can't stay here though, not after I ... I shouldn't have said those things ... John is ... he was different before."

"Don't apologise for sticking up for yourself." Harvey studied him for a moment. "Did you mean what you said about Warden Commander Garret being right?"

Arthur drew a long breath, and Harvey wasn't sure he was going to answer, but he gave a decisive nod. "I should have left with him when I had the chance. I thought John would see reason eventually."

Harvey glanced around before saying quietly, "Go to The Leaping Cow in Little Brook. A friend will meet you there." He clapped Arthur on the shoulder. "You're braver and smarter than John ever gave you credit for. It takes real guts to stand up to those you consider your friends."

"Thanks, Bryce," Arthur said, and with one last resigned look at the barracks door, he headed off towards the gate.

Harvey drew a breath. He needed to draft a letter to Niall telling him about Arthur and sending someone to Little Brook to collect the warden. There was also the vessel he had learned about last night— surely that was something Niall and the others needed to know about. For weeks he had been in control. But after the last several hours, he felt like he was about to dive into waters far deeper than he had accounted for.

CHAPTER EIGHTEEN

GARRET

Garret studied Nea's face as he carried her limp body through the woods. If it hadn't been for the gentle flurry of her keen beneath his skin, her blue lips and corpse-pale cheeks would have convinced him she was dead. Rourke had explained that it was a kind of magical stasis that was holding her life force at the very edge of death, and the only thing stopping her from slipping away entirely was the beating of Garret's own heart.

Declan found it fascinating, of course, and had spent much of the journey discussing the theory of it with Zephyr and Rourke. He was walking just ahead of Garret now, his hands flashing through the air animatedly as he chased a theory.

When they'd first emerged from the memory trap, it had been strange to see Declan alive and well. Garret had seen Declan's lifeless body for himself, been there as Nea performed the rite. But even in their world where the dead didn't walk as freely as they did here, Declan had managed to find a loophole. Or had he?

He glanced at Nea again. Would it have turned out the same if Garret had never encountered her on the road to Little Brook? Would the sending have worked if another necromancer had performed it? Or would Declan be out there haunting someone else? He hadn't had a chance to ask Nea. In truth, he wasn't sure if he really wanted to know. He had wondered though if Declan's predicament might have been a result of her magic, which worked so differently to that of other necromancers, and not Declan's own.

"If you need a rest, I can take over for a while," Wade said from beside him. "She's heavier than she looks," he added with a chuckle when Garret cast a curious glance his way.

"I can go a bit longer." They had been taking turns carrying Nea ever since they left the city.

Wade studied his face and then nodded. "Frell bit off more than she can chew this time."

Garret's jaw tightened.

"Don't fret, Garret. If anyone can fix this, it's Moira," Wade said calmly.

"It shouldn't need fixing. I should have realised earlier. Nea tried to tell me something was wrong, but—"

"She didn't want to endanger you." Wade gave him a pointed look. "Frell knew you were a threat from the start. Why do you think she trapped you in the devourer nest? Then you managed to survive that, so she threw you into the Sorrow Wood. She didn't expect Nea to go running in after you though. The tea might have clouded Nea's mind and given Frell access to her memories, but there are things it can't take away."

"I didn't need protecting." He tightened his grip on Nea. "I could have helped her if she'd just let me."

"There is enough trauma in her past connected to not being able to protect those she cares about. Maybe she couldn't bear the thought of adding your name to the list of souls whose suffering she could have prevented."

"You seem to know an awful lot about Nea's past."

Wade rubbed a hand over his face and let out a sigh. "I assure you I was against Frell's plan from the start, but I was there when she was trying to alter Nea's memories. I'm also the one who pointed Declan in the right direction to find you in the devourer nest. But he doesn't know that, and neither does Frell—though she probably suspects it."

Garret chewed the inside of his cheek. "Could you have prevented this?" He nodded towards Nea. *You can't save everyone.* How many times had she told him that?

Wade shook his head. "None of us could have. Maybe if Nea hadn't fought so hard, but then she'd be Frell's puppet, and I don't believe that's a better fate than this. He's going to kill her, you know?"

"Who?"

"The Usurper. He's going to use her keen to free himself from the Night Estate and claim the Sovereigns' power for himself, then he will kill her."

"The Usurper? I thought the Shadow Man was at the Night Estate."

Wade shook his head. "He was once, eons ago, but the Usurper stole the mantle of Shadows and claimed its powers for himself. Now he sits in a prison, mostly of his own design, and calls himself the Master of Shadows. He's the reason all this has come to pass, and he's the one responsible for the corrupting disease that plagues your mages."

Garret shifted his grip on Nea. "Why Nea? Because she is a deathborn?"

"Yes and no. The sole reason deathborn exist is to be a vessel for the Usurper's soul. So, yes, as a deathborn Nea *is* an ideal candidate though he could really inhabit any *body*. More importantly though, she's a Daughter of Shadow—most likely the last of her kind."

"And that is different to a deathborn?"

Wade let out a low whistle. "Oh, very much so. The Usurper himself was a child of Shadow—the Shadow's first son, no less. He killed his sister and set her soul wandering the wastes beyond the Sorrow Wood, then he trapped his father and stole his mantle."

"Are you saying Nea is a descendant of the Shadow Man?"

"Descendant is a loose term when it comes to beings like Nea. She was chosen for a purpose, and yes, some essence of his blood runs in her veins, but not in the sense of him being her literal ancestor ... Just like you and the Bright Mother. That connection makes you and Nea two sides of one coin." He flipped a coin in the air and caught it before turning it over to show the rose on one side and the eight-pointed star on the other.

Garret let out a huff of breath. His mind was reeling. "What do you mean about me and the Bright Mother?"

"You have no idea, do you?" Wade cast a glance at Nea. "You didn't ever wonder why the pair of you are drawn together like a seam in cloth?"

Drawn together? He wasn't sure that was the case. They'd only met a few months ago, and whilst circumstances had meant they had grown close, it wasn't anything more than that. Or was it? Declan certainly seemed to take amusement in pointing it out, and there had been moments when ... He shook his head.

Wade was still playing with the coin. "When the sky is torn and the worlds collide, when hope is lost and the dead doth rise, then will walk the saviours of the sun and night: a child of Shadow and a child of Bright."

"Where have I heard that before?" Declan swung around to face them.

"It's a piece of an old ballad," Rourke offered. "Most of it has been lost to time, but a few verses remain."

"Of course! That is why your keen is so *weird*. It's not because you're a warden at all!" Zephyr exclaimed.

"I am sorry, but you've lost me," Declan said. "Garret is definitely a warden. At least he feels like one ... for the most part. Well, he did before he went and got his keen mixed up with Nea's."

"That's just it though. How did their keens become tangled?" Her antennae twitched and straightened.

"He channelled it by accident when he was trying to isolate the corruption—"

"Exactly!" Zephyr bounced from foot to foot and clapped her hands. "Frell had no idea what was sitting right under her nose," she said with a bright smile.

"I still don't follow. It was the corruption that allowed him to channel Nea's magic, and he was touching her at the time. Mages can share or swap keens in certain circumstances; though it is rather challenging, it is not impossible. And Nea had already proven that she could share her keen with *apparent* ease when she was helping Nora stabilise her magic. I had assumed that the combination of Nea's abnormality and the corruption giving it a boost had been what enabled Garret to—"

Zephyr grabbed his face and stopped him mid-sentence. "Okay, calm that beautiful brain of yours for a moment and *listen* to me." She released him and drew a deep breath. "It wasn't anything to do with Nea. Except it was a little bit, but we'll get to that. It was all Garret because ..." She was so excited she was practically vibrating.

"Shadow's teeth, Zeph, just get it out." Wade chuckled.

"It's because Garret is—"

"A brightling," Garret said.

Zephyr deflated. "You already knew?"

"A brightling?" Declan studied Garret. "No, I would have noticed." Then his expression changed. "You knew and didn't tell me? How long have you known?"

Garret shifted his grip on Nea. "A few days. Nea told me she suspected it was the case after we encountered my mother's spirit in the forest."

"Here, let me take her for a bit." Rourke stepped forward, and Garret carefully handed Nea to him.

"Does being a brightling really mean I have some essence of the Bright Mother in my blood?" He stretched and shook his arms to relieve the tension as he directed the question at Zephyr.

"Without a doubt. Brightling are chosen by the Mother. The way the stories tell it, they are the product of failed abortions or pregnancies that would have ended in tragedy if the Bright Mother herself had not intervened. They are usually born keen-less but exhibit the ability to channel the keen of mages around them," Zephyr said.

"Nea said as much, but I've never been able to channel anyone's magic except hers." He shook his head. When he had channelled her magic in the forest, she had said it was his keen not hers that he had used.

"What aren't you saying, old boy?" Declan asked.

"The night Nea followed me into the Sorrow Wood, I used her magic again. But it was different to the first time."

"Different how?" Declan took a step towards him.

Garret rubbed the back of neck. "It was like it belonged to me, not her." He cast a glance at Nea then at his hands.

Declan let out a low whistle. "And you were born at midsummer."

Garret ran his hands through his hair. His mind was reeling, and he wished Nea was awake. He wasn't sure he was ready to discuss this with anyone else. He trusted her judgement and her careful way of explaining things.

"We're lucky Frell didn't realise."

Zephyr said at the same time Declan asked.

"Did Nea say how she thinks this happened? Like, did your mother try to purge her pregnancy or was there something else that went wrong?"

Of course Declan would be curious about the finer details.

"My mother took a tincture of pennyroyal and brightsbane, and you've spent enough time with Margot to have an idea of what that does."

Zephyr's intake of breath overshadowed every other sound. "She must have been desperate. That could kill her as easily as the babe." Her golden gaze settled on Garret. "Why would she risk killing herself in the process?"

Garret rubbed the scar above his lip. "Because she couldn't live with thought that I would grow up and become like ... my father."

"Frederick?" Declan asked.

"Evard."

"*Evard*? Mother's tits, how long have you known? Does Nea know?"

He nodded. "I learned the truth that night in the Sorrow Wood. And Nea knew for quite a while, or rather she suspected it, but my mother's spirit confirmed it."

"Does Evard know?"

"We're not sure. Nea said he was experimenting with bloodlines in the hope of creating a mage like her. She wondered if I was a result of that, but she was certain that Evard didn't know I was a brightling."

Declan rubbed his hands through his hair, causing it to stand on end. "Well ... shit. You're taking it surprisingly well, old boy."

"Honestly, I'm too worried about Nea to give too much thought to anything else right now."

"On that note, we should keep moving," Rourke said. "We need to reach the tribe before nightfall, and standing around in the forest isn't going to get us there."

"Rourke is right. We can continue this discussion once Nea's awake." He didn't want to think about what might happen if they couldn't wake her.

The lengthening shadows had merged into the smoky darkness of dusk before they reached the edge of a small village. It was set into a rocky slope that led to a sheer cliff face. Rourke passed Nea back to Garret and moved to the front of the group as a pair of thickset warriors crossed their spears and blocked the path.

"You dare to bring strangers here," the male guard said as he studied their group. "And *Nundle*, no less." His lip sneered over the word.

There were similarities to Rourke in the line of his jaw and the set of eyes. His skin was the same rusty tone, but where Rourke's tattoos were intricate coiling patterns, this man's were sharp and angular. The second guard tilted her head and met Garret's eye as he studied her. Her skin bore similar geometric patterns to the other guard, but beneath the tattoos it was a softer shade of orange. More like the pink-touched hue that toned the sky at sunset than deep rusted metal.

"They have no allegiance to the witch. They risked their lives—"

"You know the law, little brother. Their kind is not permitted to enter the village, and as for them"—he jutted his chin at Garret and Declan—"they—"

"Uther." The female guard laid a hand on his arm and tilted her head towards Nea. "They've brought the *deera solvec*." She stepped towards Garret, and he tightened his hold on Nea.

"The what? Was that the old tongue?" Declan glanced from the guard to Rourke.

"It means Daughter of Shadow," Zephyr said quietly, but her attention was not on Declan. It was on the group of Rourke's tribesmen who had come forward to see what was going on.

"Where's Moira?" Rourke asked them.

"She's in the Womb of Stars and is not to be disturbed. *Deera solvec* or not." Uther tapped the butt of his spear on the ground. "I will not permit entry into the village without—"

"Hackles down, Uther. You're just embarrassing yourself," an old woman said.

The crowd parted, revealing her. Though hunched with age, there was litheness to her limbs that suggested she had been as formidable as Rourke in her prime. Her skin was a shade somewhere between Rourke and the female guard's, the tattoos that covered it were smooth and swirling. Did the tattoos signify family or station? Perhaps station, as Uther was Rourke's brother and they had different markings.

The woman leant heavily on a dark, twisted staff at the top of which was an elegant rose in full bloom. Cupped by the petals at the centre of the rose was a large diamond-shaped amethyst.

Her pink-hued eyes settled on Garret before dropping to Nea, and a quiver of magic twitched down Garret's spine. Declan must have felt it too because he shifted his feet, his own prickling keen rising and charging the air.

"Well. I was expecting you to get her here in one piece, but we'll have to make do with what we have," she said to Rourke in that tone that Garret's grandmother had used when she was chiding him for skipping out on his chores. "Bring her." She turned around quicker than her age should have permitted, the movement shifting the deep-grey braid that hung to her hips.

The crowd parted farther to let Garret pass, and the others fell into step behind him with Rourke at the very back. They followed the woman through the centre of the village and up a winding path that led to the base of the cliff where a pair of massive doors covered in intricate carvings were set into the stone. The left door was a display of swirls and circles interspersed with roses, which had been painted shades of purple. The right door had ochre and rust-coloured eight-pointed stars carefully placed among precise geometric patterns.

"You're taking her straight into the womb?" Rourke asked as the woman stepped up to the doors.

"You've left me no choice. She is of no use to anyone in that state. I only hope that she is not too far gone to bring back."

"What do you mean 'not too far gone'?" Declan paled slightly. "Is she ... she's not ..."

"Dead?" It was the same blunt tone Nea sometimes used. "She's as close as you can get without fully slipping over. If Rourke hadn't anchored her life force to tall and broody here, she'd be lost to us entirely now." Her eyes narrowed as she studied Declan. "Though you know a little about walking that line between life and death. Her work, is it?" She indicated Nea.

Declan opened his mouth then closed it again before raking his fingers through his hair. "I am not sure, to tell the truth."

Moira didn't take her eyes off Declan as she thudded the butt of her staff on the ground, and her magic quivered down Garret's spine again. The amethyst at the top of the staff lit up, and a seam of rainbow light shone between the doors before they grated slowly open.

Behind the doors was a wide corridor carved into the stone. They followed it into a chamber with luminescent crystals set into the ceiling and walls. At the centre of the chamber was a stone altar in front of a pool of water that glowed a soft turquoise.

"Alright, take her into the pool. It will dissolve the last of the witch's magic and cleanse you both."

"Moira," Rourke said, drawing her attention. "You need to tell them."

"Tell us what?" Garret asked.

Moira's mouth tightened and she inhaled deeply. "She has gone too far to simply be reconnected with her body. The only way to bring her back without *damaging* her, or you, is to complete what Rourke started and strengthen the bond he formed between you."

Zephyr gave a sharp intake of breath, and Wade swore.

"You can't mean a death ward?" Declan said.

"If it doesn't work, it will kill them both," Wade said.

"I have no concerns about it not working," Moira said flatly. "Provided he is willing to pay the price." She indicated Garret. "Though given the death grip he's had on her body since you arrived, I doubt he will object."

"Garret, you know this will tie your soul to Nea's permanently? She would never ask that of you—she said so herself." Declan touched his arm.

"I know." He swallowed and studied Nea's face. "But I also know that she would risk everything to do what's right. And if she was listening right now, she would tell me I'm an idiot and I can't save everyone ... But I *can* save her. I need to save her ... It's becoming clear that this isn't just about curing corruption and stopping Evard. We need her, Declan." He met Declan's eye. Whilst he had come to terms with the fact that Declan probably wouldn't be able to return to their world, he had assumed Nea would. And from the moment he had watched the pallor of death take over her body, he had known he couldn't face whatever was to come alone. "*I* need her ... whatever the cost."

Declan let out a low whistle. "I wish she'd been awake to hear that little declaration." His gaze switched to Moira. "Alright, what do we do?"

"You? Just stay out of the way and keep your mouth shut." She turned to Garret. "Into the pool you go. We've wasted enough time."

Shifting his hold on Nea, Garret carried her to the edge of the pool and drew a deep breath before wading out to the centre where the warm water lapped against his waist. Moira made a dipping motion with her hand, and he lowered them both completely under the water.

The bottom fell out from beneath his feet, and he found himself suspended in a vast sea of stars. Far below, he could see Nea wandering a labyrinth of rose hedges. She seemed to be chasing a flock of glowing birds. He glanced at her lifeless body still in his arms as his lungs began to ache, starving for air.

He resurfaced, magic prickling over his skin as warm rivulets of water ran off him and spattered against the rippling surface of the pool.

"Quickly now. On the altar with her," Moira said.

Garret did as instructed, carefully laying Nea down and brushing her wet hair away from her face.

"Alright, give me your arm." Moira held a dark-bladed knife—one that Garret had seen before with roses carved into the hilt.

When Garret offered his arm, she reopened the thin scar on his wrist and then did the same to Nea. She pressed the wounds together, holding them in place as magic charged the air in the room. Ice burned along Garret's veins, and his breath came out in a white cloud. Then heat chased the ice, burning heat that dried his throat and threatened to consume him.

At last Moira released him and stumbled backwards. Rourke caught her before she fell. A white streak was forming in her hair. She drew starved gulps of air but straightened, batting Rourke's hands away as she approached Garret.

He dropped to his knees as she took hold of his arm. When had his body grown so heavy? Moira turned his wrist upward and traced her finger along the thin lines of dark violet that formed a rose where the cut had been on his forearm. He glanced at Nea's arm where it hung over the side of the altar. The pale flesh was also marked by lines, though these ones were a fiery orange in the shape of an eight-pointed star. Garret touched his fingers to the mark on his arm. The cool kiss of Nea's keen seemed imbedded beneath it. He blinked. The edges of his vison were dimming.

"What now?" Declan's voice asked, but he seemed so far away.

"Now we wait," Moira replied as the world shifted around Garret and the closing darkness consumed him.

CHAPTER NINETEEN

MARGOT

Warren held the journal out to Margot, and she shook her head, wrapping her arms around herself. She didn't want to know what it said. Not now while guilt and sorrow and a burning sensation she couldn't quite place were tearing through her body, all warring for precedence. She gulped air, trying to shift the constriction in her throat as she raked her fingers through her hair.

The door banged open and Emil rushed in. His gaze darted from Penny to Margot to Warren and then back to Margot as confusion wrinkled his brow.

"What happened?" he asked, Dale appearing in the doorway behind him.

"Nea ... she ..." Penny shook her head and swallowed. "She's dead."

Emil gripped the door frame. "How?"

"We don't know," Penny replied. "But the journal we couldn't open ... the enchantment was linked to her life force and it just lifted."

Something bumped against the back of Margot's legs and she fell backwards, only to be caught by the bed. This was worse than Kalhanna. After the purge, she hadn't known the truth either way, and that gave her hope. But there was no way Nea could be alive if the journal was open. Was there? Was Warren mistaken about the nature of the enchantment? He had to be. But if he was not and Nea was dead, did that mean Garret was too? If he wasn't, there was no way he could return from the Between without Nea's magic to work the portal. Another wave of dread lifted bile into the back of Margot's throat. They hadn't discussed how they would get home, had they? In fact, Nea had avoided the subject.

"Mother damn her!" Margot's knuckles stung and she pulled them back from the wall to study the grazes that stood angry against her flesh.

"Margot," Penny said softly, the cloying kiss of her keen rolling across the back of Margot's skull.

"No, Penny. I want to feel this. I *need* to feel it." She pressed her fingers against the grazes. Instinct told her to heal them, but the hot sting of pain was cutting through her inner turmoil, soothing it.

The sensation of Penny's magic retreated, and Warren cleared his throat, giving the journal a little shake in Margot's direction. A loose paper fluttered free and landed by Emil's feet. He retrieved it and held it out to Margot.

Her name was the only word written on it, the 'M' slanted slightly to the right and the rest of the letters a delicate mix of loops and curves. She shook her head. "I can't ... You read it."

Emil drew a steady breath and unfolded the parchment. "Dear Margot, I am sorry." He paused.

"Is that all it says?" She swiped the itchy wetness away from her cheeks. She needed to bundle herself into one of Molly's hugs and never let go.

Emil licked his lips. "If you are reading this, then I didn't manage to stop Evard. I am sorry I didn't warn you sooner. I thought I could put an end to his plans without getting anyone else involved. However, as part of it concerns the repository at Kalhanna, I could not dissuade Francesca and Tobias. I sincerely hope their involvement hasn't cost them what it has cost me.

I know you would have helped if I had told you the whole truth, but Evard has become completely unhinged and I could not knowingly put you in that kind of danger. More than that, I would never ask you to give up the teaching position at Loch Bastien. Not when you seem to have finally found your place there. Your new friends sound like good people. I would have liked to meet them.

Anyway, I am rambling now. I guess I don't want to say goodbye or maybe I don't know how to. If Evard is still a threat, this journal will give you the answers you need—at least some of them. Take it to Mateus in The City of Stars. He will be able to help you. All my love, Nea."

"The City of Stars? That's in Osmar," Dale said, breaking the silence that had fallen when Emil finished the letter.

Emil cleared his throat. "If Nea thinks—thought Mateus could help us, that needs to be our next stop before we return to the others at Del Harol."

"We are close enough to the border here. We could slip into Prahma, then we can ride inland to Meddar and cross the Bright Strait there," Penny said. "Though it would be faster to find a boat in Prahma and cross the Fathoms."

Emil said something, but Margot didn't hear it over the ringing in her ears and the oily mass of coils that was stirring in the bottom of her stomach. "Why bother?"

Everyone turned to her.

"We've lost so many people to Evard. Francesca, Adam, Dhen, Tobias, and everyone else at Kalhanna. Now Declan and Nea and most likely Garret. What's the point in trying to defeat him?"

Penny's hand left a burning sting against Margot's cheek. "Snap out of it. We don't know for sure that Nea is dead." Her dark eyes widened.

"If the enchantment on the journal was—"

"Not helping, Emil!" Penny growled over her shoulder. "The point is, Nea wouldn't want you to give up. *Molly* wouldn't want you to give up. Yes, people have died. Lots of innocent people who deserved better, but those deaths are all in vain if you turn tail and run now. Nea has given us a path to follow, and if we do nothing then those deaths and all others that come will be on our heads." She whirled around and snatched the journal from Warren. "We have to stop Evard no matter the cost! It's what Nea would do." Her fingers squeezed the book so tight they grew pale from the pressure.

Margot touched her fingers to her still-burning cheek. "It's too much, Pen. I can't ..."

"You don't need Nea to hold your hand, and she would certainly tell you that herself if she were here." Penny touched her shoulder gently. "I'm sorry I slapped you but falling apart is not a luxury we have right now. We need to reach Mateus and find out what he knows, and then we need to get this box as far from Evard's reach as we can."

"The Arcanarium might not be a bad place for it," Warren said.

Margot studied the box and gave a nod. "You said the safest course of action was to put it inside a host. I'll do it."

"Margot, you have no idea what it could do to your keen," Penny said.

"You're right. But we have to stop Evard whatever the cost."

"But—"

"I've made my decision, Penny!" Her fists clenched as she settled her gaze on Warren. "Let's get this over with."

Warren gave a nod. "The rest of you, out." He waved Penny and the two men towards the door. "You're absolutely sure of this? It will most likely be permanent, and as Penny said, there is no telling what having it inside you could do to your keen."

She swallowed and picked up the box. Magic crooned across her fingers and slid into her core. This is what it wanted, what it needed. It could help them, but first it needed to be set free. "I am certain."

"Very well." He held his hand out, and Margot placed the box on his palm. His keen swelled in an icy cloud, then the chains shone violet before dropping to the floor. Warren opened the lid and twisted his fingers over the opening. A thin coil of silver smoke twisted out and formed a shifting orb. He took hold of Margot's hand and guided the orb towards her open palm. As it hovered just above her skin, his eyes asked her one last time if she was sure.

She nodded, not trusting herself to speak, and he pressed the orb into her skin. Her keen flared, grabbing hold of the invading magic and twisting it into something new. Nausea quivered through her stomach and her knees grew weak. She stumbled back onto the bed and clamped her fingers over her palm, holding it to her chest as a voice slipped across her mind. *Thank you.*

"Well?" Warren's hand touched her shoulder, and she opened her eyes; she wasn't sure when she had closed them.

Studying the silver spiral on her palm, she reached for her keen. It felt no different to before and the mark on her skin purred in silent contentment. "I feel fine."

Warren nodded. "Well, there's no going back now. I believe it was the right choice, but it may be one you come to regret. Now that I have healed your friend and answered your question, you need to clear off." His tone was soft like he was only half serious, but Margot didn't want to overstay their welcome. She gathered her things and went outside to Penny and the others.

"Well?" Penny asked as her keen brushed lightly across the back of Margot's skull.

"Nothing untoward." She held up the silver-marked palm. "See?"

Penny pursed her lips then nodded. "Here." She held out Nea's journal, and Margot licked her lips.

"I don't want it."

"Put it with the other one for now. If Nea wanted us to take them to Mateus, then that is what we are doing."

Margot took the journal with a sigh. Nea's keen still clung to the cover, and the mark on her palm seemed to pull towards it like it recognised its own kin. She swallowed the lump that had risen in her throat and tucked the journal into her bag, giving Penny a nod. "Let's go find Mateus then."

Margot hadn't been to Prahma in over a decade, but it hadn't seen much change. It was still a hodgepodge of Beldaren and Osmarian culture. The market that ran through the centre of the town was bright and loud and smelled of rich spices and livestock. Given that Penny's horse had been killed in the fenlands, she was riding with Margot. Margot followed her directions, guiding the horse through the mass of merchants hawking their wares, to a large mud-rendered building.

An official-looking woman with a quill and a ledger was standing on the steps arguing with a squat merchant in a scarlet waistcoat. He threw his hands in the air and snatched the slip of parchment she held out to him before storming past Penny as she dismounted.

The clerk turned her attention to their small group, her mouth tightening as she studied them. "If you are here to see Percival, you are too late. He left for Dendara an hour ago."

"We're not here to see Percival," Penny said.

The clerk's dark eyebrows lifted. "You are not?"

Margot shook her head as Penny said, "No, we are seeking passage across the Fathoms."

The clerk tapped her finger against her ledger and pursed her lips. "The ferry across the Fathoms is no longer in service. If you are heading to The City of Stars, you can cross the Bright strait at Meddar." She moved her sharp gaze to the next person in line.

"Wait," Penny said, and the clerk flicked her an impatient look. "Can you tell me if Captain Wren is in town?"

The clerk's mouth twisted as though she had tasted something particularly sour. "The *captain* can be found in the warehouse district. She is under strict orders to depart the town as soon as possible given her involvement in the *incident*." She then shooed them away and snapped her fingers at the person waiting behind them.

"Well, she's a little ray of sunshine," Emil quipped as they led their horses away.

"Wren? As in Wren and Gendry?" Margot asked.

Penny nodded. "If they have closed the ferry service across the Fathoms, we might be able to convince Wren to take us. Provided she hasn't left yet." She picked up her pace, weaving carefully through the crowd as Margot and the others followed leading their horses.

They made a quick detour to the stables and left the horses with the hand before heading into the warehouse district. The district was aptly named given that it was little more than a run of warehouses that backed onto the bay. Ships of various sizes were pulled into the long docks or moored farther out. It was just as loud as the market but not nearly as bright. Workers and ship hands darted about hauling boxes and crates and yelling all manner of profanities at each other. Molly would have loved it.

Penny made a beeline for the large ship moored in the farthest dock. She dodged easily around nets and between workers as though she had done it a hundred times before. As she neared the ship, a bear of man with a thick, dark beard and a scar that ran from the corner of his left eyebrow and over his nose to his right cheek stepped out to block her path. He folded his arms and scowled at her, then a wide smile broke the beard in half and he scooped her into a hug that lifted her off her feet.

Once back on the ground, Penny straightened her clothes and turned to the group. "This is Gendry, and this is Emil, Margot, and Dale." She pointed to each in turn.

As Gendry's dark eyes studied them, a prickle of magic itched up Margot's spine and set her hair on end. Storm mage. And a particularly powerful one, but she didn't get the sense that the keen was coming from the man in front of her. She tilted to look around his bulk, her keen-sense guiding her gaze to a short woman with robust curves and a cloud of flame-coloured hair.

"That's the captain," Gendry said, following her line of sight with a grin. "Nastiest little spitfire this side of Quel'Sapar."

The woman barked an order at a young sailor and then stormed towards them, the fringe on the bottom of the silk scarf tied around her hips fluttering with her movements. "And who do we have here? Penny! Stars above, I didn't think I'd see you again so soon." She clapped Penny on the shoulder with enough force to send her staggering.

"It's good to see you, Wren."

"And who have you brought with you, hmm?" Wren studied the rest of them.

"This is Emil and Dale, and that's Margot," Penny replied. "We need passage across the Fathoms."

Wren let out a low whistle. "Not many will make that journey these days, Penny. With the leviathan on the hunt and the maelstrom, it's much safer to go inland and skirt back."

"We don't exactly have the luxury of time. Nea—"

"Surfaced again, has she?"

Margot and Penny shared a look as Penny said, "Yes, she did, but …"

Gendry's face fell. "What happened?"

"We're not sure exactly, but we have reason to believe she's dead," Emil said.

"Was it Evard?" Wren asked.

Margot shook her head. "No. How much do you know?"

Wren folded her arms and rocked back on her heel. "Enough to figure out she was in way over her head and too stubborn to ask for proper help. Why do you suspect she's dead?"

Margot fished the journal out of her bag. "There was an enchantment on this that seemed to be tied to her life force, and it lifted."

"Nea's crafty though, and not so easy to kill. Perhaps there's another explanation for the enchantment failing," Gendry said.

Margot shook her head. "It's unlikely. But regardless, we need to get to The City of Stars, and we need to get there as soon as we can."

Wren released a long breath. "I'd like to help you. Any friends of Nea's are friends of ours, but crossing the Fathoms has always been dangerous. Now it's practically suicide."

"The maelstrom isn't a new threat though," Penny said.

"No but it has become unstable and it's movements unpredictable. It would prove challenge enough even without the leviathan," Gendry said. "The cursed beast has taken near a dozen ships to the deep in as many weeks. It's why so many are anchored in the bay. The captains' union decided it was too risky to attempt passage even before the authorities stepped in and closed the trade route."

As Gendry spoke, Wren moved to a low table covered in what looked like large sheets of oiled parchment. She shuffled through them and pulled one to the top, smoothing it down with her palm almost reverently before glancing their way and meeting Gendry's eye.

"Come now, lass. I know that look; you're not thinking about the Shadow Trench? That's where the Bright forsaken thing came from!" He stomped over and glared at the parchment.

Margot joined him. It wasn't parchment but some kind of oil-treated fabric with marks and lines that Margot couldn't decipher sprawled across its surface. It was clear enough that it was a map, but it was unlike any that she had ever seen before.

"The maelstrom doesn't cross the trench. If we skirt the edge of it and cross here"—Wren touched a spot on the map—"then we only have the leviathan to contend with."

"We're not equipped to take on the beast. The admiral—"

"The admiral is wedged so far up Percival's arse he won't notice we've stolen his ship until we're through the break." She grinned.

"*Stolen* his ship?!"

"*Borrowed.* I'll return it ... eventually. It will take too much time to steal that fancy harpoon he had installed, and we've nowhere to mount it anyway. So we might as well take the ship and put it to use. The admiral is too precious to do it himself. What's the point of having an arsenal if you're not going to use it?"

Gendry's cheek bulged as though he was pressing his tongue into it. "You do realise if the admiral catches us, we'll be ostracised from the union or worse?"

"We're as good as ostracised anyway."

"Which one is the admiral's ship?" Emil asked.

"The big fancy one." Wren pointed at the impressive ship anchored closest to the opening of the bay. "Don't let looks fool you. She's the second fastest vessel in these waters, and she has enough firepower to put a decent dent in that leviathan without breaking a sweat."

"If the admiral can do something about the leviathan, why hasn't he?" Emil asked

Wren shrugged. "He's a coward. Most men who hide behind their wealth are." She turned her attention back to Gendry and batted her eyelashes. "Come on, Gen. Don't tell me you haven't fantasised about running your hands over her wheel and feeling her shudder beneath you."

"We're still talking about the ship, right?" Emil quipped.

Gendry ran a hand over his face. "It's up to the crew. We can't sail her by ourselves, not if we're taking on the leviathan, and I won't order them to risk their lives because you're having a feud with the admiral."

Wren clapped her hands together. "Let's get this boat packed and anchored in the bay. We can talk to the crew there."

Less than an hour later, they were standing on the deck of The Azure Queen and Wren had just run through the plan to steal the admiral's ship. Most of the crew looked excited for the challenge. A few, however, didn't want to risk the voyage into the Fathoms and across the trench, which was understandable. Margot wasn't sure she wanted to either, but it seemed that she had been swept up by forces beyond her control yet again.

She slipped her hand into her bag and touched the journal; the mark on her palm throbbed in response to Nea's residual keen. With a steadying breath, she glanced out at the break in the rock wall that led to the fathoms—she could really use some of Nea's bravery right now.

They waited until nightfall before piling into several small boats and quietly navigating to the foot of the admiral's ship. One of the crew threw a grappling hook and caught the rail before deftly climbing out of sight.

Moments ticked by and then a thump sounded, and a rope ladder was rolled down. Wren caught it and darted up it, followed by Penny and Gendry. Emil indicated Margot go next. As she started up the ladder, it shook and slid to the side, and she shut her eyes, bitting her lip and gripping the rope white-knuckle tight.

"Keep moving," Emil whispered from beneath her.

Drawing a deep breath, she started climbing again. As she reached the rail at the top, a large hand grabbed the back of her shirt and hauled her onto the deck.

"It gets easier with each ship you infiltrate," Gendry whispered with a grin.

Margot had been expecting the crew of the admiral's ship to fight back, but Wren's men had them rounded up in no time.

"You have two options," Wren said as she paced in front of the bound crew. "You can be lowered to the waiting boats and taken safely back to the dock or you can remain on this vessel and aid us in taking on the leviathan. Any attempts at mutiny will see you tossed into the Shadow Trench."

The crew all shared a look.

"So, what do you want to do? Go back to dock and find a seedy mug of ale and a warm bed?" Most of the captives nodded. "Or come with us? I could use a few hands, and I pay fairly, not like your admiral."

A pair of identical women at the back of the group raised their hands. "We'll come with you," they said.

"I thought you bound them all securely." Wren cast a glance at her bosun, Rufus.

He shrugged. "Tight enough they'll have purple fingers if you keep gasbagging any longer."

"He did a fantastic job. It took us much longer to slip out than normal, but we love a challenge," one of the women said, lifting a coil of rope.

One of Wren's brows rose, and a satisfied sort of smile crossed her lips. "What are your names?"

"I'm Pippa, and this is Kiki." They stepped around their old crewmates.

"A pleasure, ladies. I am Captain Wren."

"Oh, we know." Pippa grinned.

"Alright, Gen, lower the rest of them down to the boats. You lot," she directed at the crew, "get to work. I want this ship through the break as soon as possible."

Everyone moved at once, and before long the anchor was lifted. Wren stood at the bow, her eyes closed. Her keen prickled up Margot's spine and stood her hair on end. A soft breeze stirred, picking up momentum until it was a steady wind filling the sails. The ship edged forward with a creaking groan, water sloshing along the sides as it gained speed towards the break in the wall of stone that ringed the harbour.

A horn sounded, and Margot chanced a look back at the dock. Shadows darted through the bobbing lights. There was a frenzy of activity as the shinning hulls of sleek, long boats were cast off.

"A little faster, my love," Gendry called down the deck.

"And risk tearing our belly on the wall and running aground?" Wren yelled back brightly. "She's a little bigger and more unruly than the Queen."

"You can handle her, lass. If those long boats catch us—"

"They won't," Wren ground out and planted her feet as a roaring gust ballooned the sails and the ship lurched. "Keep her steady now, Gen."

The wall of rock pressed in close on either side of the ship as the first of the long boats neared.

"Not today." Pippa sent a ball of fire flaring towards the boat. The men inside bailed out of the way, some ending up in the water as the fire spread across the wood. Kiki held her hand up for a high five, and as Pippa slapped it, Kiki's keen washed across Margot. With a flick of her fingers, the mage summoned a wave of water that capsized the burning boat.

"Easy, Gen. You're too close on the port side," Wren yelled.

"She'll make it." Gendry gripped the wheel as rocks screeched along the side of the ship.

Then they emerged into open water, and the crew let out a whoop.

"They'd be absolute fools to follow us out here," Rufus said.

"Still, it won't hurt to put a bit of distance between us and the wall," Wren said as the gale started to decrease. "Nice work back there, you two," she added to the twins.

"Is that the maelstrom?" Margot pointed to the patch of sky in the distance that was devoid of stars. Occasionally it lit up with a coloured flash of light. Not exactly lightning, more like mage light: purple, pink, orange, blue, green ... It almost made her eyes water, and she couldn't imagine what it would be like to be closer.

"It's a thing of beauty, isn't it?" Gendry said. "Legend says that it is a remnant of whatever those mages did that sunk Port Brenna back in the day."

"So, it's not just a storm?"

Gendry chuckled. "No, lass. It's not *just* a storm any more than the leviathan is just an oversized whale."

"Best be getting some rest now. We should reach the edge of the trench by morning. Dara will let us know if the maelstrom moves or there's any sight of the leviathan." Wren indicated a girl of maybe seven at best who looked like even the slightest breeze could knock her off deck.

The girl had a cloud of black ringlets and deep-brown skin that hinted Faridean heritage. She studied Margot with curious eyes that were so pale a green, they were almost colourless. A flutter of magic caressed Margot, and the girl nodded. She wasn't a mage, but she wasn't completely keen-less either. A seer perhaps? Keen-touched in some way, that was certain.

CHAPTER TWENTY

NEA

Her body was a pinprick of heat and light, too far away to reach. She knew she was forgetting something crucial, but the longer she floated here in the muffled darkness, the farther away her thoughts drifted. Then she couldn't remember her own name, but she knew her purpose. She was an empty shell, a vessel for darkness and death.

Light fractured the darkness like a mirror shattering, bringing with it scolding heat and memories.

So many memories.

A name.

Her name.

Nea.

Her head was heavy, her vision blurred, but it was Garret who stood on the other side of the bars. Even if she couldn't feel his keen, she would know him by his scent anywhere: clove with the underlying notes of leather and steel.

She stood and gripped the bars. "Garret? Is it really you?"

"It's me." His voice was like the roll of soothing fingers down her spine, and when his hand brushed hers, heat sung along her arm and settled behind her navel.

Safe. She gripped his hand, not wanting the feeling to leave her. "I knew you'd figure it out."

"How do I get you out of there?" he asked as he examined the bars of the cage.

"You don't." Frell entered the room, and if looks could kill, Garret would have dropped like a stone. "I knew you would prove trouble. Now you will leave this place and return Nea to the warehouse, and I will let you live."

"She isn't really here," Nea said. "I think to break this cage you need to figure out what she took from me."

"What she took from you?" Garret turned back to face her. "She couldn't take anything. She tried but failed each time. She ..." Recognition flashed in his grey eyes. "She took your pain and your anger and your guilt. All the things that you use to keep yourself prisoner."

A smile pulled across Nea's mouth. "Well done." The floor tilted, and she caught herself on her hands and knees as weakness rattled through her body.

"Look what you've done!" Frell yelled. "Get out of my way. She's useless to me if she dies."

"This is your—"

"Garret ..." She didn't want her last moments to be listening to him argue with Frell's reflection.

"How do I fix this?" His voice was laced with pain and uncertainty, and he reached for her but didn't actually touch her as though afraid she would collapse into dust as the cage had done. She just might if the heaviness in her bones was anything to go by.

She shook her head. "You can't." She ran her fingers along the edge of his jaw, savouring the feel of him. "You need to find Rourke and get him to send you home. Tell Margot I'm sorry—" She didn't get to finish what she wanted to say as the world went dark.

❧

Impossibly tall hedges pressed in from both sides, creating a narrow road which seemed to stretch into infinity. Mist pooled along the path in ghostly drifts. Above her the sky was a deep blue that faded to black, broken by glittering stars and a sickle-shaped moon. She took a step, and roses began to bloom on the hedges—large velvety blooms a shade that was somewhere between pale pink and lilac. She lifted a finger and touched the closest flower. It shivered under her touch then discoloured to a soft grey. The ashen hue spread through the surrounding blooms like a drop of ink in water.

Nea looked back the other way. She could hear familiar voices, but only fragments of their conversation reached her.

"Help her."

"I'm not a healer ..."

A cold had seeped into her bones, numbing the tips of her fingers. She rubbed them together then hugged herself as her breath clouded in front of her. Turning away from the voices, she started moving forward again towards the flicker of light that darted through the mist.

The farther away from the voices she walked, the brighter the light grew until it solidified into a cloud of small lark-like birds made of pure starlight. The birds undulated through the mist in swirling patterns as though chasing a swarm of gnats.

She lifted her foot to take another step—

"I wouldn't go any farther that way if I were you," said a voice behind her, familiar but foreign at the same time.

The voice belonged to a man with eyes the shade of dark amethysts. The waves that brushed his shoulders were the same moody storm-grey as her own. He was leaning against the hedge, careless of the thorns that gripped at his midnight-blue cloak. As he shifted, the pinpricks of light that studded the plush fabric shimmered like stars.

"Why?"

He chuckled at her question and pushed off the hedge. "Because only death lays that way, but you already know that, don't you?"

She knew for certain now.

"I underestimated the ward mage. I would relish the challenge his tenacity gave me if it hadn't placed you in this current predicament."

"And what predicament is that?"

He gestured to the swarm of bright birds. "You are so close to the precipice, and if I let you fall, then who knows how long before another of your calibre comes along." He held his hand out. "So, come. I'll make sure you get back to where you are supposed to be."

She didn't take his hand. "It would inconvenience you if I were to follow the flock?"

"Greatly." The word was almost snarled, and he lunged forward, his fingers closing vice-tight around her wrist. He spun her, slamming her against his chest as he pointed her the way she had come. "I do look forward to meeting you under more suitable conditions." His breath stirred her hair as he whispered against her temple, then he gave her a shove that sent her stumbling.

She caught the hedge beside her to stop from falling, then she started running towards the voices that were now calling her name.

Nea turned another corner and threw her hands in the air as she was confronted with yet another long mist-shrouded passage. She slumped against the hedge, ignoring the thorns that grabbed at her clothes and hair.

"What do you want from me!" she yelled at the sliver of moon above. The starlight birds had long disappeared.

A flash of light lit the sky and streaked towards the ground. Nea pushed off the hedge and ran towards it. The branches shifted, trying to block her path as she barrelled around corners and leapt through closing gaps.

Just ahead she could make out a figure getting to his feet. The hedges groaned as they drew together to block her path. It was too far. She'd never make it in time, not with her lungs burning and her legs heavy from running. No. She would not give in. Forcing her feet to move, she charged for the closing gap, and with a yell she leapt through. The branches scraped against her skin and pulled her hair free from its braid. Her momentum carried her straight into the other person, and he caught her with a staggering step backwards.

Strong arms wrapped around her, cradling her against his chest as his face buried in her hair. The embrace was safe and warm, despite the dampness of his shirt, and she didn't want it to end. The whole time she had been in this maze, she had been a soul flying untethered, and finally she had found an anchor drawing her home. Her fingers twisted in the sides of his shirt, gripping the fabric tight as she burrowed as deep as she could in the familiar scents of clove, leather, and steel. *Safe.*

"Nea? Are you alright?" His chest vibrated against her ear, and his hand gently stroked the back of her head.

"No, I'm not. How did you get here?"

He searched her face. "I guess it's my penance for messing around with strange and unpredictable magic." His thumbs traced small circles on her arms, and his grip tightened slightly.

"What sort of strange and unpredictable magic?" She leaned back but didn't let go of his shirt. She was afraid if she did the hedge might swallow him up and she'd be alone in the mist again.

He rubbed the back of his neck. "I let Rourke tie your life force to mine to buy us time to save you."

"You did what?" She released him and retreated a step. "Do you realise how dangerous that is? It could have killed you just as easily as saved me?"

"I understood the consequences, but I don't think that is what brought me here."

She put her hands on her hips. "What are you not telling me?"

"I—"

A scream shattered the air around them, cutting him off. There was something all too familiar about the sound.

"Nea!"

She spun around as Margot's voice echoed through the dark branches. A section of the mauve blooms was darkening to a deep red—a bloodstained path leading her past Garret and deeper into the maze. "Nea, please. I need you!"

Garret caught her arm as she went to step by him. "It's not her."

The rational part of her knew he was right, that it was most likely a trick of this realm. But what if it wasn't?

"No, please ... NO—" The words ended in a scream that turned her blood to ice, and she pulled free of Garret to run towards the panicked voice.

"Nea, wait." Garret implored as his footsteps sounded behind her.

She rounded another corner and the hedges opened out into a wider area. Sitting in the middle of the space was Margot, her golden curls stained with ash and blood and a body slumped across her lap. A body that haunted Nea's dreams. She started forward again but a warm weight tackled her, knocking her to the ground.

"Stop and think." Garret's breath stirred against her ear.

She looked back at Margot and then at the patch of ground directly in front of her—or what should have been ground but was a wide void dropping away to nothingness.

A wicked smile curved across Margot's mouth and she disappeared in a cloud of violet smoke and starlight-hued feathers. Garret let Nea up but kept a hand on her arm as he drew away from the edge of the pit.

"That was too close," he said. There were small tears in his shirt, and his cheeks were covered in scratches as though he had climbed through the hedges.

Nea should have known better, but this place had scrambled her thoughts. "I'm sorry. I don't know what came over me."

He let out a breath. "I understand. When I heard the screams in the forest, I thought it was Nora. I knew it couldn't be, but something inside kept asking *what if it is?*"

Nea bit her lip. "*I* should have known better though. I should have *felt* it. It was a childish mistake for a necromancer to make. One that could have gotten us both killed."

He crossed his arms. "You're only human, Nea."

The hedges had been closing in, and the path opened up again. This time it was lit with golden sunshine though the sky above still bore the banner of night.

"That path looks too enticing to be true or am I just being overly cautious?" Garret asked with half a smile.

"Oh, it's definitely not what it seems, but we don't have much choice unless you fancy trying to climb the hedges." She indicated the branches that had blocked off their other path. "What were you trying to say before the apparition cut you off?"

He rubbed the scar above his lip, his grey eyes clouding with something—doubt? "We can discuss that later. Right now we should focus on getting out of this maze." He moved towards the sunshine-filled path, but she stepped in front of him, blocking the way.

"No. It's important; I didn't listen to you and nearly went head first into the void for it. I think if we are to get out of here, we need to work together. And for that we need complete honesty. How did you get here?" He'd said he had tied his life force to hers, and it was a concept she understood in theory. But it was magic that had not been practiced in eons, and she couldn't recall ever reading anything about enchanted mazes.

"You have to realise there was no other way to save you."

She didn't like the sound of that.

"Rourke took us to an elder of his tribe, Moira, and she finished what he had started when he tied our life forces together ... She created a death ward." He held out his right wrist, pushing the sleeve back to reveal a tattoo-like mark.

A death ward. The words seemed to take on a life of their own as they hung in the air between them. Cold dread clawed up the back of Nea's neck as she studied the faint purple lines twisting over his skin and forming a rose. She bit her lip and touched her fingers to the mark. It was cool, unlike the skin around it, but that wasn't all. Her keen sang along the lines. Not trapped and trying to get out, but stable and content as though it was right where it belonged. She examined her own arms and found a deep orange eight-pointed star on the inside of her left wrist. Garret's keen radiated from the mark in a warm thrum: steady, safe, home.

Boiling anger replaced the dread. Did he realise what he had done to his own soul? Mother damn him and his insatiable need to save people. She bit down on her lip and took a step back. "You should have let me die. How many times have I told you that you—"

"Can't save everyone. I know that. But I *could* save you."

"By saving me, you've damned yourself."

"I knew the price, and I paid it anyway. We can't—"

"I would have never asked—"

"Damn it, Nea, will you let me finish?" His tone cut through her, and the sunshine dimmed as thunder echoed through the hedges. "I know you would have never asked for this. I know that because I wouldn't have asked it of anyone either. You accuse me of having to protect everyone, of having to save them, but you're just as bad for it. You gave up your own son and ran away from everyone you care about just because you wanted to protect them. I watched you sacrifice pieces of your humanity to stop Evard from hurting Margot, and I know that you would have done it again and again until there was nothing left. I know because that is exactly what I would do."

She bit her lip. "But it's your *soul,* and by shackling it to mine, you will *never* be able to escape me." Oily coils were stirring in her stomach. "Death spoils everything it touches, especially necromancers, and I don't want it to spoil you. You deserve better than that ... You're a good man, Garret, and I'm ... I'm a monster. The things I have done, the things I have stood by and allowed to happen ..." Prickly heat blurred her vision. "I don't *deserve* to be saved."

"You're wrong."

"I—"

"Do you know what I went through to break you out of Frell's prison? I've seen your past, Nea, some of the worst moments from it. You were reacting to actions of others. You didn't choose to kill those soldiers because you just *felt* like it. You attacked Evard because he threatened you after you tried to stand up for what was right. You killed Harold to protect Margot."

She shook her head. "I still chose how to react. I didn't have to attack Evard or kill Harold. The soldiers at Kalhanna were different. I did want them dead for what they had done. I didn't just lose control of the darkness inside. I *let* it take over. We all have to make choices, and I chose wrong. I always choose wrong, and I am afraid that this time you did too."

Thunder echoed again and wind howled, snapping at her hair and clothes. The ground shuddered, and Nea staggered backwards as an impossibly tall wall of branches erupted between them, blocking them off from each other.

"Garret!" She threw herself against the hedge, ignoring the bite of the thorns against her palms. The idea of wandering the mists alone again pressed clammy fingers to the back of her neck.

"I'm still here. Are you alright?" His voice called through the hedge.

"I'm fine." *Physically at least.* Her emotions were warring with each other: anger at what he had done and fear for his safety, and something else. Something she didn't want to acknowledge because when she did it would change everything irrevocably. "I'm sorry." She rested her forehead against the branches as the wind died down and the thunder became a distant rumble. "I'm not ungrateful. I know I should have just said thank you like any normal person would."

He made a sound on the other side of the hedge. Was it a laugh? "You don't need to apologise. I understand. But I don't believe I chose wrong. I'm not a good person either, Nea. Sure, I try to be, but there are moments in my past that are as dark as yours. Each one a scar, but it is our scars that make us who we are."

She bit her lip and inhaled deeply, then something behind her barked.

"Was that a dog?" Garret asked.

Nea turned around. A lanky hound was sitting in the middle of the path. His rough, midnight-blue coat was covered in silver spots that seemed to glitter as he wagged his tail patiently.

"Yes," she replied to Garret's question.

The dog got to his feet and gave another bark then started trotting away only to stop and glance back over his shoulder as though waiting for her.

"I think he wants me to follow." She didn't want to leave Garret, but they couldn't just sit here waiting to see what happened.

"Then you should follow."

"But what about you?"

"I'll be fine. We have to find a way out of this maze. But, Nea, please be careful."

She bit her lip. "You too." The hound barked again. "Alright, I'm coming now."

As she followed the hound, the hedges closed behind her and a soft snow started to fall. The air grew colder until her breath fanned out in small white clouds. She kept moving forward. The dog stopped every so often and glanced her way as though checking she was following.

Just when Nea was beginning to think she couldn't go any farther, a warm glow appeared. It was emanating from a large door in the hedge. The handle was a big rose carved out of dark metal that shone with the iridescence of oil on water. The dog sat in the snow and flicked his snout towards the door. Gingerly, Nea tested the handle. It turned easily and the door pushed open. But as she went to step through, the ground fell out from beneath her and she plummeted down an icy tunnel before being spat out into the middle of Evard's throne room.

Evard was sitting on his mahogany throne, his chin resting on his tented fingers. Leith stood to his right, a mask of onyx hiding the upper half of his face as he stared out over the heads of the masked dancers that whirled all around Nea.

Nea got slowly to her feet and brushed her hands on the front of her clothes, only to find them replaced with a gown of lilac lace that just hugged the edge of her shoulders. The lace and silk bodice met a skirt made from layer upon layer of gossamer fabric that reminded her of feathery spider webs. Her hair was a heavy weight piled on the top of her head. The dancers closest stopped and stared, the eyes behind their masks familiar. As she studied them, blood stared to creep from under the edges of their masks. She swallowed and stepped backwards, but the floor was slick, and she slipped.

A hand caught her wrist, steadying her. Its owner yanked her forward, and she crashed against his chest. He was wearing a mask of black metal, but she recognised the hate-filled dark eyes: *Willem.* No, he was dead. She looked back at the bleeding dancers. One by one, they removed their masks. Francesca, Adam, Dhen, Tobias, Millicent ... Her heart leapt into her throat.

Willem dragged her through the crowd to the foot of Evard's dais, the lilac skirt growing heavy with blood as it trailed across the soaked ground.

"My, my. You have been a naughty girl, haven't you?" Evard said, his lip curling over his teeth in a sneer. "You fought your true nature for so long, but it won out in the end anyway." He stepped down and took hold of her wrist, leaning forward until his cheek brushed hers and his breath whispered hot against her ear. "No matter how carefully groomed we are, nature will always win out in the end."

She wanted to break free, but her body was not listening to her mind.

Evard rolled the sleeve of her gown up to show the inky marks of corruption. He traced them delicately with his finger. "If only you had accepted the truth sooner. So much turmoil could have been avoided, so many lives would still be intact. But no matter. Their deaths serve our purpose. *Your* purpose." He dropped her wrist and touched the other, the one with the orange star. "Oh, he tried so valiantly to save you, but you can't be saved. *What does death touch that it doesn't spoil?*" As he traced the star mark, the skin beneath his finger burned and burst open, bloody lines replacing the orange. "Would you like to see what became of him?"

She wanted to shake her head, to scream: No, this wasn't real. This wasn't her. But it was. She was capable of all this and more. She was a vessel of death and destruction. That was what she had been created for and no matter how hard she fought, it would always end the same.

The doors opened, and Garret was dragged out. His face was partially obscured by a pink-gold robrillium mask. Blood stained the front of his shirt in a wide bloom of deep scarlet and ran from the raw lacerations that boarded the shackles around his wrists. The guards, half-carrying half-dragging him, threw him on the ground at Nea's feet.

Her ribs strained against the bodice of her dress as her lungs cried out desperately for air. Evard's palm in the centre of her back was too hot. "Such a waste." His lips seemed to caress the words. "No matter." He pressed something into her palm, oily and ice cold: the handle of a dark-bladed dagger. "You know what must be done." His breath stirred the hairs on the side of her neck, his tongue lightly brushing her earlobe.

No. One of the guards grabbed a fistful of Garret's hair and tilted his head back, exposing his throat. Garret's grey eyes met hers, betrayal and loathing swirling in their stormy depths. No, she couldn't do this. It wasn't her. She wasn't Evard's puppet—she wasn't anyone's puppet.

"Perhaps you need a little more *incentive*." Evard snapped his fingers, and Margot was brought out. Tears ran in streaky paths down her cheeks. "I'll let you choose which one you kill. The one who sacrificed everything for you or the one you would sacrifice everything for."

Nea swallowed and tightened her grip on the hilt of the knife. "You're right. I do need to choose." She twisted the weapon, grabbing hold with both hands as she drove the blade under her ribs as hard as she could. Hot blood rushed over her hands, and the floor dropped out from under her as Evard roared.

The ground beneath her was cold and wet. Something was nuzzling against her ear making small whimpering sounds. She sat up and the dog's deep indigo eyes met hers. He licked her cheek and pressed his nose under her chin, wuffing hot breath across her neck.

She let out a sob and pressed her face into the fur of his shoulder. "That's not me," she whispered. "I can't become that—I won't."

The dog whined and sat back, his head tilted to one side.

"I can't sit here in the snow feeling sorry for myself. Where to next?"

The dog barked and trotted a short distance away. Nea scooped up the bloodstained skirt of her gown and followed after him.

After tromping through the snow for what felt like hours, a cavern of ice appeared. The opening was wide and dark. The dog barked and pointed his nose towards it. Nea shook her head. The last door she had gone through had been traumatic to say the least.

The dog's nose pressed into her hand, then he grabbed a chunk of her skirt and pulled her to the opening. She shook her head again. "I don't think I can face what is in there."

The dog let out a huff and gave her skirt another tug, tearing the gossamer fabric. The wind picked up, sending flurries of snow into the air, and the dog growled at something behind her. She spun around, but there was nothing there. Then the hedges started groaning and slamming together. She backed up until she was at the opening of the cavern. Her foot slipped, and she fell into the icy tunnel.

She slid down the slick ice until it spewed her out into a warmly lit room. There was a mirror and a basin on a pedestal. Rose-scented steam was rising from the water in the basin. Nea studied her reflection in the mirror. Her hair was hanging half-undone in a messy tangle, the lilac fabric of the dress was stained with blood and torn. So much blood—hers and others. She rubbed at her cheeks, leaving red smears. Her attention snapped to her hands—so many stains, some older and some new.

"Nea?"

She froze. Garret was standing behind her. He looked just as dishevelled as she did.

"Are you hurt ...? Is any of that yours?"

"Maybe ... I don't—" She rushed to the basin and started scrubbing. The water turned scarlet in an instant.

"Nea ..."

She scrubbed harder as ash caught in her throat and screams rang in her ears.

"You're not there anymore," he said softly like he was soothing a wild beast. "You're safe."

Safe. The word jolted through her and she knocked the basin, sending scarlet water splashing over the floor. She backed away from the widening puddle and dashed her hands on the front of her gown. They came away red again and a whimper escaped her as she studied the patches of sticky blood that marred the delicate cloth of her skirt. She had to get out of this dress. The sides of the bodice were constrictor-tight and tightening by the minute as she tried to suck air into her starved lungs. Her fingers gripped the lace across her back, searching for the tiny buttons that held it closed, but her hair kept getting in the way, tangling with the tackiness that stained her fingers.

"Easy now." Garret's voice was soothing as the warm weight of his hands touched her shoulders.

Calm flooded her body: *safe*. Garret was safe and steady like true north on Wren's enchanted compass.

"Deep breaths." He drew a breath and let it out again as though demonstrating. "Let me help you ..."

The bird fought, tangling its legs tighter in the ribbon as she approached. It tried to hop away but collapsed onto its side, its chest rapidly twitching as it panted in panic.

"Hush now. I'm not going to hurt you." She edged closer, keeping her voice calm, and the bird struggled away from her.

She lunged forward and grabbed hold of it, carefully restraining its flapping wings. It pecked at her fingers.

"Stop that now! I am trying to help you."

It struggled and pecked her again, this time drawing a tiny line of blood and causing her to drop it.

"Why won't you just let me help you!" she yelled, but the bird only panted and blinked back at her as she rubbed at the tears that were running down her cheeks. Why was she crying over some stupid bird who would rather die than let her help?

"Nea, what's going on?" Margot asked softly, her hand falling on Nea's shoulder.

Nea dashed the tears away and forced a smile onto her face. "Nothing, Margot. Just a stupid bird that doesn't want to be saved."

Margot looked at the struggling bird. "Oh, poor thing. Here, let me help." Margot slipped her shawl off and dropped it over the bird. Then she scooped it up and freed its legs, presenting them to Nea.

Nea sniffed and carefully unwound the ribbon, then Margot set the bird free. It flew off into the trees.

A tremor ran though her, scattering the memory. "I'm the bird," she whispered.

"Sorry?" Garret asked, drawing her attention to his reflection in the mirror.

Nea had spent her entire life not allowing others to help her because she was terrified of letting them see how vulnerable she really was—how broken. She'd run from everyone she ever cared about because she didn't want them to offer help she would refuse— had to refuse. As scared as she was of them knowing the truth, she was just as scared of hurting them because of what she was.

"Everyone wants to help me, but I fight them every step of the way because I am too scared to let them. If I accept help ... then they'll see the truth, and I can't ..." She closed her eyes. "I'm not strong enough to face another Kalhanna."

Garret's fingers tightened gently on her shoulders. "We're all scared, Nea, but you don't have to face it alone. You are punishing yourself for something you couldn't control. What happened at Kalhanna was the result of Evard's cruelty and thirst for power. You asking for help had nothing to do with it." He met her gaze in the mirror. "Forget about Evard and the Master of Shadows and everything else. What do you need in this moment right now?"

"I need ..." The dress didn't feel quite so tight now her panic was fading, but the bloodied fabric was starting to dry tacky and itchy against her skin. "I need to get out of this Bright forsaken dress."

CHAPTER TWENTY-ONE

GARRET

The thunder that had been growing steadily louder boomed, rattling the hedges and heralding a bitter wind that snapped at their clothes and hair. He opened his mouth to speak as the ground between them shuddered and branches burst from it knocking them both backwards.

"Garret!" There was desperation and an edge of fear to Nea's voice as she called his name.

"I'm still here." He gripped the hedge, ready to climb it, but it reached so far into the inky sky above that he couldn't tell where it ended. "Are you alright?" He rested his forehead against the branches.

"I'm fine."

Her voice was thick, and he gave a half-smile; he wouldn't call her out on that lie.

"I'm sorry." At her words, the thunder died to a distant rumble. "I'm not ungrateful. I know I should have just said thank you like any normal person would."

A laugh escaped him. He had known she wasn't going to take the news well, but he still wouldn't change what he had done. "You don't need to apologise. I understand; but I still don't believe I chose wrong. I'm not a good person either, Nea. Sure, I try to be, but there are moments in my past that are as dark as yours. Each one a scar, but it is our scars that make us who we are."

She was silent for so long that he was about to ask if she was still there when a dog barked.

"Was that a dog?" he asked.

"Yes."

She sounded as confused as he felt.

"I think he wants me to follow."

He could sense her hesitation even through the hedge. "Then you should follow."

"But what about you?"

"I'll be fine." He was starting to realise that the harder you fought the inevitable in this realm, the harder it came back to bite you in the end. "We have to find a way out of this maze. But, Nea, please be careful."

"You too," she said softly, and the dog barked again. "Alright, I'm coming now."

Garret let out a huff and turned to face the mist-filled path between the hedges. A light snow was starting to fall, though the starry sky above was completely clear. He glanced down at his still-damp shirt.

"Mrr-ow?"

His head snapped up at the sound. A large cream-coloured cat with golden tabby markings was sitting in the middle of the path watching him. Its large silver-grey eyes seemed unfathomably deep.

"So, if Nea is supposed to follow the dog, does that mean I need to follow you? Is this some kind of test then? Like one of Declan's stories?" He rubbed his arms to stir some warmth into them.

"Mrr-owp." The cat tilted its head as it regarded him. Then it stood and stalked forward to wrap itself around his legs before wandering back down the path with a flick of its tail.

"Alright then." He drew a breath and followed the cat. Declan was going to have a field day with this story when they got back. *If* they got back.

As the cat wound its way through the gathering drifts, Garret noted that its coat seemed to repel the steadily falling flakes. An ability he wouldn't mind himself as his feet grew more and more numb and his shirt pulled against his back as it stiffened and froze to his skin. They rounded a corner in the hedge and his grandmother's cottage came into view.

The cat sat and preened its paws.

"I am guessing I need to go inside there."

Its tail flicked but it made no sound.

Great. Last time he had been inside his grandmother's cottage in this realm, it had been a trap. He looked back the way he had come but the hedge was blocking the path again.

With a resigned sigh, he walked over and tested the handle. The door swung open at the slightest touch, but it wasn't his grandmother's kitchen on the other side. It was Evard's throne room. Bodies covered the floor, and in the middle of them was Declan standing as though frozen to the spot. Garret lifted his gaze past Declan to Evard's throne, but Evard wasn't sitting in it—Nea was. Evard was standing to the right of her, his hand sitting possessively on her shoulder.

A dark crown with red gems was resting on Nea's hair, which was free in tumbling curls over her back and shoulders. The gown she wore was the same blood-toned scarlet as the stones in the crown. A split up one side to her hip allowed the pale expanse of her thigh to show through. She appeared to be wearing elbow-length black gloves, but on closer inspection the lacy marks were actually the stains of corruption. Garret swallowed.

"So nice of you to finally join us." Evard's lips pulled into a cold smile. "It's a shame you missed most of the fun. She is truly magnificent, isn't she?" His fingers tightened on Nea's shoulder, but she was sitting calmly, her violet eyes staring straight into Garret's soul with no sign of their usual softness. "This is what she was created for, you know?"

"No, this isn't her," Garret said calmly.

"I understand your reservations. The truth is a cruel mistress, but you need to see what will become of your folly. You cannot hope to save her when you couldn't save any of them." Evard held his free hand out, and Nora came running through the bodies, the ends of her silver hair stained with blood and a dark-bladed knife clutched in her hand.

"Did you bring me another sacrifice?" she asked as she leant against Nea's knee.

For the first time since Garret had arrived, Nea moved. She lifted her hand and ran a finger delicately over Nora's cheek. "No, my pet, this one belongs to me." She took the knife from Nora, and Garret noticed the inky marks that stained the girl's arms.

Nea stood, knife in hand, and stepped down from the dais as Evard rubbed a fatherly hand through Nora's hair.

"Nea ..." The rest of his words died on his lips as she closed the distance between them.

"I tried to warn you, Garret. This is what I am. A monster. It is my purpose, and you cannot stop it, no matter how hard you try." She lifted a hand to cup his chin.

He caught her fingers and pulled them away from his skin. "No. You are not her. She believes this is what she could become, but she won't."

Nea's tongue darted along her lip in a way that reminded him of Amelia. "You still believe that after seeing the destruction that follows in my wake?" She turned and moved to Declan, her hand stroking his chest as she stepped around him. Her fingers laced in his dark hair and she yanked his head back, exposing his throat. "If not for me, you could have saved your brother." The dark blade flashed, and a red gash opened across Declan's neck. Nea gave him a shove and he sprawled at Garret's feet. "And your niece would still be the sweet little girl you remember. How easily she took to the darkness, but then I do recall telling you that death spoils all it touches in the end."

Garret stared at Declan's body and the steadily growing puddle of blood that was reaching towards his toes.

"Cat got your tongue? Or are you simply accepting the inevitable?" She stepped over Declan's body, the skirt of her gown dragging through the blood. "Perhaps you need a reminder of what I am capable of on a larger scale."

The throne room faded, and they were standing in the aftermath at Kalhanna. Bodies littered the ground—three times as many as had actually been there. Margot was picking her way through the corpses, tears streaming as she called out for Nea.

"Nea didn't do this. It was Evard," Garret said.

"Yes, Evard threw down the order, but he did it for *me*." She stepped closer again and he could feel the heat rolling off her body. "I don't have to kill you. The Master wants me to. You're a loose end that could ruin all his careful planning," she whispered. This close he could see the softer lilac flecks in her violet eyes. "I told him you could be swayed to our cause. After all, you can still feel it, can't you? The seed that was planted." Her hand pressed over the side of his ribs and the hot itch of corruption swelled as though the wound was new.

He swallowed.

"We've both been used as pawns in an eternal game. Pieces to be moved and exploited, but we are more alike than Evard knows. We could cast him aside and claim this new world for ourselves, rule like we were born to—not just as king and queen but as gods." She gripped the front of his shirt, a wicked smile pulling across her lips as she drew him towards her. "All you have to do is acknowledge the truth."

He shook his head, trying to clear his thoughts.

"There is no point in fighting it." Her breath stirred along his lip.

"Nea ..."

A smile curved the corner of her mouth and she tilted her head back, waiting for him to close the distance.

"... would rather end herself than become you." He took a step back.

She let out a snarl and drove the knife towards his chest, but he caught her wrist and squeezed until she was forced to relinquish her hold on the handle.

"She might believe she doesn't deserve saving. She might not want my help. But I refuse to believe that she would allow herself to fall so far into the darkness."

Nea gave a frustrated growl, her nails raking across his cheek as her body contorted before disappearing in a cloud of purple-black smoke and pale silver feathers.

"Mrr-ow?"

Garret glanced at his feet where the cat was sitting watching him with those liquid-silver eyes. It rose and placed its front feet against his knee as it brushed its face along the side of his thigh and purred.

"I'm fine," he answered the cat's unspoken question and rubbed his hands over his face, wincing as his fingers dragged over the scratches. Now he knew why Nea always used that lie. It was far easier than having to name all the emotions churning inside.

"Mrr-ow."

"Do you mind if we go somewhere warm that is not full of demons or whatever that was?"

"Mrr-owp."

He hadn't realised just how much resentment a cat's face could show until now.

"I've had my fill of enchanted tests. I feel like I have leapt from one to another since we got to this Bright forsaken realm. I just want a chance to sit down and not have to second guess everything around me." And he was officially reasoning with a cat.

The cat made a sound that could have been amusement and then, with a flick of its tail, started wandering away down the path.

"Right. Off we go again." Garret fell into step behind it, hoping this time it led him to the real Nea or a test that was a little less alluring. He shook his head and drew a steadying breath. There had been a moment there when he had wanted to give in.

As they rounded another corner of the hedge, a large midnight-blue dog came into view. He barked happily and trotted over to have his ears scratched by Garret. The cat rubbed against the dog's side, its tail flicking under his nose.

"If you're here, where's Nea?" He assumed this was the dog who Nea had encountered.

The dog flicked his nose towards an icy maw in the hedge. Garret stepped up to the opening and studied the glittering tunnel of ice that sloped into darkness.

"In there? You're sure?"

The dog barked, and the cat settled beside it to preen itself again.

Garret shook his head and sat at the top of the slope. "If this is another of those ridiculous tests ..." he muttered as he pushed off and went rocketing down the slope.

He stumbled to his feet in a large room. Nea stood with her back to him, studying her reflection in an ornate full-length mirror. The skirt of the lilac gown she was wearing was torn and covered in blood. Her hair was hanging in a messy tangle down her back, though half was still pinned up in an elaborate coil. Her attention dropped to her hands and her breath hitched.

"Nea?"

She froze, her violet gaze meeting his in the mirror. It was his Nea.

The band of pressure around his chest loosened. "Are you hurt? Is any of that yours?"

"Maybe ... I don't—" She moved to the basin and scrubbed at the blood on her hands.

"Nea ..."

She ignored him or couldn't hear him. He wasn't sure which. But she was scrubbing so hard she was going to rub her skin raw. Her breathing had increased, and he was sure if he could see her face, she would have that haunted, faraway look in her eye that she got when she was dragged back to Kalhanna.

"You're not there anymore." He tried to keep his tone soft and even. "You're safe."

A shock ran through her, and crimson water splashed onto the floor as she knocked the basin. She retreated from the puddle as it reached for her toes, wiping her hands on the front of her gown as she did so. Fresh blood stained her fingers. Her breath hitched, then she let out a sound he'd never heard her make before: a tiny gasping whimper. She grabbed at the back of her dress, the wet blood on her fingers tangling with her hair.

As her motions grew more frantic, Garret closed the distance between them and after a moment's hesitation, rested his hands on her shoulders. "Easy now."

She stilled at the sound of his voice.

"Deep breaths." He drew one of his own and let it out slowly. "Let me help you ..."

Her breathing slowed, and she was silent as though gathering her thoughts. Then so softly he might not have caught it if he hadn't been watching her mouth in the mirror, she said, "I'm the bird."

"Sorry?"

Recognition flashed in her gaze as it met his in the mirror. "Everyone wants to help me, but I fight them every step of the way because I am too scared to let them. If I accept help ... then they'll see the truth, and I can't ..." She closed her eyes and swallowed. "I'm not strong enough to face another Kalhanna."

Of course. There was more to it than that, but the scars of Kalhanna were the freshest, the deepest. He gave her shoulders a gentle squeeze. "We're all scared, Nea. But you don't have to face it alone. You are punishing yourself for something you couldn't control. What happened at Kalhanna was the result of Evard's cruelty and thirst for power. You asking for help had nothing to do with it." He met her gaze in the mirror. Acknowledging the past was important, but right now it wasn't what she needed. What either of them needed. "Forget about Evard and the Master of Shadows and everything else. What do you need in this moment right now?"

"I need ... I need to get out of this Bright forsaken dress."

Not exactly what he was expecting. He lifted one hand and hesitated.

"Are you going to help me or not?"

He brushed her hair forward over her shoulder, revealing the long run of tiny fabric-covered buttons secured by thin loops of ribbon. He started at the top, but the loops were tight around the buttons and his fingers were suddenly slick and shaking.

"Just rip the fucking thing," she growled.

Gladly. He gripped the fabric either side of the buttons and drew a deep breath then gave a hard yank in opposite directions. Threads tore and buttons pinged off the walls and furniture. He stepped back as she twisted out of the gown then kicked it across the floor as though it were trying to bite her.

In her thin shift, with her eyes bright and cheeks flushed, she was truly a magnificent sight. Her gaze snapped up to meet his, and he cleared his throat, turning his eyes away.

"Thank you," she said.

The room shifted and they were standing in the kitchen of what looked like a small farmhouse. It wasn't his grandmother's, but it was similar. A door opened and the dog and cat came trotting through. The cat leapt onto a seat by the fire as the dog flopped on the floor panting.

All traces of the blood that had covered Nea were gone, along with the torn gown and basin. Two piles of clothes had appeared on the table, Nea's satchel and Garret's sword were with them. Items neither of them had seen since they stepped through the portal at Del Harol.

Nea picked up the satchel and hugged it to her chest, then she shivered. "We should probably put on something warmer." She indicated her shift and his shirt, which was starting to drip as the warmth of the fire melted the ice from the snowstorm.

"I'm not going to turn down a dry change of clothes." He grabbed his bundle and scanned the room for somewhere to change and give her some privacy. "Ah. I'll just … let me know when you're dressed." He kept his back to her as he placed his things on a chair and stripped off.

He dressed quickly, and after a few moments, Nea said, "Okay, you can turn around now."

She was wearing the outfit Wade had given her—the one Declan had joked made her look like a pirate queen.

"Tea?" she asked.

He nodded.

As Nea went through the motions of making tea, Garret sat by the fire and coaxed the warmth back into his toes. The cat leapt onto his lap and purred as he ran his fingers through its soft fur. When Nea gave him a cup and went to sit, the dog barked and flicked his nose towards the teapot.

"You want a cup?" she asked, and the dog wagged his tail. "Alright." With a bemused look, she made two extra cups.

"About time," a man said from the floor where the dog had been. He was vaguely familiar, with long storm-grey waves that brushed his shoulders.

The cat leapt from Garret's lap and moved towards Nea. It hadn't gone three steps when its body shifted into that of a voluptuous woman with long starlight-coloured hair. "Oh, leave them alone. They've been through quite an ordeal to get here. No thanks to you." She took one of the spare cups and turned back to the fire, her silver eyes sparkling as she gave Garret a wink.

"Like you are truly guiltless in the matter, my love." The man unfolded himself from the floor and took up another chair.

Nea handed him a cup of tea and sat in the chair closest to Garret.

"Sorry to break up the delightful little moment I am sure the pair of you were about to have, but there will be time enough for that once the world is set to rights," the man said. "We just need to get you both back on the right path."

The woman rolled her eyes and sipped her tea. "Give them a minute to catch their breath. Not all of us have been trapped in a labyrinth with only ourselves for company for an eon." She settled her gaze on Nea. "Never mind him, dear. He does care, otherwise he wouldn't have bothered creating you in the first place."

Nea blinked. "I'm sorry. What do you mean creating me?"

"See, I warned you this would happen. Neither of them has any idea of what is going on." The man took a large sip of his tea.

"Is that true? You really don't know?" the woman asked gently.

Nea shook her head. "We know that I'm a deathborn and suspect that Garret is a brightling."

A warm smile pulled across the woman's mouth. "He most certainly is. That tyrant thought he could play at being a god and force me to create a brightling for him. As if I would fall for that. He did give me a perfect opportunity to create one of my own choosing though." She smiled warmly at Garret.

"You ... but that means ..." Nea's tea sploshed over her fingers as she leant forward. "It's not possible."

"You are in the Between, my darling. Anything is possible," the woman said.

"Almost anything," the man said. His violet eyes were a shade or two darker than Nea's, making them almost indigo. "And it was almost a wasted effort. You're lucky they created the ward, or we'd have one useless brightling and no anchor."

The woman rolled her eyes again. "Tch, your isolation has certainly made you an old sour pot." She licked her lip and turned her attention to Garret. "Do you have questions? You should have questions."

"They can wait. Our priority needs to be getting out of this maze and finding the source of corruption so we can get back to our own realm." He touched his side. The skin still burned as though the corruption seethed under it, but he had checked the mark when he dressed and it was still a milky silver, the voices that accompanied the infection blissfully silent.

"Pragmatic as always. I love all my children, but you are my favourite."

He glanced at Nea. Her lip was pressed between her teeth as she studied him. "Is the corruption bothering you again?" She flexed her silver-stained hand as she spoke.

"It's fine. Just something that happened during the test."

"Do you mind if I check it?" She moved towards him, and for a moment the corpse-filled throne room flashed across his mind. "If it—"

"It's fine!" He leapt to his feet. The room was so hot and the mark on his side was crawling as though covered with ants. Images kept flashing across his mind and soft lips whispered against the back of his ear.

"Garret ..." Her voice was calm and her fingers cool as they tentatively touched the back of his hand. "Show me, please?" Concern shone in her eyes; soft eyes full of sadness. Not like the other Nea who radiated only icy cruelty.

He didn't move as she slid her hand under the hem of his shirt and lifted it to examine the mark. Her cool touch was soothing against the feverish skin, and he inhaled slowly.

"It appears fine. But what happened?"

He glanced over the top of her head at the woman who was sitting on the edge of her seat watching them with an indulgent smile. The man was much more reserved, almost on guard like he was waiting for something.

"I saw a different version of you. She was everything you fear you could become, and when she touched the corruption mark, it seemed to come back to life. Now it feels like it did back in our realm. The only difference is the nagging voices are gone."

She met his gaze. "Did this version of me ... did she ..." She twisted her fingers together and took a step back. "What did she do?"

"She tried to convince me that she was you, that the things I was seeing were inevitable, that we can't escape the darkness to come so we should just embrace it. And, Nea, for a moment ... I wanted to."

The corner of her mouth quirked. "But you didn't."

"Obviously not, given he *survived* the test." There was a note of sarcasm in the man's voice.

"What was it like for you?" Garret asked.

She rolled her lip between her teeth. "You saw the blood." Her nonchalant tone broke on the last word. "I was in Evard's throne room, and there were masked dancers ... all the people who have died because of my choices. And then Evard ordered the soldiers to drag you out ... The look of betrayal you gave me as Evard told me to kill you."

"And did you?"

"Obvi—ouch!" the man said.

"Shssh," the woman reprimanded.

"I couldn't. So Evard had Margot brought out and he told me I had to choose one of you ... and ..." Her voice wavered.

"Please tell me you didn't choose to save me over Margot?"

She shook her head. "Evard wanted me to embrace the darkness. He needed me to. And I knew if I chose to kill one of you, I would lose myself entirely. Not only that, Evard would make sure whoever I didn't choose would die anyway. If I let Evard win, if I embraced darkness the way he wanted me to, there would be no hope of saving our world. So, I did the only thing I could ..." She swallowed. "I removed myself from the equation." Tears glittered along her lashes and she swallowed again.

"This realm is horrid."

"That's an understatement." She let out a small laugh, and he chuckled in response.

"It's a wonder the pair of you get anything done with all these heart to hearts."

"Never mind him. He's just bitter because he's had barely any company for an eon. Try being the pretty little pet in that tyrant's cage. I'd gladly swap," the woman said with a scowl in the man's direction. "However, he is not wrong. The longer you are separated from your bodies, the harder it will be to get back into them. To do that you have one final test. One you must face together. If you fail, you will die, and all hope will be truly lost for both worlds."

"No pressure," the man muttered.

"This final trial, what does it entail?" Garret asked.

"I cannot tell you." She must have read the expression on his face because she laughed. "Not because I don't want to, but because I do not truly know. However, it awaits through that doorway." She indicated a pair of doors that hadn't been there before.

They were carved from stone. Along the seam where they met, the left door was adorned with half a rose and the right half an eight-pointed star.

"We cannot follow through that door, but you'll be just fine without us. I know you will," the woman said.

"Let's go then," Nea said, her hand slipping into Garret's. "There's no sense in delaying any longer." She gave his fingers a squeeze.

Garret almost didn't want to step through. Whatever was on the other side would not be pleasant.

As Nea placed her palm on the right-side door, the star lit up in bright orange lines, her keen stirring along his spine in cool swirls. He lifted his hand and touched the rose door, his own keen rising and twisting with Nea's until the two became white-hot. The rose glowed lilac and the doors flew open. His body lurched forward as an invisible force grabbed hold of him and dragged him through.

CHAPTER TWENTY-TWO

HARVEY

"To what do I owe the pleasure of this little visit?" Amelia cooed as she glided around a door frame and stalked towards him. Her bare toes stopped short of the marks on the floor.

Harvey cleared his throat and glanced over his shoulder.

"You have nothing to fear. I'll warn you of any *undesirable* company."

He turned to face her. This was foolish; he shouldn't be here. Did he honestly expect her to give him straight answers? And what if Leon or Catriona caught him? It was the middle of the night, but that hadn't stopped them visiting her before.

She cocked a hip, resting her hand on it and tapping her chin with the skeletal fingers of the other hand. "Such dilemma written on your face. I would so love to be privy to what is churning inside that mind of yours." Her tongue darted over her lips. "Perhaps I can guess at why you are here? Of course it's not because you wanted to spend some *quality* time with little old me ... You want to know if Leon is any closer to freeing me ... or perhaps what his haughty necromancer friend is up to."

"Answers to both would be good. But first, why didn't you come out when they were here the other night."

A smile that might have been pretty once pulled across her lips. "I suspected you were the mysterious voyeur." The smile was replaced by a scowl and the wrinkling of her nose. "I don't like them."

"You don't *like* them."

"They work for Him."

"Evard?"

The malice that touched her features at the mention of Evard almost made him take a step back.

"No. Not that fool of a king who thinks he can bully his way to immortality. He's nothing more than a pawn who lost himself early in this little game. No, they work for the one who took the mantle but cannot wield its power. *He* works through that unsuitable vessel of flesh that calls himself king."

"Vessel of flesh?"

The smile returned. "Ah yes, you're curious about the necromancer and what he plans."

"He mentioned a vessel at Hartswood."

She nodded. "It makes the most sense to shackle me into the flesh of another, but that has been tried before and what you see is the result of that little experiment."

"So, you're not Amelia?"

"I am both Amelia and not her. She's in here with me, trapped and dormant in the cage of her own mind. She fought so hard to keep her body, but in the end, I won out. I will always win. It is a shame Nea is so far from their reach. Her body is one I would gladly inhabit. So much raw power tied up in such a pretty package."

"Who are you then?"

She traced her fingers along the neck of her nightgown. "It matters not who I am in the grand scheme of things but what I can do." Her fingers hooked around the fabric and yanked it sideways, revealing a star-shaped amber mark that looked an awful lot like a brand in the space between the edge of her collarbone and her shoulder. "I was a test while they waited for a more suitable candidate."

"Why are you telling me this?"

"I like you."

She said it so simply, but he wasn't sure how it made him feel. "Thanks, I guess. A more suitable candidate for what exactly?"

The corner of her mouth quirked. "To be *His* queen. The seat of the gods requires both a king and a queen. A sovereign of Bright"—her fingers brushed delicately over the brand—"and a sovereign of Shadow." She touched the purple birthmark. "He wishes for a reign of death and destruction, and the only way to get that, to tip the balance in his favour, is to pervert the rules. Trick the *seat*."

Harvey blinked and ran his hand through his hair. He couldn't make head nor tail of this, but he was sure Niall would find it all fascinating. "If you're some failed experiment, why find another vessel to put you in? Why not just leave you here and be done with it?"

"Their ideal candidate has proven persistently insubordinate. Such a waste given she was essentially purpose built. However, it is not the soul that inhabits the body so much as the potential of the body itself. At least, that is what they say. Amelia's body was unsuitable as she was not a necromancer herself. So, failing putting me in Nea, I guess the consensus is *any* necromancer will do."

"That's Kieran's plan then—to find a necromancer and put you inside them." He swallowed the lump that rose at the thought. Maybe the temple was right about mages. No one should have the kind of power Amelia was talking about.

She shrugged. "It is what Evard wants. Kieran, however, is harder to read. His mind is delightfully winding and sordid."

"Oh my, what do we have here?" The voice was smooth as silk.

Amelia's lip curled into a sneer. "Come to try and tempt me out with poisoned words and brutish compulsion again? Bryce could teach you a thing or two about how to woo a lady." Her tongue darted over her lips.

"Bryce, is it?"

Harvey turned, keeping his eyes downcast and his expression apologetic.

"I know you. You're Trenton's recruit. The one who has John's drawers in a tangle." Catriona reached for his chin, but he took a step back. The barrier containing Amelia prickled against his spine and the coin in his pocket grew warm. "Hmm, you're nothing special," Catriona added.

Had the coin been reacting to her magic?

"Tell me though, why does the *creature* deign to speak with you when it disregards all requests from your betters?"

Harvey drew a breath. If he gave Catriona a reason to suspect him then there was no way he was getting out of this alive. "I—I don't know." There was some truth to it.

"Really?" Catriona's sapphire eyes settled on Amelia behind him. "Do you care to enlighten me, wraith?"

Amelia gave an indulgent chuckle. "Bryce is polite and doesn't call me nasty little names. He might be afraid of me, but he doesn't treat me like a tool, a means to an end."

"If he is so afraid of you, why is he here in the middle of the night?"

"My allure is strongest in the dark hours. Just ask Nea ... Oh wait, you can't, because Leon let her get away. *Twice.* You know if he fails a third time Evard is going to break his neck then have Kieran resurrect him. He won't be as much *fun* when he's a mindless reanimation."

Harvey edged away from the barrier so he could see both Amelia and Catriona. The coin grew hot again and Catriona touched her temple.

"Get out," she growled.

"Oh dear. Are you not strong enough to overcome little old me? Nea had no problem. Then again, she had help from Garret."

Catriona took a step towards the barrier, her brow furrowing.

"You don't like being compared to her, do you? That's what happens when you accept a political marriage to someone who has given their heart to another. It's a shame seed can't set in that bitter womb of yours. Then you might not have been second to Nea in everything." Amelia rubbed a hand over her lower abdomen. "But she stole that from you too."

"Get out of my head!" Catriona roared, and the coin in Harvey's pocket grew so hot he was surprised it didn't burst into flames.

Amelia laughed. Not the indulgent chuckle from before, but bitter and cruel in a way that stood the hairs on Harvey's arms on end. "You wanted this. You wanted to *talk*."

Catriona was now at the barrier, her hands pushing against empty air and her cheeks flushed.

"Amelia," Harvey said quietly. "Let her go."

Amelia's silver-blue gaze switched to Harvey. "She needs to learn; if she wants to rattle the bars of the wolf's cage, then she'd better be ready for the teeth."

"I think she understands now." Harvey took a step towards the barrier.

Catriona gave a strangled gasp and dropped to the floor.

"Now you know what you are *playing* with." Amelia tilted her chin and let out a haughty breath before slipping away into the shadows.

"Thank you." Catriona's voice was a strained rasp.

"How did she do that? I thought the barrier contained her."

Catriona's eyes narrowed as she studied him. "Perhaps John is right to be wary of you."

Harvey shrugged. "I can call her back. I'm sure she would happily finish what she started."

"I don't know how she can extend her magic beyond the barrier, but she didn't just use her magic. She perverted my own and turned it against me. We need to be more careful."

Harvey got the sense she was talking to herself.

Running footsteps reached them moments before Leon and Kieran rounded the corner.

"What's going on here?" Leon's attention landed on Harvey. He stalked forward and grabbed Harvey's arm, yanking him away from Catriona. "What did you do?" Leon demanded, inches from his face.

"Nothing ... I." He glanced towards Catriona. "She—"

"It was my fault." Catriona's voice was quiet. "Bryce merely stepped in to help, and it's lucky he did."

Harvey did his best to keep the shock from his face.

"I warned you that the creature was not to be underestimated." Kieran's tone was dry.

"Amelia," Harvey said automatically.

"What was that?" Leon gave him a shove.

"Her name is Amelia. She doesn't like being treated with disrespect."

The smile that crossed Leon's mouth was cruel. "So, you've had dealings with her, have you?"

Harvey shook his head. "Only once. I made the mistake of crossing this hall as a shortcut." He kept his voice level and his eyes downcast. "She likes to harass people, and most know better than to mess around with her." He flicked a look in Catriona's direction. "If you are safe now, I would gladly return to the barracks."

"And what exactly were you doing inside the fort so late at night?" Leon asked.

"I was sharing supper with my sister. There hasn't been much of a chance to see her since joining the guard. I was on my way out when I heard her highness scream." He swallowed. One word from Catriona and his story would come undone.

"So gallant of you," Kieran drawled. "Most would leave her to her fate."

"But Amelia can't cross the barrier," Harvey said. "She just likes to play games with people."

"You seem to know an awful lot about the creature for a lowly soldier." Kieran stroked his chin. "And you are the soldier who John has concerns about ... Perhaps we should get your sister here and ask her a few *questions*." He threw a look at Leon.

"Your sister's name?" Leon asked.

Lorie was the first name that came to mind but then the coin grew hot in his pocket. "Tessa," he said, hoping Catriona was simply trying to coax him into revealing the name, not attempting to read his mind.

"Surely this is something that can be done away from this hallway," Catriona said, studying the pooling darkness Amelia had disappeared into.

"Here is fine." Leon folded his hands behind his back and started walking away. "I suggest you don't move. If I return with your sister to find you have run off, I won't hesitate to kill her."

It didn't take Leon long to return with a wide-eyed Molly. She met Harvey's gaze with a stern frown as Leon shoved her against the wall. "Now, Tessa, we have a few questions for you. Firstly, what have you been up to this evening?"

"I don't see how my activities have any bearing on whatever is going on here."

"Humour us." Leon smiled delicately but his tone still held a razor edge.

Molly glanced from one face to another before landing on Harvey.

He licked his lip, wishing that she could read his mind. If she took a wild guess and her story didn't collaborate with his ...

"I did my duties and then turned in for the night."

Shit.

Leon's smile was predatory.

Molly met Harvey's eye again and he silently implored her. "Of course, that was after my brother visited me for supper. Next thing I know, you're pulling me from my bed and dragging me here."

Harvey could have sighed with relief, but he kept his features neutral. If Leon caught them both in the lie, then there was no telling what he would do. He had been proven to have a vindictive temper, one Harvey was happy to bear the brunt of, but he didn't want Molly getting hurt because of him.

Leon's eyes narrowed as he flicked a look in Harvey's direction before focusing on Molly again. "Did your brother mention anything about coming down here to visit the creature?"

"Amelia? No, he's not an idiot." She gave Harvey a look that said quite the opposite. "We're told daily to avoid this wing as much as possible, and I doubt a few weeks on the guard has erased the warning from his mind."

"Perhaps I could enlighten you, little brute." Amelia slid from the darkness.

"What did you call me?" Leon spun to face her, and Molly edged closer to Harvey.

"Would you prefer boar? Thug? Mongrel? Bastard?" Her grin widened with each word.

Leon strode forward and made a grab for her, but the rune marks flared to life and a flash of light threw him backwards.

"You don't like the truth, do you? No one really does."

Leon's face went white.

"Unhand him now, demon," Catriona said, and the coin grew hot.

Amelia must have been using her magic on Leon.

"Do something." Catriona whirled on Kieran, who was leaning against the wall examining his fingernails.

"To what end? You are the mind mage. You should be able to control her."

"Her magic should not be able to extend beyond the marks." Catriona thrust her hand at the glowing barrier.

Kieran shrugged. "A loophole perhaps. If so, one I might be able to exploit."

"Such sordid thoughts behind such a handsome face." Amelia crooned as Leon gripped his skull. "Oh, Nea is in for quite a violent experience once you get those filthy hands on her, isn't she? That is, if you *can* get your hands on her. She's proved rather slippery."

"You!" Catriona pointed at Harvey. "She listens to you—tell her to stop."

"I don't—"

"It was not a request!" The coin grew white-hot.

Harvey licked his lip. "Let him go, Amelia."

"He won't hesitate to kill you or your pretty *sister*. He'll enjoy every minute of extending her agony until she begs him for release. And he has the audacity to call me a *beast*."

"Amelia ..." Harvey said softly.

"He will be the death of you and all you hold dear."

Leon fell onto his arse panting as Amelia disappeared again.

"Interesting," Kieran said as he studied Harvey. "If the creature responds to you, we can use that." He looked to Leon. "I believe it is time we went to retrieve a vessel."

"Nea is—"

"Beyond our reach. We can make do with another."

"Are we free to go now?" Harvey asked as he took hold of Molly's arm.

"Hmm? Yes." Kieran started to wave them away. "But tell Trenton we will be needing a contingent of soldiers to be ready to leave at first light."

"For what purpose?" Harvey asked.

"To ride on Hartswood of course."

Molly gasped, and Kieran's gaze narrowed as it switched to her. "Isn't Hartswood the home of the necromancers?" She recovered quickly.

"Indeed."

"Come on, Tess." Harvey gave her arm a tug. "I'll walk you back to the servants' quarters."

Molly was silent until they were well away from the south wing. She glanced over her shoulder then punched him in the arm.

"What was that for?"

"Are you completely insane?" she hissed. "Why were you snooping around Amelia again?"

"I wanted to know what Leon was planning to do with her."

"You can't trust anything she tells you. Her whole purpose is to manipulate and corrupt." She bunched her fists.

"I know," he said softly. But every encounter with Amelia had been, well, not exactly pleasant, but she seemed like more than just a cruel ghost who existed only to corrupt.

"We need to leave."

His attention snapped to her face. "We can't leave now. How do you think that will look?"

She cast another glance around the hall. "You promised me that at the first sign of trouble we—"

"I know. But Kieran was suggesting they attack Hartswood."

"Exactly. Do you know what is at Hartswood?"

Harvey shook his head.

"It is a sanctuary for the young and the elderly. Most necromancers aren't even there. They are off travelling or living in far-flung towns. Hartswood is where they go to train when they are young and live out their days when they are old."

He rubbed a hand through his hair. "Kieran intends to put Amelia inside a necromancer."

"How? I thought only Nea could do things like that." She opened and closed her fists. "And why bother with getting past the sentries at Hartswood? Just kidnap one of the other necromancers out there." She indicated the world at large with a sweep of her hand.

"I think he intends to put her in the body of someone easy to manipulate and groom. I think he intends to put her in a child."

"Shit." She started pacing then stopped dead and turned back to face him, her cheeks ghost white in the shadowy hall. "Harv, Nea's son is at Hartswood."

"Nea's? Does that mean ..."

She nodded. "Leith is the father, and until there is a legitimate heir, Henry will be next in line. I have to beat Leon and Kieran to Hartswood. You can stay here if you want, but I'm leaving right now."

"Wait." He caught her arm as she started to march away again. "I'll come with you—I just need to deliver the message to Trenton and then we can leave."

"Be quick." She hurried away.

Harvey half-collapsed against the wall. He'd wanted excitement, but now he definitely felt as though he had bitten off more than he could chew.

The forest around them was one of the creepiest Harvey had ever trekked through. The trees seemed to move when you weren't watching, and dark, vaguely humanoid shapes darted at the very corner of your vision. Beside him, Molly walked in silence, her eyes trained on the path straight ahead of them.

They had removed the enchanted bands that hid their true identities not long after departing Fort Braemar. Changing back had been just as painful, and every so often he would get a jolt as though his body wasn't quite finished settling into its old shape.

After a while of feeling like they were walking in a giant circle, they came to a large stone that stood in the middle of the path. A series of twisting circles and swirls were carved on its rough surface.

Molly glanced around. "Hello? Old lady ghost, are you around? We need to get through."

"Ah, Mol, what are you doing?"

"There's supposed to be a spirit here to meet us. Then we cut our hand, smear blood on the stone, and eat a glowing flower that tastes like licking the bottom of a shoe. Then we can pass safely on to Hartswood."

"What happens if you just go around the stone?"

"I don't know. When I came here with Margot, we had to do the ritual."

Harvey shrugged and stepped past the stone. He walked a few metres then a bubble of force hit him. Something tugged deep inside his gut as the world lurched and Molly and the stone appeared in front of him again. "So that didn't work," he said as she gave him a look over her shoulder.

She placed her palm against the stone. "Spirit, please come out. We need to get to Hartswood to warn them about Leon and Kieran."

"Agatha," an age-soaked voice said behind them. "That is my name, girl."

Harvey turned to study the stooped woman who had appeared behind him. She had a cloud of milk-white hair and sharp blue eyes that glittered with unfathomable knowledge. As Harvey studied her, her form shifted and Nea appeared. No, not Nea. This woman had skin a shade or two darker and eyes the colour of fine-cut emeralds. The rest of her features were a near complete match for Nea's, though perhaps a tiny bit sharper.

"Those with ill intent will not be able to pass the wards," she said in the accented tones of an Osmarian native.

"We don't mean any harm," Molly said.

"We are aware of that, but these men who are coming will not be able to pass the ward, so this fuss and bother is completely unnecessary." Her form shifted again to a tall man with a stone-grey goatee and deep purple eyes.

"So, you won't let us pass?"

"Calm down little, spitfire. You are both permitted to pass once the offering has been received." The spirit shifted into the old woman again. She indicated the stone with an open palm. "You may proceed."

"Alright, give me your hand, Harvey," Molly said as she pulled out a knife.

Harvey licked his lip then held his hand out. Molly didn't hesitate to slice a stinging line across his skin. As the blood welled, she grabbed his wrist and pressed his palm to the stone. Then she did the same with her own. The bloody smear shifted, twisting its way along the spirals and then into the ground. Vines with delicate white flowers sprouted from beneath the stone. Molly plucked two of the blooms and held one out to him as she popped the other in her mouth and chewed quickly before swallowing with a grimace.

"Go on, Harvey. They taste awful but it's all part of the ritual and look." She held up her palm as a green glow spread across the cut and sealed it leaving the skin beneath unscarred.

"Alright." He took the flower and popped it on his tongue. "Hey, it's not so—Mother's tits!" He chewed faster and then forced it down. His fingers grew warm and tingly as the slice started to glow and heal. "Now what?"

Molly shrugged. "Now we keep heading to Hartswood." She stepped around the stone and started down the path.

Harvey followed her, waiting for the pressure from before to hit him. But after a moment of resistance, nothing happened. He glanced over his shoulder, but the shifting spirit was gone and so was the large stone, leaving only a dark twisting path that disappeared into the trees.

They eventually emerged from the forest into a wide meadow of gently swaying grass dotted with wildflowers. Across the field was a low cobblestone wall and beyond that a sprawling manor house that almost resembled a small castle. Molly led him across the meadow and through the gate into a wide garden. Stone paths criss-crossed through the raised garden beds from which all manner of vegetable and herb tumbled in overcrowded delight.

Peals of laughter and excited shouts reached them from somewhere beyond the house as Molly moved through the garden, careful not to disturb the bees that drifted lazily from plant to plant.

Around the back of the house was another garden. This one was bursting at the seams with tumbling bushes of brightly coloured flowers that led to a large hedge of red roses, beyond which was a field of cows lazily grazing. Farther out still was a grove of what looked like various fruiting trees.

Harvey wasn't sure what he had been expecting, but this place was like he had stepped into another world.

"Hello," a bright voice said beside him, and he glanced at the little girl who had joined them.

She had large eyes that were an interesting shade of hazel perhaps: blue–green with yellow flecks around the centre. Flowers were braided through her hair, which was the silver colour of moonlight on water.

"Ah, hello."

"Nora," a woman called, and the girl glanced over her shoulder.

"Over here, Mama. We have visitors."

"Abigail would have said ..." The woman stepped out the back door of the house and stopped when she noticed them. "... something." She pushed her thick auburn braid over her shoulder and straightened her apron. "We weren't expecting anyone, and you're not necromancers. How did you get past the sentries?" Her nose twitched, and the coin in Harvey's pocket grew warm. "What are you?" Her eyes, a similar shade to Nora's, narrowed and she settled her hands on her hips.

"We're keen-less," Molly responded and pulled the disc of pink metal out of her pocket. "I am Molly, and this Harvey. I've been here before, so I knew about the offering."

The woman took the coin from Molly and inspected it before handing it back and rubbing her fingers together. "I'm Bridie, and this is Elenora. If you are here for Abigail, she is out in the grove."

"Nora, you were supposed to be finding us." A girl with stone-grey ringlets came skipping over. "Oh, hello, Molly!"

"Hello, Kenna," Molly replied.

The girl stuck her fingers in her mouth and turned to let out a massive whistle.

A young boy around twelve came running from the front of the house straight past another. The second boy was on the back end of his lanky teenage years, probably around fifteen with snow-white hair. On his shoulders was a young boy with a tussled mass of stormy waves. The smaller boy wriggled until he was let down, then he ran to Molly and threw a hug around her legs.

"Margie?" he asked, his grey eyes blinking owlishly.

Molly shook her head. "Margot isn't with me."

"Oh, you haven't met Bran!" Kenna exclaimed. "Bran, this is Margot's"—her head tilted, and she twisted her mouth as though searching for a word—"wife, Molly, but I don't know her friend."

"Harvey," he offered.

She gave a nod and continued, "And that's Pierce. He's Nora's brother." She indicated the boy with blond hair.

"Nice to meet you. Nonna and the others are out in the grove. Agatha called a meeting," Bran said.

"The sentry spirit?"

Bran chuckled. "Yeah, that's her."

Harvey shared a look with Molly.

"You have some idea what that might be about then?" Bridie said. "Come on. I'll take you to the others." She led them through the gate in the rose hedge and then across the field and out another gate into the grove. A collection of shoes were lined up neatly just inside the second gate. Both Molly and Bridie slipped theirs off as well.

Molly gave a little squeak and shifted her feet. "You never get used to that."

Harvey pulled his boots off, and as his bare toes settled into the grass, a vibration jolted along his spine, standing his hair on end. He smoothed it down. "What was that?"

Bridie chuckled. "Magic saturates the ground here." She guided them across the grove to a circle of people: a tall woman with sharp features and short ash-grey hair and a man with dark hair and a leather apron over his clothes; two elderly women, one who looked like an older version of Nea and one with the same hazel eyes as Nora and Bridie; and lastly, her mouth splitting in a wide grin, was Sonia.

"I should have known you pair were the ones who caused all the commotion," Sonia quipped.

"Sonia," the woman who resembled Nea said, drawing her attention. "You go with Hazel and Angus."

"Nonna, I don't think that leaving now is a good idea. What if—" the short-haired woman started, but Nonna cut her off with a wave.

"They won't get past the wards."

"But Kieran—" She snapped her mouth shut and threw a glance at Bridie.

"Kieran?" Bridie met Nonna's gaze. "What about Kieran?"

Nonna cleared her throat and waved Sonia and the others away. "Off with you. You know what needs to be done." She waited for the others to leave before inclining her head to Molly. "It is good to see you again, Molly, but who is your new friend?"

"Harvey," he said and held his hand out.

She shook his hand. "Abigail, though most around here simply refer to me as Nonna."

"And which do you prefer?"

She gave a soft chuckle. "I'm too old to be bothered by what the youth call me. This is Camille." She indicated the other woman who had pulled Bridie aside and was talking to her in a hushed tone.

Bridie had gone slightly grey, and her hand was pressed over her mouth. All around them the branches of the trees groaned. "Reel your keen in, girl," Nonna reprimanded.

Bridie gave a gasping sob and the trees stopped moving. "I'm sorry."

"It's alright, my dear. You've had a nasty shock. Honestly, if I thought my man was dead and he suddenly turned up on the wrong side of the war I would lose it a little too. Sit." Nonna's gaze shifted to Molly. "Would you mind running to the kitchen and getting the bottle out of the basket on the upper shelf?"

Molly gave a nod and hurried off.

"Don't forget the cups," Nonna called after her, and she gave a wave over her shoulder.

"Now you, boy, sit."

Camille had settled next to Bridie and placed an arm around her shoulders. Harvey sat on her other side.

"Tell me everything you know," Nonna said as she folded herself onto the grass across from him.

Where to start? He ran his hand through his hair. "Kieran is working for Evard. We believe he wants to remove Amelia from the south wing at Fort Braemar by putting her in another body, specifically the body of a necromancer. He thinks he will find the perfect vessel here."

"Kieran would never." Bridie shook her head. "He's a good man ... He was always a good man."

Nonna pursed her lips. "He was always a little infatuated with power. Not a good trait for a necromancer. Perhaps Evard perverted that infatuation, or perhaps he is working for Evard under duress."

Harvey shook his head. "I doubt it. He certainly didn't act like someone under duress. Amelia mentioned something about tricking the throne of the Bright Mother."

Nonna's eyebrows lifted slightly. "He seeks to exploit a loophole." She shared a look with Camille.

"We should have told them the truth from the beginning. Instead, by keeping them apart, we've allowed the very thing we were trying to avoid to happen regardless," Camille said as she rubbed small circles on Bridie's back.

"We can't know that."

Camille's mouth tightened at the corner. "If Kieran manages to move the thing inside Amelia to another host, a necromancer no less—"

"It won't work. They would need either Nea or Garret to be the host, and they are well beyond Kieran's reach—the only saving grace of them running off into the Between."

"Are you certain? Kieran seemed to think that any necromancer would do, or that is what Amelia said."

"Amelia appears to have told you rather a lot," Nonna said as Molly returned with a brown bottle and a handful of cups.

"He was warned about her, but he's a bit of an idiot," Molly quipped as she joined them on the grass.

Nonna studied him for a while. "Any necromancer won't do. It will pervert the magic and blow a hole clean in the barrier. The last time that happened, an entire city was sunk into the sea."

"Wait, did you say Garret could be a host as well?" Harvey asked as Molly offered him a cup. The liquor inside stung his nose, bringing with it the memory of heavy fists and his mother's pleading cries. He shook his head.

"Sorry, Harv, I didn't think."

"It's alright."

"Yes, Garret would make as good a host as Nea, perhaps even better if they could corrupt him as well."

"But wardens can't get corruption," Bride said.

"Actually, they can, and Garret did," Molly said, drawing the attention of the three other women.

"What? How?" Bridie leant forward.

"We're not exactly sure, but he was wounded in the fight at Fort Braemar and the wound was corrupted. It happened to another warden as well, nearly a year ago now; Peter."

"Corruption from a wound—that is impossible," Bridie scoffed, but Nonna and Camille shared one of those looks again.

"Not impossible, but if Garret has been corrupted that changes things entirely," Nonna said.

"Why? What are you not telling us?" Molly asked.

"What *is* Garret?" Bridie added.

"Garret is a brightling, probably the last this world will ever see." There was a tone in Nonna's voice that cut right through Harvey, twisting the feeling that he had bitten off more than he could chew into a deep seed of dread. He didn't know what a brightling was or how Garret came to be one, and deep inside he wasn't sure he wanted to know.

CHAPTER TWENTY-THREE

Margot

A shout woke Margot, and she rolled out of bed. She rubbed her hand over her face to chase the dregs of her dream from her mind: fire and ash, dark bodies marching across bloodstained earth. The room lurched to the side, nearly throwing her off her feet. She blinked, and slowly the realisation of where she actually was came to her.

There was another shout and a ratcheting noise from above. She pulled her boots on and staggered up the steps of the hold as the ship rocked and vibrated again.

The deck was in chaos. Sailors shouted at each other and raced about as sure-footed as mountain goats despite the turbulent sea that assaulted the ship. The foreboding clouds of the maelstrom with their rainbow lighting were so close Margot could smell the electric tang of ozone and something else—something almost sweet. A roll of thunder echoed, sounding more like the cackling laughter of a tyrant than the bone-shaking boom she would expect. She didn't have time to process that though as something slammed into the side of the ship and she was tossed to her hands and knees.

Emil's face swam across her vision as he hauled her to her feet. "Alright there, Margot?"

"What's going on? I thought someone was going to keep an eye on the maelstrom," she shouted over another mind-numbing peal of thunder.

"They did, but the maelstrom is unpredictable even with a lookout. It's not the problem though—" His words were cut off as he staggered to the side when the ship lurched again. "The problem is that!"

She followed the line of his finger to the massive head of a beast that was sticking above the waves. It looked like something you'd find in one of Nonna's stories about the Between. A massive head that was somehow both equine and reptilian with a ruff of purple finger-like appendages that stood around its head in a strange leathery mane. It twisted its long neck, the iridescent green scales reflecting the flashes of light from the maelstrom.

"Get down." Emil knocked her to the deck, his body pressing her against the soaked wood as he shielded her head. "Sorry," he said as he helped her to her feet. "It spits acid."

The ratcheting sound she heard before started again, then Gendry let out a yell and pulled the handle on the harpoon. The bolt shot through the air, slicing a path across the creature's neck.

"Wren, my love, I don't think this is a fight we can win," he yelled.

The captain appeared next to Margot. "If you could shoot straight it wouldn't be problem."

"I'd like to see you try with that thing crashing the ship about like a dingy."

Rufus loaded another harpoon, and Gendry made an adjustment as the leviathan dropped out of sight beneath the churning water.

"Grab on to something," Wren bellowed.

Emil pressed a rope into Margot's hands. She gripped so hard her knuckles ached, then the ship started to tip. Gravity dragged against Margot as she was tossed into the air. A wall of water hit her almost too fast for her to take a breath. Salt and grit stung her eyes as she squeezed them tight. Her fingers slid along the rope, threatening to let go as foamy water washed over her again. She tightened her grip as her lungs cried out for air. There was a second's relief as wind touched her cheeks. She gulped a ragged breath as she was tossed under again.

Something tangled in the back of her shirt and yanked her backwards. The water dragged over her as her throat constricted and her chest strained, desperate for more air than the tiny gulp she had managed.

She was rolled onto a hard surface. Feet thudded around her; a hot hand was pressing the side of her neck.

Her eyes flew open, and Gendry grinned down at her. "Close one that was. I don't know what would be better—drowning or digesting."

She blinked.

"It prefers to swallow its prey whole," Gendry offered.

"Fire!" Wren bellowed, and Margot craned her head around. Emil had taken over control of the harpoon.

The bolt sailed true and hit the creature in the centre of the neck. It let out a wail and thrashed before hitting the side of the boat again. Then it turned in the water and charged away.

The maelstrom had overtaken the ship. Magic thrummed in the air around them standing Margot's hair on end and making her skin glow a soft green. The mark on her palm grew warm, expanding over the skin of her forearm in intricate circles before receding again as Penny's had done in Warren's hut.

The other mages on the boat were all glowing as well. Penny a soft pink, Kiki a vibrant blue and her sister, Pippa, a warm orange, and Wren the silver-blue of lightning. Even Emil was glowing in shifting shades of silver and dark grey.

"As pretty as this little light show is, we need to get out of here," Gendry said.

However, walls of water had lifted on three sides, giving them only one available path—straight into the centre of the storm. The strange laughing thunder cackled, and the boat surged forward under a wind that was not Wren's doing. All around them multicoloured lightning struck the water. With a great roar, a whirlpool opened directly in front of them. The ship was sucked in as easily as if it was an errant scrap of flotsam.

Wren shouted something but it was lost in the roar of wind and water.

Gendry's heavy arm gripped Margot around the waist as he balled his fist in one of the ropes that secured the main sail.

The storm seemed to hold its breath for a heartbeat, then the boat tipped, and the raging ocean swallowed them.

Margot groaned. The ground beneath her cheek was sticky and rough. Her hair was plastered to her forehead in gritty chunks that itched. She sat slowly and brushed the sand from her skin. All around her the beach was littered with debris from the ship. A short distance away, Emil was helping Pippa to her feet, their skin still glowing softly. Farther along, Penny, Dara, and Rufus were picking through the wreckage, checking the bodies that littered the sand.

"Has anyone seen Wren?" Gendry asked as he lifted a broken piece of ship off Kiki and helped her up. She stumbled and winced in pain; her hand came away from her side stained red.

No one answered him.

"Go look. We've got everything under control here," Margot said as she moved to Kiki and helped her sit on a crate so she could inspect the wound. It was a decent-sized gash but didn't appear too deep. Margot healed it quickly and turned to the others to check if anyone else needed help.

One by one, the rest of the crew emerged. Most were bedraggled and waterlogged but otherwise appeared unharmed. Aside from the glow, which was slowly receding, the storm didn't seem to have affected Margot's keen all that much. Maybe it was a little less effort to draw the source, and the healing itself didn't seem as painful or taxing for the patient.

Finally, Gendry reappeared carrying Wren. "Put me down, you great oaf. I told you I am fine," she grumbled and battered his chest with her hand.

He gave her a look but set her on her feet.

She took one limping step and groaned.

Margot hurried forward. "Let me see to that, Wren."

Wren nodded and glanced at Gendry. "Head count if you would, my love?"

"Oh, my *love* now is it? A moment ago, I was a *great oaf.*" His attempt at an irritated glare was spoiled by his smile.

"You're still an oaf, but you're *my* oaf." She beamed.

Despite being attacked by the leviathan and then literally swallowed by the maelstrom, everyone seemed to be in good spirits. Margot turned her attention to Wren's leg. Her magic washed over the limb and found the weakness—a clean break—it would still be painful to fix. Mending bones always was. "Sorry, Wren, it's broken, which means this will be painful."

Wren waved her concern away. "It'll be worse if you leave it."

Margot rubbed her fingers together then placed them on Wren's leg above the break. She let her keen wash out in a warm rush and pulled the bones into place before melding them together.

Wren gritted her teeth and her skin glowed brighter as a bolt of lightning struck the water. "Shadow's teeth!"

"All accounted for," Gendry said as he returned. "And I believe we are somewhere between Gesar and Tikut."

"That far south?" Wren rubbed her lip. "Strange. I would have expected us to wash up somewhere near Hedar. The fathoms don't even extend as far as Gesar."

"Unless we were magically transported. What if the maelstrom is a portal?" Margot said, reminding herself forcibly of Nea in a way that sent a pang through her chest.

"Perhaps. That would explain the stories of missing ships," Wren said. "Anyway, we should gather what we can here and see if we can't find a town."

As everyone moved off to search for anything that was salvageable, Margot stared out over the calm waters to the horizon. She hadn't had time to think about Nea or the journal since the day before. Both journals, along with the rest of her things, were likely beneath the ocean, or if they had made it to shore, they would have been ruined. Whatever knowledge Nea had left for her was lost. She hurried through the wreckage, flipping over boards and crates, searching for any sign of her bag or the journal.

"Margot, are you alright?" Emil asked as she charged past him.

"Nea's journal!" she barked out, not stopping her frantic search. "I need to find it."

"Alright, you *need* a break," Penny said calmly, the smooth fingers of her keen working over the back of Margot's neck. "Sit. If it survived the wreck, we'll find it, and if not, well I am sure Mateus will know enough to point us in the right direction even without it."

"But ..." Margot wilted under the pressure of Penny's magic, collapsing onto the sand and letting out a breath that was somewhere between a sigh and a sob. She pressed her face into her hands. It wasn't just the knowledge the journal held; it was her last lifeline to Nea. Pressure built behind her eyes and she rubbed her fingers against them. "I can't face this without her, Pen," she said the words so softly she was sure Penny wouldn't hear them.

"Nonsense," Penny said, crouching in front of her. "You don't need Nea or Declan or anyone else. Nea knew that, which is why she entrusted the secrets in that journal to you. You are far smarter than you give yourself credit for."

"It's not intelligence I am worried about, Pen." She shook her head and chewed the side of her thumb. "I'm not brave like Nea. I don't have the stomach to do the things that must be done ... I can't ... I couldn't ... I'm not a killer."

"Nea's not a killer either." Penny's dark brows lifted. "Okay ... she's taken lives before, yes, but never in cold blood. You don't have to change who you are to be the hero. And Nea isn't asking you to be the hero anyway; she's just asking you to clean up her mess. And cleaning up Nea's messes is something you have a lot of practice with, no?"

Margot gave a wet chuckle. "I guess. I just wish I could be more like her."

"Impulsive and dangerous?" Emil quipped. "Honestly, the world could do with a few less Neas and few more Margots as far as I am concerned. I'm sure Garret would agree if he were here."

Penny laughed. "I dare say so." She rose to her feet and stretched as Pippa came wandering over with Margot's bag.

"You're in luck. Not sure if anything is salvageable, but here you go." She held the waterlogged bag out. A tiny crab scuttled over the surface and she flicked it off with grimace.

"Thank you." Margot took the bag and gingerly opened it. Everything was soaked through, but she burrowed until she found the journal. Cool magic frosted her fingertips as they brushed the spine and pulled it out. The cover was water damaged like everything else in the bag. She gingerly opened it and her heart sank. The delicate loops of Nea's handwriting were broken and smudged, complete sections indecipherable. She pushed the journal back into her bag and turned her hot eyes to the hand Emil was offering her.

She let him pull her to her feet and give her a hug. The familiar smell of clove that he shared with all wardens washed over her. Emil wasn't generally a hugger—a trait he shared with Nea—but he always knew when Margot needed more than soothing words. Like Nea and Margot, Emil had been pretty much raised by Nonna and the others at Hartswood. And because of that, he was as much a brother to her as Ivan was despite not sharing any blood.

When he pulled away, he patted her shoulders. "All good then?" His amber gaze searched hers.

She nodded. "As good as I can be. I'm sorry, Emil. This must be hard for you too."

He shrugged. "You know Nea always has a back-up plan. She's slippery like that."

"But the journal—"

"Maybe Warren got it wrong." He said it too quickly, but she would let it go this time.

"Maybe." She shouldered her bag and wandered over to where Wren and Gendry had gathered the crew.

She wished she could share Emil's hope, but something inside told her that this time hope would just lead to bitter disappointment. If only Molly were there. Mother's grief she missed Molly.

CHAPTER TWENTY-FOUR

Nea

They landed on the main street just outside the Bright Temple in the capital. The sky above was a churning mass of dark clouds rent with flashes of technicolour lightning. *The maelstrom.* But what was it doing above the capital? Nea glanced at her arm. The mark was glowing a vivid orange against the soft lilac of the rest of her skin as her keen reacted to the proximity of the storm. Beside her, Garret was glowing in shifting shades of silver and gold, the mark on his arm a bright violet.

"Do I want to know?" he asked.

"It's the maelstrom. The enchanted storm that plagues the Fathoms, but I don't know why it's here." Cackling thunder drowned out her words. "We need to—Amelia?" Nea's attention snapped to the waifish girl stalking towards them. She was glowing a soft shade of pink, but then lilac shifted over her skin followed by a dark charcoal grey. Her dirty nightgown had been replaced with a form-hugging dress of emerald silk. The neckline of the garment was a low scoop that left the corpse-white expanse of her chest bare. The purple birthmark she shared with all deathborn stood out in stark contrast, but so did the star-shaped brand on the opposite side of her collarbone.

"You finally came." Amelia swept in and pressed a cold kiss to each of Nea's cheeks before doing the same to Garret. "Are you both ready? We're in for quite a treat."

Nea had stiffened, pinned in place by some invisible force when Amelia embraced her, but now she took a step back and shook her head. "I should have realised. He's had the brand all along, hasn't he?"

Amelia cocked her head to the side, her normally lank hair so glossy now that it reflected the flashing light from the clouds above. "Are you honestly surprised? You're not His first *pet*, you know? He's been playing this game for an eon, and we have finally reached the conclusion."

"Evard—"

Amelia's bark of bitter laughter cut her off. "No, my darling *sister*, not Evard. The Master."

"The Usurper?" Garret asked, and Amelia's lip curled.

"That is what some choose to call him, but he has stolen nothing, only claimed what is his by right."

"Who are you really? Who did they jam in that body when they killed the real Amelia?"

A sinister smile rolled slowly across Amelia's lips. "I thought you would have figured it out by now. You're an intelligent woman, and even if you weren't, blood calls to blood, kin knows kin."

Nea drew a breath and let her keen roll over Amelia.

The girl's smile deepened.

"Evette?"

She curtsied.

"Evette? Samson's wife?"

Amelia turned her attention to Garret as he spoke. "The same. He valiantly tried to save me, but he was a fool who could not accept the inevitable. You're not a fool though are you, little princeling?"

Garret's jaw tightened.

"What's wrong? You know the truth now, and maybe you always suspected it. *Blood calls to blood* after all." She took a step closer to Garret and he rocked back, but that same compulsion from before pressed on them. Nea pushed against it, trying to free herself.

Amelia's fingers traced the edge of Garret's jaw and then skimmed down the side of his neck, over his chest, to the edge of his ribs where the scar from the corrupted wound was. "Do you want to know a little secret about corruption?" She rose on the tips of her toes to press her cheek against his as she whispered, "It can only flourish in those who have a propensity for darkness, for chaos. Just ask Nea. Oh, she fights it more than most, but she knows the truth. She always has. I didn't need to seed that corruption in her. It was already there, waiting for a chance to get out to take over. It had been since Kalhanna. Hadn't it?" She directed the last at Nea.

Nea shook her head, and Amelia gave a simpering laugh. "You've always been an appalling liar." Amelia turned to Garret again. "You don't lie though, do you? Not to yourself at least. You liked that little taste of power. You crave more." She pressed her hands against the centre of Garret's chest, her lips a hair's breadth from brushing his. "I can show you a whole new world brimming with power and promise. All you have to do is ask."

Garret was shaking, his keen burning bright under his skin as he fought the compulsion. But the harder they resisted, the harder that force pressed down.

The realisation made Nea stop struggling. The pressure lessened; not enough that she could move freely, but enough that her keen could find the chinks in Amelia's armour. There had to be some thin crevice that Nea's magic could burrow into.

As she focused on Amelia, the air before her began to flicker as though she could see the source itself overlaying the world. There were patches that seemed thinner than others, and she *knew* if she levered her keen into them, she could tear them wide open, and the entire fabric of time and space would be laid bare to her. *It's your birthright,* a voice whispered at the back of her mind. The voice wasn't sinister and cloying like corruption but almost fatherly. *Don't fear it. Claim it.*

She hesitated, casting a glance at Amelia and Garret. She wasn't afraid that Garret would give in, even if he was himself. He would fight just as hard as she would, and he would rather destroy himself than surrender to it. That is what this was ultimately about, this challenge. About facing that temptation and trusting yourself not to give in. That's what her challenge had been—not just here in the labyrinth, but always. Always was she presented that choice; exposed to the heady allure of what she could become. It was new to Garret though, and it was clear in the depths of his gaze just how hard he was fighting, just how afraid he was that he would lose himself.

The ward mark started to itch, and she dropped her gaze to it. The vibrant orange was dimming the longer Garret struggled. She focused on the feel of his keen under her skin. The warm numbness. It tangled with her own, transforming into something new. A crack formed in the compulsion restraining her and she forced the new power into it, tearing it open.

Amelia gave a hiss and released Garret, her attention fully on Nea. The compulsion hit her again, nearly knocking her to her knees, but she gritted her teeth and grabbed hold of the soul that was housed in Amelia's body. She twisted it, and Garret drew a ragged breath as the compulsion dropped entirely.

"You. Won't. Win," Amelia ground out through her teeth, panting with each word. A small bead of blood ran from her nose and along the edge of her lip. "The seed—"

Amelia's words cut off in a wet gurgle as Nea ripped through the fabric holding her together. Her body didn't slump to the ground but disintegrated into a cloud of purple-black smoke and starlight feathers.

Nea drew a steadying breath and turned to face Garret. He swallowed and refused to meet her eye.

"Garret ..." she said softly and took a step towards him, but he rocked back on his heels.

"I need a minute." He lifted his hands and moved away from her.

She studied his shoulders as he raked his fingers through his hair and cursed under his breath.

"I know what you're feeling. You're reliving every choice you've ever made, wondering if there's some sign that you're not really who she said you are. It's new for you, but I've lived nearly my entire life second-guessing every thought, every action, wondering if this is the time that I give in entirely. She was right; Kalhanna changed me, twisted something inside because I let it in—I needed to. I told you already that I gave in to the darkness inside, let it take over to kill those soldiers. I did that because I knew if I didn't, I wouldn't be able to kill them, and I knew if I didn't kill them, they would take me back to Evard and I would lose myself anyway. So I chose to lose myself on my terms."

He spun to face her and let out a breath. "I don't trust myself to keep fighting it."

She gave him a sad smile. "I know. But you will keep fighting." She took a step towards him. "When we were separated before, you were given a choice. And you chose to believe in my better nature. You *trusted* that I wouldn't give in. I don't even trust myself, but you trusted me anyway. This is the same. *You* don't have to believe that you are good a person; *you* don't have to trust that you'll never give in because the promises are so sweet and you are only human. But *I* believe in you ... I trust you."

The second the words left her lips, the churning sky stilled, and the world seemed to hold its breath.

"How can you?"

She shrugged. "How can you believe in me? Trust me? You've seen what I am capable of. You know I am impulsive and reckless and curious ... And the Shadow favours such traits as they are easier to corrupt." She bit back a smile. "I've had the door out of this labyrinth before me the entire time, but we both needed to realise a few things about ourselves and each other before I could see it. We are two sides of the same coin, Garret."

Recognition flashed on his features. "Wade said that exact same thing."

"Did he?"

"Yes, and he knew about me being a brightling."

"He did? Did Frell?"

He shook his head. "Wade didn't seem to think so, and Zephyr didn't know until Wade started comparing your connection to the Shadow Man to my connection to the Bright Mother." He cast a glance at the frozen storm above them. "You said you know the way out."

"Yes, Amelia just helped me figure it out ... Whether I can use it is another matter."

Drawing a deep breath, she turned her attention to the air around them, finding a place where the source was thinner, and worked her keen into it. The source pushed back against her, and pressure built behind her eyes. She gritted her teeth and reeled her keen in before holding her hand out for Garret to take. "I need a boost."

"A boost?"

"Do you mind if I borrow your keen?"

He took hold of her hand, and the marks on their arms grew brighter as the steady warmth of Garret's keen mixed with her own. It was gradual at first then the extra power zinged up her spine and set her teeth on edge.

Focusing on the thin section of the source, she worked her keen into it again, widening a crack until she had made a small hole. The pressure behind her eyes returned and she gripped Garret's hand tighter as the coppery scent of blood reached her. She lifted her free hand to touch the trickle that dripped from her nose and gritted her teeth, giving a final push of power.

With a sound like ripping cloth, the crack sprung open, and the world dropped out from under them.

It was different to travelling through the stone portal. Instead of the stretching, constricting, out-of-her-body-and-in-it-again sensations, it was like walking down a road. Scenes flashed by at a near-sickening speed, but she kept her eyes straight ahead, her mind focused on the pull of her destination. She didn't know what that destination was—maybe she should have given that some thought instead of taking a leap of faith. However, something inside told her it was alright. Her keen knew what it was doing even if she didn't.

Then her body appeared below her, lying on a stone slab in a strange cavern that was lit by hundreds of glowing crystals. Garret lay on the ground beside her, his lips blue like her own as though they were both at that very edge of death. She stepped forward and touched the centre of her own chest.

The world flipped and heat flooded her veins, then her eyes flew open. Above her, crystals glittered like multicoloured stars as she willed feeling into her stiff limbs. Her head swam and her vision doubled as she slowly sat. She rubbed her eyes and stretched, trying to dispel the sensation that her skin had changed and somehow the fit was not quite right.

Her gaze fell on the body lying on the ground beside her. *Garret!* She moved too quickly, her legs coming out from under her as she stumbled to him.

No breath stirred his chest. Her fingers pressed into the cold skin of his neck, searching desperately for a pulse. Nothing.

"No, no, no," she whispered and felt for the edge of his keen. It was a warm throb but—it was inside of her. That is why her body felt wrong—it was trying to house two souls. "You bloody idiot, Nea." She pressed her hands over her face and drew a ragged breath. How in the Mother's name was she going to fix this?

"Nea?" Her attention snapped to Declan as he approached. "Thank the Bright you're okay." He rushed to her and swamped her with a hug but then his gaze fell on Garret, a furrow forming across his forehead. "Why isn't Garret back? Is he ...?"

Nea shook her head. "I think he's inside me."

"*Inside* you?" Declan's brows nearly met his hairline. "How?"

"I'm not sure exactly. I borrowed his keen to make a portal, and everything was fine until we emerged on this side and I rejoined my body."

"Back up. You borrowed Garret's keen to *make* a portal? How? Can you do it now?"

"We have a more pressing issue. We need to get Garret back in his own body, then I promise I will let you help me experiment with making portals."

"Excellent." He clapped his hands together. "So how do we extract Garret? Should I get Moira? Or Rourke?"

"Probably. If Moira is the one who performed the ward, she might know what's going on."

"Hang tight. I'll go get her." He hurried towards the door then stopped and turned to face her. "No experimenting without me."

"Declan!"

"I'm going." He disappeared, and Nea studied Garret's face.

She touched the backs of her fingers to his cheek. His skin was ice cold, and the deathly pallor made the scar on his lip stand out. She'd never asked him how he got it, but he'd had it a long time because the teenager she had met in the memory field had also had it. Though his had been much fresher, closer to newly healed.

Garret's keen swelled under her skin, almost drowning her own keen out, and the mark on her wrist burned. She lifted her arm and glared at the faintly glowing lines of the Bright Mother's eight-pointed star then rolled Garret's arm over and inspected his mark. The lines were a faded violet, almost grey. "I wonder ..." She pressed the two wards together and channelled the source into them until the lines grew white-hot, then she pushed the sensation of Garret's keen through the mark on her arm into his.

Ice and fire erupted in waves down her spine and spots danced across her vision, threatening to toss her into oblivion. Panting, she dropped Garret's wrist. The lines of his death ward glowed bright violet for a moment then died again.

The fit of Nea's body shifted, snapping back into place, and Garret sat up.

"Shadow's teeth!" He gripped his head.

"Are you alright?"

His gaze moved to Nea as she spoke.

"I think so. Though I feel ..." He rubbed a hand over his face then glanced around as though looking for someone. "Wasn't Declan here?"

"He's gone to get Moira."

"Good. I think. Did you ...? Were you ...? Was I ...?"

Nea held in a laugh. "When we emerged from the portal, we both ended up in my body. I am not sure how, but I've fixed it now."

"You managed to get him back in his own body then?" Declan arrived with an elderly woman in tow.

"Yes." Nea stood.

The older woman was leaning heavily on a staff with a large rose carved at its top. The amethyst set into the centre of the carving was pulsing with a rose-coloured glow. Her eyes, a strange shade of soft pink, studied Nea's face for several heartbeats as her keen, which felt like nothing Nea had ever encountered, rolled steadily down her spine.

The woman gave a satisfied nod. "You did well." Her gaze switched to Garret, who was getting gingerly to his feet. "You both did. Come. Rourke should have the restorative ready, and we have little time to waste."

"How long were we gone?" Nea asked as she followed the woman who she assumed was Moira.

"Long enough that I was beginning to believe the ward would fail."

"And if it had?"

Moira stopped and fixed Nea with a look that suggested frustration. It was one Nonna wore when Nea asked a question she already knew the answer to.

"Why did you risk it?"

"My options were limited thanks to your run in with Frell." Her tone was dry, and the corner of her mouth twitched into a frown. "I hoped the divine blood you share would be enough. That the bond already forming between you would not break under the pressure of what was required. The Lady Bright assured me that would be case, the Shadow, however, was not so certain. I am pleased that he was wrong this time." She started moving again.

"And what happens now?"

"Now we make sure you have a handle on the power you unlocked. That shouldn't be a problem though. Getting Garret to unlearn several decades of living as a ward mage and teaching him how to use his brightling powers is going to be another thing entirely."

"Does he need to?"

Moira's mouth twisted. "It will be much easier if he does. Right now, however, you both need to recover before we can start putting you through your paces." Her tone was final, and Nea got the sense that for now she would not entertain any further questions.

CHAPTER TWENTY-FIVE

GARRET

"I am fucking trying!" Garret threw his hands in the air and stalked away from Declan.

For the better part of the day, he had been attempting to channel Declan's keen the way he had Nea's. But no matter how hard he tried, all he could do was sense it and suppress it. They had to be wrong. He wasn't a brightling. Channelling Nea's keen had, in fact, been a result of the corruption and then the jump through the portal.

Footsteps sounded behind him. "I'm sorry. I just need a break," he said without turning to face Declan.

"Then let's go for a walk," Nea said, and he spun around.

"Where did Declan go?"

"I sent him away."

She seemed calm, calmer than he had ever seen her as though something inside had changed.

"I think we just need to give up. Being able to channel your keen was a freak accident, not some sign that I am this divine creation. You were right. It is just a string of coincidences."

One iron-grey brow twitched up. "What is this really about?"

"It's not about anything. We're wasting our time here when we should be hunting down this Usurper and putting him in his place so we can cure corruption and go home."

She touched her fingers to the faded grey marks on her arm. "What Amelia said—"

"It has nothing to do with Amelia!" He clenched his fists; he could still feel the barbs of Amelia's keen burrowing under his skin, whispering across the back of his mind. If he unlocked that power hidden within, there would be no turning back.

Nea folded her arms. "Come on. There's something I want to show you."

He studied her back as she walked away, deliberating whether or not he should follow her, but when she stopped at the edge of the path and half-turned to glance back his way, he nodded and caught up.

She gave him a small knowing smile but said nothing as she continued out of the village.

The path wound into the forest, and soon the smooth stones were replaced with a spongy moss that led them right to the edge of a crystalline pool. Glowing fish danced through the water, occasionally flitting to the surface to test drifting leaves and other flotsam.

"You are still approaching your keen from the perspective of a warden," she said as she moved to the edge of the pool.

"Because that is what I am. I can't change how my keen works— it's instinctual. You know that."

She studied him over her shoulder. "Do you know that the majority of how we interact with our keen, with the source, is learned and not, in fact, instinctive? It does become instinct. But it is a tool we hone over time."

"Maybe for mages it works that way, but wardens—"

"You're not *only* a warden, Garret." She let out a huff and turned her attention to the water. "You need a change of perspective." Her fingers went to the fastenings on her waistcoat, and she slipped it off then bent to remove her boots.

"What are you doing?"

"Do you trust me?"

He did, didn't he? That was what the whole labyrinth had been about figuring out, hadn't it? Yes, he trusted her, but could she trust him? Should she? They hadn't spoken about what happened in the labyrinth, but something critical had changed. They had almost crossed that invisible line in the past, but now it felt like something greater than he could handle, especially when he'd had a taste of what the corruption could really give him—of the way his future could go. She didn't deserve to be dragged into that, not after everything else she had been through. He let out a breath. "I trust *you.*"

"Good. Well, what are you waiting for?"

His gaze shifted to her. She was standing waist-deep in the water, the thin material of her slip clinging to her damp sides. The glowing fish swirled around her legs and away again.

"I don't know how going for a swim is going to help."

She splashed him. "We're not going for a swim. You are getting a long overdue lesson on *perspective.* So come on."

With a sigh, he slipped his clothes off and placed them beside Nea's, then he stepped into the water, finding it warmer than he was expecting. As he waded out to where Nea was standing, a quiver of unfathomable magic stirred up his spine. "Alright, now what?" He folded his arms.

She rubbed her fingers along her lip, but the movement couldn't hide her smile. "Now close your eyes and take a deep breath."

He did as he was told.

"Another. You're still too tense."

As he took several more long, slow breaths under her instruction, the world around them seemed to come to life. Birdsong echoed through the trees, accompanied by the rustling of leaves and gentle lapping sound of the water against the rocks at the edge of the pool. Directly in front of him, Nea's breath matched his own.

"Good," she whispered. "Now tell me what you hear."

"Birdsong, the breeze in the leaves, the water lapping against the shore."

"And what do you *physically* feel?"

"The fish stirring around our legs, the water, the slight chill on the breeze."

"Alright. Now ..." She took hold of his hand and pressed it against the centre of her chest.

His breath caught for a moment in his throat.

"This time, what does your *keen-sense* feel?"

Cold was the first thing that came to mind. Nea's keen was always cool, almost soothing, but at times it was the deep breath-stealing cold of a winter blizzard. He got the sense though that that wasn't what she meant. With another outward breath, he let his keen smooth along the edges of hers. Instinctually, his keen was looking for the weaknesses, the points where it could cut her off from the source. That was his suppression rising.

"Ignore that instinct, brush it aside and move beyond it," she whispered, her fingers flexing against his as her skin warmed under his palm.

Brush it aside? How? Something else was lurking under the instinct. He focused on that deeper feeling, coaxing it forward. Then he could feel the shroud of source that lay over every inch of her.

"That's it."

Last time he had felt this had been with that spirit in the Sorrow Wood, and his keen had gotten tangled in that shroud, tearing it apart like a flimsy piece of cloth. What if he got tangled again and Nea couldn't stop—

Her fingers touched his cheek, scattering the rising panic. "Inhale ... Exhale ..."

"I—"

"You won't hurt me. You can't accidentally rip someone's soul from their body—it takes sustained effort and control."

He swallowed and shook his head. "What if—"

"Garret, trust me. I wouldn't ask this of you if I didn't know you could do it ... and if I didn't trust you."

After several deep breaths, he centred himself again and found the shroud.

"Good, how does my keen feel now?"

"Like waves on the shore, pushing and pulling."

"Like breathing," she whispered.

"Yes, or a song building and falling."

"Exactly. And how does that compare to the warden part of your keen?"

He turned his focus inward. The warden part of his keen was easy to find; it was silent and numbing, and there was no ebb and flow, just a steady urge to suffocate the connection to the source. Beneath that, however, there was something else, bright and burning. He focused on the sensation and lifted it to the surface. It was much like Nea's keen, pulsing in waves, but it came with the urge to learn, to grown, to consume—

Nea gave a sharp intake of breath, and he opened his eyes.

"You found it." It was the widest smile he'd ever seen her give, full of warmth and delight, and he couldn't help but smile back. "I was worried we would need to figure out a way around my father's block before you could find it. You'll master it in no time at all with a little more practice."

He rubbed his fingers along his top lip. He'd forgotten what she had said about the part Niall played in his past. Why had he locked that part of Garret's keen away? The thought brought with it the reminder that Evard was his father, who had without a doubt raped his mother. And unable to live with her grief, or maybe her guilt, she had tried to kill Garret before he had even been born. His entire life had been a series of lies and hidden truths.

"Garret, look at me."

He obeyed. There was always a deep sadness in the depths of her gaze, and now he truly understood it. She had lived her entire life knowing she was different and having to keep it a secret from those who she cared for most. She had been treated like an abomination and abandoned by her mother all because of what she had been born. Is that what his life would have been like? It had been, hadn't it, before Niall came along and took his memories? Had he just been a pawn in some divine game ... had Nea? Anger tightened the back of his jaw, but it softened as a small smile touched the corner of Nea's mouth.

"Do I need to remind you that knowing the truth now doesn't change who you have always been in here?" She touched the place over his heart. "Or here?" She brushed his hair away from his temple.

He caught her hand as it slid away from his face. So many thoughts and emotions were churning inside, he wasn't sure which he should focus on. But Nea was an anchor stopping him from getting swept away. He released her hand and brushed a lock of hair behind her ear. His fingers lingered on the side of her neck, his thumb smoothing along the edge of her jaw. Her breath seemed to pause for several heartbeats, and she closed her eyes.

"Nea—"

"Would you please just kiss me already?"

A tremor ran through him and he wasn't sure he had heard her correctly. He toyed with his scar to prevent himself from just grabbing her and—"Are you sure?"

"Yes." It was barely a whisper, and he might not have caught it if he hadn't been watching her mouth.

He touched the edge of her jaw again, committing the feel of her to memory. She pressed her cheek into his touch and gently kissed the pad of his thumb as it rolled over her lower lip. Slowly, he slid his hand around the side of her neck and titled her head back as he lightly brushed his lips against hers.

A soft moan escaped her. The sound seemed to signal a shift for them both. Nea pressed her body against his, her fingers lacing into his hair. He captured her lower lip gently between his teeth as his hands slid down her sides and around the curve of her hips. She made another sound, her free hand sliding between them to trace along his jaw. His grip on her tightened and he backed her to the stone shelf at the edge of the pool. She gave a little shiver as his hands dropped lower, cupping the backs of her thighs and lifting her. Her legs closed around his hips, pinning their bodies together as she arched against him in a way that brought a primal groan from his core. He looped one arm around her to support her as the other hand studied the curves of her body, over one breast and then behind her neck. Her fingers fanned out over his chest before moving up and grabbing his hair again. She gave a delicate tug that sent a shiver to his toes as her lips left his to press against his throat.

"Nea ..." His voice was raw and husky.

"Yes?" she whispered, her teeth brushing the side of his neck as her legs tightened around his hips and the source around them gave a delicate quiver.

"Are you sure you want—"

"*Yes.*"

"Where did you and Nea disappear to yesterday?" Declan asked as he joined Garret outside Rourke's hut and handed him a cup of tea.

Garret inhaled the smooth scented steam rising from the brew. "We just took a walk in the forest. She thought it might help me clear my head."

Declan's mouth twitched. "Just a walk? You were gone quite a while."

Garret shrugged and flexed his fingers. He could still feel the soft curves of Nea's body. "Anyway, I think I am ready to give channelling your keen another try."

Declan looked like he wanted to say more, but he took a long drink from his cup instead. "Alright let's do it."

They moved to a small field at the end of the village and Declan held out his hands. "So, I have been thinking, what if I fed my keen into you the way Nea did with Nora? You'd be able to feel it intrinsically, and it might override that instinct to suppress."

"Part of the walk yesterday was Nea showing me how to move past the suppression. However, it's not a bad idea." He took hold of Declan's hands, and a wild zing like a shower of sparks ran down his spine as Declan pushed his keen beneath Garret's skin.

The warm numbness of suppression rose, and he gritted his teeth, forcing it back and allowing the bright part of his keen to take over, that hungry need to consume and learn rising with it. Ice prickled around him and the mark on his wrist lit up, the lines glowing vivid violet against his skin.

Declan let his hand go and the feeling immediately dissipated, but the churning brightness of storm magic prickled under the skin of his fingers. He flexed them and met Declan's eye.

"Well?"

"I don't know."

"Try something."

"Like what?" He opened his hands in front of himself and a silver-blue spark jumped across his fingertips.

Declan clapped. "Did you see that? Can you control it?"

Control it? He hadn't been able to actively control Nea's keen even though he could channel it. Channelling and controlling, it would seem, were two very different things.

With a deep breath, he thought about what Declan's keen *felt* like when he used it. It was bright and flashing, raw power that was somehow elegantly controlled and discrete despite its unbridled nature. Thunder rumbled. He gave his fingers a little flick, fanning them out as he did so like he'd seen Declan do a hundred times before. An arc of silver-blue lightning shot across the field and struck the thin trunk of a tree, sending a shower of bright sparks into the air.

"Shadow's teeth!" Declan exclaimed.

Shadow's teeth indeed. Garret studied his fingers.

"Can you do that again?" Declan was practically bouncing. "You should try a different keen. We need someone else, someone different—I'll get Zeph! Or Nea—both. They both need to see this. Don't move!"

"Declan, wait ..." But Declan had taken off across the field already.

Garret shook his head as he studied the smouldering tree.

"It would appear you've had a breakthrough." Nea's keen rolled in cool fingertips down his spine as she joined him. "Can you summon Declan's keen as though it is your own like you did mine or do you need to be in contact with him?"

"I don't know." He studied his fingers and tried to summon the static prickle again. A single spark quivered across his fingertips then died.

One of her stormy brows twitched up.

"What?"

"You're overthinking it again. Magic isn't a *thinking* thing; it's a *feeling* thing. I thought we covered that yesterday."

Her words stirred up images from the day before. Her hips pressed against his, back arched as—"We need to talk about what happened yesterday."

"We probably should ... however, maybe it is better if we focus on finding the Usurper and getting out of the Between first."

"Do you regret—"

"No." She shook her head. "It's just ... complicated. I never expected to survive Kalhanna, and ever since ... I don't know. Yesterday was the first time in years that I felt ... *alive.* But there is so much at stake that if I allow myself to be distracted, if I lose focus and Evard and the Usurper do win, then ..."

"I understand. So we accept that it happened, and we focus on what is important right now."

A sad smile quirked the corner of her mouth. "But if we survive the end of the world, then I promise we can make up for lost time."

He grinned and pressed a kiss to her forehead. "I'll hold you to that."

"Well, well, well," Declan purred.

"Leave them be," Zephyr said, her tone playful.

Nea took a step back, leaving a cold void in her wake. She was right though. Feelings were distracting, and not only that—they were something that tyrants like Evard lived to exploit.

"Have you made any progress at all or have the pair of you just been standing around making eyes at each other?"

"Go on. Get it all out of your system," Nea said with an eye-roll.

"Oh no, for months I watched the pair of you dance around each other. I am going to savour this." Declan grinned.

"Declan—"

"Boundaries," he finished Garret's sentence for him. "Fine." The playful gleam in his gaze diminished slightly. "Back to business then. Did you manage to channel my keen again?"

Garret rubbed the back of his neck. "I haven't tried."

"Well, what are you waiting for? The sooner you get the hang of this the sooner we can go after the Usurper. Do you need me to lend you some keen again?"

"No, I need to try without it." He lifted his hands and studied them. Declan's keen churned beside him, but under his own skin was only the warm numbness of suppression and the cool throb of Nea. Her keen had spiked, rattling the source and frosting the surface of the pond when they had—

"Focus, Garret." Nea's voice brought him back to the moment.

How had it felt to use Declan's keen? A static prickle rolled over the back of his neck and down his arm. *Right.* He lifted his hand as the static built to an unbearable rush of pins and needles. He flicked his fingers and fanned them towards the tree, forcing the rush of energy out of his body. It burst forth like a charging bull, sending an aftershock up his arm that made his back teeth ache.

The trunk erupted in a shower of splinters and sparks as the bolt of lightning hit it dead centre.

Zephyr clapped and bounced on the balls of her feet. "That was amazing."

Garret studied his fingers.

"Yes, well done. But don't let it build so much before you release it. It's about finesse, not bludgeoning." Declan ran his finger along his lip.

Nea's words to Nora rang across the back of his mind: 'The source is our ally, not our slave. We don't order it around; we work with it.'

With a nod, he let the static build again. It came easier this time, his instinct to suppress rolling aside to allow it to the surface. He could feel the tipping point, the moment when he could lose control of it and held it back. It was like drawing a bow string. He inhaled slowly then, as he exhaled, he let the power free. Lightning shrouded the tree once more.

Declan clapped him on the shoulder. "Now you're getting the hang of it."

CHAPTER TWENTY-SIX

Margot

After several days, they entered Dalthera, The City of Stars. Margot had never set foot in the city, but she'd heard enough stories regaling its breathtaking beauty. Those tales did not do the city justice at all. Glittering stone buildings were set into the mouth of a long-dormant volcano, and at the centre of the city, on a raised plateau of dark stone was the Arcanarium. With its twisting towers and emerald-painted rooves, it overshadowed all but the gleaming palace beyond it.

Wren made a noise beside Margot as she studied the path into the city. "Once we enter the city proper, we'll go our separate ways. We will be in town for a few days though, and if you should need anything you will be able to find us in The Dancing Goat at the southmost end of the docks."

"You can't show us to the Arcanarium?"

Wren shook her head forcefully. "Penny knows the way, and you'll get a better reception if you're not seen cavorting with 'no greats and pirates'." She dug in her pocket and pulled out a sea snail shell. "Here."

It was the iridescent purple–green of an oil slick on water with copper stripes that shimmered across its surface. As Margot took it, a flicker of magic skittered up her arm.

"If—when you find Nea again, give it to her. She'll know what to do with it."

A lump blocked Margot's throat and she tilted the shell towards Wren. "Nea is—"

"She's not dead. I can feel it in my bones."

Margot closed her fingers around the shell, pressing it hard into the centre of her palm. She wanted Wren to be right, but she couldn't allow herself to hope—not this time.

Wren gave a nod and clapped her on the shoulder. "Remember, if you need us, you'll find us at The Dancing Goat." She then slid her hand into Gendry's, and they wandered off after the rest of the crew who were dispersing into the city.

Margot turned to Emil, Penny, and Dale, who were standing a short distance away talking softly. Penny looked up and gave her a small smile as she approached. "Ready?"

With a nod, Margot slid the shell Wren had given her into her bag. "As ready as I am going to be."

The walk to the base of the plateau was short, but it led them through a busy market and then into a run of houses, each more magnificent than the next. The rooves were painted a myriad of colours, from a deep russet red to a startling magenta, and on through the spectrum to a vivid cornflower blue that was so close to the shade of Molly's eyes, it made Margot's heart ache.

There were two options to reach the Arcanarium at the top of the sheer wall of dark stone that shone like glass: a zigzagging set of stairs that were carved into the rock wall itself or one of the large, gilded elevator cages controlled by an age-hunched man with a stark white beard and a pair of rust-coloured overalls.

They chose the elevator, but as they slowly ascended, they discovered the stairs that had looked steep and daunting from the ground were actually a slow incline with alcove gardens and other small sections carved out alongside them every so often. Margot almost regretted they hadn't taken the option to explore the path.

At the top, the doors rolled open to reveal a wide courtyard. By the base of the stairs that led into the Arcanarium itself was a table, behind which sat a mage with an emerald-green waistcoat and ledger. He gave them a haughty once-over as they approached, his mouth barely twitching as his gaze found Penny. "Penelope, it has been too long since you have graced these walls. Who, may I ask, are your *interesting* acquaintances?"

"Felix, a pleasure as always." Penny swept forward and kissed each of his cheeks. "May I present Margot, Emil, and Dale. We are here to see Mateus if he is available."

"Arcanius Mateus is a busy man these days. I can see about an audience, but I cannot make any promises."

"Come now, Felix. We're old friends, and I believe you still owe me for helping you with Josiah."

A shift flickered across Felix's face so fast if Margot hadn't been watching him, she wouldn't have noticed.

"What is the nature of your visit?"

Penny studied Margot for a few moments before answering. "Nea sent us in relation to a sensitive matter. I am sure you understand the need for discretion."

Felix gave a short nod. "Very well. If you will follow me to the atrium."

He led them into a wide room that reminded Margot of the Del Harol room of reflection and conservatory combined. A fountain sat bubbling in the centre of a wide rectangular pool in which long-finned fish a motley of reds, oranges, white, and black drifted lazily. Potted plants and stone benches took up nearly every available bit of space. And scattered about the room were small groups of mages conversing or studying.

Felix left them to wait while he went to notify Mateus, and Penny moved to the edge of the pool. She brushed her fingers across the surface of the water and the fish swarmed towards them searching for food.

Margot wandered over to one of the plants with large fan-shaped leaves and a spike of coral-pink flowers rimmed with blue. Niall had a similar specimen in his collection. From memory it was a Faridean native, and the flowers were used for some kind of poultice, or was it a tonic? She turned to ask Penny if she could remember the name of the plant when Felix returned with a man whom she assumed was Mateus.

'An exquisite example of human beauty,' Penny had said, and she wasn't wrong. Even Margot could appreciate the line of his jaw and way his deep bronze skin contrasted with his starlight-toned hair. His hazel eyes, more brown than green, were full of a deep intelligence, but a hint of playfulness glittered in them as his mouth split into a wide grin when he spotted Penny. He stepped around Felix to sweep forward and press a kiss to each of her cheeks.

"Hello, Mateus," Penny said as he released her. "I would like you to meet my friends Margot, Emil, and Dale."

"It is so nice to put faces to the names."

"I am sorry?" Margot asked.

"Nea has told me much about you," he clarified. His voice was thick and luxurious, like spiced honey. "You are here at her request, yes?"

"Yes." Margot cast a glance around at the other mages in the atrium. "Is there somewhere we can speak in private?"

One of Mateus's pale brows rose, and he exchanged a look with Felix. "My office should suffice. Come, it is this way."

Mateus sat back in his seat, Nea's ruined journal in front of him. He hadn't said anything as Margot and Penny had told him everything that had happened from Kalhanna up until the enchantment on Nea's journal had died. He rubbed his fingers across his brow and looked out the window. "No wonder Nea wouldn't reveal her associate. Evard ..." He shook his head.

"So, did you ever find this *Book of Souls*?" Emil asked.

Mateus shook his head again. "It went missing centuries ago, but I expect Nea knew that already."

"Do you know what might have been in the journal?" Margot tried to keep her voice steady.

"No. However, Arcanius Greffon should be able to undo the damage."

"Can he be trusted?" she asked, and Mateus studied her before answering.

"I believe so, and we can be there the whole time he has the journal."

"Do you think the enchantment was tied to Nea's life force?" Emil asked, sending a bolt of tension through Margot's shoulders.

"Without having felt the enchantment myself or knowing what the journal actually contains it is hard to say. I wouldn't put it past Nea to do something like that if matters are as dire as they appear to be." A frown crossed his features. "If it is indeed the case, then I am sorry to hear it. She was one of the best of our generation."

Margot swallowed to try to shift the lump in her throat. "How long will it take to get an audience with Arcanius Greffon?"

"Not long. I'll have Felix send for him." He pressed his fingers to a disc of black stone set into the top of his desk and the cool flurry of his keen stirred the air. "He'll be on his way shortly. Can I offer any of you some tea?"

"It has been too long since I have had a cup of proper Osmarian jasmine," Penny said with a smile.

Mateus nodded and touched the stone disc again.

They didn't have to wait long at all. A maid came in with a tray of tea things, and shortly after her a man who looked surprisingly like an older version of Declan, his jaw was perhaps a little squarer, skin a shade darker, and he wasn't quite as tall. His green eyes, though, held the same sparkle of easy humour.

He took the cup the maid offered him on her way out the door and then turned to the room. "So, Mateus, you didn't invite me here simply to take tea."

"Can you mend this?" Mateus picked up Nea's journal and lobbed it towards Greffon.

He caught it one-handed without spilling even a tiny drop of tea, and his keen built; a soft whispering that promised potential. "Should be easy enough," he said with a nod. "Which of you does it belong to?" he asked them all, but his gaze fell on Margot.

"Nea." She chewed the side of her thumb.

Greffon examined the journal. "If it belongs to Nea, why isn't she here herself?"

"There was an enchantment on the journal, one that we believe was tied to her life force, and several days ago it lifted. So, we have reason to believe she's ..." Emil shot a look at Margot and took a long sip from his cup.

"I see ..." Greffon frowned. "That does make it more complicated. Thankfully though I know enough about Nea's keen that I should be able to perform a reconstruction easily enough. I'll need to take it down to the vault though."

Margot shot Mateus an alarmed look. He had implied that they would be able to be present whilst Greffon had the journal. It wasn't that she didn't trust Greffon, but she didn't like the idea of letting her last lifeline to Nea out of her sight.

"If you don't mind, Margot and I would like to accompany you to the vault. Penny and the others can go and secure lodgings while they wait." Mateus finished his tea and placed his cup aside.

Greffon studied Margot and then gave a small nod. "That should be fine."

A dizzying rush of breath entered Margot's lungs. She wasn't sure whether she felt more relieved or anxious about the prospect of finally discovering the secrets held in those pages.

The vault was like the other repositories that Margot had been in with the addition of clerks, who were human-sized golems of various materials from a warm mustard-yellow clay to a dark ebony wood. The clerks weren't the only difference. Archivists and other mages were gathered at tables and in private alcoves giving the whole place a feel of life that the repositories back home could never hope to achieve. After all, with very few exceptions, Beldaren mages seemed to possess a distinct preference to lock away possibly dangerous relics and anarchist manifestos rather than study them and risk inciting change. That was probably why they were in the mess they were in now.

As they crossed the large hall, Mateus and Greffon were greeted by various other mages, and at one point a girl of probably nineteen bounced over with a heavy tome, the ribbon bookmarks hanging out of it fluttering as she moved.

She gave Mateus a wide smile before turning to Greffon and showing him something in the tome. "Is this an example of Hebrion's law?" The excited tone of her voice and the glitter in her eyes were so like a younger version of Nea that Margot drew a deep breath.

"Yes. Now you need to compare that to the passage in section four and outline the moral implications as theorised by Hebrion himself. You might also find the Diabella manifesto holds a pertinent argument."

The girl gave Greffon a wide smile. "Thank you, Arcanius." She gave him a nod then hurried away again.

Greffon headed off across the room once more to a door at the back that was guarded by a clerk made from a glistening dark metal with robrillium designs set into its limbs and across its chest. The clerk nodded to Greffon—the movement accompanied by the sound of metal plates sliding together. "Greetings, Arcanius Greffon.

Arcanius Mateus. If you wish to proceed into the deep vault, then you must register your guest." The clerk's glowing eyes settled on Margot and a jolt of magic ran across her shoulders.

"Quite right you are," Greffon said, and his green gaze landed on Margot. "This is Margot, a healer from Beldaren."

The clerk inclined its head. "You will need to sign in." It tilted a ledger towards her.

"Certainly. Where's the pen?"

"No pen." It lifted an index finger and a long needle emerged from the tip.

"It needs your blood," Mateus said.

"Oh." Margot pressed her fingertip against the needle and coaxed a bead of blood to form. She pressed the blood against the next empty line on the ledger and it shone rose gold before stretching across the page and forming a very precise copy of her signature.

"You may proceed." The clerk stepped away from the door to permit them entry.

On this side of the door the vault was much more like the vaults she was used to—right down to the dusty cobwebs that gathered in the corners. It would seem that there were magics even the Osmarians didn't want the general masses privy to. Greffon led Margot deeper into the vault and then into a room which was bare save for the obsidian slab at its centre. Rune marks glimmered in a myriad of colours around the plinth, and they flared brighter as Greffon neared.

"Wait," Margot said as he went to lay the journal down. "Can you mend this one as well?" She drew the other journal out, the one that hadn't been sealed by magic. Even though she knew what it contained already, it was a memento of Nea's life before Kalhanna that Margot wasn't ready to give up.

Greffon took the journal from her, then Mateus drew her to the edge of the room. They stood in silence as Greffon laid the journals on the slab and lifted his hands over them. That strange blossoming keen curled through Margot's hair and the rune marks burned so bright she had to squint to see what was happening.

A cool thread of a keen so familiar it brought a lump to her throat twisted with Greffon's, and the journals lifted off the slab. The rune marks shifted into the air around the books, forming two glowing rings encircling them. Greffon gritted his teeth and Nea's keen spiked, causing the source in the room to shudder.

For a moment, the fabric of the world peeled back, and Margot met Nea's violet gaze.

"Margot?"

Before she could respond, the source slammed back together, and she was leaning against the wall with Mateus's cool fingers pressed to her brow.

His hazel eyes reflected concern as he studied her face. "We nearly lost you for a second there. He's almost done." He gestured to the plinth.

The journals drifted lazily onto its smooth surface as the rune marks died down to the soft glow they had been before. Greffon picked up the first journal and flipped it open. With a small nod, he handed it to Margot, and she opened it, not sure what to expect.

Evard has the Book of Souls. I am not certain how it came to be in his possession, but there is no mistaking it. He has been different of late: cruel and calculating in a way he never was before. If I did not know any better, I would say he has been possessed, but he bears no other hallmarks of that being the case. It could simply be the book's influence on him ...

Margot scanned the rest of the page, her heart leaping into the back of her throat. She then flipped through the book. It appeared from the few brief passages that she read that Nea had outlined in no uncertain terms exactly what she believed Evard was planning, and if he succeeded then they were all doomed.

"What is it?" Mateus asked, his hand falling on Margot's shoulder and causing her to jump.

"Evard has the *Book of Souls,* and Nea thinks—thought ..." She chewed her thumbnail and then flicked her gaze from Mateus to Greffon. "... that he wanted to use it to tear a hole in the barrier. To bring the Between crashing down on our realm so he can steal the mantle of Shadows and claim the sovereign thrones for himself."

Greffon swore.

"Impossible. Even if Evard was a mage, it would be close to impossible for him to achieve such a feat." Mateus ran his hands through his hair.

"Nea didn't seem to think so, and it appears that she outlines exactly how he plans to achieve it; taken straight from the pages of the *Book of Souls* itself, no less." Margot closed Nea's journal. "Also, she believed he might have been possessed—that it is not, in fact, Evard calling the shots but someone or something else."

"She was certain?"

Margot shook her head. "Apparently, even though she suspected it, she could not confirm it. And for someone like Nea to not be certain of a possession ..."

Mateus nodded. "We need to get to Beldaren immediately."

"With the Fathoms impassable it will take us weeks just to get to Fengate, but to get all the way to Del Harol? Do we have that much time?"

"Evard has not cracked the code yet, and with Nea out of the picture, it will take him time to find a loophole."

Greffon said as Mateus asked.

"Why Del Harol?"

"That is where Niall and the others are. Niall is probably our best bet of figuring out a way to sabotage Evard's plans. But why is Nea so important?" Margot directed at Greffon.

He rubbed his chin and shot a look at Mateus. "Because she's not exactly human herself."

Nonna had suggested as much. "Do you know what she is?"

Greffon shook his head slowly. "There's an old ballad that

mentions a child of Shadow and a child of Bright. Children of the divine blood. The first mages were assumed to have held the blood of the sovereigns, but occasionally, when times got particularly bleak, a child would emerge who was a little too different—more powerful, more prone to leaving chaos in their wake."

"Like a brightling?"

Greffon tilted his head. "Yes. But brightling are children of the Bright, and they come with a set of fairly specific hallmarks. I suspect Nea is a child of the Shadow. Niall told me enough when he sent her here to piece together that theory."

Margot tightened her grip on the journal. "What if both a child of Bright and a child of Shadow existed at the same time?"

"Then we'd be likely facing an event of apocalyptic proportions."

A stone dropped into the pit of Margot's stomach. "Then we'd better get moving."

CHAPTER TWENTY-SEVEN

NEA

The source quivered in front of her, a swirl of lilac forming as she focused on the point where the fabric was the thinnest. She worked the fingers of her magic into it, steadily forming a tear. It was getting easier each time she tried, but the process still left her breathless and with a pounding headache that threatened to drag her into unconsciousness. With a deep breath to centre herself, she gripped the edges of the tear and pulled in opposite directions. The portal sprang open; she was met by a flickering void of coloured lights. Margot stood before her, such a deep sadness in her whiskey-brown eyes that Nea's heart gave a flutter.

"Margot?"

The portal snapped shut, the recoil of magic forcing her back a step.

"You mustn't lose focus like that," Moira said. "If you want to be able to get home once you've dealt with the Usurper and found your cure, then you need precise control."

"I know." She rubbed her face with a wince. Her brain felt like it was trying to escape through her ears. "We've been practicing all afternoon. I could use a break."

Moira fixed her with a calculating stare. "Am I driving you too hard? Rourke always said as much."

"You're somewhat unforgiving, but Nonna is the same, so I am used to it."

The older woman nodded slowly. "Your control of it certainly seems to be increasing. What changed just now?"

"I saw Margot."

"The one who is a sister but not by blood."

"Yes, exactly."

"Curious. You actually saw her, or you thought of her?"

"I actually saw her. I felt her first—I think, but then it was like I could have reached out and touched her through the portal."

A wide smile formed on Moira's lips. "Excellent. I would say you managed to form a portal back to your world and it pulled you to the closest anchor, or maybe the strongest. One more test, I think."

"Just the one?" She was growing tired of this realm and its seemingly constant need to test her.

"Yes," Moira chuckled, "just the one. I want you to focus on a location you know and see if you can open a portal to that specific point. Finding Margot was an accident, but if you can target the opening then my work is done."

"Any location?"

"Any location that you know, though it will be easier if you have an emotional attachment to it."

"Alright." Nea closed her eyes and felt for the edges of the source again. When she found them, she opened her eyes and eased her keen into the cracks, forcing past the pain that built inside her skull. As the shimmering portal started to form, she drew up an image of her father's study. The portal opened and on the other side was her father's desk.

His head snapped up and a wide smile crossed his mouth. "Well now, someone has learned a new trick."

Beside her Moira gave a satisfied nod. "Can you reach through?"

Nea wasn't sure she wanted to try. What if she stepped through and the portal shut, and she couldn't open it again? Garret and

Declan would be stranded in the Between and she would have no way to reach them.

She lifted her hand and reached towards the portal. She'd been able to travel short distances here in the Between with no problem, but she wasn't jumping the barrier. As her fingertips met the middle of the portal, they pressed against a slight resistance. Then with a deep breath and her father watching her curiously, she pushed through. It was like stirring treacle with her fingers. The sensation pulled over her arm and then she met the cool air on the other side. Her father bolted from his chair to come around the desk to her. His fingers gripped hers and she let out a relieved gasp.

"You seem to be having quite the adventure."

"That is an understatement. We'll be home soon, and I can tell you all about it, but right now I need you to let my hand go so I can close the portal." Her voice sounded thin, and a sheen of sweat had broken out on her brow. Her corrupted arm was the one on the other side of the portal and a burning itch had started under her skin, building the longer her arm stayed there.

Her father released her hand, and the portal snapped shut the moment she withdrew her fingers from it. Moira was saying something beside her, but she couldn't hear it over the rush of blood in her ears. The corruption no longer itched but a voice was braying across the back of her mind.

You will be mine and now that you've unlocked the gift of your divinity, I will use it to take what I am due.

"Nea?" Moira touched her shoulder, and a tremor ran through her, scattering the voice.

"The corruption—" Her attention dropped to her wrist, but the marks were still a pale silver. "We need to get to the Night Estate."

Moira nodded. "I believe you're ready."

Later that evening, they were all gathered outside Moira's cottage. Zephyr had drawn a map of what she knew of the Night Estate and Wade was busy sewing. His keen reminded Nea of Arcanius Greffon's—the flicker of creative potential.

"I still don't understand what the outfits are for," Nea said.

"The full moon masquerade. It is our best bet to get in unnoticed, though ..." He studied her hair. "I am not sure how I am going to disguise that."

"Do we need to disguise it?"

"It's instantly recognisable to those who know you, and the Usurper will be looking for it."

Nea twisted her mouth. "We could dye it."

"Pointless if you ask me," Rourke said from his spot across the fire beside Garret. "No matter how you disguise Nea, the Usurper will know her. *She* cannot hide from him."

"Then what do you suggest? Just truss her up in a pretty bow and toss her to the wolf?"

Rourke shook his head and gave a low rumbling laugh. "Always so dramatic. But the idea has merit. He'll be so distracted by Nea the rest of us can go about our business unnoticed."

"Surely he would suspect a trap," Garret said.

"Perhaps, but he is so conceited and so sure that eventually he will get what he wants that he should be distracted long enough to give us an opening."

"And what exactly are we looking for?" Declan piped up.

"A mirror," Rourke answered.

"A mirror?" Declan's brows knit together.

"Is he using a spirit-glass?" Nea leant forward. "Of course. A spirit-glass would allow him to project himself like he does, and if he has enough power, he could use it to communicate across worlds. Then once a mage *tapped* in to his signal, he could take root in the part of their soul that was connected to the source." She leapt to her feet, bumping Wade as she did so. "Why didn't I think of that before? Evard didn't encounter him through the *Book of Souls;* he encountered him through the spirit-glass! If I had just—"

"Okay, my lovely, you need to slow down. Not all of us have *all* the information, remember?" Declan said with a grin.

"We need to destroy that spirit-glass if we can find it. That should be enough to break his connection to our realm. It won't heal the current cases of corruption, but it will prevent new ones. And without his constant influence, we should be able to isolate the infected portion of his victims' souls and cleanse him out like any ordinary possession." She clapped her hands together.

"What about Amelia?" Garret asked. "Or others like her who can seed corruption?"

"That is trickier, but I am hoping if we break the Usurper's hold on our realm enough we should be able to sever his connection to Amelia as well. And that should make her easier to destroy ... at least in theory ... Regardless, if we destroy the Usurper's spirit-glass, we will weaken him considerably and we will have an easier time mopping up the mess back in our realm."

"Well, it sounds like we have a plan then," Zephyr said as she plopped herself down next to Declan. "Offer Nea up to the Usurper to distract him while the rest of us sneak in and find his spirit-glass. Then we destroy the mirror, and you jump back ... to your realm." She gave Declan a sad glance. "And the Usurper should be weakened enough that you can destroy him from there."

"Maybe." Nea tapped her chin. "Though that doesn't help the Bright Mother or the real Shadow Man reclaim their power and right the balance."

"Because you are only focused on part of the problem." Moira joined them. "If you weaken the Usurper's grip on your realm, it will take him some time—perhaps centuries—to lick his wounds, but he will get his power back eventually. The only way to be done with him is to reclaim the power he stole from the sovereigns and release them from their prisons. You know this already." Moira levelled her gaze on Nea. "And you know what must be done to achieve it."

Nea shook her head.

"You can shake your head all you want but at the end of the day, that is what must be done."

"It's too dangerous. If we miscalculate, if breaking the glass doesn't sufficiently weaken him, then we risk—"

Moira slammed the butt of her staff on the ground. "You are too smart for that sort of catastrophic thinking. Breaking the glass *will* weaken him and then you need to draw him to your world and finish him. You were created for this very purpose; you both were." She tilted her head in Garret's direction.

"How do we draw him to our world?" Declan asked.

"By tearing down the barrier," Zephyr replied.

"But that will free him completely, won't it?"

"Yes," Nea said, "and if we haven't sufficiently weakened him, the only way to stop him will be to unseat him by claiming the thrones of eternity for ourselves." As she said it, realisation hit her, and she threw a sharp look at Moira. "That's the only answer, isn't it? Even if we weaken him. The only way to fix everything and prevent this from happening again is for Garret and me to take the thrones. That is why you knew the ward would work and why we were *created*."

"A child of Bright and a child of Shadow. There is enough divine blood in you that you will be up for the feat."

"But that is exactly what he wants. It's why he's been manipulating Evard all this time, setting all the parts in just the right place." Nea clenched her fists and paced a few steps away.

"He wants to claim the thrones for himself. He cannot do that without a consort—there needs to be balance. His plan is to manufacture a consort and place her on the throne only to trap her and take whatever power he can from her. The same way he did the sovereigns. You can claim the thrones and then free the sovereigns and return them to power. That is not an option he would give you."

Nea rubbed her hands over her face. "I need to clear my head." She stalked away, her thoughts churning.

The path she followed led her to a small garden. Wild bushes of roses scented the air with their heavy blooms, almost overpowering the soft aroma of the lavender as Nea brushed by it. She sat on one of the cool stone benches and raked her fingers through her hair.

Footsteps crunched on the path, and the scent of clove mingled with the roses and lavender as Garret stopped in front of her. She shifted sideways on the seat to make room for him, and as he sat, she lent her shoulder against his.

"It's an impossible ask," she said.

"Moira seems to think it's simple enough."

"Of course she does. Everything is not riding on her shoulders."

"You are not bearing the weight alone." He placed a hand on her knee and gave it a gentle squeeze. "We can only take it one step at a time."

She turned to face him with a small smile. "True enough. We have to *survive* tricking the Usurper before we can achieve anything else."

"I believe in you if that helps?" There was a note of humour in his voice.

"Surprisingly, yes." She licked her lip. It had been easy enough to say they could ignore what had happened between them until everything was set to rights. But with him this close, the subtle pull of his keen and the steady feeling of safety it invoked ... She drew a slow breath. "We should probably be getting back to the others."

"Probably." He didn't make a move to get up.

"I mean, there's a lot to plan before we head to the Night Estate."

"That there is." He made a move that time, but Nea grabbed his hand.

"Wait." She stood. Their chests were almost touching. Her fingers laced through his and she moved them to the small of her back as she rose on her toes and pressed her lips against his.

Ever since they had emerged from the labyrinth, she hadn't been able to control her feelings. It was strange. She had never felt this way about anyone in her past. She'd come close with Leith, but there was something about Garret, maybe it was the ward or the divine blood. *Two sides of one coin.*

"I thought we agreed—"

She bit down lightly on his lower lip, cutting his words short and eliciting a soft groan from his throat. The sound of it stirred up memories of the other day by the pool and she tightened her grip on him.

The arm around her waist tensed, closing the distance between their bodies as his tongue swept across hers and the fingers of his free hand tangled in the hair at the nape of her neck. She wanted to get lost in the kiss like she had before, but they were too exposed here. The source lurched and then they were standing in the clearing by the pool again.

They broke apart, and Nea let out a small laugh. "Sorry about that. I guess I haven't exactly got it under complete control yet. I was wishing we were somewhere more private."

Garret scanned the clearing, his gaze settling on the large stone slab that edged the lake, and he rubbed the scar above his lip. "So?"

"So." She bit her lip. "We're a pair of idiots if we think we can just act like nothing happened. It is distracting, and it will likely get both of us killed."

"Thank the Bright you figured that out." He wrapped his arms around her and pressed a kiss to the top of her head.

She gave his chest a small shove. "You agreed with me easily enough."

He shrugged and tilted her chin upwards. His lips were tantalisingly close. The ward mark warmed under her skin, humming with the power of their melded keen. "I knew you'd figure it out." He closed the distance with a kiss that set her aflame and sent shockwaves through the source.

❧

Nea smoothed her hands over the silky fabric at her waist and met Zephyr's gaze in the mirror. Zephyr's crystalline eyes sparkled as she took one of the pins from between her teeth and wove it into Nea's hair, restraining the unruly waves into an elegant updo. Her own azure hair was arranged in a collection of braids scattered with pale gold ribbons and beads and looped about her skull in an intricate maze of coils and folds.

"There. Just one more thing." Zephyr brushed her hands together and reached for the mask that was lying on the table beside her.

The sight of the dark lace brought the masquerade Nea had encountered in the labyrinth to the forefront of her mind, and her mouth went dry. She held still though as Zephyr positioned it over her face then secured it into place by pinning the ribbons into her hair.

"How is everything coming along in here?" Wade pushed through the curtain behind them and stopped short. "Oh, my stars."

"It's perfect, isn't it?" Zephyr did a little twirl and the skirt of her gown brushed Nea's.

Wade was certainly a master. The pale gold silk of Zephyr's gown was a perfect complement to the blue tones of her hair. The delicate detailing of black lace that ran over the shoulders and asymmetrically across the bodice made the otherwise simple dress stunning.

Nea's gown was something else though. The bodice started out a darker shade of lilac where it clung to her shoulders, the criss-crossing sections of gossamer fabric shifting to a deep, almost black, midnight-purple as it fell in smooth swathes to make the skirt. It would have been lovely just as it was, but when she moved, the tiny crystal beads that dotted the entire gown lit up like a field of stars, transforming it into something spectacular. Zephyr had placed similar crystals in the loops of Nea's hair and dusted her shoulders and cheeks with an iridescent powder that made her skin shimmer like moonlight.

Wade let out a breath. "It will be impossible for anyone to ignore her, which will make our part in the festivities easier. Come on. The others are waiting."

As Nea and Zephyr stepped out of the cottage, Declan let out a low whistle. "We should attend balls more often."

"Where's your fancy outfit?" Zephyr asked as she moved towards him.

"I don't need one, remember? Whilst you, Wade, and Nea are having a grand old time charming the other partygoers, the rest of us have actual work to do." With a wolfish grin, he pressed a kiss to her cheek. Declan sobered as his attention shifted to Nea. "You look breathtaking, my dear, but are you alright?"

"I'm fine. Just ..." She rubbed her hands down the front of her gown and Wade made a noise.

"It will be fine," Garret said behind her, and she half-turned to face him. His gaze did a sweep over her form before settling on her eyes. He took a step towards her and lifted a hand—

"Don't touch her. You'll smudge all my hard work," Zephyr said as his fingers inched towards Nea's shimmering shoulder.

Garret lowered his hand. "What about that?" He pointed to the ward mark on the inside of Nea's left wrist. "Won't the Usurper know what it is?"

Wade nodded. "Which is why I have these." He held out a pair of long midnight-purple gloves with moons embroidered around the opening and crystal beads sewn on in a scattering of stars that petered out towards the wrists.

Nea took them from him and slid them on, flexing her fingers.

"Are you all ready?" Moira asked as she and Rourke joined them.

"As ready as we can be," Wade answered.

"Wonderful. There is no time to waste."

Nea drew a steadying breath and stepped away from Garret. It was getting easier to find the doorways in the source now, like they were waiting for her to reach out. And when she thought of it, it really wasn't too different to finding the barrier, rather it was an extension of that feeling. She touched the closest doorway, and it sprang open, revealing the location Moira had shown her before: a smooth path of silver cobblestones leading to a massive hedge maze, and at the centre of that maze, a spindle-towered castle that seemed carved from the glistening grey stone of the mountain behind it.

People dressed in all manner of elegant finery wandered along the road through the clear path in the hedge that cut right to the castle doors, which were open, allowing golden light to spill out into the dusk. Nea spotted a patch of vivid pink hair; the woman it belonged to turned and her crystalline gaze met Nea's as an arrogant smile curved her mouth. She tilted her shepherd's crook in a tiny salute before turning back to the path.

"Frell," Wade said beside Nea. "She could pose a problem."

"We can handle the witch," Rourke said. "Come on." Without another word, he stepped through the portal.

Wade, Declan, and Zephyr followed him.

Garret hesitated, his hand finding Nea's.

"Ready?"

"I have to be."

"You'll both be fine, and as I will not be seeing you again once you step through that portal, good luck and trust each other—even if you don't trust yourselves." Moira gave them both a little shove in the direction of the portal and they stepped through together, nearly colliding with a woman in the widest hoop skirt Nea had ever seen.

As they started down the path towards the palace, Nea's stomach was doing backflips. Everything was riding on their success tonight, but weakening the Usurper was just the start. And if they did succeed, would she be able to muster the courage to see this thing through to the end?

CHAPTER TWENTY-EIGHT

HARVEY

Click-whoosh-thud. "Bullshit!"

Harvey opened one eye as Molly swore. He was sitting with his back against a tree while she practiced with a borrowed crossbow Angus had unearthed from some forgotten corner of the storage shed. And whilst it had once been 'a beautiful instrument of death,' it was now 'a dusty web-shrouded piece of junk'—Angus' words exactly when he had offered it to Molly.

She had cleaned it up, removing decades of grime and oiling all the parts until they shone in the sunlight. You could see how elegant it had once been with its carving of green-painted vines and pink-gold robrillium mechanisms.

"Angus told you it was a lost cause. It was probably just some pretty ornament to hang on the wall and never meant to be fired."

"She's seen her share of battles, Harv. This wear here and here, you don't get that sitting on a shelf." She lifted the bow and examined the sights. "I think the sights are still out and this mechanism here needs some more work." She settled next him and selected a tool from the open roll on the grass. "Any word from Leith?" she asked.

"He was leaving Del Harol this morning with some of the others. They should be here soon, though Nonna seems to think it will be unnecessary. Even with Kieran's help, she's confident that Leon and his men won't get past the sentries."

"Mages." Molly grunted. "They put too much stock in their powers, and that makes them forget that desperate men can move mountains when they set their minds to it. Kalhanna should have proved that they are not as untouchable as they think they are."

"You do realise Margot is a mage?"

"Yes, but she's different." She fiddled with the problematic mechanism. "Shit!" Her finger slipped, the tip slicing open and smearing a line of blood along the rosy metal. There was a pink-toned flash of light then the robrillium absorbed the blood.

"What just happened?" Harvey asked.

"I have no idea," Molly said, pressing her thumb against her bleeding fingertip.

"You found Meleta's bow," Nonna said, drawing both their attention. "Strange that it would appear now and choose a keen-less to wield it."

"I'm sorry—Meleta?"

"She was a battle mage who fought in the Bright wars. Her bow was considered lost, most likely at the bottom of one of those deep pools in the Fenlands."

"Surely this isn't the same bow," Molly scoffed.

Nonna's mouth twitched at one corner and she studied the bolts that littered Molly's target. "Try firing it again."

"There's no point until I fix the sights and un-jam this." Molly indicated the part that had sliced her finger open.

"Humour an old woman." Nonna opened her palm towards the target.

"Fine." Lifting the crossbow, Molly levelled her sights on the target and drew a slow breath as she depressed the trigger.

Click-whoosh-thud. "What the fuck?"

The bolt had landed dead centre in the target, a wave of force rattling the other bolts around it free so that they rained down on the ground. Molly turned the crossbow over, examining it from every angle. "That's impossible."

One of Nonna's dark grey brows lifted.

"I mean, the sights are still way out, and I am good, but I am not *that* good."

"You don't happen to be harbouring a secret keen you haven't told anyone about?" Harvey asked with a grin as he moved to inspect the bolt. It had driven so deep into the target he wasn't sure he would be able to pull it out.

"No." She placed the crossbow on the grass and took a step back. "No offence, Abigail, but this bow can go right back to where it belongs."

"Oh, it is right where it belongs. It chose you for whatever reason, so you might as well get used to it." Nonna chuckled and meandered away towards the gate. "Look sharp now—we have company."

They followed her around the front of the manor where a group of riders were dismounting: Leith, Niall, Haley, Jasper, Janey, Ryan, and a handful of Leith's personal guard.

Janey gave Harvey a small wave as he approached, a wide smile splitting her lips as she rapidly signed. "*I missed you.*"

"*I missed you too.*" Harvey signed in response.

She looked different, having traded her usual skirt and blouse for a pair of buckskin-coloured pants and a spring-green tunic that made the golden flecks in her green eyes stand out. He ran a hand over the back of his neck as he dragged his attention to Leith, who had said his name. "Sorry, Leith. I missed that."

Leith gave him a knowing grin. "I need to know everything you can tell me about Kieran's plan."

"There's not much that I didn't cover in my letter. He plans on coming here and taking a necromancer to use as a vessel to put another soul in ... possibly Amelia's." Out loud it sounded like the most impossible idea ever, but history would suggest that mages who sort to achieve the impossible rarely failed, for better or worse.

"And you believe he won't get past the sentries, Mother?" Niall asked.

"Kieran?" she scoffed. "Someone like Nea or Mateus or even Bran with a little more training might be able to. But it would be a feat requiring a mammoth degree of finesse and raw power, and Kieran has neither in any great quantity."

"Well, that's a scathing reference," Jasper said, and his twin, Haley, nudged his shoulder.

"You're absolutely sure?" Leith asked, and Nonna gave him a look that could wilt the flowers in the garden behind him.

"The only other way he could get past the sentries would be to damage the lock-stone."

"Can't he though? It's just a giant rock," Molly said.

"It is a giant, *enchanted* rock that does not exist solely in this realm. To damage it enough to disable the sentries, he would have to trade his soul, and his sense of self-preservation is too strong for that."

"So, we rushed all the way here for no apparent reason then," Jasper said.

Nonna shifted her heavy stare to him, and his mouth pressed into a thin line. "We appreciate the concern, but Hartswood is in no danger. Still, this visit affords us an opportunity to discuss what we know of Evard's plans and develop a strategy for dealing with them."

A commotion sounded behind them, and Harvey twisted to investigate. The gaggle of Hartswood children were watching them over the top of one of the garden beds. All but Henry ducked out of sight when they noticed they had been caught. Henry tilted his head as he studied the adults. Did the air just grow cooler? Harvey shook the feeling off and turned back to the others. Niall was studying him. His violet gaze, so like his daughter's, flicked from Harvey to the boy and then to Leith and back to Henry again.

"Perhaps we can continue this discussion once we are settled," Niall said.

"Of course," Leith said. "If it is not too much of an imposition, Abigail?"

She waved his words away. "Come. We have more than enough rooms."

As Abigail led the others away, Niall caught Leith's arm. "Wait."

Once the bulk of the adults had cleared off, the children emerged from their hiding place. Henry wandered over and looked up at Niall then Leith and then nodded to Harvey.

"Ah ... I'm not sure if you knew," Harvey said.

"Henry, what are you doing?" Nora came running over and grabbed the boy's arm. "I'm sorry. He's a bit odd sometimes. Nonna thinks his keen is mixed up because he belongs to Nea."

"Henry?" Leith said, and he crouched in one fluid motion. "Nea's Henry?"

Nora's eyes widened as Leith's gaze fell on her. "Yes, but she never told me she had a son. I don't know if Uncle Garret knows either. Henry looks like him or that is what Mama says. He has uncle Garret's eyes."

"Garret?" Leith rocked back.

"Yes. Do you know him? You do look a little like him, but he's not quite as pretty as you."

Harvey bit down on a laugh.

"Yes, I know Garret. He's a good friend." Leith held his hand out. "I'm Leith."

"Oh, the prince, and you're Nea's father." Her hazel gaze switched to Niall, who nodded.

"Niall."

"I'm Elenora, but most people just call me Nora, and this is Henry ... but I already told you that."

Henry placed a hand on Leith's knee and then looked up at Niall. "Bad people are coming."

"Henry!" Nora reprimanded.

"It's alright." Niall crouched to Henry's height. "Did you hear Nonna and the other adults talking?"

Henry shook his head. "I dreamed it."

Niall tapped his chin.

"He's a necromancer though," Leith said as he studied the stormy shade of Henry's hair.

"His keen is all messed up," Nora provided.

"I don't think it is *messed up*. It is just different." Niall chewed his lower lip as he studied the boy.

Nora frowned at Niall, her hands going to her hips. "*Nonna* said that Nea's blood and her connection with the source made him different. It messed him up, and you should know that you never argue with Nonna. Not unless you want to spend all afternoon scrubbing the stones in the main entryway ... twice."

"Mother is not as infallible as she would have people believe."

"Infallible?"

"She's not always right; she gets things wrong sometimes." Was that a bitterness there? An old wound perhaps. "Anyway, yes there are bad people who want to come here, but the sentries will keep us safe."

Henry shook his head. "They won't. I dreamed it." He then gave Leith's knee a pat and wandered away.

"Henry, wait!" Nora started after the boy then spun around and gave Leith a short a curtsey. "A pleasure to meet you, your highness ... and you too, Niall." She darted away.

Leith stood and scratched the underside of his chin. "Do you think he's right?"

Niall pressed his lip between his teeth. "It is rare for one to be both a mage and seer, but Henry's keen is indeed very different compared to other necromancers. Much like Nea's was at his age. Mother decided that it was better to lock away the parts of Nea's keen that did not pertain to her necromancy. In Nea's case, it was easy enough given that the necromancy was much stronger than everything else."

"Do mages do that often?" Harvey asked, and they both turned to him as though they had forgotten he was there. "Lock away things they find undesirable?" he clarified.

Niall's mouth quirked at the corner, the movement highlighting the features he shared with Nea. "Not often. It is not easy and can cause irreparable damage to the mind or body. And the younger the mage, the easier it is to manipulate their keen. But not just any mage can do it. Mind mages, some necromancers and healers, possess the skill required, but the latter are very rare."

"So, who did it to Nea?"

Niall bit his lip again and flicked a look at the ground. "I did."

"Did you do it to Garret too?"

"Garret?" Leith looked from Harvey to Niall. "Garret is a warden."

Niall rubbed his fingers across his forehead. "It seems you've learned rather a lot." He glanced at Leith. "Garret is complicated. He's a warden, but he's also a brightling; a child of the divine blood. And yes"—he glanced back at Harvey—"I locked away the part of Garret's keen that wasn't warden, but we all agreed at the time it was the best course of action."

"Who is we?" Leith asked.

"Mother, Camille, and myself. Warren disagreed with us, of course, but over the years I have realised that he was right. What we did to both Garret and Nea was wrong." He let out a small huff and shook his head. "If you were wondering, Harvey, no I didn't do it to you and I don't know who did."

The words hit Harvey like a punch to the gut, sending his breath out in a whoosh. "*What?* I'm not—I've never been—I'm *keen-less.*"

Niall nodded knowingly. "I thought so too, but there is something about you. Have you ever noticed anything strange? Been able to feel things that the eye couldn't see?"

"No." He shook his head. "Why would anyone do that anyway? I was just an ordinary kid from a poor family whose stepfather beat his mother to death after too much drink." The words were out before he could stop them, and he turned away from the look on Niall's face.

"Harvey—" Leith started.

"I don't want to discuss this further." He stormed away. Where was Garret when you needed him? Or—*Janey*. He rounded the corner of the manor and there she was, leaning on the gate, watching the cows grazing lazily in the field. The sunlight caught her chestnut hair, lighting up the scarlet tones and making it appear more red than brown. As he approached, her attention shifted to him, a bright smile on her lips that faded as she took in the look on his face.

You couldn't hide anything from Janey. She was too good at reading people. She placed her hand lightly against his arm, her eyes swimming with concern as the corner of her mouth pulled down. "*Want to talk?*" She signed.

"I don't know."

Her lips pursed as she studied him, and then she shot forward and gave him a hug. Margot had once said Janey used hugs like medicine, and she wasn't wrong. No matter how bad you felt, Janey could soothe it with a hug.

"Niall thinks I'm a mage and someone locked away my keen. It's ridiculous." Her hair tickled his nose as his breath stirred it.

She pulled back and studied him again, tracing her fingers along her lips. The air around her seemed to grow warmer, but then again Janey was always warm.

He'd just assumed her fire magic made her run hotter than most other people, but what if he was feeling her keen? Nonsense! He was not a mage. He couldn't feel people's keen.

"*Walk?*" She signed, then indicated the grove at the other side of the field.

"I don't think a walk is going to fix this."

She punched him lightly in the ribs then took a step through the gate, beckoning him over her shoulder as she headed across the field.

Harvey followed with a sigh. "You don't believe him, do you?"

She stopped and nodded then tapped her temple and shrugged.

"You knew? How? Why didn't you say anything thing?"

She gave him a wry smile and gestured to the ragged scar across her throat. "*It doesn't change who you are.*" She signed, and then her finger thudded against the centre of his chest.

Was Harvey the only one who didn't know? "But—"

"Harvey." She touched his cheek, the thick, strained tone of her voice stopping his racing thoughts more than the touch itself. She licked her lip and her gaze shifted to her feet. "*I like you. Mage or not.*" She signed.

"I like you too."

She shook her head and opened her hands. It was something he had seen her do when she was trying to find the right words. A soft blush edged her cheeks as she touched the centre of her chest twice then pressed her palm over her heart.

He blinked and his smile made his cheeks hurt. "You *like* me."

A wide smile crossed her lips and she nodded.

"I *like* you too. Would you mind if I kissed you?"

She made a face like she was thinking about it then nodded again.

Harvey slipped his fingers around the back of her neck and she lifted on her toes to meet him. Their lips grazed each other, and Janey's shifted into a smile; his own lifting to echo it. It was short and sweet and over far too soon for Harvey's liking, but Janey pressed one more kiss against his mouth then another against his cheek before linking her fingers with his and urging him to continue their walk.

He could never have imagined a more tumultuous day.

They stepped into the soft grass of the grove after removing their boots, and a jolt ran up Harvey's spine. The light feeling the kiss had given him departed almost instantly. Something big was coming.

A desolate howl rent the night air and Harvey sat bolt upright in bed. Footsteps pounded in the hall and shouting erupted. Harvey leapt up and ran for the door, grabbing his sword on the way. Leith, Niall, and Nonna were just outside the main entry, attention fixed on the forest that led to the manor.

"A false alarm?" Leith asked.

Niall shook his head, but Nonna said, "It must have been. I told you Kieran can't—"

The world shook, nearly throwing them from their feet, and a bolt of yellow light flew into the sky above the forest, illuminating the trees below in a sickly glow.

"Mother, get the children down to the repository. Bran too," Niall said.

"What's going on?" Bridie emerged from the manor with Haley and Janey.

"Kieran has breached the sentry ward," Niall responded.

"He hasn't yet, and he won't succeed," Nonna said.

"Mother, for once in your life will you not be a stubborn arse and just do as you are asked?" Niall clenched his fists and turned to the others. "Wake everyone and tell them to prepare for an attack."

"On it!" Haley gave Niall a small salute and hurried inside.

"Mother, please take the children to the repository. If I am wrong, you can say I told you so later, but it is better to be safe in this instance."

Nonna let out a huff but went back inside the manor as another bloom of yellow lit up the sky and the earth gave a stomach-tossing lurch.

"What do you want the rest of us to do?" Harvey asked.

Niall's mouth pulled into a grim line. "Just be—"

They were thrown back by a wave of force. Thunder boomed so loud it left Harvey's ears ringing as he gained his feet.

A chasm opened up, swallowing the trees as it charged towards the manor. Camille appeared beside Harvey, her arms outstretched, nightgown fluttering in the unnatural wind that had arrived with the thunder. With an angry howl, the chasm halted in its tracks, spewing a cloud of dust and gravel that rained down on the small group now gathered in front of the manor.

Camille let out a panting breath and fell onto her hands and knees with a groan. Harvey rushed to check on her, but she waved him away, dabbing the trickle of blood from her nose. "Go. He's past the lock-stone."

Janey joined them and slipped her arm around Camille's waist to help her to feet. She gave Harvey a small smile then flicked her head towards the forest.

He drew a breath before joining Leith and the others as a swarm of dark shapes breached the tree line.

As the enemies advanced across the field, a strange scent filled the air. It had a distinct tang to it like smoke bush combined with the thick all-pervading scent of—

"Death," Niall said beside Harvey has he inhaled. "He's raised himself half an army."

"Raised an army?" Molly asked, pointing her crossbow towards the line of soldiers. "They're reanimations ..." she answered herself and at Niall's nod added, "... that sick fuck."

"Indeed," Niall said.

When the enemies were halfway across the field, the front line broke into a shambling run. Abigail stepped forward, and a section of attackers stopped in their tracks, limbs jerking and heads rolling on their shoulders as one by one they dropped to the ground.

The rest of the line neared the garden, and those gathered there sprang into action. Harvey whirled his sword through the air and cleaved the head off a reanimation. The half-decayed body crumpled to the ground, limbs still twitching. He charged towards another opponent but before he reached his target, its body erupted in flames. He glanced at Janey and she gave him a small wave before darting away into the fighting bodies.

The next solider he met was not a reanimation.

"Micha?"

Micha stopped and tilted his head. "Do I know you?"

"No. But why are you fighting alongside Kieran?"

"Because he threatened them all with death and reanimation if they refused," Trenton said, driving his blade through the chest of a charging reanimation as though to prove his point.

A blur whooshed past them and a crossbow bolt went slicing through the chests of two undead, dropping them instantly. Molly let out a whoop as she slid to a stop beside Harvey. "Best bow ever!"

"Molly?" Trenton asked.

"Yeah, we can talk later. Right now there's a whole horde of creepies that need killing." She darted away again.

Harvey gave a nod. "If you're thinking about switching sides, now is the time to do it."

Trenton and Micha nodded. "I'll find Callie," Micha said and disappeared into the fray.

Trenton opened his mouth to say something as an agonised howl filled the air. Harvey whirled around. Abigail dropped to the ground, her hands clutching her chest as a soldier advanced on her. Harvey charged forward, leaping over prone bodies, and swung his sword. It hit the attacker at the point his shoulder met his collarbone and grated downward. The soldier staggered backwards and his gaze met Harvey's before his knees buckled and he fell to the ground.

Abigail was still letting out a soul-tearing wail. She clutched at Harvey's arm as he dispatched another reanimation.

"The grove," she rasped and tugged him towards the back of the manor.

Harvey let her lead him through the fighting bodies. Word had obviously gotten out to Kieran's soldiers as some like Micha, Callie, and Trenton were now fighting alongside Leith's men and the mages.

When they rounded the corner, Abigail's grip on his arm slipped at the sight of the grove ablaze. The sound that came out of her was part scream of rage, part sob, and she rushed through the fighting bodies, her fists clenched. Halfway across the garden, she flicked her hands to the sides, fingers splayed wide. A purple flash pulsed outwards; it hit Harvey as a wall of ice that rattled through his chest and left a crawling sensation at the back of his skull. All around Abigail, reanimations dropped, and the soldiers fighting stopped to stare.

A scream sounded inside the house, and Harvey edged towards it.

"Go! I'll handle things out here," Haley yelled.

He didn't need telling twice; he raced inside. Bridie was backed into a corner. Her lip was split, and the side of her face was the deep red of a blossoming bruise. Camille was on the ground, unmoving beside her. Harvey kicked the attacker—Leon—in the ribs, driving him back.

Leon snarled as he levelled his sword on Harvey. "Where's Nea?"

"How should I know? She went running off with Garret." Harvey edged around, putting himself between Leon and Bridie, who was checking her grandmother.

"You must know something. Garret keeps you in high confidence. There is not a plan that goes through his mind that he doesn't run past you."

"Are we flirting or fighting? Because right now I prefer the latter." Harvey tightened his grip and vaulted forward.

Leon blocked it easily but that had been Harvey's intention. He stepped within Leon's defence and brought his elbow up under Leon's chin. Leon's teeth gave a satisfying clack, and he swore, shoving Harvey back with a fist to the ribs.

As Harvey staggered backwards, Leon pressed forward, whirling his sword with deadly precision. Harvey dodged and darted out of reach, earning another snarl.

"You think your speed will save you? Have you forgotten how easily I bested you before?"

The screech of metal on metal filled the air as their swords met again.

"I should have killed you when I had the chance," Leon panted.

"Maybe you should stop talking and focus, then you wouldn't keep losing your prey." Harvey grinned and gripped Leon's wrist, driving his thumb into the tendons just below the base of his palm.

Leon's grip on his sword wavered and it clattered to the floor. Harvey forced him against the wall and levelled the tip of his sword on his throat.

"Do it," Leon spat. "Or are you too soft like Garret?"

Harvey tensed his grip and a horn sounded. Leon used Harvey's momentary distraction, forcing him back and collecting the edge of his jaw with his forehead. As Harvey shook off the daze, Leon ran for the door.

"Are you alright?" Bridie asked, placing her fingers on his arm.

Harvey shook his head again. "He just rattled my skull a bit. Is Camille?"

"She should recover. I moved her to Abigail's study." She stepped out the door Leon had exited through. "They're retreating?"

"Most likely they got what they came for."

The colour drained from her face. "The children!" She raced past Harvey and disappeared along a corridor.

He followed her as she took the stairs to the basement two at a time. Bran was slumped against the last step and she nearly tripped over him. "Bran!" She gripped his shoulders and he winced.

"I couldn't stop them." He coughed. "They broke through the wards like they were nothing."

Bridie released him and rushed to the door at the end of the hall that was hanging open. Kenna and Pierce appeared. There were tears on Kenna's cheeks as she rushed to Bridie and burrowed her face against her.

"Where are Nora and Henry?" Bridie asked, the thick tone of her voice telling Harvey she already knew the answer but was too scared to say it out loud.

"They took them," Pierce said.

"Who?"

"I didn't know them. A woman and man, but Kieran was with them. The man, he was dressed like a warden, but he was keen-less," Bran replied.

"Leon," Harvey growled.

"Who did they take?" Niall asked as he appeared at the top of the stairs.

"Nora and Henry," Harvey replied.

"I tried to stop them, told them to take me instead, but Kieran wanted Nora." Bran winced and leant against the wall, his hand going to his ribs.

"We have to go after them right now!" Bridie said. "Before they get too far away."

"We can't go running off without a plan."

"Fuck making a plan! That bastard stole my daughter! I'll tear his fucking throat out."

The foundations shuddered and Niall gripped the wall. "What in the realms was that?"

"It felt like the source just buckled; do you think the destruction of the grove had something to do with it?" Bran asked.

Niall didn't answer. He turned on his heel and hurried away. Harvey shared a look with Bridie and Bran then followed him.

Outside, the others were gathered around Leith, all except Jasper, who was nowhere in sight.

"What's happening to the source?" Haley asked. She was leaning heavily on Janey, a bloodstained hand pressed to the tear in the side of her warden leathers.

The mages and wardens present all winced as the world gave another shudder, this one accompanied by an ear-splitting sound like the crack of a whip, only infinitely louder.

CHAPTER TWENTY-NINE

GARRET

When they entered the hedge maze, Rourke drew Declan and Garret along one of the side passages. Garret cast a glance back at Nea as Zephyr linked their arms together and drew her up the stairs to the ornate entryway. A hand on his shoulder pulled his attention to Declan, who flicked his head to indicate Rourke waiting for them a short distance away.

"They'll be fine."

"Frell—"

"After what she did to Nea, Frell should be the worried one. Come on. We have work to do."

Garret gave a nod and followed Declan.

They headed through the maze, farther from the sounds of the ball, and soon they came to a shadowed door in the side of the building. Servants hurried in and out carrying trays and pitchers. After a tall man with an emerald-green waistcoat entered, Rourke moved forward. He caught the door as it started to swing shut and pushed his way inside. The servant turned and puffed out his chest, ready to reprimand them, but Rourke's keen flared. The man's eyes rolled back in his head and he slumped against the wall. Garret darted forward and caught the empty tray he had been carrying before it hit the floor.

They hurried across the room and through a door that led to a long hallway. Music, accompanied by the distant rumble of people socialising, drifted from somewhere to the right as they crept along the corridor. So far, Zephyr's map of the castle had been accurate enough. They just needed to reach the end of this hall and take the door to the left that would lead them to the chambers where Zephyr said the Usurper liked to entertain his more *important* guests. Hopefully, the spirit-glass would be somewhere there. If not, they would have to find a way up to the private quarters as the master suite was the next best guess at the glass's location.

Quiet murmurs and giggles rose above the distant sounds of the ball, and Garret pressed against the wall as a door flew open between him and the others. A dishevelled couple came barrelling out into the hallway. They all but collided with the opposite wall, the man's hands roving over the girl, hiking her skirts up as he smothered her in a series of noisy kisses. Garret cleared his throat, but they didn't seem to notice him, so he lightly stepped around them and caught up to Declan and Rourke just as they reached the door to the Usurper's private entertaining rooms.

The door opened into a large chamber. Guests littered the space, lounging on ornate daybeds and mountains of pillows. Servants moved through the room with pitchers of wine and trays of decadent pastries.

Declan let out a low whistle. "This is my kind of party," he whispered with a grin as a girl with slender rabbit ears poking out of her honey-coloured hair winked at him.

"Focus," Garret said.

"The Usurper is fond of decadence and debauchery," Rourke muttered as they started across the room.

A hand caught Garret's arm, a jolt running down his spine as a compulsive keen settled over his shoulders. His suppression rose, brushing the compulsion away, and he turned. His eyes met Frell's crystalline gaze, and her lips rolled into a polite smile that barely contained her sneer.

"To think your *tenacity* nearly cost Nea her life, and yet here we are at the very outcome you fought so hard to prevent." She traced her finger around the rim of her glass, the liquid inside shimmering from burgundy to gold then back again. "I can't believe you are not keeping a better eye on her. After all, the Master can be so very persuasive. With the right words, I am sure he'll have Nea dancing to his tune before the night is through."

Garret clenched his jaw.

"Cat got your tongue or are you finally accepting the inevitable? She is made from the stuff of gods. The second she realises that and claims her birthright, you and your world will be no more than an afterthought." She took a sip.

"You know nothing of Nea's true nature."

Frell gave an indulgent laugh and shifted forward, her skirt brushing Garret's legs as she whispered, "Oh, you are so very wrong about that. I have seen the inner workings of her mind, touched the fabric of her memories. I know her true nature intimately." She took a step back. "Do enjoy the party."

Garret drew a breath and looked around for Declan and Rourke, but they had disappeared. He headed through a door at the side of the room and caught sight of Nea. The man beside her, who was wearing a midnight-blue cloak and had storm-grey waves brushing his shoulders, had his palm splayed across her lower back as he guided her around a corner. Where were Zephyr and Wade?

"Garret!" someone hissed across the hall from him, and he followed the direction of the voice.

Wade was leaning out an open doorway. He beckoned Garret into the room and closed the door behind him with a snap. "What did Frell have to say?"

"She seems pretty confident the Usurper is going to coerce Nea over to his side."

Wade shook his head. "She's going to be bitterly disappointed then, isn't she?"

Garret nodded. "Any luck finding the spirit-glass?"

"Not as yet. Zephyr and Declan have gone upstairs to look, and Rourke has gone to check the library. The Usurper's not likely to keep it somewhere in plain sight though, especially with the likes of Frell wandering around. She might think he trusts her, but he's just using her devotion as a means to an end." He smoothed his hands over the front of his royal-purple jacket. There were rolling waves with ships and sea monsters embroidered around the cuffs and hemline.

"Do you have any ideas where it might be?"

"We could try the conservatory. That's where he keeps his most prized *possessions*, but I doubt the mirror will be there. I think it will be somewhere far more private."

"Like his rooms upstairs?"

Wade nodded. "That's why Zephyr and Declan went there. It can't hurt to try the conservatory though, and if we have no luck we'll go upstairs and join the others."

"Alright, lead the way." The sooner they found this spirit-glass, the better.

Wade led him along the hall and into a glass-walled conservatory. The room was huge and full to the brim with plants and various statues and relics on marble pedestals. They followed a winding path into a circular courtyard at the room's centre.

A gilded cage took pride of place in the space. Inside the cage, lounging on a velvet-covered chaise, was an all too familiar woman in a pale gold gown that skimmed over her form, highlighting every curve. She stood as they approached the bars of her cage and her starlight-coloured hair tumbled free to her waist. A sadness touched her silver eyes as they settled on Garret. "You shouldn't be here."

"I shouldn't?"

She shook her head. "If he learns of you then he will change tactics. He knows that he cannot truly control Nea the way he wants to, but he persists with her because she presents the easiest option for accomplishing his goal. But you ..." She lifted her hand as though reaching out to touch him, but her fingers curled back as they neared the bars. "You need to leave."

He shook his head. "Not until I find his spirit-glass."

"You seek to destroy it then. That's clever, and it might just give you the edge needed to overcome him. But, Garret, you must be careful. You and Nea both. You are walking a very dangerous line, especially now that you are bound by the death ward." Her mouth twisted and her gaze fell on Wade. "Darius, it has been too long."

"Your grace." Wade gave her a curt bow. "I am sorry that I failed to keep Nea safe from Frell."

"The fault is not yours to bear. Frell has been given powers she was never meant to possess." She let out a soft breath. "He keeps the glass in his private rooms on the second floor."

"I believe you will find this next part of our tour very enlightening." A velvety voice echoed through the garden.

"Go," the Bright Mother hissed.

Garret and Wade ducked down a path just as the Usurper appeared with Nea. Her mouth dropped open when she saw the Bright Mother in her cage. Garret knew he should go, but something had him rooted to the spot.

Nea approached the bars and lifted her hand.

The Usurper caught her arm. "I wouldn't get too close if I were you. She can be terribly spiteful when the mood takes her; can't you, Mother?"

The Bright Mother tilted her chin and stared down her nose at him.

"It is unlike you to be at a loss for words. Do you see who graces my arm? And you told me she would never submit. But she comes bearing the most delightful proposition." He linked his fingers though Nea's and drew the back of her hand to his lips. "Don't you, my pet?"

Nea stiffened and her keen spiked; ice charged along the lines of the mark on Garret's wrist.

"Come on. We have to go," Wade whispered through his teeth.

"But what is this?" The Usurper grabbed Nea's wrist, his fingers pressing over the place where the ward sat. Garret gritted his teeth as pain sliced through his skin and Nea gasped, snatching her arm free.

"Oh, you clever girl." He inhaled and then slapped her hard across the face.

Wade grabbed Garret's shoulder and pulled him back as he started forward. "We have to find that mirror. Come on. Nea can handle herself."

"Where is the brightling?" The Usurper pressed Nea against the bars of the Bright Mother's cage.

She twisted in his grasp, her keen fluctuating wildly as purple shimmers littered the air around her. "I don't know what you're talking about. Frell—"

Another resounding slap cut Nea's words off. "Don't lie to me," the Usurper roared.

Garret couldn't watch this any longer, but if he intervened now then the whole plan would be ruined. With a deep breath, he turned to Wade and nodded. They left as quietly as they could.

They met with Declan, Rourke, and Zephyr outside the door that led into the Usurper's suite. It was locked of course, a thin coil of magic rippling across the wood. Garret rested his palm against the centre of the door and let his suppression rise. The magic pressed back, radiating heat down his arm and leaving the tips of his fingers tingling.

"It's a complex ward, but I am sure we can break it. Here, let me try," Wade said, handing Nea's satchel to Garret and pressed his hand to the wood.

Wade's keen rose in a playful flurry before settling to a deep enigmatic throb that promised unfathomable potential. He clicked his tongue and directed his keen towards the door. A jolt of energy ricocheted out of the wood and pushed Wade back a foot before it went bouncing down the hallway.

Frell appeared around the corner, her hand lifted to catch the bouncing bolt of energy. It exploded against her palm in a shower of yellow and brown sparks. "Ah, now I've figured out your little game," she said sweetly, giving her fingers a little shake that sent another burst of sparks towards the floor. "Clever but short-sighted, and whatever will you do when Nea surrenders to the Master's charms? And before you spout that nonsense about her being a fighter with ironclad morals—it is her *destiny*. She cannot fight it any more than the caterpillar that eats his ways into oblivion to become a butterfly."

"Stand aside, Frell. You are outnumbered," Wade said.

A sinister smile slid across her lips as she turned her focus to him. "I knew you were misguided, Darius, but I didn't take you for a complete fool. You know you cannot win against me." She lifted her shepherd's crook and a bolt of dark lightning arched from the hook straight at Wade.

"No you don't!" Zephyr leapt forward, her hands out in front of her. She caught the ball of energy and sent it back towards Frell.

"You have always been blinded by that bleeding heart of yours, Zephyr. I will not permit you to ruin everything like you did last time." Frell flicked her fingers and a cloud of dark metal flashed through the air.

Zephyr waved her hand and the shards of metal thudded into the wood of a nearby door. "No, Frell, you are the one who is blind. As soon as the Usurper gets what he wants, he will cast you aside. You think he will make you queen of everything? He will not even allow Nea that privilege and she was purpose built for it. He takes what he believes he is owed and does not care who he has to trample to get it. You sold your soul and locked your people into a contract with a traitorous upstart who has no intention of holding up his side of the bargain."

Frell let out an aggravated growl. "You know nothing—"

"No! You refuse to accept the reality. You have to because if you don't then everything you have done, every manipulation, all the blood and fractured souls that stain your hands has all been for naught." Zephyr stamped her foot. A ripple of azure magic shifted over her form.

Frell eyes widened and the knuckles of the hand gripping the crook grew pale. "You wouldn't dare," she growled.

Zephyr lifted her hand and the crook shuddered in Frell's hold. Zephyr pressed her lips together and curled her fingers inwards as she made a snatching motion. The crook jumped towards her, dragging Frell's arm with it.

"You won't win. You willingly gave up your power, or have you forgotten the pact you signed?" Frell ground the words out through her teeth.

"I was naïve to believe the sweet whispers the Usurper fed me— fed us all. Unlike you, however, I made sure my pact came with a loophole." She made the snatching motion again. The crook shone azure blue and broke free of Frell's fingers. It flew into Zephyr's outstretched hand, knocking her into Declan, who caught her shoulders to steady her.

"What do you think you're doing?"

"Taking back what is mine!" Zephyr slammed the crook on the floor. It shattered and a wave of force rushed out.

The magic hit Frell, knocking her backwards with a scream. She dropped to her knees and her form contorted until a bright pink sheep was standing in her place. Zephyr rubbed the centre of her own chest, azure magic flickering in the air around her as she approached the door. She touched her palm to the wood, and it exploded inward, sending splinters flying.

"What about her?" Declan asked as he studied the sheep with a curious smile.

Zephyr shrugged. "She'll turn back eventually, but that's not our concern." She stepped past Garret into the room.

It was a large antechamber. Bookshelves lined one wall but instead of books, they contained jars of every shape and size imaginable. Inside each was a different-coloured orb of glowing mist that swirled and shifted. Garret had seen something like this in Penny's memory from Kalhanna. "Are those souls?" he asked.

Zephyr's lips pressed together as she studied the jars. "Pieces of souls, yes. Payment for every pact signed with the Usurper."

"What's this one for?" Declan asked, indicating a long-necked glass flask in a cage of robrillium that was sitting on a pedestal in front of the shelves.

Zephyr's brow furrowed as she shot a look at Garret.

"Nea," Rourke said. "Once he gets a piece of her soul in there and stoppers the flask, her power will be his for eternity."

"Then we need to make sure that doesn't happen," Garret said, moving towards the flask. If they destroyed it—

"Don't touch it!" Wade grabbed his arm.

"If we destroy it, he can't use it to trap Nea."

"It can't be destroyed—not by simply smashing it at least. And if you touch it then it will take its payment from *your* soul. Best to just leave it for now and focus on finding the spirit-glass."

"Any ideas where to start?" Declan asked, spinning in a slow circle as he examined the room.

"It doesn't look like it's in here," Zephyr said. "Maybe one of the adjoining rooms?" She indicated the two doors in opposite walls.

Rourke crossed to one and tested the handle. It swung open easily and inside was a sunken pool, the water it contained steaming gently.

"Of course, a personal hot spring on the *second floor* makes so much sense," Declan quipped.

Garret's gaze, however, had settled on the black glass mirror sitting on the mantle across the room. It looked an awful lot like the spirit-glass that Nea had repaired in the Loch Bastien repository. He moved towards it, but as he neared the tiles at the edge of the pool, the water bubbled to life and a massive octopus heaved itself out. Its skin changing from a deep burgundy to a vibrant orange with blue spots as it charged towards him.

He darted out of the way and drew his sword. The creature, which had collided with the wall, rounded on him, lifting itself up on four of its arms to reveal the large acid-green beak at its core.

As the octopus hurtled towards Garret again, he swung the sword and severed two of its arms. Black ichor gushed to the floor, sizzling and pitting the tiles around the edge of the pool. The creature shrieked, its skin flickering between orange and icy blue.

Lightning shrouded the creature as the prickles of Declan's keen stirred the air. "Get to that mirror. I've got it under control." He grinned as the creature rounded on him.

Garret gave a nod and raced around the edge of the pool. But as he reached the mirror, another octopus fell from the ceiling, landing in the water and sending a splashing wave out in all directions. Garret ignored it as he leapt towards the mirror. The second his fingers brushed the glass, the colour drained from the world as it flipped.

He found himself standing in the centre of a meadow. He'd been here before in a memory of Nea's, one in which she killed a wolf. A man stood across from Garret. He had a scar down his left cheek and eyes so pale a blue they were almost colourless. His features flickered to those of the Usurper—dark grey hair and indigo eyes— and then a back again. He had his hand twisted into the ruff of the very wolf Nea had killed. Garret spun around. Behind him, Nea and Emil were still having their mock sword fight. Margot was sitting a short distance away weaving flowers together. As Garret's gaze returned to the man, he released his grip on the wolf, and keen unlike any Garret had felt before stirred the air. The wolf charged at the children and the man grinned as his face changed to that of the Usurper again.

Nea screamed—the wolf yelped, and the air grew still.

"Found you." The man grinned and started to take a step forward, but his face shifted again, and the Usurper's voice whispered out of his mouth. "No, we don't need to claim her yet. Let her powers mature while we get everything else in place. Knowing that she does exist is enough for now." The scene faded and Garret turned, looking for a way out, but a swirling silver mist shrouded him, undulating in twisting waves as far as the eye could see. He rubbed his top lip, toying with the scar, and took a step forward. The world dropped out from under him.

Cold tiles pressed against his back and someone touched his cheek with a wet hand.

"Come on, old boy." Declan's normally light tone was thick.

Pain seared Garret's chest, along with the urge to cough. He rolled sideways and spat out a mouthful of water that tasted like salt and sand. After several more fits of coughing, he wiped the back of his hand over his mouth and met Declan's eye.

Declan let out a relieved sigh and rocked back on his heels.

"What happened to the mirror?" Garret asked as he sat and pressed the heel of his palm to his throbbing forehead.

"It shattered the moment you touched it. The blast sent you into the water and ..." Declan pushed his wet hair back from his forehead. "I think I got a little taste of what you went through after ... Little Brook." He tried to summon his usual lopsided smile, but it fell flat. "Don't do that to me ever again."

"You know that's a promise I can't make." Garret clapped Declan on the shoulder. "Was it the right mirror at least?"

Declan shook his head.

"It appears that it was a decoy. We should have known the Usurper wouldn't make it so easy to find," Rourke said.

"Well, only one door left to try," Wade said from the other side of the room. "Come on. We're running out of time."

When they entered the second room, they found an extremely large four-poster bed covered in throws and pillows. The wall across from the bed was made completely from mirrors.

"He's got a thing for his own reflection it would seem," Declan said as he moved over to inspect the wall, his keen prickling the air. "None of these feel magical in origin though."

"It has to be here. The Bright Mother said this is where we would find it."

"She certainly has loose lips. I shall have to punish her for that later." The velvety voice of the Usurper sounded from the doorway. He stepped into the room carrying an unconscious Nea.

"What have you done to her?" Wade demanded.

The Usurper looked down at her and shrugged. "Oh, nothing that the barer of the other ward can't cure." He laid her delicately on the bed and ran a finger down her cheek. "So, which of you is it? Hmm?" He turned to face them and tented his fingers.

They all shared a look, and Rourke shook his head.

"Before you decide to try and trick me, I should warn you that giving you the option to tell me of your own free will is just a formality. I will have the truth one way or another."

How were they going to make it out of this one? They shared another look, and Wade took a step forward.

"Come now, Darius. I know it's not you or Zephyr. It could be the brightlander, but that is doubtful. More likely it is one of our human guests. Did you know"—his indigo gaze shifted between Declan and Garret as he took hold of Nea's limp arm and removed the glove with a deft tug—"that the wards connect the souls of the bearers in such a way that if I was to do this ..." He traced a finger along the lines of Nea's ward mark, his keen flaring in a cloud of breath-stealing cold. The skin around the mark split open and blood ran along her palm as he dropped her hand.

Pain sliced Garret's wrist as though his mark was the one being flayed open. The Usurper grinned and shook his head. "The more you fight it, the more damage you will do to her. Are you willing to risk killing her to keep your identity from me?" As he said it, glowing lines of orange fanned out from Nea's mark, leaving bloody tracks along her skin as they raced up her arm. "I'd decide quickly if I were you. If the curse reaches her heart—"

"I'm the one you're looking for," Garret said, stepping forward, and Wade swore.

The Usurper chuckled. "How disappointing. I was hoping for more of a fight, but alas ... It is so very easy to manipulate people when emotions are involved. I can't actually kill her without killing you, did you know that? I doubt you did, or you wouldn't have so gallantly given yourself away under the pretence of saving her. The ward ties you together so intimately that one cannot perish without taking the other, and I wouldn't risk losing you both."

Zephyr moved up to Garret's side. "You can't leave her arm like that. Will you let me heal her?"

The Usurper glanced at Nea and then gave a wave of his hand. "Sure."

Zephyr hurried to the bed and touched her fingers to Nea's wrist. Azure magic drifted over Nea's skin, drawing the marks that covered her arm closed and leaving thin scars in their wake. She then cast a glance at the Usurper, but he wasn't paying attention to her, his gaze firmly on Garret.

"Mother was clever. I had no idea of your existence until tonight, but you've been touched by my influence, haven't you? I can feel the burrs of it under your skin. If you supplicate yourself before me, I would be willing to free you from the corruption."

Garret shook his head.

"Don't be a fool now. Eventually the corruption will win, and you will be mine anyway. I'm just allowing you the choice to join me willingly. Nea turned me down one time too many and look what her pride cost her." He indicated Nea's prone form without looking at her.

Zephyr chose that moment—her fingers touched Nea's brow and her keen spiked.

Nea gave a rasping gasp and sat as the Usurper whirled to face Zephyr with a roar. He stopped short, however, as Nea's keen pressed down on him, a look of fury in her eyes.

"You can't rip my soul from my body, my dear. Remember you already tried that once this evening?"

Nea gritted her teeth, and a trickle of blood ran from her nose.

"Now, now, don't go killing yourself just to spite me."

Her hands shook and her breath panted over her lips. "I will end you even if I have to sacrifice myself to do it." She tore the remaining glove from her hand as she spun around and then slammed her palm against a small disc of black glass set into the headboard of the bed.

The room gave a violent shudder.

"NO!" the Usurper roared and lunged for her.

Nea's keen burned along the lines of Garret's ward mark but it was burning too bright and fading fast. He charged forward, shoving the Usurper aside, and placed his hand over Nea's, letting his keen wash out and join with hers. A fissure formed in the glass under Nea's hand and the mirrors all around the room lit up with images of their realm. Nea gasped as her eyes fell on one that depicted a sprawling manor house under siege.

"You're too late, my dear," the Usurper snarled. "Just like Kalhanna all over again."

Nea's keen gave one last spike and the glass under her palm shattered, sending shards flying outward. She tore away from Garret, purple magic shimmering in the air as both her hands hit the mirror showing the attack. The mirror split up the middle, a wide portal opening and bringing with it the scent of smoke and death. Nea jumped through and Garret charged after her.

CHAPTER THIRTY

NEA

Garret, Declan, and Rourke disappeared down one of the side paths in the maze before they reached the stairs leading to the doors of the castle. Nea paused and let out a breath. Zephyr linked her elbow through Nea's, careful not to brush against her shoulder.

"They'll be fine," she whispered and tugged Nea forward. "We just need to keep the Usurper distracted."

When they reached the top of the stairs, Wade touched Nea's arm. "I'm going to make the rounds then meet up with others. Remember, keep him occupied as long as you can. We're going to need every minute you can give us." Then he slipped away, waving and saying a loud greeting to a woman in a chartreuse gown with a high collar of peacock feathers.

Zephyr gave Nea's arm a squeeze, nodding in greeting to those who acknowledged her as she brought Nea to the edge of the room. She took two glasses of soft-pink wine from a passing servant. "Try not to look so on edge. We're at a party, remember? You're supposed to be having fun," she whispered as she handed one of the glasses to Nea.

"I dislike parties," Nea said taking a sip of the wine. It had a definite note of sweetness that left a soft fizzing sensation on the tip of her tongue. "For someone who seems so eager to have me in his possession, he is being remarkably illusive," she said as she took another sip.

"Come on." Zephyr downed the liquid in her glass in one gulp and then placed it aside. "Let's get you out where he can't help but take notice." She took the glass from Nea and placed it aside with her own then grabbed her hand and dragged her out into the whirling dancers.

Zephyr guided one of Nea's hands to her shoulder and took hold of the other one before preceding to lead her across the floor. One by one, the couples around them drew back until there was clear space circling them.

The music changed, the crowd parted, and there he was looking so like the actual Shadow Man with the deep-grey waves of his hair brushing his shoulders and his midnight-blue cloak falling behind him.

Zephyr released Nea and dipped into a low curtsey. "Your grace," she said softly and took a step back.

The Usurper barely flicked Zephyr a look as he slowly approached Nea, his body moving down the path made by the stilled dancers with a feline grace. Nea fought the urge to roll her eyes at the dramatics.

"I knew you wouldn't be able to stay away," he said as he reached her, then he took her hand and pressed a kiss to the back of it. "Are you ready to take your rightful place?"

Nea let her gaze drop then studied him through her lashes, her head tilted in a way she hoped was coming off as coy. "Perhaps." She bit her lower lip lightly. "I will admit that recent events have opened my mind to the *possibilities* that an alliance could cultivate." She flicked a look at Zephyr, who had backed away farther into the crowd.

The Usurper slipped a hand down her waist and deftly spun her out into a slow twirl as the music changed again. "The *possibilities*?" he purred as he drew her back in.

"Yes, but we can discuss the particulars of such an alliance later. I prefer not to mix business with pleasure." Hearing the words coming out of her own mouth was almost painful.

"I cannot fault you for that." The dancers around them had started moving again, and he guided her through them as Zephyr had done.

She caught a flash of azure hair and gold gown ducking down one of the passages leading away from the room as the Usurper spun her out again. Now all she had to do was keep him occupied long enough for the others to find the mirror. As her attention returned to the Usurper, she found him watching her, the depths of his indigo gaze unreadable.

"Perhaps you would like a tour of the estate? As far as prisons go, it is certainly *divine*." He danced her to the edge of the room and led her out a door into a long hallway. "I believe you are rather fond of libraries." Hand splayed across her lower back, he guided her through an ornate set of double doors into a grand room.

Bookshelves stood in nearly every available bit of space, creating a labyrinth that led to a wide set of stairs that accessed the mezzanine level.

"Magnificent, isn't it? I have tomes here from all corners of both your world and mine. Think of the hours you could lose in here, the discoveries you could make ... If you remain agreeable, I will relinquish the secrets of this room and so much more." He brushed his fingertips along the side of her neck as his breath whispered over the shell of her ear, "Let me show you."

As he steered her through the maze of shelves, she let her fingers trail along the spines. A myriad of different keens plucked at her skin and stirred through the air. He paused before a set of glass of doors and took hold of her chin. She fought the urge to take a step away as he tilted her head back.

"I thought you far more verbose than this. Are you so enamoured that it has stolen your words?"

Drawing a breath, she caught his hand and removed it from her chin. "I am just considering what you have to offer."

The corner of his mouth curved. "Perhaps you are starting to regret fighting your destiny for so long ... Would you like to see my favourite possession?"

He didn't give her a chance to answer, just reached behind himself and pushed the doors open to reveal a glass-walled conservatory at least five times the size of the one at Del Harol. The huge room was full to the brim with plants, statues, and relics, many unlike anything Nea had seen before. She would love to explore every inch of the space if there weren't more pressing matters at hand.

"I believe you will find this next part of our tour very enlightening," he said, placing his hand against her lower back again and leading her into the room.

The path ran to a gilded cage in the centre of a courtyard, and inside it stood the Bright Mother. Her lips pulled into a tight line as her silver gaze fell on the Usurper, but there was a sadness in that gaze as it met Nea's.

Nea took a step forward and lifted her hand towards the bars. Magic zinged across her fingertips and settled along the lines of the ward at her wrist.

The Usurper caught her arm. "I wouldn't get too close if I were you. She can be terribly spiteful when the mood takes her; can't you, Mother?"

The Bright Mother tilted her chin and stared down her nose at him.

"It is unlike you to be at a loss for words. Do you see who graces my arm? And you told me she would never submit. But she comes bearing the most delightful proposition." He linked his fingers though Nea's and drew the back of her hand to his lips. "Don't you, my pet?" His dark gaze bore into hers and the ward burned under her skin. His grip on her fingers flexed and something flashed behind his eyes as his lips hiked up at the corner. "But what is this?" He grabbed Nea's wrist, his fingers pressing over the place where the ward sat.

Nea gasped as pain laced outwards from the mark, up to her elbow, and into the centre of her palm. She snatched her arm free, covering the wrist with her hand as she rocked back.

"Oh, you clever girl." Ice laced his tone. He inhaled then slapped her hard across the face.

The force of the blow made her bite her tongue, but she resisted the urge to cry out.

"Where is the brightling?" He gripped her shoulders, slamming her against the bars of the Bright Mother's cage. The proximity of the bars charged the air around her and her keen responded, flaring out of her control and sending shimmers of lilac dancing around them.

Fighting hard to reel her keen in, she levelled her gaze on the Usurper. "I don't know what you're talking about. Frell—"

He slapped her again, cutting her words short. "Don't lie to me," he roared.

Nea bit the inside of her cheek and struggled against him. She drove her keen along the seams that held him together and pulled. Spots swam across her vision and pain sliced through her mind.

"You can't use that little trick on me, my dear," the Usurper panted. "I. AM. A. GOD!" With each word, his keen pressed down, suffocating her.

The spots grew bigger, but she gritted her teeth and forced her keen to latch onto his soul again. "No, you're not. You're a greedy little bully who wants to bludgeon his way to godhood." She tugged at the fabric holding him together, and he snarled.

"You cannot defy me. I own you!" He snapped his fingers, and a wild itch tore at the skin of her right arm as the corruption marks flared to life, bringing with them a wild rage that burned through every inch of her. A crushing compulsion rooted her to the spot, the weight of it making her knees shake.

"Your thirst has truly made you blind if you thought that your win would come so easily," the Bright Mother said. "She fights you still, even under that compulsion, and she will destroy herself before she lets you control her."

The Usurper glared at the Bright Mother. "She can fight me all she wants. I only need her *keen*. I don't particularly care what package it comes in, regardless of how lovely its current one is. She will be Father's last mistake and that brightling will be yours."

"We shall see. However, it is good that you are used to the taste of disappointment." Her mouth curved into a smile, and the Usurper's top lip pulled back in a snarl. "While you waste your time here, others are closing in on the anchor of your powers. What would happen if it were to be sundered? What would that mean for your grand plan?"

The Usurper let out a roar and the compulsion pressed down harder, stealing Nea's breath and forcing her into oblivion.

A bright blue butterfly fluttered through the darkness. Nea lifted her fingers and it alighted on them, a quiver of warm magic rolling down her arm at the contact.

Her eyes flew open. Above her was a heavily curtained canopy. Something was wrong. The pressure in her chest was a warning.

Zephyr's worried gaze swam into her vision. "Breathe," she whispered.

Nea drew a breath, the pain of the air charging into her lungs drawing a starved gasp from her lips. She sat and the man beside the bed whirled, a savagery on his features as he lifted a hand towards Zephyr. Nea didn't think—she grabbed the edge of his soul, her keen tearing through her veins in shards of dark ice.

As a pair of indigo eyes met hers, she realised it was the Usurper. Hot fury chased the ice from her blood, and she gripped his soul tighter.

He gave a short step, his knee bumping into the side of the bed as he fought her. His mouth pulled into an overconfident sneer. "You can't rip my soul from my body, my dear. Remember, you already tried that once this evening?"

The corruption screamed in the back of her mind and she gritted her teeth as the metallic scent of blood tickled her nose.

"Now, now, don't go killing yourself just to spite me." A flicker of concern shone in his eyes, not for her but for himself.

She let out a panting breath, willing her hands to stop shaking. He was right; her body would give out before she managed to do any real damage to him. A tremor of magic reached her, a distinct pull behind her naval, a doorway ... a—spirit-glass! Behind her. "I will end you even if I have to sacrifice myself to do it," she growled pulling the glove from her right hand as she turned, searching wildly for the mirror. It was smaller than she expected: an oval of black set into the other decorative elements in the headboard of the bed. She vaulted forward, slamming her palm against that small disc and sending her keen into it. Her magic found a fissure in the glass, and the room shuddered.

"NO!" the Usurper roared.

Her keen wasn't enough. She pushed more of it into that crack, willing it to shatter, but she needed more. It craved more—like the corruption.

A heavy hand pressed over hers. Warm keen washed through every inch of her, melding with her own and giving it a boost. *Garret.* The fissure rose to the surface of the glass under her hand, and the mirrors around the room lit up. Scenes from their own realm appeared: Evard's throne room, Loch Bastien, Fengate—Hartswood. Her heart gave a jolt as dark figures moved through the smoke that shrouded the scene. Something else shifted deeper; a sense of unfathomable sorrow that tightened in iron bands around her chest.

"You're too late, my dear," the Usurper snarled. "Just like Kalhanna all over again."

No! She pushed everything she had into the mirror and her head swam, her vision dimming for a second before the glass under her palm shattered in a dark cloud. Shards flew through the air, pain scoring her cheek and burning through her fingers. She couldn't worry about that right now. Leaping off the bed, she reached for the barrier between worlds. It was thinner over the mirrors. Pain jolted up her arm as she slammed her palms against the one that contained the scenes from Hartswood. Her keen radiated out and the glass split up the centre, opening a doorway that brought the scents of smoke and death with it.

Praying she wasn't too late, she leapt through.

Cold fingers dragged over her skin as she met the resistance of the barrier at the other side, but she pushed harder, and it burst open like a flower head dispersing seed.

Heat shrouded the air around her. Ash rained steadily down on her skin as dread and sorrow and anger warred in her stomach. She fought back the urge to vomit and spun in a slow circle to take in the burning trees around her.

"The grove," she whispered around a ragged intake of breath and hot tears that refused to fall.

"Nea, wait!" Garret yelled from behind her, but she was already running towards the manor.

A cracking sound to the left warned her before a large branch broke free. Garret grabbed her, pulling her out of the way as it hit the ground where she had been in a shower of sparks.

The garden on the other side of the field was littered with bodies, but Nea didn't recognise any of them. Her keen swelled forward, and she touched the back of her hand to her mouth. They had been reanimations, every single one. Bile rose again and the first tear rolled, bringing a tightness to her throat. She pressed the heels of her palms to her forehead. *Don't shut down now.*

"By the Bright!" Zephyr exclaimed as she joined Nea.

Nea blinked through her tears at her. She appeared completely human: her eyes were a deep burnished gold, hair a lustrous shade of blue-black, and her antennae were gone.

"Who would do such a thing?" she said aghast as she caught Nea's eye. "To reanimate so many ... the soul price would be ..."

Nea shook her head. She was afraid to open her mouth.

"Garret?" a familiar voice sounded, drawing Nea's gaze to the man picking his way through the bodies.

"Jasper? What happened?" Garret asked, stepping forward to greet him.

"Evard," Jasper said bitterly. "More accurately, Kieran under Evard's orders. He was looking for a vessel." Dread rolled like thick mud down Nea's spine.

Thunder clapped and the flames hissed as torrential rain started to fall on the grove behind them. "Declan?! You're supposed to be dead," Jasper exclaimed.

"I'm as shocked as you, Jasper old boy. However—"

"I need to find Nonna," Nea said, cutting Declan's remark short.

"She's with your father out front," Jasper said.

Nea nodded and hurried that way, Garret close on her heels. They rounded the corner. There were more bodies, but Nea didn't check to see if they bore familiar faces. Her father and Nonna were standing with Leith, Harvey, and a man Nea didn't recognise who wore the green and saffron of Evard's guard. Another group of people, including Molly and Janey, were standing farther away with Bridie and Camille.

Niall's attention shifted to Nea and his keen washed over the back of her neck.

The others turned to face her.

"Nea?" Nonna said. "How did you get here?"

Nea shook her head. "Who did he take?"

"What?"

Heat seared up her spine and she flexed her hand, causing a spike of pain across her fingers as the skin of her wrist began to crawl. "KIERAN! Who did the fucking bastard take?"

A jolt ran through Nonna's body at Nea's tone. "Nea, perhaps you should calm down," Nonna said smoothly.

"I am perfectly calm." The source trembled and the earth gave a shudder. "Kieran came here to find a vessel, so unless he is among the dead, who did he take?"

Nonna's gaze flicked to Garret. "He took Elenora and ... Henry."

It was a punch to the stomach, and Garret caught her elbow as her knees gave way. "How long ago?" he asked, his voice thicker than usual.

"An hour, maybe. It happened during the fight, so we cannot be sure."

"Right." Nea shook Garret's hand from her arm and marched towards the house.

"Nea, where are you going?" Nonna called after her.

"To get Nora and Henry back and tear Kieran's Bright-damned soul from his body."

"You can't go running off on a rash impulse."

Nea spun to face her grandmother again, ignoring the dragging claws that were scraping across the inside of her skull. "Do you know what he intends to do to that sweet little girl?"

"He won't be able to. He doesn't possess the brand."

"He does have the brand, but regardless of that, he doesn't need it. Evard has the *book*." Her hand was aching, and she glanced at the blood that was drying sticky on her fingers. Little shards of black glass stuck to her skin in places. She squeezed her fingers in a fist, the burst of pain cutting through the rage and rising voices.

"You're in no state to go running off on a rescue mission."

"I'm *fine*!" The air around Nea frosted as the source trembled.

"You are clearly not fine," Nonna said tightly. "You—"

"I don't care! This is my mess, and I am going to fix it one way or another." She started away again, but Leith moved in front of her. "Get out of my way," she growled.

"Nea—"

"Damn it, Leith, MOVE!" The source cracked like a whip and the burning itch of corruption brayed triumphantly. She couldn't let it win, not before Henry and Nora were safe.

Leith swallowed and lifted a hand to reach for—

"Don't you dare touch me."

He drew his hand back. "Nea, you really should listen to Abigail. You can't help anyone in the state you are in."

"Leith," Garret cautioned, "let her pass."

Leith rubbed a hand over the back of his neck and stepped out of her way. She brushed by him. "We need to keep our heads and make a plan before we go running off. She's in no fit state—"

"I know," Garret said, "but she asked for some space and you need to respect that."

She didn't hear what either of them said next as she entered the manor and took the stairs to the sleeping quarters two at a time.

After throwing the door to her old room open, she barged in and slammed it so hard it banged against the frame and bounced open again. With a growl, she shut it and pressed her forehead against the cool wood. White-hot rage fuelled by her fear was tearing about under her skin. With a ragged breath, she pushed away from the door and turned to take in the room.

A little collection of rocks had been arranged on her desk and a drying crown of flowers hung over one of the bedposts. A blue shawl with vines embroidered on it lay across the foot of the bed. With a sigh, she brushed her fingers through the fringe along its edges. The remnants of Nora's keen clung to the fabric and pervaded the room, mingling with Nea's own.

Moving to the closet, she traced her fingertip over the carvings until she found the lock mechanism. The false floor popped open with a soft click and she summoned a mage light. The lilac-hued glow fell into the hidey-hole. Her journals were gone. *Margot.* She raked her fingers through her hair only to have them tangle in the loops Zephyr had arranged. With a snarl, she pulled them free and found the fastenings of her gown. Ignoring the pain that spiked through her fingers, she tore at the buttons, then slipped out of the dress and left it in a pool on the floor.

The action had caused fresh blood to well from her injured hand and she stormed to the desk, throwing the drawer open with more force than was necessary. It slid completely free and crashed to the floor, spilling its contents.

"Fuck!" She snatched up the drawer, scattering its contents further, and hurled it against the far wall with a roar.

A hot tear rolled down her cheek and she brushed it away. Her gaze landed on a small journal amongst the other items that had been in the drawer. Nora's keen clung to the cover in icy flutters. With a sniffle and a sigh, she picked it up and placed it on the desk beside the stones. She blinked back the tears and started to tidy the rest of the mess.

When she found the sewing kit she had originally been looking for, she rifled through it and pulled out a needle.

Her mage light cast a soft lilac glow across the skin of her palm as she held her hand out and removed the larger shards of glass.

Garret's keen reached her before his knock against the door sounded. "Nea?"

"You can come in."

He opened the door and entered. The corner of his mouth tightened as his grey gaze found her. "Are you—"

"I'm fi—fuck." The needle slipped, driving into the side of her finger.

"Will you let me help?" he asked gently.

She stiffened but then nodded and turned in the chair to face him, showing him the injured hand and holding out the needle. He moved over and took hold of the hand, gently rolling it in the light as he examined it. Then he used the needle to carefully dig out the remaining shards. He didn't say anything while he worked, but the way his mouth was pulled, she wouldn't have been surprised if he was grinding his back teeth.

"You seem awfully calm," Nea said when she couldn't take the silence any longer.

The corner of his mouth twitched. "Well, you are worked up enough for the pair of us ... I don't think I've ever seen Leith so chastened." He placed the needle aside. "Do you have anything to put on this or should I get Jasper?"

"There's a medicine kit in the closet. There should be some salve in there."

He retrieved the kit and dressed the hand in a neat bandage. "Are you sure you don't want Jasper to take a look at it?"

"It will be fine. The wounds are mostly superficial." She got up and found a change of clothes in the back of the wardrobe.

Garret sat on the vacated chair and ran his finger along his lip as he watched her while she pulled the beads from her hair and then combed it out and braided it. "Are we going to discuss the corruption or were you hoping I wouldn't notice?"

She froze and pressed her tongue into the side of her cheek as she inspected the corruption marks. They were still a milky grey. The way it was scraping across the back of her mind, they should have been jet black. "You can feel it?"

He gave her a look. "I would have guessed after the outburst down there, but yes I can feel it. I am fairly sure every mage and warden from here to Mother's Deep can feel it."

She swallowed. "Is yours?"

He shook his head. "Not yet, but mine was never as advanced as yours."

She rubbed her hand over her face and sat on the edge of the bed. "I can endure it long enough to get Nora and Henry back from Kieran, but ..." She shook her head. "After that ..."

The bed depressed as he sat beside her, his shoulder pressing against hers. "We'll figure it out."

"And if we can't?"

"Let's just focus on one thing at a time. Do you want me to see if there is any of Margot's treatment here? Or get a pair of bind-shackles?"

She chewed her lip. "Not shackles. I need to be able to access my keen."

"Do you think that's wise? If the corruption—"

"Becomes a problem, you know what has to be done."

"No." He shook his head and got to his feet, pacing away from her. "You cannot ask that of me. It's not that simple anymore, and in truth, I would have had a hard enough time doing it before. But now ... Nea, I'm sorry, but I can't."

She crossed to him and touched the back of his hand. "I'm sorry. You're right. If the roles were reversed, I couldn't either ... I'm so scared and angry and"—she swallowed—"and I can't tell what is the corruption and what is me."

He cupped her cheek, the numbness of his suppression brushing over her like a warm blanket. "Then do you really need your keen or is that the corruption manipulating you because *it* needs your keen?"

The suppression had stilled the grating voices and dampened the hot, crawling sensations. She drew a long, slow breath and covered his hand with her own. "Alright. You may have a point."

The corner of his mouth twitched. "What do you want to do?"

"Go get the shackles ... and my father."

He brushed his lips against her hers lightly and then left. She flopped onto the bed, pressing her hands over her eyes as the departure of his suppression gave the corruption free reign of her body again.

Not long after Garret left, a knock sounded, and the door creaked open. "Nea, may I come in?" Bran asked.

"Of course." She sat.

One side of Bran's face was swollen and covered with patches of purple and black. His lip was split in a way that would leave a scar even if healed by magic.

"Oh, Bran, why haven't you let Jasper heal you?"

"It's nothing. There are others who need help first." He ran a hand through his hair. "I'm really sorry, Nea. I tried to stop them."

She waved his apology away. "Sit down."

When he did as he was told, she inspected the wounds. He'd cleaned himself up well enough, but the lip would need a stitch or two if he wasn't going to let Jasper tend it. "Who did this to you?"

"I don't know him. Harvey said his name was Leon. He was dressed in warden armour, but he wasn't a warden, and there was a woman with him, a mind mage with black hair and blue eyes."

"That's Leon." She nodded. "And Catriona by the sounds of it. You're lucky he didn't kill you."

He nodded. "I think he was going to, but Catriona made him stop." He studied his fingers. "The look on Nora's face as they dragged her away ..."

"Bran ..." She crouched down. "... you did nothing wrong."

"Nonna told me that, but why do I feel like I should have tried harder? Why are necromancers so useless in a fight?"

"You're not useless."

"But I couldn't do *anything* to stop him."

The board outside the door creaked as Garret and her father returned. Bran drew a heavy breath and started to get up.

"Where do you think you're going?" Nea asked.

"You're obviously busy. I don't want to get in the way."

"Sit back down." She pushed the jar of salve into his hands. "Put some of that on your lip. It will help until you get it seen to. Did you bring the shackles?" she asked, turning to Garret.

He nodded, and she held out her wrists.

"Why do you have bind-shackles?" Bran asked, starting to rise from the chair again.

"It's the only way to stop the corruption," Nea said as Garret closed the first shackle around her wrist.

"What about Margot's treatment?"

"My case is too advanced, Bran. This is the safest way."

"I suppose it doesn't matter anyway. It's not like necromancy can help you in a fight—"

"Stop that! It's not your fault."

Bran's gaze dropped to his feet and he rolled the jar around in his fingers.

"Quite right," Niall said as Garret placed the second shackle around Nea's wrist, and the corruption was silenced.

"You have the key?" she asked, and Garret held out the leather thong around his neck. The pink-gold key sat neatly against the seer stone. He tucked them away under his shirt again.

Niall clapped his hands together. "Right, now, what did you want to discuss?"

"I'm going after Kieran—"

"I'm coming with you." Bran leapt from the chair.

"No, you're not. Leon almost killed you once."

"Nea, please, I have to. I was supposed to keep them safe."

She let out a sigh. "It's too dangerous—"

"Don't give me the same spiel Nonna would; I'm not a child anymore." He turned to Garret.

"Don't look at me. I know better than to go against what Nea wants."

Niall laughed. "You learned that the hard way I imagine."

Nea ran a hand over her hair. "Fine, but you need to let Jasper have a look at you first, and you can only come if he believes you are well enough."

Bran got up and darted between Niall and Garret. "Jasper!" he called as his footsteps pounded along the hallway.

"You're sure that's wise?" Niall asked.

"No, but if I didn't let him come, he would follow us anyway. You know what he's like when he gets an idea in his head."

"Indeed. Now you didn't just summon me up here to tell me you're going after Kieran, did you?" He leant against the door frame.

She blew out a breath. "No. I want the truth. Why did you lock away part of Garret's and my keen, and why did you decide not to tell us what we were?"

"Ah." He sucked his lip between his teeth. "We thought if we locked away your keen and kept you from each other then we could avoid all this. When Evard realised that his experiments had failed, he would give up. I knew he wouldn't, but I wanted to believe he would. And I regret that I let Mother and the others convince me it was the right course of action."

"Kept us from each other? Why would that matter?" Garret took Bran's vacated chair.

"Because—"

"Blood calls to blood. You thought if we encountered each other, it would undo what you had done. And it did, didn't it?"

"A more romantic person would say you were destined to be together. You are two halves of one whole, and nothing in the known realms could keep you from each other. There is some truth in that, but from a much more practical perspective, you are two halves bound by one destiny. A destiny that could either save the realms or destroy them." He shook his head. "If Evard had known the truth about either of you, this all would have ended sooner. What we did to you both was wrong, but it did buy us time. And Evard still doesn't know the whole truth, does he?"

"No. If he even suspected he had a brightling right under his nose, he wouldn't be messing about with fragmented souls and deathborn. Garret, maybe you should stay—"

"You're in just as much danger as I am. Or did I get that part wrong?" He cast a glance at Niall.

"You are correct. Whilst a brightling, and a corrupted one at that, is more desirable, a child of the Shadow will do in a pinch, especially since part of Garret's keen is somehow now woven with yours." He shot a look at Nea, and she shifted. "Care to enlighten me as to how that happened?"

"That's not important right now."

Her father's brows lifted, and he folded his arms as he pressed his tongue into his cheek. "Fine. If you won't tell me, I am sure Garret will or I could just pluck the information straight out of either of your minds."

"You wouldn't."

"When we were in the Between, Nea almost died, and the only way to save her was to bind us together with a death ward."

"Have the pair of you taken complete leave of your senses?"

"It was the only option, and I wasn't going to just sit back and let her die."

"Show me." Niall pushed off the wall and held out his hand.

Nea rolled her sleeve back and placed her wrist on top. The lines of the mark were muted orange, closer to apricot, and Niall frowned as he brushed his fingers over them.

"It's hard to tell with the shackles. Garret?"

"You want me to remove them?"

"No, I want to see your mark."

When Garret held out his wrist the way Nea had done, Niall traced the lines, and they glowed a deep violet.

"Well, I will say I am impressed. I've never seen an actual death ward. I don't think anyone has for several centuries, perhaps half a millennia even. I would like to study the ward. Have you noticed any changes to your keen? Or anything else?"

"It is easier to lend keen to each other, but otherwise I have noticed no difference. At least our skin has stopped lighting up when we touch," Nea replied.

"Your skin?"

"In the Between before the ward was created, our skin would glow if we touched, and Garret's keen had gone completely dormant. Everything fixed itself though after the ward."

"Interesting. Do you think it was something to do with going through the por—"

"Can we discuss this later? I don't want to delay going after Kieran much longer." Nea stopped her father's musing.

"I guess there are other more pressing issues. But don't think you are getting out of it or explaining why a man who is supposed to be dead is suddenly walking around alive and well."

"Have you finished your tantrum?" Nonna asked as they joined them.

"Mother," Niall cautioned.

"I am fine," Nea said.

Nonna's mouth twisted but she said nothing.

"Right, have you met Trenton?" Niall indicated the tall man in the uniform of Evard's guard standing beside Leith.

"I do not believe I have." She held out her hand and Leith caught it, studying the bandage.

"Do you need a healer? Jasper is—"

"It will heal well enough on its own," she said, waving away his concern. "I'm sorry I snapped at you before." She tugged her hand free.

"It's alright."

She nodded and turned to greet Trenton.

"Trenton believes that Kieran is not taking the children back to Braemar, but rather he's going straight to the capital," her father said, and the soldier nodded.

"What about Amelia?"

"What about me?"

They all spun around. On instinct, Nea reached for the source, ready to clamp down on Amelia's soul, but found only numbness as she remembered the shackles.

"Oh, come now, if I meant any of you harm then I have had ample time to act on that impulse." This Amelia was different, cold and calculating, less unhinged.

"It was very cleaver of you, Niall, to anchor the bars of my prison to the lock-stone." She smiled and then let out a little laugh.

"How did you get here so fast?" Niall asked.

Amelia shrugged. "One moment I was sitting in my cage and the next I was standing at the foot of the dead stone. I am simply here to warn you." She took a step towards Nea, but Garret moved to block her path. "So protective. It is a shame you won't be able to save her; in the end, even that ward will fail you." Her gaze dropped to Garret's wrist and she lifted her hand as though she would touch it. "The offer I presented earlier is still there should you realise you are on the wrong side of what is to come." She turned away and started walking back towards the forest. "You'd better hurry if you want to save the girl," she said over her shoulder, then she disappeared.

"Did she just use a portal?" Garret asked.

Nea shook her head. "I can't really tell without my keen-sense, but I don't think she was completely corporeal. Kind of like Declan before we went into the Between."

"But we could all see her."

"What ward was she talking about?" Nonna asked.

"It's not important right now, Mother," Niall said, but Nonna had already settled a heavy gaze on Nea.

"She was talking about a death ward."

"Shadow's teeth. What in the known realms would compel you to even consider such a thing? I wouldn't expect Garret to be aware of the danger, but you should certainly know better."

"Mother," Niall cautioned.

"It was my doing and there was no other choice," Garret said, settling his cool grey gaze on Nonna.

"There is always a choice."

"You're right. There was another choice; I could have let Nea die. But that is a choice I would never make, and frankly the ward is no one's business other than Nea's and my own."

Nonna snapped her mouth shut, and Nea bit back a grin.

"Right, now we need to go after Kieran. If he is heading for the capital, that buys us a little time," Garret continued.

"What about Amelia though? We can't just leave her roaming around, can we?" Harvey asked.

"We have little choice in that now," Niall responded.

"She's likely to go to Evard. They ultimately want the same thing, even if they want different versions of it," Nea added.

"Alright, so what's the plan?" Leith stepped forward.

"You will go back the Del Harol. Garret and I will go after Kieran."

"I will not sit on my hands this time."

"You can't risk it. Once we deal with your father, the people will need a leader. If you get yourself killed, they will be put through unnecessary turmoil in times that are already going to be confusing and hard."

"I have to get Henry back. If Father ..." The tone of his voice sent a pang through Nea's chest. She knew what he was feeling. She'd been drowning in it since Nonna told her they had taken Henry. Two years ago, she had sent him away out of sheer necessity and her heart still broke every morning she woke up and he wasn't there cuddled into her side.

"I *know*, Leith, but you need to listen to your head, not your heart."

"Nea is right," Garret said, "and a smaller group can move quicker and more quietly, which we will need in this instance."

Leith studied Garret then gave a resigned nod. "Who do you want to take with you?"

"Declan," Nea and Garret said together.

"Harvey and Molly," Garret added.

"Zephyr. And I promised Bran that he could come too," Nea finished.

"Alright." Leith drew a heavy breath. "When are you leaving?"

Nea met his worried gaze. "Right now."

CHAPTER THIRTY-ONE

MARGOT

The Dancing Goat was full of people, but Wren was easy enough to spot even without Gendry's bulk standing behind her. Her scarlet hair caught the light and her voice carried as she slammed the fist of the man she was having an arm wrestle with against the wood of the table and leapt to her feet. "I'll be taking that boat now."

"Come on, Wren. I can pay you some other way."

"You had your chance and you just blew it. Unless you want to try for best—"

"No. I'm done." The man dug out a slip of parchment and handed it to Wren.

"Perfect." You can have her back once I've met up with the Queen in Mother's Deep.

"If it is passage to Mother's Deep you want, I can just take you. There's no need to commandeer my bloody ship."

Wren leant across the table and patted the man on the cheek. "No, but it's more fun this way." She rocked back and caught Margot's eye. "Now, if you'll excuse me, I have other business to attend to."

When Margot reached the table, Wren tapped the seat beside her. "Did you find Mateus?"

"Yes, and we need passage back to Beldaren."

"Depends on where in Beldaren you need to go. I can't take you to Prahma."

"What about Fengate?"

Wren let out a whistle. "Port's a bit shallow for the likes of the Queen, and if the tide is not in our favour, we'll get stuck there. But we could get close along the coast between Fengate and Kalhanna or we can make port at New Brenna."

"The coast above Kalhanna is fine." Margot didn't want to go to the capital if she could avoid it.

Wren nodded. "How many people and how soon do you want to leave?"

"Five. Penny, Emil, Dale, Mateus, and myself. And as soon as possible."

"Well, you're in luck. I've just secured myself a ship. We'll take a short detour to Mother's Deep to collect the Queen, then head to Beldaren. Should be a fairly smooth journey as we won't need to cross the Fathoms this time." She stood. "Meet me at the docks in an hour."

The hour went fast as Margot rounded up Mateus and the others, and they found their way to the docks.

"I almost didn't believe you would be joining us, Mateus," Wren said as she joined them beside a ship that was a similar size to The Azure Queen. The figurehead of this ship was a large swan, wings stretching along the sides of the boat as though it was coming in to land.

"Yes. I can't say I am looking forward to the journey, but desperate times."

Wren clapped him on the back. "You'll be fine. I have a tonic that will help you get your sea legs faster."

"It's whiskey, isn't it?"

Gendry let out a roar of a laugh.

"You get sick sea, Mateus?" Margot asked.

"I don't enjoy travel on water for many reasons. The nausea is one of them."

"The nausea I can help with. I'll make you a tonic—one that's not whiskey. It probably won't take it away completely, but it will take the edge off."

"I would appreciate it."

⁂

I fear that I have wandered too far into the wolf's den. I made a discovery today, one that I wish I could forget. A little over two decades ago, Evard was doing experiments with magical bloodlines. His hope was to breed a new type of mage—as though mages are some type of livestock! The moral implications of such a 'breeding program' alone.

There was a large dot of ink on the page as though Nea's pen had sat at the end of that sentence for some time.

*Worse than that, his experimenting seems to have extended beyond the mere careful selection of bloodlines. It appears, from the notes I uncovered in his private vault, that he was actively trying to produce either a deathborn or a brightling. Not only did he subject his female test subjects to pregnancy, often against their will, but he then proceeded to administer a range of tonics from the simple, pennyroyal and brightsbane, through to the more complex. He then had the bodies of the **failed experiments—***

The words were heavy like Nea had traced them multiple times and they had bled through to the next page. She had been furious when she penned this entry. Margot would have known that from the tighter loops of her handwriting, even without the icy prickling of her keen clinging to the page.

"If you frown any harder, you're going to have a permanent dimple between your brows," Emil said as he sat beside her and leant his head against the siderail of the boat. Margot's mage light bobbed between them, casting pale green highlights in his black hair.

She rubbed her fingers over her brow and handed the journal to him. "Why didn't Nea tell us any of this ... She had proof of Evard's— atrocities. At least some of them."

Emil scanned the page and let out a low scoff. "Just how long has Evard been scheming? I mean, if what Nea is outlining here is true, he's been at it since before some of us were even born." He tapped the page with his index finger. "He obviously gave up on this 'breeding program'. Do you think someone found—Shadow's teeth, did you see this?"

She took the journal from him and read the lines he was pointing to:

Did my father know of Sophia's involvement in Evard's experiments? Is that the reason I am a deathborn? I cannot believe my father would take part in something as deplorable as this. It is more likely he didn't know and Sophia hid the truth from him. I would like to think that Sophia wouldn't deign to let Evard perform such experiments on her, but what if she did? Does Evard know the truth about me then?

Margot snapped the journal shut with a blink. "That's enough for today."

"Did you know Nea was a deathborn?"

She nodded. "Yes, but I only learned of it recently. She told me after she and Garret returned from Loch Bastien."

"Nonna said Garret is a brightling, didn't she? Do you think he's one of these experiments too?"

Margot chewed the side of her thumb, wincing as she accidentally pulled a tag of skin free. "I don't know. Maybe ... I think it's unlikely though. The focus of this"—she scrunched her nose up—"'breeding program' was to cross *magical* bloodlines, and Evard's bloodline hasn't produced a mage in several centuries. It would be counterproductive for him to—"

"Hold on. Are you suggesting that Evard is Garret's *father*? Shadow's teeth!" He shook his head as though trying to clear it. "Does Garret know?"

"I don't think so, and I don't believe Garret was a direct result of Evard's experiments."

Emil puffed his cheeks as he let out a breath.

They sat in silence, the gently rolling motion of the boat knocking their shoulders together every so often. Margot's eyes slid shut and she inhaled the salty air. The sounds of the crew members laughing and swearing as they played a game of dice reached her.

"Why though?" Emil suddenly asked.

She opened one eye to regard him. "Why what?"

"Why bother with all the effort to breed some kind of *super* mage?"

Margot shrugged. "His ultimate goal is to tear down the barrier and claim the thrones of eternity for himself. At least, that is what he thinks will happen. Nea is pretty clear that she doesn't believe that is how it will actually play out. She believes the Shadow Man is calling the shots and using Evard to influence things on this side of the barrier somehow. She's not as clear on the *how* of that, but she keeps referring to it as some kind of possession."

"I'm sorry I asked." He chuckled. "You ever wish we could jump back in time and just pretend this is all someone else's problem or, I don't know, maybe get rid of Evard before he became a real threat?"

"Only all the time. But honestly, if the Shadow Man is the true driving force behind everything, then getting rid of Evard will only fix our current problems until the Shadow finds another minion to do his grunt work."

"You sounded almost as jaded as Nea just now." He grinned.

She nudged him with her shoulder then stood. "I should turn in for the night. I need to gather my thoughts before I discuss what I read today with Penny and Mateus. Good night, Emil."

"Good night, Margot." He got up as well and wandered over to the group playing dice.

Margot sighed and headed down to the hold. She tucked the journal into her bag then climbed into her bunk and hugged it to her chest. If this ship went the way of the admiral's, she didn't want to risk losing the journal. She blinked at the bunk above her as she let her thoughts wander to Molly. Her bright blue eyes, how the sun lit up the buttery tones in her creamy hair, the soft curves of her body, and the way she tilted her head and purred when Margot explored them. The thoughts brought a shifting pang of regret and loneliness to her core, but even that was better than trying to piece together the monstrosity that was Evard's ultimate plan.

Mateus's mouth was pulled tight as he flipped through the journal.

"Wait—that section there." Penny leant over his shoulder and touched the page. "Nea calls this"—she pointed to the golden whirl on her hand—"a piece of the Bright Mother. A key. But both Nonna and Warren said it was a brightling. Was Nea wrong?"

"Doubtful," Mateus said as his eyes skimmed the passage. "It could be both."

"Both?" Margot asked, leaning against the rail of the ship. The sky above was a clear blue scattered with fluffy drifts of pure-white clouds.

"To create a brightling, the Bright Mother would have to give them some essence of divinity. A literal piece of herself would do the trick," Mateus replied.

"So, does that mean Nea has a 'literal piece' of the Shadow Man inside her?" Penny asked.

"No. Deathborn are not divine creations like brightling."

"But Nea's not a true deathborn. Nonna said she was a deer sola or something like that," Margot said.

"Deera solvec?"

"Yes, that's what it was."

Mateus gave a small laugh and shook his head. "Well, that certainly explains a lot."

"What does that mean?" Emil asked.

"Nea's always been different, but I could never quite put my finger on why. Knowing she's a deathborn and a deera solvec though ..."

"Yes, but what is a deera solvec? Nonna said it made Nea some kind of anchor," Margot said.

"In a sense I guess it would, but that is a crude way to put it. A deera solvec is a literal Daughter of Shadow, a direct descendant of the Shadow Man. Or so the old stories say." His cheek concaved as though he were biting the inside of it. "It explains why she can manipulate the souls of *both* the living and the dead."

"So, could this give me that same ability?" Margot indicated the silver anchor mark on her palm.

Mateus held his hand out, and she laid hers on it. The cool kiss of his keen swelled through her as he traced the mark with a fingertip. "I don't think so. It *is* programmed for a specific purpose, but I couldn't tell you what it is. I don't feel that it is a true anchor though ..." He shook his head. "No. I am certain it's not. But I have no idea what it might actually be; I've never encountered anything quite like it before."

Margot closed her fingers over the mark as it hummed under her skin. It seemed to like the feel of Mateus's keen the same way it did the residue of Nea's on the journal.

"Is that all a deera solvec can do? Manipulate souls?" Penny asked as she sat next to Margot.

"They can also rend holes in the barrier. Legend says they can physically jump realms on a whim, and it was a deera solvec who invented the portal network. Ultimately, like brightling, they are conduits of raw power."

"Are they the opposite of brightling then? If a deera solvec is a Daughter of Shadow, is a brightling a Child of Bright?" Emil asked.

Mateus nodded. "In essence, yes, they are opposites, but not in abilities. This warden friend of yours is a brightling?"

Margot nodded. "So we were told."

He tapped his chin and flipped forward a few pages. "Nea had no idea about his existence?"

"No. They only met about eight months ago. Garret didn't even know what he was. At least that is what Nonna implied, and I am inclined believe her. I never suspected he was anything other than a warden, even if his keen did feel a little different at times."

"Different?" Mateus leant forward.

"Deep ... and rife with secrets," Penny offered. "Like something lingers under the numbness of his warden gifts."

"So, exactly like Nea's."

"No," both Penny and Margot said.

"It's deep like Nea's," Penny continued, "but where Nea's keen is full of the kind of secrets you *don't* want to know—the dark and unfathomable, the chaos from which everything originates—Garret's is soothing and warm, and full of welcome secrets. Exactly how I imagine the Bright Mother herself to feel, and I wouldn't have recognised it if not for this." She held her marked palm out. "After I allowed him into my memories, this mark was brighter as though something in his keen had revitalised it."

Mateus inspected Penny's palm then sat back and scratched his chin. "What do you make of all this, Emil?" He settled his hazel gaze on Emil, who shrugged.

"I'm still trying to catch up on the whole Nea-is-a-deathborn thing. But how ... how does someone get a literal piece of a god inside them?"

"There are many ways. The old myths tell of consuming something you shouldn't or saying the wrong phrase at the wrong time, or more simply, the god pushes through to this side of the barrier and touches the soul in question," Mateus replied.

"But the Shadow man can't cross the barrier; he's been trapped for an eon in the Between, hasn't he? So how could he touch Nea's soul?"

"A convenient combination of events—"

"Or a predestined one," Penny said, cutting Margot off.

Emil flicked a look between them.

"Nea was born at midwinter when it is said that the barrier between worlds is permeated to allow the dead to visit their loved ones," Margot said. "Nonna believes that Nea was never intended to be a deathborn. She was a true stillborn, and we know from reading this"—she indicated the journal—"that Sophia may have been part of Evard's *experiments*."

"Not to mention that Nea's bloodline routinely turns out highly skilled and powerful mages supposedly because of some pact her ancestors made with the Shadow himself before the Bright war," Mateus added.

"A long line of powerful rule-breaking mages. Sophia possibly being experimented on by Evard—whether she knew it or not—whilst she was pregnant with Nea. A thinner, more easily breeched barrier. A child who may or may not have been meant to be a deathborn but whose soul was left lingering at the point between life and death just long enough." Margot counted the points off on her fingers.

"Okay, I can see how all that adds up." Emil swallowed. "But what about the Bright Mother and Garret?"

They all shook their heads.

"There aren't any clear indictors that his mother was part of Evard's experiments in trying to create a brightling or at least a mage powerful enough to breech the barrier. Perhaps it is a mere coincidence," Penny said.

"I'm starting to think there's no such thing as coincidence." Margot folded her arms.

"I am sure, for those not caught up in the eons-old machinations of the gods, that simple coincidence does, in fact, exist."

Margot shot Mateus a look.

He shrugged. "What is it the temple says? We are not given more than we can endure?"

"That is bullshit fed to people so they accept their lot in life and still pay lip service to the Mother regardless of their hardships." A quiver went through the mark on Margot's palm as though it agreed with her sentiment.

"When did you get so bitter with regard to the Bright, Margot?" Emil asked as he traced his finger along his lip.

She let out a huff and shook her head. "I don't know. In the old stories she often came to the aid of the heroes, but she always took her pound of flesh for assistance granted. If she truly was so benevolent and loved her children as much as the temple would have us believe, then why exact such heavy payment from her faithful."

"Because magic does not come without a price. The havoc that pulling too much power reaps on the body should tell you that," Penny responded.

"It wasn't really a question, Pen."

"Oh, I know, but I've been watching your crisis of faith fester since we left Del Harol, and I am sick of it. If Nea were here, she'd likely give you a clap up the back of the head for spending so much time contemplating your navel."

"She would not."

"No, perhaps not. But she would certainly have something to say about it, wouldn't she?"

"And then some." Emil laughed.

The sound of Emil's laughter shifted the claws that had gripped Margot's heart the day the enchantment on Nea's journal had lifted. A laugh of her own bubbled free, and Penny joined her.

"Well, you're certainly a mirthful lot. Haven't been drinking too much seawater I hope," Wren quipped as she joined them. "I just wanted to tell you we'll be in Mother's Deep by evening. And once we get the Queen sorted, we'll have you at the drop-off point along the coast above Kalhanna in less than a day."

"Excellent," Mateus said as the others sobered. "I, for one, cannot wait to get my feet back on solid ground."

CHAPTER THIRTY-TWO

HARVEY

"You can stop staring, Molly. I'm not going to disappear," Declan said with a grin.

"You were *dead*. Garret saw you, and I don't think he would make a mistake about something like that."

"I found a loophole, apparently."

Bran poked Declan's arm with his index finger. "It's so weird. You don't *feel* like a reanimation, but you don't exactly feel human either. Kind of like ... Nea or Garret, like you've been touched by *something*." He cast a glance towards Nea where she was sitting taking notes.

"That's because he's not a reanimation. More likely he is some kind of deathwalker," she said without looking up.

"Of course!" Zephyr exclaimed, her golden eyes shining. She had come from the Between with Nea and the others, and though she looked human, there was something uncanny about her. "That explains why your keen glitters the way it does. It was fractured by death and then reset. Like the shattered pieces of a mirror."

Bran whistled. "That is some seriously complex magic! Do you know how you did it?" He sat forward, blue eyes appearing almost green in the light from their fire.

"Not in the slightest. But I suspect it had something to do with creating a pocket between worlds to leave a message, and then that reacted in some way to Nea's keen," Declan answered.

"Wait, are you the spirit that was hanging around her back in Dunhold?" Bran asked.

"Yes, that would be me." Declan chuckled.

Harvey's attention shifted to Garret, who was sitting beside him carving a small piece of wood. He had been very quiet, which wasn't exactly unusual for Garret, but Harvey was surprised he didn't have more to say about Declan's sudden reappearance.

"We can theorise about it all later," Garret said without looking up. "Right now we need to focus on what we are going to do when we find Kieran."

Though Nea seemed to be able to create portals, her keen was currently bound by the pair of rose-gold shackles around her wrists.

Harvey didn't mind tracking Kieran instead of using a portal; he wasn't fond of the idea that they could step out of a doorway into the centre of Kieran's camp and find themselves quickly overcome.

He flicked a glance to Nea. She was sitting on the opposite side of the fire, a journal propped open on her lap. The pale purple orb of light Bran had created for her floated around her shoulders, casting strange shadows across her face. She seemed completely absorbed by whatever she was writing. And Harvey hadn't failed to notice the concerned looks Garret flicked her way every so often.

"Can we come up with a plan without knowing the details? Like where Kieran is taking the children and how many people he has with him for a start?" Molly asked.

"We know Leon is with him and maybe Catriona. John—"

"And Arthur too, I imagine," Declan said before taking a sip of his tea.

"No. Arthur is at Del Harol. He had a falling out with John and left the order."

"Really?" Declan's dark brows rose.

"Yes, and it was about bloody time," Molly said. "John is not a problem anyway. Leon is the one to watch out for. Being commander of the order has gone to his head. I still don't understand the wardens following a keen-less," she added.

"Most of them are not. Leith said only those from Loch Bastien and the capital are under Evard's thumb. The rest seem to have disappeared."

"They're dead then?" Declan asked.

Harvey shook his head. "Some for sure, but not all. I'd say, like Arthur, they are figuring out which side of this they want to be on and going into hiding before Evard can get to them. He's been too focused on whatever Kieran is doing to be worried about chasing down a few rogue wardens."

"Kieran will be taking Nora and Henry to the catacombs under the Bright temple," Nea said, drawing all their attention.

"The ones Sonia and Margot escaped through after the rescue mission from Evard?" Molly asked.

"The same." Nea took a sip of her tea. "It makes the most sense—unless ..." The colour drained from her cheeks. "No. He wouldn't—"

"You're doing that thing again, lovely," Declan said gently. "None of us are mind readers remember?"

"He could be taking them to Kalhanna." She said Kalhanna the way she always did—with a little intake of breath first like that one word was heavier than the rest.

"Why Kalhanna?" Molly asked.

"The source is scarred there, which makes it easier to breech, and Evard wouldn't want to create a breech too close to the palace; he'd want to avoid the risk of another Mother's Deep. No, Kalhanna is perfect."

"What about Amelia? She seemed to think Kieran wanted to put her in the vessel."

Nea shook her head. "That would be easier, but she has her own agenda and that makes her too unpredictable. I imagine they have another soul they want to put in Nora. But who ...? Johanna maybe?"

"But Johanna wasn't a necromancer, and isn't that what is needed?" Declan asked.

"No, but she was deathborn ... Unless, of course, Kieran has found a way to somehow anchor Evette to a new host. It's not impossible, especially now that the wards binding Amelia have been sundered. Kieran lacks the control required though—" She leapt to her feet, knocking her tea over in her haste, her wide eyes glittering in the firelight.

"Nea?" Declan stood.

"There is another option, and it's not good, not good at all."

"And that is?"

"What use is a lock pick when you have the key?" she whispered.

"That's what the deathborn at Dunhold said to you, isn't it?" Garret asked.

She nodded. "I hope I am wrong, because if I am not, Kieran is going to attempt to anchor the Usurper himself to Nora's body."

"That won't work though, will it?"

Nea opened her mouth then closed it and shook her head.

"No. More likely it will kill her and blow a hole clean in the barrier," Zephyr said as she swirled her cup, studying the contents before taking a sip.

"That's what the Usurper wants though, isn't it?" Declan asked, flicking a look from Zephyr to Nea.

"Yes, but not like that. He wants to be the one controlling every minute detail of the plan, because what he is trying to achieve requires the right parts in the right places at the right time. If Kieran changes even one small step, it will alter things for the Usurper and not necessarily in his favour," Zephyr answered.

"And if Kieran knows that ..." Nea and Zephyr shared a look that sent a quiver of ice down Harvey's spine.

"He's always been infatuated with power—Abigail said as much," Harvey offered, and immediately wished he hadn't because Nea, Zephyr, and Declan all looked his way. And whilst Zephyr and

Declan merely appeared curious, the look on Nea's face turned his stomach to water. Most of the time she was calm despite the sorrow that lived deep in her gaze, and Harvey had seen her angry enough to reduce a grown man to ash with a simple glare, but he had never seen her ... *afraid.*

"Do you think Kieran is going rogue then?" Declan asked, drawing Nea's attention back to him.

"Maybe ... I can't be—"

"Don't bullshit, Nea," Molly said. "You know something. If you didn't, you wouldn't be carefully choosing your words to try and hide the details. You keeping secrets and trying to fix this yourself is what got us all in this mess in the first place. So now is your chance to do this right before the world goes to shit—more than it already has." She leapt to her feet.

"Molly—"

Garret started as Nea said.

"No, she's right. Evard planned on taking one of the Thrones of Eternity for himself; the Usurper convinced him it could be done. But the Usurper was just using Evard because he was easy to manipulate. Kieran is another story entirely. He has never agreed with the rule about necromancers not using their power to raise the dead. He once said, 'Why would the Bright give us that power if she didn't want us to use it?'. It's a grand argument for a weak mind. Having power is not about exploiting it—it's about knowing when and when not to use it. Just because you can do something, doesn't mean you should.

Kieran isn't a suitable vessel for the Usurper, nor is he powerful enough to serve as a consort. However, if the Usurper was crippled and caught off guard, Kieran could steal enough of his power to seize one of the thrones. To do that he needs the Usurper here in our realm in a body that is easily exploited. That's why Kieran took both Henry and Nora. One to fail and blast a hole in the barrier, and one to anchor the Usurper to in the aftermath."

Garret stiffened beside Harvey and swore. He placed his carving aside and inspected the line of blood that marred his thumb before casting a heavy glance at Nea.

She gave him an apologetic look, her mouth twisting under her teeth as something unspoken seemed to pass between them.

"And if this is what he is planning and he succeeds?" Molly asked the question Harvey was dreading.

Bloody mages. No one should have the type of power Nea was talking about.

"We can kiss our arses goodbye," Declan answered.

"Quite. However, if we can stop him before he destroys the barrier, then we can find the thrones for ourselves and put an end to all of this for good."

"But how? Obviously not just anyone can sit on these thrones, otherwise Evard or Kieran would have done it already," Harvey said.

Nea pointed at Garret and then herself. "Both of us can. It's what we were both made for—a last-ditch effort by the sovereigns to reclaim their power."

Molly let out a whistle. "Okay, so step one: stop Kieran from blowing a hole in the barrier, and step two: find some ancient, enchanted seat and make sure either Nea or Garret sit on it. But what happens then? Wouldn't that make whoever takes the seat the supreme ruler of the known realms? That's this Usurper's plan, isn't it?"

"We just need to take the throne and then choose to give up the divine part of ourselves. It will be enough to pull all the other parts back together and free the actual sovereigns."

Molly puffed her cheeks out. "And Kalhanna is the best place for Kieran to do all this?"

Nea gave a curt nod. "The source is extremely thin there. That might have been Evard's plan all along—weaken the source enough so that breaking the barrier would be easy for even someone like Kieran to accomplish."

"Then why not just create a portal and send us there so we can ambush him?" Harvey asked.

"If I am wrong ..." She brushed her fingers against her right wrist and then sat and shook her head. "It's more likely that I am right, but the amount of source I need to channel to make a portal is too risky with the corruption. And just in case I am wrong, then tracking them is still the best option. When their destination becomes clear we can worry about getting there ahead of them."

"Well, this discussion has certainly given me a headache. So that means it's time for bed," Molly said with a small smile. "Goodnight."

After a chorus of goodnights, Declan, Zephyr, and Bran also turned in, and Nea returned to her journal, though her pen didn't touch the page for a long time.

Harvey edged closer to Garret. "Before the attack, Niall told me I was like you," he said softly.

Garret glanced sideways at him. "A brightling?"

"No, not that. He said I was probably born a mage and someone locked my keen away. Have you ever noticed anything?"

"When we first met, I assumed you were keen-touched. Still do if I am being honest. The way you move in a fight—" He shook his head. "I wouldn't have thought you a mage though. Regardless, it doesn't change who you are." He shot a conspiratorial smile in Nea's direction, but she didn't appear to be paying attention.

"Janey said as much."

"She's a smart woman. You should listen to her."

Harvey nodded, a small smile touching his lips. "Niall said very few mages have the ability to lock away keens like that without damaging the person they are doing it to. And he didn't do it to me, but who else would have?"

"How old are you?" So Nea was listening.

"Twenty-eight."

She nodded. "And who are your parents?"

"My mother was a farmer's daughter from Varth, and I don't know who my father was. I was always told he was a member of the king's guard and died before I was born. Mother didn't like to speak of him, especially once Shane came along."

"Shane?"

"My stepfather."

Nea's eyes narrowed as she studied him, then they shifted to Garret and she made a note in her journal.

Harvey exchanged a look with Garret, who shrugged.

"And you're certain your mother wasn't a mage?"

He shook his head. "She used to know when things were going to happen, and she'd say strange things sometimes, but Shane—I'm sorry, Nea, but I don't want to talk about what he did to her."

Her brow pinched and a deep sorrow filled her gaze. "I am sorry. We don't need to talk about it."

"Why all the questions about my mother anyway?"

She bit her lip and made a few notes in her journal. "From the sounds of it, your mother was a seer. And the timing is right ... I wouldn't have thought anything of it except the Bright Mother said something when we were in the Between."

"Which part?" Garret asked

"The part about the tyrant trying to force her to create a brightling. I know Evard was experimenting with"—she flicked a looked between them—"bloodlines."

"You're not suggesting Evard is Harvey's father?"

She shook her head. "No. At least, I don't *think* he is. But Harvey could be the result of those experiments, and when he was found to be *unsuitable,* he was cast aside."

"Wait, why would you jump to the conclusion that Evard is my father?" Harvey asked, but the realisation hit him before Garret had a chance to respond. "Did you know? Does Leith?"

"No and no, but that's unimportant right now," Nea replied. "The question is why did Evard stop his experiments? You would have been one of the last, given the time frame."

"Do you think I am a result of this experimentation as well?" Garret asked her.

"No. If you had been, he would have known about you from the start, and there would have been no need to keep playing god." Her tone was tight as she said the last few words.

Harvey studied Nea for a few moments. "You know an awful lot about Evard's plans. More than you let on before."

"I *was* his arcane advisor for a while," she said neatly, smoothing her hands over her knees.

"Could you undo what was done to me?"

She tilted her head, her violet gaze seeming to stare straight through him. "Would you honestly want that?"

He rubbed the back of his neck. "I don't know."

"I can't. My father could, or Penny, if you really want it."

"Are you saying I could have had a choice?" Garret asked, a small note of humour in his tone.

"No. But Harvey is not a brightling, and he doesn't have the Bright Mother herself breathing down his neck to save the world from her megalomaniac offspring." Her mouth curved into the barest of smiles, but the level of intimacy it conveyed left Harvey shifting in his seat and he wasn't even on the receiving end.

"Right," Garret said with a half-smile of his own, his finger tracing the scar that cut his top lip.

They didn't talk much more after that. Nea turned back to her journal and made a few more notes before heading to bed, and Garret finished his carving then flicked his bedroll out close to Nea's and lay down.

Harvey sat a while longer watching the flames. What in the realms had they stepped in? Mages playing at being gods and dragging them towards the end of the world. If Nea was right and Kieran succeeded ... He shook his head. It was hard enough trying to come to terms with what Niall had told him. All this uncertainty was a new feeling, and he didn't like it. *It doesn't change anything.*

Both Nea and Janey had told him that, and Janey ... He pressed his fingers to his lips then banked the fire down before sliding into his own bedroll. He might have more questions than answers and the world might be spinning out of his control, but thoughts of Janey brought a sweet stillness to the chaos.

They had been tracking Kieran's group for several days. Most of the soldiers who had joined him for the attack on Hartswood returned to Fort Braemar, but a small group, including Leon and Catriona, continued on.

As they neared Kalhanna, they made a final push to catch up with Kieran. And when night fell, Harvey and Garret went out to check the camp.

Crouching low, they stuck to the shadows of the barn that Kieran had chosen to bed down in for the night. As they edged along the hedge that paralleled the barn wall, muffled voices drifted from inside. Then the door rattled open, and Leon stalked out.

"Where do you think he's going?" Harvey whispered, and Garret shrugged.

They waited until Leon was a good distance away and crept around to find a vantage point where they could see through the open door.

Catriona sat behind Nora, her fingers working through the girl's silver hair as she braided it, singing softly. The knees of Nora's pants were torn and there was a faded stain on the front of her tunic that resembled dried blood. Henry was on the floor next to her curled on his side and hugging a piece of fabric—it looked kind of like a shawl. His eyes were open and staring out into the dark. Garret shifted and swore. Henry sat bolt upright, blinking in their direction. The coin in Harvey's pocket grew warm.

"What is it?" Catriona stood and moved towards the door.

"Most likely nothing, like the last dozen times." Kieran's bored tone drifted into the night.

Garret caught Harvey's eye and indicated he follow as they crept farther into the shadows.

When they were a safe distance away, Harvey asked, "What happened?"

"Henry was using his keen. If either Catriona or Kieran had bothered to check, they would have felt me."

"Should we go back and get the others?"

Garret nodded. "This is probably our best chance."

A sound drew their attention to the opening of the barn again. Leon had returned with a small group of soldiers and Evard himself.

"Perfect timing, my lord," Kieran said as he stepped out to greet them. "Shall we proceed to the ruin?"

"Yes, just as soon as I have seen this vessel you have chosen," Evard said.

Kieran gave a slow nod and disappeared inside only to emerge again a few moments later with Catriona and the children.

Henry glanced towards their hiding place, and Garret took a few steps back into the shadows of the trees. "Come on," he whispered, and drew Harvey away.

"Did you find them?" Declan asked as they returned to the camp.

"Evard is with them now and they are moving to Kalhanna. Whatever they have planned, it looks like tonight is the night," Harvey said.

"We have to hurry then," Nea said, pushing to her feet and securing her satchel over her shoulder. She studied the shackles around her wrists and let out a long breath before holding her hands towards Garret.

"You're sure?"

She nodded. "I need my keen for this. I'll have to risk it."

Garret pulled a leather thong from around his neck. A smooth grey stone with a hole through the middle and a pink-gold key were hanging from it. He took the key and lightly brushed his thumb along the underside of Nea's wrist as he touched it to the first shackle.

A tremor ran through Nea's body as the second shackle fell away, and she rubbed her hands over her arms before pressing her fingers to the centre of her forehead as though a sudden headache had sprung up.

"Are you—"

"I'll be fine." She retrieved the shackles and slipped them into her satchel then lifted her hand.

"Should you risk making a portal?" Declan asked.

Nea shook her head. "Probably not, but it's the fastest way. We can't risk Kieran and Evard getting a chance to perform the ritual."

The air directly in front of Nea's fingers flickered, and her lips drew together in a tight line. The tips of her fingers turned black, the silver marks that stained her forearm darkening to an iron grey. The flickering air formed into a perfect oval just big enough for a person to pass through. "Quick now. I can't hold it open too long." She stepped through and disappeared.

"The first time is a little rough, but you get used to it," Declan said as he followed her, dragging Molly along behind him.

Bran grinned and leapt through, followed by Zephyr.

"He's lying. It doesn't get any better." Garret gave Harvey a nudge towards the portal.

A little rough was an understatement. It was like that moment going down a flight of stairs when you missed a step and your stomach dropped as you realised there was only open air between you and a bone-jolting tumble. The fall didn't come though. Instead Harvey's body was compressed and twisted before being unceremoniously spat out on the other side.

He took half a dozen steps before the world stopped violently shifting and he found his footing. Nea was a short distance away, rubbing small circles on Molly's back as she leant forward, her hands on her knees and her face ashen.

"Never again," Molly was repeating in a hushed tone.

Harvey examined the room they had appeared in. The roof was collapsed in one section and small plants had taken root in the piles of debris in the corners. A quiver ran through Nea, and she swallowed as Garret placed a hand on her shoulder.

"Nea," he said softly, "if you need—"

"I'm fine." She didn't look fine. She looked—spooked, for lack of a better word.

"You don't—"

"I said I'm fine!" she snapped, cutting Declan off.

He lifted his hands in surrender. "Alright, now what?"

Nea gave her arm a savage flick. The corruption marks were completely black from the tips of her fingers across the back of her hand where they disappeared under the edge if her sleeve. "Kieran will set up out in the courtyard. We should—" Her attention shifted to the door. As did that of the other mages and Garret.

"Are we too late?" Bran asked.

"We're not too late yet, but we need to get out there now. He's starting," Nea said, striding towards the door.

"Right. Let's do this then." Molly readied her bow and followed Nea.

CHAPTER THIRTY-THREE

GARRET

The air outside was wrong, but not for the same reasons as inside. In the hall, it had been the prickly aftermath of what had happened several years ago. Out here the feeling was new, and it was rippling outwards from Kieran, who wielded a glowing branding iron.

Leon held Nora in front of Kieran, her pale back exposed to the night through the torn fabric of her shirt. Garret clenched his fists, ready to charge down the stairs, but Declan's hand landed on his shoulder as Nea stepped forward.

"Let the children go, Evard."

"And why would I do that?"

"Because in their place you get my complete loyalty. No more fighting the inevitable. I will submit to your will." What was she doing?

"You cannot trust her, my lord," Leon growled.

Evard lifted a finger in Leon's direction, not taking his eyes off Nea. "And what of your friends? Will they *submit to my will?*" His cold, grey gaze swept over the others and settled on Garret. *Submit? Not bloody likely.*

Nea shook her head. "They will take the children and leave. And you will let them."

"Or what? You are terribly outnumbered, my dear."

"We don't need her, my lord. Let's just kill her and get on with it," Kieran said.

"I should warn you, Evard. Kieran has no intention of granting you that which you seek. As soon as he uses that brand on Nora, it will rend a hole in the barrier. The result of which will likely kill most of those present, yourself included. Then he will take the Usurper's power and claim it for himself."

Evard's gaze shifted to Kieran.

"Lies, my lord. You know that Nea would say *anything* to get what she wants." Kieran adjusted his grip on the brand.

The king gave a humourless chuckle. "She might spin words to hide her true intention or to get what she wants, but she has never been an adept liar. You, however ..."

Kieran's mouth tightened. "I am sorry, my lord. I wanted to draw this out a little longer. I had hoped to see the look on your face when you realised that *you* had become *my* pawn and I had claimed the results of all your years of careful planning for myself. No matter." He lifted a hand and a guard near Evard stepped forward, drawing his sword. There was something strange about the guard. It was similar to how the devourers had felt in the Between. Nea clearly noticed it as well, her head tilting as her keen stirred the air around her.

"Stand down," Evard growled.

"He will not listen to you," Kieran said before his gaze flicked to Nea and he gestured to all the guards present. "Beautiful, aren't they, Nea? So refined are the strings holding them together that you had no idea. Did you?" He lifted his hand again and all the soldiers except the one restraining Henry snapped to attention and drew their weapons. Were they reanimations? The bodies left at Hartswood hadn't *felt* like these men.

"Now if you are quite finished with the interruption, I would like to get on with it." The end of the branding iron lit up purple again and he tilted it towards to Nora.

Nea's keen spiked, and she disappeared only to reappear between Kieran and Nora with a loud crack. She lashed out, catching the shaft of the brand and driving it back towards Kieran. He grunted as the end he still held hit him in the centre of the chest.

"I'm not the only one who learned a new trick then," he said, twisting the iron and trying to wrench it free from Nea's grasp. She won though, snatching it from him and spinning as Leon made a grab for her. The brand swung through the air and she caught Leon's cheek with it, the skin splitting open as he let out a snarl.

"Bran, get Nora," Garret ordered as he started down the stairs, taking them two at time.

An arc of lightning shot past him and hit one of the guards around Evard at the same time a crossbow bolt felled the solider holding Henry. The child rolled across the ground then pushed to his feet and started running in the direction of Nea.

"I've got him!" Harvey leapt past Garret and raced to intercept Henry.

Garret reached Leon and landed a boot in his side, knocking him off course as he made a lunge for Nea.

"Your bitch has made me bleed for the last time," Leon said, touching his fingers to the split on his cheek as his gaze settled on Garret. "I wanted to savour this. Maybe make you watch while I defiled every inch of her ... but I'll have to settle for hearing her scream as I tear your throat out in front of her instead."

He leapt forward, the strike sending a jolt along Garret's arm as their swords met.

"You know Willem told me what he was going to do to her during the purge in graphic detail? She leaves a mark on all she touches." As Leon goaded Garret, he shifted around, moving into position.

Garret, however, took advantage of the opening Leon's familiar feint created.

Leon leapt back with a growl.

"You've always been sloppy on your left side. Maybe if you spent less time talking you could focus on your technique."

With an enraged flourish, Leon pressed forward again, forcing Garret back with the fury of his blows.

Nea's keen rose in icy spikes then cut off almost instantly. Garret fought the urge to spin around and look for her. Leon latched onto the momentary slip in focus, his blade tearing a stinging path across Garret's cheek as he dodged a second too late.

"Oh look, now we're matching." Leon grinned. "I hope John doesn't kill Nea before I get the chance to have some fun with her."

Lightning crackled through the air, exploding in a shower of sparks behind Garret as John swore and Nea's keen flared to life again. John let out a rasping scream as the cold pressure increased. The scream ended in a wet gurgle, and the source gave a shudder.

"You're doing my work for me, it would seem," Kieran droned.

"You always were lazy," Nea quipped.

Garret didn't hear what happened next as Leon made another charge towards him. The momentum made them switch places, and Garret caught a glimpse of Nea and Kieran grappling for the brand over Leon's shoulder.

"And you were always a pretentious bitch. I guess being singled out your whole life will do that to you, but it ends tonight. The Shadow's powers will be mine, and you will be no more than a footnote in some historian's journal."

Nea let out a yelp as he kicked her in the ribs, snatching the branding iron from her fingers. "You want the Shadow, Kieran?" she snarled and tackled him, knocking him to the ground. "Then have it!" Her hand pressed over his cheek and her keen dragged cold fingers down Garret's spine. When she pulled her hand away, it left a perfect print of black webbing over one side of Kieran's face. She grabbed the iron, the end glowing a vivid purple again.

"You wouldn't risk putting him in me." Kieran scuttled away from her.

"No, not you." She spun and leapt onto Leon's back, driving the lit-up brand into his cheek. Leon struggled, trying to throw her off but she held firm, her keen frosting the air as she hissed something in his ear that Garret didn't catch. She let go and staggered backwards as the source gave a violent jolt accompanied by the sound of tearing cloth.

"What have you done?!" Kieran roared.

"Exactly what you wanted." She stopped beside Garret.

"Are you alright?"

"I'm fine. We have to move." She lifted an arm and a portal spang to life before her fingers. "Bran!"

Bran came running with Nora, followed by Zephyr, then Harvey carrying Henry. Nea waved them through the portal.

"Garret, you need to go. I can only keep it open so long."

"Nea—"

"Please go now." The tone of her voice cut through him and he took a step towards the portal. "Wait."

As he turned to face her, she pressed her lips against his. The kiss was desperate and hungry, laced with salt from her tears, and there was a finality to it that dropped the bottom out of his stomach.

"I made a promise, remember? And this time you have permission to save me." After one last touch of her lips, she pushed him through the portal.

Garret staggered backwards, water splashing around his legs. He could still see the scene playing out at Kalhanna through the oval in front of him. Nea grabbed Declan and shoved him towards the doorway. She said something Garret couldn't hear over the howling wind that had risen as the tear in the sky widened.

He needed to get back there. The portal was starting to fray at the edges. He had to move now. Declan collided with him as he took a step towards the portal. The mage's hands gripped Garret's shoulders, restraining him.

"I have to—"

"Nea told me to make you stay. If you go back through the portal, the magical blast will kill you. She can't stop it." As the last words left Declan's lips, the ground beneath their feet shuddered and a brain-scraping whine filled the air. There was a flash of light, and the portal slammed shut.

Everything was eerily quiet.

"Uncle Garret?" A small hand brushed his fingers. "Are Nea and Molly ... are they?"

Garret shook his head and glanced away, realising as his gaze landed on the portal arch at the other end of the pool that they were in the room of reflection at Del Harol.

"They'll be alright," Declan said.

"No one could have survived that. Did you see the way the stones were buckling? And if that last blast didn't kill them, it would have knocked them off the cliff—they're both tough, but still only human. A fall like that would ..." Harvey shook his head. "Sorry," he added in Garret's direction with a downcast look.

"They have to be alive—at least Nea does—because Garret still is," Declan said.

"How does Garret being alive have anything to do with Nea?" Harvey asked.

Garret pressed his fingers to the inside of his right wrist. The sensation of Nea's keen was there under his skin, but it was weak and distant unlike it had been before. A hand landed on his shoulder and he lifted his gaze to meet a pair of too-familiar violet eyes.

"What happened?" Niall asked. His voice had an oddly fragile lilt to it.

Garret shook his head. "I couldn't stop her." The urge to hit something rose with the words. "She knew. The whole time she knew she wasn't going to be coming back with us." A pang worried his side, a shifting of itchy fingers just under his skin.

"I imagine so. What happened though to Kieran and the others?"

"Kieran had replaced Evard's entire personal guard with reanimations. It seems he has been planning a hostile takeover for a while," Harvey replied.

"They weren't normal reanimations though," Bran said, and all eyes turned to him. "They were clever, and the strings holding the souls in the bodies were so intricate you couldn't tell they were undead."

"Kieran did have a good gloat to Nea about that. It's not something that would have easily escaped her notice," Declan said

Bran nodded. "Because normal reanimations are crude puppets and easily identifiable as such. I don't know what sort of pact Kieran made in order to learn how to create them, and I am not sure I want to know."

"So Evard is dead then?" Niall asked

"I lost sight of him in the fight," Harvey said. "But John is dead and ... Kieran, I'm not sure exactly what Nea did to him."

"She gave him corruption," Garret said.

"Nea did what now?" Declan's brows nearly disappeared into his hairline. "She said she would never do that. That she wasn't even sure she could do it. And regardless, destroying the mirror was supposed to have prevented new cases of corruption, wasn't it?"

Garret shrugged. "Well, she did. I saw it myself." The itch at his side grew more insistent and he folded his arms.

"What about Catriona?" Leith asked, drawing Garret's attention to where he was sitting with Henry in his lap.

"I didn't see her," Garret said, glancing at the others who all shook their heads.

"She had a fight with Kieran, and he left her behind. He told her he'd deal with her later," Nora said.

"A fight?" Niall asked, and Nora leant against Garret's leg.

"Yes, she didn't want him to *hurt* us. She tried to use her keen on him, but he had Leon put bind-shackles on her and tie her up."

"Why the sudden change of heart?" Harvey asked no one in particular.

"Cat is ... complicated," Leith said with a half-grin. "Seems I have a type," he added under his breath.

Niall gave him a sympathetic look, and Declan chuckled.

"And Leon?" Niall prompted.

They all shared a look.

"The bad Shadow is inside him now," Henry said.

"The Usurper, but how?"

"Nea," they all said a once.

Niall shook his head. "Why would she?"

"Nora?" Bridie hurried into the room with Abigail on her heels.

"Mama!" Nora let go of Garret and splashed through the water as she raced to her mother and threw her arms around her.

"Putting him in a keen-less is actually a very clever move," Abigail said.

"Clever how, Mother?" Niall asked.

"The scarred source at Kalhanna was always going to be a threat. There was no way to mend it without breaking it first. Nea knew that the power required to put the Usurper in a host would be enough to tear the barrier there. A tear can be fixed after the initial destruction. But which host to use? Too dangerous to put him in another mage, so Kieran was out of the question. But by putting him in Leon ... She's simply moved him from one prison to another."

"Surely the body itself doesn't matter," Declan said, and Abigail fixed him with a familiar soul-scraping stare.

"The body does matter, which *you* should well know. Put him in Nea or Garret and kiss your arse goodbye before sunup. In another mage you might buy yourself a few weeks, but a keen-less? That's almost as good as a permanent set of bind-shackles."

If Nea had effectively shackled the Usurper, why were whispers sliding across the back of Garret's neck? The itch was becoming pricklier the longer he ignored it. He drew on his suppression and smothered it, but the second his focus wavered, it was back again with a mocking laugh that reverberated inside his skull.

"So that's it then. This Usurper is no longer a threat?" Leith asked.

"No, he's still a threat—just his teeth are blunted. But blunt teeth can still break skin, and if he manages to find the thrones, keen-less or not, it won't matter. There is also the little complication of the tear above Kalhanna to contend with now. Until it is sealed, things from the Between will be able to pass freely into this world," Abigail said.

"So, we focus on the tear then?" Harvey asked.

"We need to locate the thrones before the Usurper does, and for that we are going to need to find Nea," Abigail answered.

"Surely the best place to start the search is Kalhanna? We can take two teams—one to search for Nea and the other to monitor the tear in the barrier and see about getting it stitched back up," Niall said.

"What about Kieran? He was dangerous enough without corruption, but if he can create more of those new reanimations ...?" Bran asked.

"He'll be sticking close to the Usurper because that is what the corruption will want him to do," Garret said and wished he hadn't as both Niall and Abigail shifted their attention to him, their keens lightly brushing his spine.

"Mother can fix it," Henry said, slipping off Leith's knee and coming over.

Garret tensed as Henry's fingers brushed his side.

"She can absorb it."

"Absorb it?" Declan asked, crouching to Henry's height.

The boy nodded. "The good Shadow told me. Mother is special. That's why the bad Shadow wanted to wear her skin."

"Okay ..." Declan straightened. "That's not creepy at all," he added under his breath.

Garret bit back a grin.

"Do bind-shackles work on wardens? If your corruption has taken over again, that might be the best way to control it until we find Nea and confirm what Henry is saying," Declan said.

"I don't know."

"They don't work on wardens, but they should work on brightling," Niall said. "And they'll prevent the corruption from spreading. Unless you would rather Margot's treatment?"

Garret rubbed his side. "I'll try the treatment for now. We'll save the shackles until they are needed."

"Alright, come with me." Niall beckoned him to follow. "The others can start working out our next move, but you and I need to talk."

With a nod, Garret followed him. They headed out of the room of reflection and along the hall to Niall's study. Once inside, Niall closed the door and rested his forehead against it. The action reminded Garret so much of Nea he had to look away, his gaze falling instead on the small stack of journals on the corner of Niall's desk. A myriad of different keens clung to the pile, but he recognised Nea's amongst the others.

After pulling out the third journal down, he opened its ink-stained cover. The edges of the pages were blacked, stained by the same spill that marred the cover most likely. But Nea's writing twisted across the pages, dodging the stains neatly.

"I imagine by now you've figured out my daughter is quite the force to be reckoned with when she gets an idea in her head ... no matter how misguided." Niall drew a long slow breath. "She's been that way since the day she was born. Mother is right; she's clever. Too clever for her own good some might say. It runs in her blood"—he gave a small smile—"but that intelligence is often blinded by her emotions in the moment. You've likely noticed that too, though she is very good at hiding it. At *mimicking normality* as Warren always put it, and he would know given they are cast from the same cloth." He moved to a shelf and rearranged a few items. "I had hoped she would stay in Osmar after her studies were complete. I encouraged it even, and for a while she seemed content to do just that, travelling about with Wren on that ship of hers. I thought if she was out of reach, then all this could be avoided. I knew I was lying to myself. Some destinies cannot simply be ignored, some moments in the fabric of time inevitable. Had Sophia not tied herself up in Evard's machinations, perhaps these concerns would be some other father's destiny." He pressed his lips together and glanced out the window.

"Sophia was working with Evard?"

"He has a way of charming people, but it didn't take much effort to woo Sophia." Niall fixed him with a shrewd stare, then the corner of his mouth quirked in the same way Nea's would have. "You need not be concerned that you've accidentally had intimate relations with your sister. There is no mistaking Nea's parentage. Just as there is no mistaking yours."

"I wasn't ... we ... that is." He rubbed the scar above his lip, and Niall gave a stiff chuckle.

"Others may accept the excuses, but I wouldn't be worth much as a mind mage if I didn't notice the minute details. Mind magic is as much about reading the body as it is the mind."

Garret shifted and placed Nea's journal down.

"Here." Niall crossed to a cupboard and pulled out a small jar. He lobbed it to Garret. "That should take the edge off that corruption."

"Thanks." Garret undid the front of his warden leathers and slid out of the jacket. "Did you just bring me here to discuss Nea?"

Niall studied him. "No, but it is important for you to process what happened at Kalhanna, so it doesn't fester, especially given that your case of corruption has returned. I am sure you've been playing the events leading up to now over again and again in your mind, trying to find the moment when you could have said or done something differently. You may have prevented *this* outcome, but at what cost? Nea's sacrifice would be unavoidable. It is just how she is built. So trying to find the fault in your own actions is a useless endeavour in this instance at least."

"I know. It doesn't stop me from cursing myself for letting her push me through the portal without more of fight though." He ran his fingers through his hair.

Niall tilted his head and toyed with his lower lip. "If it makes any difference, Declan is correct in assuming that Nea is, in fact, still alive. Were that not the case, we certainly would not be having this conversation."

"I'm more concerned about what could happen to her if Leon—"

"We can't focus on what might happen to her. We need to plan our next move. If Nea manages to escape Leon, she will likely head straight to the Arcanarium in Osmar."

"Why there?"

"Because she will be doing what she does whenever she is presented with a seemingly impossible task ... She will gather information. The Arcanarium is the best place to do that."

"You don't think she will return to Hartswood or here?"

Niall's brow lifted and he ran his finger along his lower lip again. "No. I think she will be focused on finding the thrones so she can put an end to this mess once and for all."

"Then I will—"

"Stay with Leith and help him coordinate efforts to close the tear and in the meantime protect the people from whatever comes through. The order is in shambles, and it needs a strong leader. From what warden commander Godfrey has told me, of all the surviving commanders, you have the best head on your shoulders."

"I'm no longer a commander though. I'm not even technically a member of the order."

"Every warden I have asked would disagree with you on that matter. And what would Nea tell you to do if she were here? Hmm?" He folded his arms.

Garret rubbed the back of his neck. He knew exactly what Nea would say, and she would be right, just like Niall was. He gave a nod. "I'll stay and help Leith." *At least for now.*

CHAPTER THIRTY-FOUR

NEA

"Wait."

Garret turned to face her again, and she grabbed hold of the front of his warden armour, pressing her chest against his as she kissed him. All around them the wind howled, the widening hole in the sky screeching in protest. Tears stung hot paths down her cheeks as she savoured every last second before pulling away. "I made a promise, remember? And this time you have permission to save me." She brushed her lips against his one last time and then gave him a gentle shove, sending him staggering through the portal.

Nea spun, searching the field. After spotting Declan a short distance away, she ran to him. "You need to leave." Gripping the sleeve of his shirt, she hauled him towards the portal. "No matter what happens, don't let Garret come back here. I can't stop the tear. It is going to send out a magical blast that will kill anyone too close."

Declan shook her hand off his arm. "What about you, my lovely?"

"I have to find Molly. Please, Declan ..." A pulse ran through the source, sending a clawing sensation through Nea's body and setting her teeth on edge. "You need to go. We are running out of time. Keep him safe." She pushed him towards the deteriorating portal.

He gave her a lopsided grin that held none of its usual mirth and leapt through.

The wind propelled Nea along as she searched for Molly. She caught a flash of blonde hair in the corner of her eye.

Molly drove the point of a crossbow bolt under the chin of the reanimation she was fighting and gave it a savage twist. "Why the fuck won't you stay dead?"

Nea let her keen tear into the reanimation and sever the strings holding it together. "Come on, Molly. We have to go!" She turned to race to the portal. But it was fading so fast, there was no way they would make it in time.

The wind picked up again and the tear above them groaned, sending out another bone-rattling pulse of magic.

"Shit! This way." She dragged Molly towards the cliff. "We have to—"

A wall of magic slammed into her back, knocking the breath from her and sending her to her knees.

"This is the part where we choose which way we want to die, right?" Molly's tone was as flat as the forced smile she gave Nea as she helped her up.

"Something like that."

The whole world shuddered, and they were tossed into the air amidst a shower of debris.

Nea reached for Molly's hand and opened a portal below them as they fell. She hoped it was enough, but her reserves were wearing thin, and the tear was disrupting her keen.

I am so sorry, Garret.

CHAPTER THIRTY-FIVE

NEA

The ground beneath Nea was gritty and damp, the air full of the scent of drying seaweed and salt. Rolling waves washed over her legs, bringing a chill to her skin and creating little furrows under her as they drew back again. She opened her eyes and crawled away from the shallows before twisting into a sitting position and casting her gaze down the beach.

Bodies littered the sand around her. Evard's men—no, Kieran's reanimations.

Prowling through the bodies was a dark shape that looked half-dog half-boar. Curving tusks protruded from its muzzle, and wiry, russet-coloured guard hairs ran along its spine. The red hairs spread out over its sides to form circular patterns across its dark coat.

Nea stood slowly, trying not to draw the creature's attention, but its gaze snapped to her and it lunged forward with a growl.

She tensed and threw her hands up, but the creature went barrelling straight past her and hit the chest of a staggering soldier who had been standing above a body with hair in a long, creamy-blonde braid. *Molly!*

As the boar-dog tore into the reanimation, Nea rushed to Molly's side and rolled her over.

She let out a soft groan, and Nea sat back on her heels with a sigh of relief.

Molly's cornflower-blue eyes blinked open and narrowed as they fell on Nea. "Am I dead? I feel like I should be." She gave a small cough and winced as she sat. "What the fuck is that?"

Nea followed the line of her sight to the boar-dog, who was sitting a short distance away, muzzle and throat dripping with scarlet and head tilted as it studied the women.

"It's friendly—I think. Though it doesn't seem to like the reanimations."

"*Doesn't seem to like ...*" Molly slowly shook her head. "Where did it come from?"

"If I had to hazard a guess, I would say it came from there." Nea pointed to the dark tear in the sky that was pulsing with multicoloured light that reminded her of the maelstrom.

"Shit. That's not good." Molly's eyes widened. "How do we fix that?"

"I'm not sure just yet ... But if the boar-dog"—the creature gave an affronted grunt—"came through, then I am certain other things will too."

"Arf!"

They both turned at the sound of a high-pitched bark.

"Arf! Arf!" A small saffron-coated terrier was bouncing through the bodies. "Arf!" He leapt onto Nea's lap, his tail wagging so fast it was a blur and his hot breath panting against the side of her neck as he tried to lick her face. Unsuccessful, he ran in circles around the boar-dog, who seemed to roll his eyes at the display.

"Is that a normal dog then or—Bright Mother's tits. What's wrong with his eyes?"

The dog had stopped his mad dash and lay on the sand beside the boar-dog, his tongue lolling out. He had fixed his gaze on Molly— his strange, colourless, multifaceted gaze. There was a patch of darker golden fur in a ring around one eye. He gave Nea a wink.

"Wade?" Nea's attention moved to the boar-dog. "Rourke?"

"Arf! Arf!" The terrier leapt up and bounced in circles again.

"Shadow's teeth, what are you doing here?"

The boar-dog, Rourke, gave what could only be described as a shrug.

"Wait. You know them?" Molly blinked, flicking a look from one dog to the other.

"They are friends of mine, but they weren't dogs last time I saw them, and they are both supposed to be in the Between."

"Like Zephyr?"

"Arf!"

"Yes, Wade is from the same ... tribe I guess is the best word—though they called themselves a troupe—as Zephyr. And Rourke is a brightlander."

Rourke grunted.

"But Zephyr appears human."

Nea nodded. "Maybe coming through the tear had something to do with it. Zephyr came through one of my portals, which, for the most part, is fairly stable magic. But the tear is wild magic and therefore completely unpredictable as to how it will effect anyone, or thing, passing through it."

"Right, well. What now?" Molly stood and brushed herself off. "I mean, we can't just sit here and wait for more creatures to crawl out of the tear, can we?"

"No. I need to get to Mother's Deep."

"Mother's Deep? Shouldn't we be heading back to Del Harol to regroup with the others?"

"You probably should, but I need to find passage to Quel'sapar."

"Quel'sapar? Did the fall from the cliff rattle your brains? Quel'sapar doesn't exist."

Nea pressed her tongue into the side of her cheek and folded her arms.

"It does exist? Then how—it's like Hartswood, isn't it? We need to make a blood sacrifice and then eat something glowing and then boom! Quel'sapar suddenly appears."

"Not quite." Nea pushed to her feet and brushed the sand from her clothes. Closing her eyes, she let her keen out, searching for the thin edges of a doorway in the source. She gritted her teeth, expecting the corruption to surge as it sensed her keen. But it was coiled tightly in the back of her mind, almost as though it was satiated for the time being.

This close to the tear, the source was ragged, rent with dozens upon dozens of holes. Beings shifted behind the fractures and tears, some waiting, some trying to squeeze through or widen the openings. It wouldn't be wise to create a portal here so close to the breeched barrier.

With a sigh, she opened her satchel and dug into it. Her fingers met with a small wooden carving, and she drew it out. It was a fox carved from a cream-coloured wood. With a soft smile, she tucked it safely away, and then went digging again until she found a smooth curve that sent magic surging along her skin and seemed to amplify the sounds of the waves beside them.

Pulling the object out, she opened her palm to show Molly. A teal and purple seasnail shell sat neatly in the centre of her hand. The copper-coloured stripes glinted in the light.

"I'm guessing you're not showing me your prized shell collection. What does that do?"

"This." Nea closed her fist around the shell and flooded it with her keen. Then when it grew too hot to hold, she pelted it as hard as she could into the ocean.

Nothing happened.

"Well, that was anticlimactic. Got any other bright ideas or small stones you want to try assaulting the ocean with instead?"

"It should have—"

A bolt of teal light shot out of the water where the shell had landed, then the surface of the ocean started to glow and boil as an unnatural wind snapped at their hair.

"Ah, Nea, are you sure—Mother's tits!"

With a groan, a large ship appeared just beyond the shallows.

"Don't tell me that came through the tear?"

Nea shook her head. "That would be The Azure Queen." She lifted her arm to wave; Rufus would be checking the shoreline with his spyglass. A few moments later, figures climbed into one of the rowboats and started to lower it into the ocean.

"Arf!" Wade went running between Nea and Molly and started digging at something in the sand.

"My crossbow!" Molly jogged over and pulled it free of the sand, giving Wade a scratch behind the ears. "Good b—ah ... Thank you."

As Molly rejoined Nea, the boat was pulling into the shallows. A lithe dark-haired man leapt out and splashed towards them.

"Emil?" They said together.

"Nea? Molly? How in the realms?" He turned back towards the boat as though he was going to yell, but Margot vaulted over the side, all but falling into the ocean. She raced towards them, sending a cascade of water in all directions.

When she reached them, she threw her arms around both of them and pressed a kiss to Molly's cheek. "Oh, Molly, you cannot believe how much I missed you. And, Nea—" She pulled back and gave Nea's shoulder a shove. "Don't you dare do that to me again!"

"Do what?"

"Don't play innocent; I thought you were dead!" Her voice broke on the last word.

"I'm sorry."

Margot drew a long breath.

"Well, I wasn't expecting to get here quite so fast, and what in the realms is that?" Wren had joined them, her hands on her hips as she tilted her head back to examine the tear in the sky.

"A breech in the barrier," Nea said simply.

"Oh, *right*." Wren glanced at the rest of her group, who were wandering up the beach.

Nea studied them. Gendry, Penny, a warden she didn't recognise, and—"Mateus?"

"Nea? It's good to see you in one piece. I believe you've had quite an adventure."

"It's still going and won't be done until we fix that." She indicated the tear. "Which is why I summoned the Queen, though I didn't realise you would all be on her." She indicated Emil, Penny, Margot, and Mateus.

"Why do you need the Queen?" Wren asked.

"I need to get to Quel'sapar."

Wren rolled her eyes. "Of course. Why would I expect anything different?"

"Speaking of different." Mateus's keen rolled in a cold press down Nea's spine. "What in the realms have you done to your keen?"

"You can probably feel the corruption." She held up her blackened fingers.

"No, not that. It feels like—"

"Garret," Margot said.

"Your warden friend?" Mateus asked.

Emil nodded.

"Oh, that's the ward." She held out her left wrist and rolled her sleeve back to show him the dark orange eight-pointed star.

"What sort of ward is that?" Mateus brushed his fingers over the mark, and the lines lit up in response to his keen.

"A death ward."

Mateus's silver-white eyebrows nearly met his hairline. "A death ward? That's ..." He touched the ward again. "Fascinating."

"Quite. But you didn't just summon us to have a chat on the beach. Are you ready to depart?" Wren asked.

Nea nodded. "Yes I am."

"I'm coming too," Molly said.

"No, Mol, not this time. It's been—"

"I know." Molly cupped Margot's face. "But someone needs to keep Nea out of trouble."

"I can go with her," Emil said.

"Perfect. Emil can take care of Nea."

"Margot, I love you, but I need to go with Nea. I made a promise to Garret to keep her safe if anything happened to him, and you know I don't go back on my promises."

Margot wilted but then brightened again. "Then I am coming too."

"No. It's too dangerous," Nea said.

"Yet it's perfectly fine for you and Molly to throw yourselves into danger."

"That's different, Margot. I don't have a choice whether I *throw* myself into danger or not. I haven't had that choice since the moment I was born. But you do have a choice." The corruption stirred in the back of her mind, lifting its head as though sensing the edge of her rising emotions.

Margot's keen suddenly flared warmly, and she looked down at her palm where a silver mark was glowing in pulsing shades of silver and apple green.

"What is that?" Nea asked.

"It's the anchor."

"The anchor? Margot, what did you do?"

"I warned her it was a bad idea to let Warren put it in her," Penny said, folding her arms.

"It wanted to help—it still does, and it wants to heal."

"Heal?"

"Your corruption. It's reacting to it."

Nea studied her blackened fingers. Something had happened to the corruption when she infected Kieran. It didn't feel as hungry anymore, and the voice in the back of her mind was softer—almost soothing. And it didn't respond to her keen the way it had before.

However, the moment her emotions flared, it came to life, ready to comply to her every whim. She closed her fingers over her palm and drew a breath before holding her hand out to Margot. "Okay. Give it a try."

Margot took hold of Nea's wrist and her keen washed over Nea's skin, pulling into the corruption marks.

Nea gritted her teeth as barbed claws dragged through the back of her mind and the corruption howled in objection. Then it lost its grip on her, morphing into something else entirely. The web-like stains on her arm discoloured to a silver grey and shifted into a series of swirling cloud-like patterns to her elbow. The marks in the centre of her palm formed a perfect crescent moon, several shades darker than the swirls up her arm.

She gave her arm a flick to dispel the prickling sensations running over her skin.

"Is it gone?" Mateus came forward and touched Nea's arm. "No, I can still feel something. Not corruption, but ... what is that?"

"My birthright," Nea said with a wry smile.

"It's not necromancy though," Emil said.

Nea shook her head.

"Because necromancy is only a tiny piece of who Nea is," Penny said. "Have you not been paying attention at all?"

"Alright, you lot." Wren clapped her hands together. "If we stand around here too much longer the tide will take us. Who's coming on the Queen?"

"I am," Nea said moving forward, and Rourke joined her, his bulk pressing against the side of her leg. Wren gave the boar-dog a curious glance but shrugged.

"Me too," Molly said, giving Margot a small smile before taking hold of her face and pressing a hungry kiss to her lips. As she pulled back, she said, "We all need to play our part to save the world."

"Since when do you believe in destiny?"

"It's not destiny. It's doing what is right." She brushed her lips against Margot's again. "I love you, and I promise I will stay safe."

"I love you too." Margot gave her a watery smile and let her go before turning to Nea and throwing her arms around her. "You stay safe too. I don't think I could survive losing you again."

"I can't make any promises, but I will try."

Margot started to pull away, but Nea tightened her grip.

"I imagine Garret will be in a bit of a mood when you encounter him next. Take care of him for me." She let go and took a step back.

"Arf!" Wade bounced in circles around them.

Nea crouched and rubbed behind his ears. "I take it you are going with Margot?"

He gave a nod.

"This is Wade," she told Margot. "Declan and Garret can explain when you reach them."

"Declan? You know I can't see his spirit—"

"He's alive again," Molly said. "It's weird, and I don't completely understand it, but it is easier to just accept it."

Margot rubbed her fingers along her brow, and Molly gave her a hug.

"Okay." Nea nodded and clapped her hands together. "Be safe, all of you."

"You should take your own advice sometime," Penny said with sly twinkle in her dark eyes as she patted Nea's shoulder.

Once the goodbyes were done, Nea and Molly climbed into the boat with Wren. Gendry helped Rourke in and then pushed off before jumping on board himself. Margot and the others waved then turned and headed along the sand.

With a slow, deep breath, Nea looked out towards The Azure Queen.

"Are you sure about coming, Molly?"

"Not in the slightest. You certainly wouldn't be my first choice of travelling companion, but I did promise Garret I would take care

of you if anything happened. So ... we're stuck together for now."
She shrugged.

Nea nodded and brushed her fingers over the ward mark. "Well,
let's hope we make it out of Quel'sapar in once piece then, because
I doubt Margot would ever forgive me if I got us both killed."

"You make it really hard to like you sometimes. You know that,
right?"

Gendry let out a laugh, and Wren said, "Yeah, but she grows on
you eventually."

"Don't worry too much about Quel'sapar. It's a shithole of place,
but the worst thing we'll face there is Vince's temper. And it won't
help that he's not terribly fond of Nea. She's rubbed him the wrong
way one too many times." Gendry grinned.

Nea scoffed. "I only ruined one party and—"

"Liberated one of his *wives*, stole a priceless heirloom and set
him on fire." Wren laughed.

"I did not set him on fire ... He did that all on his own."

Molly was staring between the two of them open-mouthed. "So,
is this Vince an important person?"

Wren made a face. "He certainly thinks so. He's a merchant
prince who likes to play at being a pirate. And he happens to have
the loudest mouth in the Court of Captains, which means he's
essentially in charge of Quel'sapar."

They reached the side of the ship and hooked the pulley ropes
to the boat.

Once on deck, Nea cast a glance back towards the beach. The
tiny figures of Margot and the others were disappearing in the
direction of Fengate. She turned her attention to the ruined tower
of Kalhanna, above which was the churning tear in the sky. Dark
shapes were falling from it, highlighted by the technicoloured
light.

She swallowed.

Allowing the tear to form had been her only option, but she hoped that by doing so she hadn't caused irreparable damage to both worlds. There was no point in dwelling on the uncertainties though. Right now, they needed to focus on what they could control and do it as fast as humanly possible. The fate of everyone in the known realms was depending on it.

To be continued ...

THANK YOU FOR READING BRIGHTLING

If you enjoyed wandering the wilds of the Between, I would love it if you left me a review either at your favourite online store or on Goodreads. And make sure you pick up the final book in Nea and Garret's story:

SOVEREIGNS

The barrier has been torn asunder. Now they must find the seat of the Sovereigns' power before the mortal realm and the Between collide, altering the fabric of the known realms forever.

Under the Usurper's influence, Leon has left nothing but destruction and undead in his wake. A chilling reminder of the future the world will face if Nea and Garret cannot find the Thrones of Eternity before the Usurper does. Hunting for clues to the thrones' whereabouts, Nea races to the enchanted isle of Quel'sapar. But with the death ward now linking her keen to Garret's, the itchy stirrings of his corruption could prove a fatal distraction.

The hunt will lead them deep into the mountains of the Spine. There they will finally face down the Usurper and learn that to liberate the Sovereigns, one of them will have to sacrifice everything.

GLOSSARY

Bind-shackles: Bands of robrillium that prevent a mage from using their keen by blocking their connection to the source. Each pair is struck with its own key. If this key is lost, that pair can only be unlocked by a warden's keen.

Brightling: Extremely rare keen-folk who have the ability to absorb and use the keen of others or turn a mage's own keen against them, even though they seem to have no keen of their own.

Corruption: A type of possession / magical disease that primarily affects mages. The afflicted become increasingly violent as they slowly lose control of their minds and their keen.

Deathborn: A mage who appears to be stillborn but reanimates within the hour following its birth. Only found among healers, mind mages, and necromancers, and even then, reasonably rare.

Death ward: (sometimes called deathbond) A type of oathing that permanently fuses the souls of two mages together. This bond is unbreakable and continues even after death. Because the souls are connected in this way, if one of the pair dies, so does the other.

Deera solvec: In the old language, it means Daughter of Shadow. Though Shadow-touched children could be any gender. Deera solvec possess the ability to tear holes in the barrier and create portals between worlds. Like brightling, they are extremely rare. However, unlike brightling, they are almost always born mages.

Devourer: A construct of thought and memory that dwells in the Between. They usually exist in nests, which consist of a Queen and her drones. They have no true shape of their own but can take on any shape they please. Usually they prefer to appear human in an effort to trick their prey.

High Mage: The head of each college of mages. There used to be an arch mage who was the head of all mages, but the position was dissolved long ago.

Keen: The soul essence of an individual or the 'flavour' of their magic. Interchangeable with the word magic, however, *keen* generally refers to the feeling of the life force of an individual and how that part of them interacts with the source as a whole. Magic is more so the direct effect they have on the world through channelling the source.

Keen-folk: A general term that covers all types of magic-users, not just mages and wardens, but seers and other gifted.

Keen-less: Those without magic.

Keen-sense: The ability to sense magic. Something all keen-folk innately have but also something that certain keen-less can possess (though this is rare).

Keen-touched: Sometimes interchangeable with keen-folk but generally used to refer to those keen-folk who are not mages or wardens. Seers and those gifted with 'low-magic' i.e. savants and prodigies who cannot control the source but have uncanny abilities regardless.

Lock-stone: A trans-dimensional construct that can be used as an anchor for magic. The lock-stone outside Hartswood solidifies the wards around the estate and protects it.

Mage: Keen-folk who have complete control of the source in one element E.g. weather (storm mages), fire, earth, water, healing, mind, death and the spirit world (necromancers) etc. There are certain nuances among the generic types of mages. For example: Sophia is a water mage, but she is particularly skilled with frost and ice magic. Declan is a storm mage who has an affinity for lightning, something not all weather mages are comfortable with.

Oathing: A kind of soul marriage between two mages. The bond dissolves after death. Often used for shorter-term pacts between individuals.

Oathbond: (sometimes called an oath ward) Refers to the connection created by an oathing.

Reanimation: Undead given 'life' by a necromancer. They are created by forcing a spirit, whether once human or not, into a corpse. They are generally mindless puppets controlled by the necromancer who resurrected them.

Robrillium: The enchanted metal used to create bind-shackles. It ranges in colour from light-pinkish gold through to a deep-rose gold.

Spirit-glass: Enchanted mirrors, usually made of obsidian or black glass, through which necromancers use to communicate. They can become corrupted and slowly steal the lifeforce of those using them; functioning ones are rare as a result of this.

The barrier: The veil between realms as seen by necromancers. It can appear a range of different ways depending on the individual interacting with it. E.g. Nea's barrier is a hedge of pale-pink and grey roses, and Nonna's is a bramble of blackberries.

The Between: A magical spirit realm that the souls of the dead are believed to pass through on their way to the grove of the ancestors.

The maelstrom: An enchanted storm that exists in the stretch of ocean between Beldaren and Osmar, known as the Fathoms. It is a direct result of the actions of a group of mages several centuries ago, actions which also led to the sinking of the city of Port Brenna (now called Mother's Deep). Not much is known about the storm. Its movements are unpredictable, and any ship that passes through it either completely disappears or is washed up as a wreck miles away from the Fathoms.

The Order: The term used to refer to the wardens as a whole. Has a specific hierarchy of splinter cells and commanders.

The Source: The fabric of the universe from where keen-touched get their powers.

Thrones of Eternity: The mythological seat of the gods and the root of their power.

Warden: Keen-folk who can suppress the keen or connection to the source in other keen-folk. Theorised to be a type of mage even though they don't channel the source. Originally called ward mages.

ABOUT THE AUTHOR

C. E. Page has been dreaming up stories of faraway places and strange magics for as long as she can remember. She lives on the east coast of Australia with her partner, Evan, two balls of pure energy in the shape of young boys, and a honey badger masquerading as dog.

An avid reader and gamer, she loves devouring a good story in whatever form it takes.

You can find out more about her and her upcoming works at: www.cepageauthor.com

www.ingramcontent.com/pod-product-compliance
Lightning Source LLC
Chambersburg PA
CBHW032112110726

47902CB00003B/560